I0586299

Also available by Ava Dunn

I Lied For You

Salt

COLD

DESERT

AVA DUNN

OLIVE
READS

COLD DESERT

Australia

Published by Olive Reads in 2023

Published by Olive Reads

Copyright © Ava Dunn 2023

The moral right of the author has been asserted.
ALL RIGHTS RESERVED
No part of this publication may be reproduced, stored in a retrieval
system, or transmitted in any form by any means electronic,
mechanical, photocopying, recording or otherwise without the prior
consent of the publishers.

9780645639346 (paperback)
9780645639353 (ebook)

Cover design by Elysia Clapin ©

Typeset in Garamond

COLD

DESERT

Chapter One

The year before Hollie Matheson went missing, I lost my mind. But this story happens mostly before then. A time before she went missing, a time during, a time after.

I have lived here in Short Point for a year now, without her. I moved here to live with my father because my mother didn't want me anymore. More to the point, she didn't want to deal with me anymore. The world is a hard place to navigate when you don't have a compass. The only way I knew how to live was by trying my best not to.

The day my mother told me I was moving to Short Point to live with my father, whom I hadn't seen in six years, I was crouched over the kitchen table, consumed by the thoughts of the roast dinner she was baking in the oven. All I thought about was food.

How many carrots could I stuff into my sleeve? How many peas could I mash into the plate and make it look like the green leaves of the painted flowers on the edge? Could I swear to my mother I'd turned vegetarian so I wouldn't have to eat the meat and gravy?

The potatoes were safe. I could eat one. That was it. No more than one. *If Mum tries to give me two, I'll chuck a fit*, I thought.

'Daisy, I have something to tell you. I'm not sure you'll like it.'

'I'm not going back to the hospital, Mum,' I mumbled, gnawing on my fingernails.

She loved sending me to the hospital. All because I wouldn't eat.

Mum explained, 'No, it's not that.' She paused as she sat at the table opposite me. She waited for me to meet her eyes before she explained, 'I've been seeing a psychologist.'

I blinked. My mum was perfect. She never needed help. The fact she'd go to see a shrink was mind-blowing. Shrinks were for the screw-ups like me.

'Why?' I asked.

'To help cope with your illness.'

I rolled my eyes. 'I don't have an illness. I am fine.'

'That's your opinion,' she said, holding a perfectly manicured hand up to me as if to shut me up. 'No, the psychologist seemed to think it would be a good idea to try something unorthodox to help both of us.'

I sat quietly and waited. This ought to be interesting – hearing the ideas of someone that had never even met me or the eating disorder that had taken over me.

Mum said, 'We get you out of this environment…and try somewhere new.'

'Like…go on a holiday together?' My nerves fluttered. I did not like the idea of going somewhere with my mother so close in contact (and having her constant supervision). Being alone and isolated from people, especially my mother, was what I needed to cope. I could exercise in private and not eat.

'No…' She took a deep breath and blurted out, 'You live somewhere else.'

My face flushed, and a prickling sensation ricocheted all over my body. I wish I'd known then that the key word was live, as in survive, but all I could focus on at the time was that my own mother was kicking me out. I worked hard at composing my face so I would not burst into tears.

'A new start for you might get you out of the habits and memories you have here,' she continued. 'I can also work on my own mental health.'

'I don't want to go,' I whispered.

She reached out her hand and took mine. Her lip trembled as she looked me in the eye and told me, 'It's not about what you want.'

It had never been about what I had wanted. She didn't get it. My whole life had been about her, and now that I really needed the help, she was kicking me out, still making it about her.

I'd been in and out of hospitals the previous year. Low iron, low potassium, low B-12, anaemia, low blood pressure, I still didn't have my period…it took a lot of visits before the doctors actually said to my mother that I might have something called anorexia nervosa.

'No,' my mother had snorted. 'She couldn't possibly; she eats like a pig.'

The doctor had checked my lower jaw and fingers. He had asked me, 'Do you vomit after you eat?'

I had stared back at him with a defiant glare. *You may think you know what I do, mister, but you can't prove it.*

He had printed out referrals and said, 'She needs to go into hospital immediately. Nip this in the bud, Mrs. Cavill. It's an insidious disease and it is deadly if it takes hold.'

Shows how much that doctor knew. There I was a year later, still alive, stronger than ever.

'I don't want to talk about this anymore,' I stated in my clearest voice to my mother. I stood up defiantly with my chin up and went to walk away, but everything went black for a second and I lost my breath. She lunged across the table to catch me but I slapped her hand away, steadying myself and my breath with a deep inhale, flaring my nostrils at her the way she had when I had been a petulant little child.

'I don't need your help,' I spat before walking away, carefully placing each foot in front of the other.

I left her alone, leaning across the table, her head down on the surface beside her outstretched hand as though she was a martyr for giving up on me, her only child. I didn't even ask where I was being sent. I didn't care anymore. She could send me to a deserted island, a big city, Uluru for all I cared.

Mum ended up sending me to New South Wales. A small town at a river mouth that led out to the Pacific Ocean.

She helped me pack a suitcase. I wasn't sure what I needed to take. How long would I be going for? Was it hot or cold there? Was I going for a week or was I going for a month? I asked Mum and all she could tell me with a thin mouth was, 'That's up to you, Daisy.'

'What do you mean, that's up to me?' I held up two different cardigans. One green, one black. 'I need to know!'

My mum gave me a told-you-so expression and quipped, 'Don't you think that I've needed to know how long, Daisy? Hm?'

She was impossible! I threw the green cardigan down as hard as I could; it floated down carefully onto my bed and made my anger harder and sharper with its lack of satisfying effect. Mum was always like this. Acted like she was so hard-done by me. Like I was a problem. She kept claiming she was trying to help me and she was putting everything into keeping me alive, but she couldn't even give me a straight answer.

We were leaving the next morning and she expected me to have everything packed and be okay with the fact I had no idea how long I was going. I may as well come to terms that she was giving up on me for good. It would have been fine with me. I didn't care about her anymore. Ever since she blamed everything about how I was on me. But I didn't want to leave Jessie, my golden retriever. As I stood, fuming, at my bedside, Jessie looked up at me from her dog-bed in the corner of my bedroom. Her ears went back and the whites of her eyes showed.

Mum closed the bedroom door on me and walked away, leaving me to cry alone with Jessie. I went to her bed and knelt down. The timber floorboards would leave bruises on my knees but I didn't care. I wrapped my arms around Jessie and breathed in her pungent scent. I wet her curly neck with my tears and slobber. She patiently sat and let me cry, placing her paw on my thigh.

I would miss her. I couldn't bear to be around my mother anymore, but I was bereft at having to leave my best friend.

Mum was sending me to live with my father. I hadn't seen my father in six years. He had left when I was eleven. The day he had left, he had woken me up at five in the morning. It had still been dark. I'd sat up in bed, rubbing my eyes.

'Daddy? What's wrong?'

The light coming from the hallway had illuminated the tears streaming down his face. He had kissed me on the cheek with his whiskers brushing against me. 'I have to go live somewhere else. I'll still talk on the phone with you every day. I'm sorry, Sprout.' I hadn't seen him since. Except, I was about to see him again. I was about to live with him. It was a surreal feeling to be leaving my home because my mother didn't want me anymore, and going into the house of the man who had left me years ago because he hadn't wanted me anymore, either.

In the morning before my big road trip to New South Wales, I attempted to lift my suitcase into the car, but my muscles shook so much I could barely lift it.

Mum bustled over and shooed me away. 'Daisy, no. Just leave it. I'll do it, like I have to do everything else for you.'

I rolled my eyes and got into the car. If I had the energy to argue with her, I would have. As we started driving, I asked, 'Can we stop for coffee?'

'No. No more coffee. If you're hungry, you have to eat.'

'I'm not hungry,' I snapped and crossed my arms and legs. If I said it enough, one day I'd believe it myself.

The drive took seven hours. I decided somewhere between Cann River and Eden to give this recovery deal a good go. Maybe I could become normal again. Recovery didn't have to mean going to the hospital. I could eat healthy foods, stay skinny and be "recovered" at last. I imagined writing my tell-all book, thanking my mother for being cruel and forcing me to recover by abandoning me with my father whom I barely knew. We'd be on all the talk shows, beautifully dolled up and smiling. I'd flick my luscious hair (mine was so dry and tangled now I'd long given up on it) and promise to all the poor girls and boys, men and women suffering with anorexia nervosa that they too could be like me. Healthy...and deathly thin. Ignoring the juxtaposition of those two words. All it took was a little tough love and dedication. Yes...I'd give this a go.

When we arrived in the beachside town of Short Point, I pressed my forehead to the window so I could look outside, past freckles of rain. The land was flat, tidal lowland, empty green paddocks on either side of the road. A man was cycling up ahead and Mum fitfully hesitated before speeding past him. I couldn't tell if she was in a hurry to get there so she could stop driving, or get rid of me.

One tall pine tree stood out on the horizon ahead, almost like a gigantic Christmas tree. It towered over the roofs of the bundles of neat houses on the right. Houses with neatly pruned native gardens, and long sloping front yards. Then over the hill, older houses that looked like fibro shacks. Further down the road, it was expensive-looking again with expansive farm properties with white-railed fences and cattle yards.

After the farms, a dark forested area loomed. I sat back, as glum as the weather and the dark trees on either side of the road as we passed through.

'Are you nervous, Daisy?' Mum asked, following the road signs and not looking at me.

'A little bit,' I admitted. My stomach was actually doing somersaults and I wanted to get out of the car and run away. Sure, this man was my father, but I hadn't seen him since I was eleven. I'd only had birthday and Christmas cards from him in the past five years. How was I supposed to live with him? I wondered if he knew how ill I was. I wondered if he knew at all. I'd have to wait and see what he said or did. What if he was a creep? Why did he even leave Mum in the first place? All I knew about him was that he was a chippy, which was slang for a carpenter.

We came out of the forest and the river came into view. It looked more like a flat lake. It was almost level with the road. Some birds flew across the road in front of Mum and she braked gently to avoid them.

'That's actually very pretty,' Mum said, nodding at the river.

I nodded. 'Yeah.'

'The beaches here are meant to be amazing,' she added. 'Do you think you'll like living by the water?'

'Lived by the water back home, Mum,' I said. 'It's no big deal.'

'That was a bay, though,' she said. 'Not the ocean.'

'It's salt water, has fish. It's the same,' I said.

'I've always wanted to see whales,' Mum replied. 'You'll let me know if you see them, won't you.'

'Sure, whatever,' I grumbled. I'd never thought about whales. They were just big things in science books and documentaries to me up until that point. I'd never thought much about them and didn't particularly care if my mother wanted to see them or not.

I cracked my neck and avoided her eyes. I kept expecting to see a town centre, but Mum followed the road to the left and then pulled up at a yellow house perched atop the double-car garage, opposite the flattest, swampiest, murkiest part of the river. The yellow house was gaudy, too bright amongst the dark greys, browns and greens of the neighbouring properties. Of all colours to paint a house, yellow? I grimaced as it glared even in the cloudy light.

'We're here.'

I gasped inwardly; this was it. This was my new house. A man came down the narrow path from the side of the house. A short man wearing a baseball cap and Blundstone boots.

'G'Day,' he called.

Oh, Dear God. That was my father. There he was. Why did he look so much shorter than I remembered him?

Mum got out of the car and I lingered while Mum handed him my suitcase. A stuffed toy I named Milky was in the boot of the car – it was a dog that was missing a lot of fluff and stuffing. I'd had it since I was four. I cringed at the thought of this man seeing Milky so that urged me to get out of the car and pick it up myself, clutching it tightly at my hip, under the cardigan I was wearing so it wasn't so obvious I needed a soft toy at almost seventeen years old.

'What's this?' Dad asked, touching it at my hip.

I tried to act like I didn't need it by scrunching it in my fist. 'Just something to remind me of my dog back home.' He didn't even know Jessie existed, which made me angry. She was a big part of my life and he had no idea. I'd begged Mum for a dog when Dad had left. Now here I was, without my dog but standing with the man whom I replaced with the dog. Surreal.

8

Dad led Mum and me into the house. There was a staircase with slippery tiled steps to the front door. Inside the house, there were gleaming dark timber floorboards that looked like Dad had buffed them, and cream walls, stained with time.

'Daisy, I'll show you your room – it's just opposite mine.'

We turned left down the hall, and on the right, there was a small bedroom with beige carpet and wooden venetian curtains covering narrow windows. I ran a finger along a blind and rubbed it with my thumb, my finger coated with light grey dust. Despite the exterior of the house being so bright, the interior was dim.

Mum nodded her head at my disgusted expression, and tried to drum up some enthusiasm. 'Oh yes, it's lovely. A lovely view to the back garden.'

The back garden was overflowing with unruly palms and very sad flocks of Birds of Paradise. My eye twitched as I took in the sloping back lawn, full of bindi prickles, no doubt.

'Yeah, but wait until you see the view from the lounge. It's to die for.' My dad beckoned us to follow him back into the main part of the house. The lounge was cramped; a blue lounge settee and matching recliners smothered the room. There was a type of wood heater called a coonarra in the centre of the room that made the viewing angle of the small television upon a square lamp table awkward. Atop the coonarra was a school photo of me, when I was in grade five. Right around the time Dad left. Seeing the photo made my back stiffen and my jaw clamp.

Dad took us out the glass sliding door and we stepped out onto the balcony. He had cluttered it with washing, chairs, tools and a discarded mattress. He gestured across the swamp and said, 'Eh?' as if we could appreciate an epic view. There was nothing but green scrublands – the river too difficult to see beyond the scrub.

Mum nodded politely.

Dad leant on the steel railing and sighed. 'I love it. It's my pride and joy. Never been so happy in a place.'

I was about to ruin all of that for him.

Mum forced a smile and said, 'Well, I think that's it, then.'

My heart lurched, and Dad spun around. 'Already? You only just got here. Stay for a cuppa.'

She nodded and I grabbed her wrist, a silent exchange, pleading, begging, imploring – please do not leave me here.

Dad rubbed at his salt and pepper stubble. 'Well, I wish you'd stay for a while, Raelene. You've had a long drive. We have a lot of catching up to do.'

'No, that's fine. That's everything I need to drop off.' She patted her hips self-consciously.

My dad walked ahead of my mother as she walked back to the car. He walked with a slight limp. I didn't remember him having a limp. He was so much older than I remembered. He peered at me from under his cap and winked a blue eye at me. I looked away.

'You really should stay for a while, Raelene,' he said to my mother. He seemed like he didn't want to be alone with me any more than I wanted to be alone with him. It was all just…so….weird.

She backed up to the car. 'No, I think it's best that you and Daisy get reconnected just the two of you. I've got a motel booked down in Eden. I'll be fine.'

'Safe trip then,' he said.

'Thank you,' she replied. I watched her get into the car, reverse out of the driveway, and drive away. I waited for the taillights to flash red, even for a second, to know that she was hesitant to leave me, but they stayed dull and she left me standing in the front yard with the man I barely knew.

I wished she had hugged me. I found out later that she didn't hug me goodbye because she could not stand to feel the bumps in my back – that it broke her heart. She bawled her eyes out on the side of the road around the corner for an hour before finally heading to Eden to rest and have the deepest sleep she'd had in months.

Dad looked to me, waiting for me to say something but I bowed my head and crossed my arms.

'I guess we'll go in, then,' he said. Again, he waited for me to speak, but my mouth remained closed. He led the way back up the stairs. I wanted to ask why he limped, but didn't want to be rude. I wanted to ask him why he left, but didn't want to start a fight. I wanted to tell him I hated him, but I would be lying. I only hated myself.

Dad escorted me into his little house and gave me the extended tour – where the forks and knives were (unnecessary), where the sugar and tea were (unnecessary), where the Wi-Fi router was (noted) and where some sanitary items were (unnecessary). He grinned at my school photo on the coonara heater. 'Eh, recognise that rascal, Sprout?'

I nodded and gazed around the room. I noted there were photos of other people too, people I didn't know. There was only one photo of Dad. He was standing on a rooftop with a toolbelt around his waist, holding up a hammer and looking chuffed with a wide grin.

'What do you want to do, Sprout?' he asked.

I forced myself to speak. 'I just want to have a rest.'

He nodded and took me to my bedroom. There were sheets folded at the end of the empty mattress. A pillow and pillowcase also awaited me to make them. I dropped down onto the bed without even bothering to make it, suddenly exhausted from the trip. Dad swung his hands together for a moment before saying, 'I'll let you rest before we get dinner.'

I curled up and closed my eyes, just intending to rest, but I slept like I hadn't slept in months.

Later, I opened my eyes later to darkness and Dad standing in the doorway saying my name.

'What?' I asked groggily, sitting up and falling back onto the pillow immediately, overcome with dizziness.

'What do you want for dinner?'

This is a very dangerous question to ask a person with anorexia. What did I want? I wanted pizza, pasta, McDonald's, chocolate, ice cream, tacos, bananas, kebabs, chicken – everything I could mush in my mouth and swallow to feel full. Anorexia, however, wanted to snap *nothing – leave me alone*, but I was determined to give this a go. Wasn't I?

'There's a Vietnamese place on the main highway, near the main part of town. Does a bloody mean Singapore noodles.'

Vegetables could be an okay place to start, so I nodded and said, 'Sure.'

He slapped his thigh with eagerness and said, 'Let's go then.'

I followed him to his ute, rubbing my hands over my arms, checking I could still link my fingers around my biceps. I sat in the front seat amongst piles of paperwork and empty energy drink cans.

Dad drove to the town and we parked outside the restaurant.

Inside, staff greeted us.

'How you?'

'Great, May. How's Anh?' My stomach shrank as I realised my dad knew these waitresses like they were friends. It meant I might see them again. Having to eat in front of people filled me with anxiety, but knowing that I might see these people again made me even more anxious because they'd remember I ate. Then try feed me more. Oh, boy.

They were friendly enough, and they had quick service, flirting with my dad jokingly. I sat with a plate of vegetables and rice noodles in front of me. I remained quiet, but the voice in my head was relentless.

Eat this, it said, *and you'll convince him you're fine. Maybe he doesn't know about it.* The ugly voice in my head grumbled at me angrily but saw reason. If I ate this, and convinced him I was fine; he'd think I had no problem and then I could get away with not eating other things. There was also a part of me that was embarrassed. How could I be such a screw-up that Mum would have to do this? I guess I kind of wanted to see if I could eat the noodles too. She was making a big deal out of nothing. I was fine.

Dad didn't watch me closely the way Mum did. He just ate his food, chewing and staring at his plate, probably wondering what the hell he could talk about with me.

After we finished eating in painful silence, we walked out.

'Would you like to go for a walk?' he asked.

My tummy was distended and painful, but the voice said *Yes, burn off that food*. 'Yes, please,' I said.

We walked around the block and then returned to the car. Dad said, 'Your school is nearby. Want to check it out? You're starting on Monday.'

School? I hadn't even considered that I'd be going to school. I didn't even go to school back home. Mum had withdrawn me because it was easier to monitor what I ate when she could see me all the time. The thought of going to school with new people terrified me. New place. New people. No friends. I nodded, trying to appear normal and excited. He drove to the school and we peered out the window at it together in the darkness.

'Looks good, eh.'

I grimaced. 'Yeah.'

Mum had pulled me out of school earlier in the year when I'd gone into the hospital the first time. I hadn't been at school in months, and now he expected me to rock up and attend school? I couldn't stop my foot from jiggling up and down all the way home and we didn't speak until we got back to his house and we went inside. I cried into my pillow most of the night. I was going to have to try to work this out. Going to school meant I'd need energy. Going to school meant people would see me. My teeth chattered at the thought of losing control of my eating. Why on earth had my mother thought this ridiculous idea of uprooting my entire life would be a good thing?

Dad and I went shopping the next day for school supplies. I managed to get away with just an apple for breakfast. Dad didn't say anything. But we hit the local department store, then he bought fish and chips for lunch. Nobody could possibly love junk food as much as my father loved it. It seemed to be all that he stuck into his mouth, along with copious amounts of energy drinks.

We sat on the grass by the beach with the white paper spread between us. Silver gulls cawed and squealed, jostling each other for prime position.

Dad picked at the chips. I fed the gulls.

'I reckon it's great you're here,' he said, mumbling and munching at the same time.

I squinted at him. It was a cool, cloudy day with a dull sky, but the sun kept peeping through the clouds and glaring. I didn't know what to say so I let him continue.

'When your mum called me to say she was going away for work – and could you live here for a few months, I reckon I nearly fell through the floor with shock.' He laughed, covering his mouth and chewed up food.

I let this bogus story my mum fed him sink in. Had she really not told him that I was suffering from anorexia nervosa and needed to go stay with him just to give her a break? Was he really that gullible?

He continued, 'We'll have a good time. It's a great place. I reckon you're gonna love it once you settle in.'

'Maybe,' I said, brushing the salt from the chips off my fingers and onto my pants. I wanted to ask why he never visited, or invited me up for a visit, but I stayed quiet.

'Plus, best fish and chips here in the whole country.' He winked.

'Yeah.' I smiled and wondered if he'd even noticed that not a single chip had made it past my lips.

Chapter Two

The next morning, I got dressed for school and straightened my limp hair, put on mascara, pulled on three pairs of socks and I stuffed my bra with tissue. I put on my shoes, picked up my school bag and with tremendous trembling, walked to my dad's ute so I could be dropped off at school. No time for breakfast. Plus, I was too nervous. I kept my mouth closed in case of projectile nervous spew.

Black Swan High School was located opposite the showgrounds and had an open-plan design to their buildings. Tall ceilings made the school dwarfed me. The court yard was void of any plants, and the bricks on the ground were raised and a trip hazard. I tripped on one and Dad caught my arm and the principal didn't even notice. The entire school was surrounded by gum trees. A vast oval stretched beyond the classrooms and made me swallow nervously. It was huge. How was I ever going to remember my way around?

Dad and the principal walked ahead of me, and were energetically touring the school. Everything around the school became a blur as I struggled to focus.

The principal gave me a map of the school and went through my timetable with me as Dad left for work. The map was marked with blue biro where I had to go and where the toilets were. The main building was open and spacious, lined with lockers, the corridors tall and decorated with student posters for activism, motivation, parties and support networks. R U OK and JUST DO IT posters conflicted each other.

The map and scribbles proved helpful and I managed to get to each class on time, drew minimal attention to myself except at each roll call when the teacher noticed they had a new student. 'Where are you? Who are you? Oh, lovely to meet you honey; I'm blah blah, feel free to ask for help blah blah blah'.

Students would turn and stare at me and I'd give an awkward smile and then we'd just get to work. I was so glad I had the text books already so I didn't have to share with anyone, encroaching on their space. I could huddle over the book myself like a little fat lump and not bother anyone.

The last class of the day was literature. The teacher had frizzy golden hair and small glasses. She was quite tanned, considering it was the end of autumn and heading into winter – I found out later that she'd spent the last two months in Croatia on a sail boat. She was energetic; she pumped her fists and gestured wildly. I smiled as she told us all about some cathedral being the scene of her busting for the loo. She had so much vigour and enthusiasm that I found myself hanging onto every word.

The class text was *To Kill a Mockingbird*. I waited for everyone to leave at the end of class to let her know that I didn't have a copy of the book. She lent me her own. Her name was written in beautiful cursive writing on the inside cover. Freda Gregg. I wished I could write that beautifully.

I traced the loops and swirls in her name with my finger as I made my way to the courtyard. I was meant to get onto the school bus. But I was full of nervous energy. I decided to walk home instead. It would take an hour and a half, and it was seven and a half kilometres. I could walk that distance. It would help burn off all the calories from eating the Asian food the other night. I walked home from school, half following the GPS directions on my phone, half reading the book. It was a straight line once I got on the main road into the town – not that it was much of a town. More like a collection of houses nestled between the river and the sea.

It was almost five by the time I got home. Dad was not home yet and I realised with dread that I didn't have a key. I was locked out.

I tried calling him.

'G'day, this is Mick,' said the voicemail message. I hung up. He seemed so excited to have me move in with him and here he was completely forgetting that he had to be home for me after school!

I groaned as ill-temper pursed my lips and the muscles around my face tightened. The way the afternoon autumn sun bounced off the yellow house hurt my eyes. The way the birds chirped irritated me. Too many boots at the front door and thongs and even too many dried eucalyptus leaves littering the patio bugged me. From all I knew of Dad, he didn't seem to have much of a logical process to things.

Tossing my school bag against the door, I sat down. *Jeez what a drag; having to sit here like a stunned mullet waiting for him.*

On my first day of school and everything. *A gal was trying to straighten up and fly right, rush home to do my homework, read To Kill a Mockingbird and whatever but nope.*

I needed to keep my mouth busy. I had some gum in my bag. I rifled around and pulled it out. Sweet spearmint. It was a lifesaver. I focused on chew, chew, swallow. Chew, chew, swallow.

Dad finally swung into the drive in his ute and I stood up, kicking my bag angrily.

'Where were you?' I demanded.

'Sorry I'm late. Got to go back to work but I can let you in.' He hurried to the door and unlocked it for me, even held it open for me to boot my bag inside.

'You're not staying?'

'Nah, love. Like I said, I've got some things to finish at work.'

'What am I supposed to do here on my own?'

'You got homework don't ya?' He smiled slightly at me over his shoulder and got back into his car. He waved out the window. 'I'll be home round seven. See ya.'

So, I hadn't been forgotten after all. Point to Dad. But I was home alone. Unattended. Unsupervised. Great. Mum never left me alone anymore, worried I'd do something stupid. I should have been celebrating this freedom but it felt smothering to be standing in that quiet little house. The kitchen was tiny. Cramped, the walls seemed to close in. The clock in the kitchen ticked loudly with each passing second. Tick. Tick. Tick…tock. Tick-tick. Tock. I opened the fridge just to see the light come on. Hello little light. Now you're off. Now you're on. Well, that got old pretty fast.

My eyes flickered to the load of the bread. I could eat a little bit of that. It might give me something to focus on instead of the crushing boredom. Nobody was around. That usually meant I could skip eating, but it also meant I could eat without pressure. I went for it. I took a slice of bread over to the living area and turned on the TV. No remotes. It was an old piece of junk still clinging desperately to 1978. I took a bite of the bread, ignoring the crumbs as I flicked through the television channels. Game show. Game show. Game show. Game show. Greek news. Italian news. Game show. Infomercial. I put down the bread and curled up on the blue couch. The cushions were lumpy and the

18

stuffing was falling out. I stared at the photo of me from grade five. I wondered if Mum was missing me yet.

I must have dozed off on the couch because the next thing I knew I was waking up the sound of the front door opening and a guy calling out, 'Oi, you here?'

I leapt up in terror, squashing the bread in my hand and squealed, 'Who are you?'

A guy in his twenties looked back at me in surprise and said, 'Oh. Sorry. Didn't mean to scare you. I'm here for Mick.'

'Who are you?' My fingers closed on the lamp beside the couch. I was only a little afraid to use it.

'Settle down, settle down.' He came into the living room and said, 'I'm Sandy. I work for Mick.' He held out a hand for me to shake. 'I reckon you're the new girl in town.'

I was so shocked that I reached up and shook his hand despite being frightened of him. 'Has he told you about me?' I asked.

'Bloody oath he told me. He's told everyone. Been excited to meet you the way he goes on about you.' The corner of his mouth lifted into a crooked smile, revealing white, crooked teeth. There was something endearing about the way he oozed easiness. It warmed me but made me want to snort with laughter. My dad didn't even know me! What on earth could he have told Sandy about me?

I settled on explaining, 'Well, okay, but he doesn't really know me really well.'

As I sat back down on the sofa, Sandy's eyes went to the squished bread but he didn't say anything. Instead, he gestured at the TV. 'So, uh…what are you watching?'

'Nothing.'

'Oh yeah, oh yeah.' He nodded and sat down next to me. An awkward moment passed where I stared at him and he stared at the infomercial.

'Can I…help you with something?' I asked. 'Because my dad…he's not even home. So, you don't need to stay.'

19

Sandy's head reeled back and he scoffed. 'Yeah, I know, I know...he just wanted me to pop around, so I'll...uh, wait.'

I scratched at my head. I didn't really want him there, but I didn't want to be alone either. He was a bit jerky in his movements, awkward and nervous. I asked, 'How long have you worked for my dad?'

'Not long.'

'Not long?'

'Not long,' he re-affirmed with a nod and a sideways grin.

'How could my dad talk about me so much in not long?'

He shrugged. 'Dunno. Guess he's not the only one in town talking about you.' He grinned and returned his attention to the infomercial. He then asked, 'Mind if I change the channel?'

I gestured that he could go for it. Sandy got up and switched through about fifteen different channels of static before he came across a blue screen with white foam and a black arrow zipping along. He sat back down but leant forward as though he'd like to kiss the screen from across the room. The clarity was so shoddy it took me a full minute to realise what he was actually watching.

'Surfing,' I said in a surprised voice. Surfing was never on the TV back home.

'Mm.'

'You like surfing?'

'Yep.'

'So, you actually surf?'

'Mm.'

There weren't many surfers back home. I had lived next to the bay, in an established town, too far south to know any of the rich people from Elsternwick and Brighton, too north to know any of the sporty kids from Dromana and Rye. I was from the middle of the bay, where the old people played lawn bowls and the derros had commission housing. The surfers were all from the northern parts (rich people that spent summers in Lorne) or the southern parts (on the end of the peninsula where the bay wrapped around to the ocean). I don't think I'd even met a surfer in real-life before.

I asked Sandy, 'Are you any good at it?'

'Huh?'

Just like that, the man's speaking and listening skills were knocked out of his head.

'I s'pose I gotta do some reading for school,' I sighed and got up. I paused at my bedroom door and noted that Sandy was still glued to the TV. He was even twitching and leaning his body as if he was surfing himself. Fish out of water, that man, I thought. Fish out of water...just like me.

Dad arrived home at seven, like he'd promised, but he brought home with him a couple of pizzas and a six pack of beer bottles. I loitered in the kitchen, feeling incredibly self-conscious. There was a large square cut out of the wall that looked into the living and lounge area, and it was as though I couldn't escape their eyes.

Sandy and my dad took slice after slice. I leant against the counter and picked at the same slice, too embarrassed to eat in front of Sandy. He didn't seem to have the same self-awareness. He chewed with his mouth open, laughed and gobbed bits of food, chugged two bottles of beer and was so animated as he spoke with my dad about the boys, football and politics.

My dad kept glancing at me before sipping the beer. He thought I didn't notice.

Once I'd tore enough of my pizza slice up, so it looked like I'd eaten a few slices, I said loudly, 'Well...I've got some more homework to do.'

One second I would be dedicated to recovering, and to not be anorexic anymore, but as I had to keep meeting new people and live in this new place, it became painfully obvious that I didn't know how to not be anorexic anymore.

Dad swallowed and asked, trying to be casual, 'Have you eaten enough?'

'Yeah, Dad...thanks.'

I smiled and then waved at Sandy, 'Nice to meet you.'

'You too, Daze.'

I cocked my head in confusion before I realised that he meant Daisy. I smiled weakly and said, 'Goodnight.'

I headed to my room and sat at the little desk. It looked like it had been picked up from the Hard Rubbish collection pile.

I was supposed to write a journal to go along with the book. I'd read more that afternoon while Sandy had been glued to the television, twitching and leaning his body to match the surfer on the screen and groaning each time the guy stacked. I really wanted to impress Ms. Gregg, so I got out a notebook and a pen and began tapping the dilapidated old desk, searching for inspiration.

What could I even write? Everything I wanted to say about the book so far began to be analysed and critiqued in my own head before it even made it onto the page.

'Be rough; be raw,' she had told the class. But I wanted it to be perfect, even when it was 'rough' and/or 'raw'.

Tap, tap, tap, went the pen, and still the page remained empty. I thought maybe some music would help. I got up and turned the radio on. The local radio station was the only one that could be picked up for kilometres. A tide report was on and seemed to go on forever with the droning of wind speeds and tidal shifts and times. Finally, some music came on. An alternative rock song with some killer interesting sounds on the guitar, singing about something being on fire.

I decided to start with the significance of the title of the book, since everything begins with a title. I made the start of writing my name in my best cursive writing at the top of the page. I decided I would only write in pretty cursive from then on. My regular handwriting was made up of boring straight letters but deceptively neat. Like a neat boy. I wrote like a neat boy. Neat. BOY.

I wanted to be more like a pretty girl. Pretty girl with pretty eyes and nice hair and lovely dialect. Boys would want me, and girls would want to be me. One of those girls that everybody admires that gets good grades and never sweats – not even in PE. They certainly didn't eat junk food. Or too much. They ate like little birds – were never necessarily hungry but had cute little wraps for lunch and Acai bowls for breakfast. With glowing skin and glowing teeth, she would be perfect. She would be me. I just needed to uphold the image.

I took a deep breath and decided to think about the mockingbird. Were they even real birds? Or was that what made the title so significant? I supposed I couldn't comment on the title after all until I'd read the book. I left the paper on the desk and decided to just go to bed.

Chapter Three

Magpies garbled and squawked outside the window at daybreak. I snapped my eyes open, startled again to find myself in a new place. I wondered how long it would take for me to wake up and not have my heart lurch in a panic at the disorientation.

I got up and went out to the shoddy balcony and sat out there with the noisy buggers. Their eyes fixed on me, their heads tilting. Sharp eyes that looked to the inside of me, waiting for food but daring me with their fearlessness.

There was frost on the porch railing and a bite to the air. I used to get up early at home, too. I'd go for a run. Six kilometres, then back home to do a workout that made me tremble. All before Mum got up for work. I'd eat one slice of wholemeal toast, masticated and spat into the glob of tissues, tucked under some potato peels in the kitchen bin. Plate being washed up just as Mum walked in doing her makeup and reading the newspaper at the same time.

Just getting up sweetie?

Yeah, just had breakfast.

That's good. Quick. Or you'll miss the bus.

But that wasn't going to be me this time. I was giving this a good hard go. I'd eaten more crap the last couple of days than I ever would have. Already I felt as though it had gone straight to my butt. Out of habit, I touched my wrists, hips, collarbones, ribcage. All still there, even after the bit of pizza yesterday.

I traced my finger along the frost on the railing and shuddered with the chill.

'Hey, Sprout.'

I jumped with surprise and looked up. Dad was standing at the back door with a mug in his hand.

'Hey.'

'Your mother says I gotta cook you breakfast in the mornings.'

'Yeah, I'm a bit of an arsonist in kitchens.' Nervous laugh.

Dad shrugged. 'I'm not working 'til nine so I can cook you whatever you want, Sprout.'

'I'm fine, thanks.'

'Eggs?'

'It's okay. You don't have to. I can get something myself. It's just Mum's way of controlling everything.' Casual shrug. 'Don't worry about it.'

'Eggs it is.'

I sat down at the kitchen table, rubbing my cold hands together as he cooked me breakfast. He didn't really say much. Just asked how I liked the school yesterday, and about what he had going on at work, and he spoke about the weather a lot. I engaged as best I could.

I ate the eggs. They were so awful. Lumpy. Cold. Tasteless. Patches over-cooked and lumps under-cooked. They made me feel like puking all morning.

At recess, I looked at my apple and felt the lump in my stomach and gagged at the thought of eating it, so I pitched it as hard as I could across the school oval. Nobody cared. At lunch, my vegemite sandwich went in the bin. Nobody cared. I walked home alone again and this time Sandy was there to open-up the house for me.

'Here to watch TV again?' I teased.

'Something like that,' he replied and parked himself down in the living room. I watched it for a while with him then retreated to my bedroom.

This time, Dad came home at six, and this time he made himself and Sandy bacon and eggs with baked beans.

I said quietly, 'I don't feel well,' and hid in the bath. Listening to Dad and Sandy talk in low, quiet voices. I couldn't make out anything they said, but I was detaching. I didn't want to hear what they were saying. I didn't care about any of it. Anorexia was winning again.

I wiped the steam off the mirror and stared into my eyes. I'd wanted to try, hadn't I? Already I felt like such a failure. I'd be better tomorrow.

I sneered at my reflection and whispered, 'You won't win,' but at the same time, a nasty voice in my mind retorted, 'Yes, I will.'

I started running again the next day. Alarm at 4:40. Back by 5:50 and in bed ready for Dad to rouse me at 6:30 for my school day. Harmless really. But it still felt like I was doing something really against the rules...and it felt like I was both winning and losing.

I repeated this routine for an entire two weeks, but got up earlier and earlier. I ran around the town; its quiet houses and streets were like an island. It wasn't far enough, so eventually I began running up to the highway to the main town and back – the same route I walked home from school. So not only was I walking almost eight kilometres a day, I'd begun to run it, too. Repeatedly.

Up earlier. Up at four. Up at 3:50. Up at 3:40. Run. Change. Pretend to sleep. Let Dad "wake me up". Get dressed. Toast for breakfast – making sure Dad saw me eat at least one slice. Brush teeth, flush the other slice of toast that I'd stuffed in my pants down the toilet, do my makeup, do my hair, pack my lunch, go to school. Recess: throw apple away. Lunchtime: throw sandwich away. Afternoon: Run home. Sandy would come over. I'd do my homework. Dinner: eat whatever Dad gave me but get rid of as much as possible. Have a shower. Purge dinner down the drain, the vomit circling around my toes. Go to bed. Repeat.

After three weeks had gone by, I finally got my own key to the house, so Sandy just stayed at work with my dad. He still came for dinner though. He'd always take the attention of my dad away so it made it easy to hide food. I was on auto-pilot. It made life easy. I was numb and detached, but I figured I was doing well. Sometimes I didn't purge. Sometimes I kept my recess apple and ate it at lunchtime. But I always got up early to go running.

Then Friday happened. Morning run. I was running late. I'd got up at three and I decided that I would try running that route three times. I was going slower. My legs were slimming down and my knees were becoming the thickest part of my leg instead of my thighs.

By the beach, I stopped to check my watch and saw that I was late. I couldn't run any faster. I was sweaty and shaky. I set-off at a fast jog, gasping for breath, then mis-stepped in a pot hole and my knee twisted out from under me. I fell to the dirt and my hands stung like mad. I brushed the dirt off my clothes and tenderly stood up. I went to take a step but my knee drilled. I needed to rest. Damn it!

'Oi!'

I almost took off bolting. It was Sandy on the other side of the road, hanging out of his panelvan, half-dressed. 'What are you doing out here so early, young lady?'

'What are you doing?' I shouted back.

He grinned and shimmied into a wetsuit. 'Going for a surf. Wanna join?' He scooped a surfboard out of the back of the panelvan and watched me limp across the road. 'What did you do, you numbat?' he asked.

'Nothing.'

'Nothin', my arse. Look at ya.'

'Just overdid it, that's all,' I grimaced.

'You be right?'

'Pfft. Course.' I played it off cool while wincing and clutching at my knee. I longed to ask Sandy to drive me home and keep it a secret from my dad. But my pride overtook me and I stayed quiet.

'All right. Well...' He looked over at the beach carpark. It was chockers and the sun was only just coming up. Surfboard bags were empty and some other people were changing into wetsuits. 'I better get cracking. Got work with your old man in an hour. I'll see you around, eh?'

'Yeah. See you around.'

He jogged off to the water line. I kind of wanted to follow him to see what was so good about surfing at six in the morning. Those guys had to be nuts. Obsessed.

If I could have sprinted, I might have made it home in ten minutes, just as Dad was getting out of the shower. But no. I couldn't. I slowly walked back home, accepting the fate that Dad was going to now know that I'd been sneaking out to go running. The gig was up.

To my relief, Dad had slept through his alarm. I tiptoed into the shower and acted like I had just got up. He rushed around the house in a mad dash. No time to make me breakfast, he told me. He was late. So, he never even noticed that I could barely walk either. No need for toast. No need for lunch. He would never even know.

Or so I thought.

After recess, I could barely stand.

A girl with long brown hair saw me limping and stopped me with concern all over her face. 'Hey, are you okay?'

'Yeah.'

Later, some girls from my art class, a year behind me – year tens doing some HSC subjects – named Ella and Devlin watched as I extracted myself from the high stool at the art bench with intrigue.

Ella asked, 'What did you do to your leg?'

Devlin added, 'We can go get you an ice pack from first aid.'

Ella added, 'Or a bit of food?'

I waved them off and said, 'No thank you.' I momentarily hoped we could have a conversation and I might make some friends, but they turned and continued their own conversation with each other. My shoulders slumped and I limped out the door, where some boys named Lockie and Mitchell huffed at me to hurry up. The first girl with the brown hair who had asked me if I was okay slammed them into the wall of the corridor and told them, 'Shut up; Be nice! She's obviously struggling to walk because of her disease.'

Tears came to my eyes and I limped faster. Later in the day, teachers began noticing I was limping into their classrooms. They asked me in each class if I was all right. I shrugged them away, and said, 'I'm fine; there's nothing wrong – my leg's just asleep.'

But by lunchtime, I gave up. I couldn't take the pain anymore. I went to the office and told them I wanted to go home. They called my dad for me. I took the phone and waited for him to answer.

'Yello.'

'Um. Dad?'

'Sprout?'

'I need to be picked up.'

'What? From school?'

'Yeah.'

'But I'm at work, Sprout.'

'I know. But, um,' I sighed. 'I hurt my knee and I don't think I can walk home.'

'What do you mean walk? You catch the bus home, don't you?' he asked.

I sighed. 'No, I walk. I don't want to catch the bus.'

'So ya hurt ya knee.'

'Yes.'

'How bad is it?'

Frigging hell, I wanted to yell, just pick me up! But I took a deep breath and said, 'I need a lift.'

'All right, all right. I'll sort something out.' He hung up so I handed the phone back to the office lady and sat out in the foyer, twiddling my thumbs for what seemed like forever. All I ever seemed to do was wait for my dad and lie to him.

The sliding door opened and I turned my head automatically and saw Sandy strut through in his work boots, shorts and a Rip Curl singlet – even though it was May. The office ladies suddenly seemed to be sweltering in the 16-degree heat because their faces burnt red and they started sweating. I grabbed my bag and followed Sandy to his panelvan and got in.

'Overdid it, eh,' he said as he chucked on his sunnies and started the car. It rumbled like a Harley Davidson.

'Yeah. I'll just go home and ice it; it'll be fine.'

'You gotta come back to my place,' he said, turning the steering wheel a thousand times to get out of the carpark and into traffic.

'Why?'

'Your dad said so. He'll pick you up on his way through.'

'But –'

'Oi, do you think this is good news for me? I usually go surfing when I knock off, not collect sixteen-year-old fibbers who have hurt their knees.'

My face burnt red. 'Then go surfing. Drop me home. My dad won't care.'

'Nah, sorry mate; you're stuck with me because I need me job.' He shrugged and added, 'Hey. It'll be right. Have a cuppa or a Milo with me. I'll help you with your homework or whatever.'

I didn't mind. Not really. I kind of enjoyed his company. I liked the way he smelled. I liked the physical area his mass used. It comforted me. A little.

I feigned a grimace and said, 'Okay.'

We arrived at Sandy's little beach house in a small dead-end street, located right next to one of the two main beaches. One beach, the one closer to Dad's house, and where I'd hurt my knee, ran in an eastward direction but faced north, towards the rock wall. It was littered with rocks and was at the mouth of the river that ran in front of Dad's house. The beach closest to Sandy's, was wilder, sandier and faced eastwards to the open ocean. The surf lifesaving club roof was visible across the road from Sandy's house. Its kitchen was even smaller than my dad's. It had '80s décor, was very narrow but it had views to rival that of a luxury apartment.

I didn't think about the Milo. I just drank it. Sip, swallow. It was easy to not worry about things when you were looking at the blue, white and green of the sea meeting the yellow and white hues of the beach.

'Did you live near the beach back with your mum?' Sandy asked.

I shook my head. 'Nah,' I said, even though I had. I had lived in a three-bedroom brick house with my mother five minutes from the bay, but I had never really cared for it. Sort of. I used to. Until the summer before last. I had started going around with a guy named Corey; used to watch him jumping off the pier again and again. He'd splash me with water and I'd giggle and squeal, pretending to hate it but I loved it. It had been good fun. Until he had jumped and landed headfirst on a submerged shopping trolley. The bay smelled like a dirty toilet after that. Other people couldn't smell it but I could.

Standing in his kitchen, Sandy gazed out the window and it was as though he couldn't be still. Every muscle twitched. He ran a hand through his hair and murmured, 'Damn it looks good out there, eh.'

The waves came in even lines, like a metronome of the sea. The water was green under the dull sunshine. I shrugged. 'I guess.'

'It'd be good to go out for a bit.'

I swirled the mug of Milo with a frown. 'I thought you went this morning.'

'Means nothin', mate,' he laughed. 'I wanna go again.'

'Why don't you then?'

'I'm looking after you.'

'I'm a big girl. I can sit here.'

Sandy narrowed his eyes at me and then looked back out at the water. He gnawed on his sun-chapped lips and then turned to me, clapping his hands together.

'Righto. I reckon we can meet halfway here. If your knee can take it.'

'What?'

He gestured to the beach. 'I'll go surfing, but you can come down to the beach.'

I dropped the mug down onto his ceramic bench and it clanged but didn't break. My eyes were as wide as my shock. 'But I can't surf.'

He laughed. 'No, you can just sit on the beach and watch and I'll keep an eye on you from there. That's if your knee can hack the distance.'

I rubbed at my knee and imagined myself sitting on the beach, watching him surf as though I was a groupie or a girlfriend. The thought of being a girlfriend made me blush – and I did wonder about the surfing scene. Sandy seemed addicted to it, the way I was addicted to starving and exercising. A higher power coming

32

over us, making us compulsive and desperate to feel how we felt in the moment. The power I felt when denying or hiding food was what kept me returning to the habit. I wondered how surfing felt. It seemed like it would be the opposite of power – being at the mercy of the ocean, though I supposed in a way it was like you were harnessing that power and becoming at one with it.

I drew in a deep breath and nodded. 'I think my knee can hack it.'

'You sure?'

I nodded. 'I can do it.' I was curious to see him surf. Visions of *The Endless Summer* and Kelly Slater came to mind. I imagined Sandy doing crazy aerials over the white walls of water like I saw on posters, dolphins leaping and rainbows shining.

Sandy's face lit up with a massive grin and he bolted into his garage and he dragged on a wetsuit like a condom before I even managed to make it to the front door. He jogged down the street ahead of me and I followed him gingerly, down the steps to the sand. When I reached the bottom, I looked back up the staircase. How I'd get back up them, I had no idea. My knee felt like something had snapped on the side.

I eased myself down and watched Sandy run into the water. I stretched my leg with the sore knee out in front of me and dug my hands into the sand. I couldn't keep them still. I lifted the sand, patted it, scrubbed it, rolled it, buried it, smeared it, flattened it, moulded it and dug it. For half an hour, I didn't even realise what I was doing. I noticed it only because I couldn't stop. It was soothing. I was getting horribly covered in sand, but it felt so good at the same time. Sand was an odd thing. It was pretty much a rock. Rock and water. Shells and fish skulls.

A spray of water landed on me and I flinched and looked up. A girl from school – the one who had asked if I was okay and told the boys to leave me alone because of my disease. She was shaking her hair and it was sprinkling all over me. I leant away and couldn't hide the disgusted expression on my face.

She stood over me, hair dripping wet, wetsuit undone to her waist. She was covered in goosebumps but had no sign of a shiver. She held a surfboard at her side, under her arm. Another surf-nut. This place seemed to have a surf-nut prerequisite for residency. She asked, 'What are you doing here?'

I buried my hands down into the cool sand as I answered her. 'Nothing. Just waiting for a mate.'

'Who's ya mate?'

'What's it got to do with you?' I asked.

'All them out there are my mates. I reckon I'd know if one of them was your mate because you'd be my mate.' She grinned.

'His name is Sandy,' I answered.

'Sandy?'

'Mm-hm.'

'You're full of shit. How do you know him?' Her words seemed nasty, but her eyes glittered. More like a challenge, a quiz.

'He works for my dad. We hang out.' I wasn't stupid. I could appreciate Sandy's attributes even though he was older than I was. Being "in" with a guy like him would get me enough respect to avoid having my hair ripped out in a territorial estrogen throwdown that this chick was barking for.

My answer must have pacified her enough because she put her board down and gestured at it. 'Sweet, right?'

'What?'

'My new board. Al Merrick shaped it, you know.'

'Oh. Yeah. I like it a lot.' I touched its smooth underside. 'It's cool.'

'Do you know people talk about you?' she said and sat down next to me.

She was closer to me than anyone had ever sat before. If I moved, I'd elbow her. She didn't seem to mind being very close to people. I answered, 'Um...no.'

'Well, they do. Everyone knows you're sick.'

I exhaled and turned my attention back to Sandy. He was paddling for a wave, keeping his face angled back over his shoulder before he decided not to go for it and angled himself away from it. The girl continued talking and I tried to not let her bother me, but she said, 'Everyone knows what you are,' like I was a leper.

My lips shook as I said, 'What am I?'

'You're anno, right?' She smiled. Then laughed a little. 'You're really skinny. It's not like you can hide it.'

I glared at her. Anno? That sounded so degrading. Like it was a joke. I snapped, 'No. I'm not.'

'Well. That's what everyone is saying,' she replied.

'Right,' I muttered and started playing with the sand again, wishing she'd go away.

A moment passed before she said quietly, 'Shit. I'm sorry. That was bitchy of me to say.'

'Was it?' I asked innocently.

'Can we start over?' she asked. She gesticulated with her hands and looked up at the sky as she said, 'I have this thing where I say things without thinking and I don't mean anything, I get into trouble all the time for it, I just can't help it, I talk and I can't stop and it's a pain but it's just like – shut up Hollie.'

Her eyes came back down and met mine, where she would have seen my own eyes staring at her sideways in a bewildered way.

She held out a hand. 'I'm Hollie.' We shook hands. Then she started digging in the sand too. It seemed to be as irresistible to her as it was for me. She said, 'And I am sorry for what I said. It's just that all the guys were real excited about there being a new girl in town. Fresh meat, and stuff,' she chortled.

'Really?'

'It doesn't happen around here very often.'

'Oh.'

'Especially such interesting ones like you.' I looked at her pointedly with my eyes raised. She continued, 'Yeah. Locals sorta stick with locals if you know what I mean.'

'Oh okay.'

'Everyone was so excited about you coming.'

'Wow.'

'Yeah, but then they saw you and they were all disappointed because of well, you know.'

I rubbed at my eye, trying not to get sand in it.

Hollie said, 'It's cool that you moved here though, more people to meet and stuff like that. It's pretty bloody boring around here.'

I smirked and agreed with her. 'Oh, I know!' I said, purposely gushing. 'It's just DEAD. And so boring.'

She was quiet. I had touched a nerve. One point to me.

'So, your dad is a close friend of Sandy's?' she asked after a minute.

'Yeah.'

'He's decent.'

'Yeah, he is.' I gestured to the cluster of blobs of wetsuits out in the water. 'Are you all friends then? You surfies?'

Hollie nodded and wrung out her hair. It was dark brown and wavy – just gorgeous. My own hair was a mousy blonde, flat and dead. I wanted hair like hers as I watched her running her hands through the thick hair.

I muttered, 'You're getting sand in your hair.'

'Oops.' She giggled and shook her hair like a bloody model. 'Yeah, so you know. We only stick together us locals. That's why I was surprised when you said Sandy was your mate. We are so close.' She put up her index finger and middle finger, snug together to show me how close she was with Sandy. I glanced out where Sandy was waiting for another wave.

Hollie said, 'He's never mentioned you to me before.'

'I haven't lived here long.'

'I know. I've seen you at school, too. You sit by yourself. Nobody's made friends with you yet.'

My stomach churned. She had noticed my weirdness, so others would have as well. I hadn't tried to make friends, but nobody had tried to make friends with me either. I was a social pariah already. Nobody wanted to be my friend. I snapped, 'Do they have to?'

'You're in if you surf. Not JUST surf either. None of that bloody weekend-surf bullshit. You gotta be good,' she told me.

'And you're good?'

She grinned. 'You bet your arse I'm good.'

'So…I guess my dad isn't a real local then either because he doesn't surf.'

'I mean us. Our group. We are the locals. We run this place. No one can touch us. No one can just squeeze in.' She looked at me pointedly. 'Unless you surf.'

'You think I'm squeezing in?' I asked.

'We look after our own is all. If you're in, you're in. If you're out, you're out.' It hurt my feelings more than it should have. Why did I care? Some clique was shutting me out. Big bloody deal. But it still hurt to know that I was the "interesting anno". I had become that weird anno at my last school. That headcase. I was normal, damn it. I'd fit in. I wouldn't be that anno girl anymore. But the thought of how stuck I was, how I'd be like this forever, made me balk. Who was I without anorexia, really? I couldn't remember the girl I was before it.

The realisation that I'd never be normal flattened me. I stood up tenderly and brushed off the sand.

'Where are you going?' she asked.

'I need to be alone.'

I limped my way back to Sandy's. My mind was quiet. I just listened to the noise my shoes made on the gravel and the pavement. The birds. The odd car going past. The distant calls of the excited surfers and the throes of the ocean hitting the sandbar. I sat on the veranda step and counted the granules of sand that had stuck to my palm. The granules kept falling off so I had to keep restarting.

After a while, Sandy walked up with his board under his arm and demanded, 'Where the bloody hell did you go? Had me thinking you'd gone into the water and drowned or something.'

'I was with Hollie for a bit,' I replied, deciding on the spot that I would test what Hollie had said about their closeness. 'She said you and her are really close.' I narrowed my eyes. 'Like, really close.'

'Does that bother you?'

I shrugged.

He groaned, 'I don't see why it should.' He lowered himself down onto the veranda beside me. His upper body was shirtless and I found my eyes being drawn into the muscles that curved outwards. It was an alien thing to me. Stomachs didn't curve outwards. Stomachs were concave. I flinched when he put his surfboard down behind me in an almost intimate move of putting his arm behind me. He added, 'We're friends.'

I sighed, 'I don't know. She made it seem like you were pretty close.'

Sandy grinned lopsidedly and his eyes glazed for a moment. 'Nah, just friends. What did she say exactly?'

'She said you locals stick together,' I muttered, looking down at the gap between my knees. 'And you're only in if you surf.'

Sandy was silent.

I looked up at him, holding my stringy hair off my face. 'She said boys were talking about me but now they've seen me, they're not interested because I'm...'

My voice cut off. I couldn't admit it. I was meant to be a different person here. I wasn't the anorexic anymore. I would never be recovered if I stayed one. To finish, I said slowly, 'Skinny.'

Sandy leaned back, pulling against his knees in a type of stretch as he mulled over what I had said. 'Well, that's kind of mean.'

I scoffed. 'Yeah.' Looking back down at my knees, I traced where one was swollen and whispered, 'Everyone was talking about me but you never even told anyone you knew me.'

'What?'

I huffed and glared at him. 'Are you embarrassed by me?'

38

His mouth dropped and his blue eyes flashed. 'What?'

'Never mind.' I stood up and he mirrored me. He blocked me from the door.

'Nah, nah, nah – wait. You can't drop that kind of bomb and walk off. Talk to me.'

I rolled my eyes, regretting I'd said it. 'Just how I felt.'

'I didn't tell anyone about you because…' He scratched his head and grimaced.

'What?' It was my turn to be confused.

He grunted before he explained, 'I didn't tell anyone because I don't want people to know I hang out with your dad. It's complicated.'

I was rooted to the spot as I wrinkled up my face and spat, 'What? Why?'

'Like I said, it's complicated.' He held out his arms. 'I'm not embarrassed by you. At all. I just didn't know how to explain who you are and why you're with me. I didn't want people asking questions.'

'So, you don't really work for my dad, then?'

'Nah,' he grinned. 'Just good…friends. Mates.'

'Is it because he doesn't surf?'

Sandy's eyes flicked to the side before he answered, 'A little. Yeah.'

'You guys are really weird,' I groaned.

He laughed in a high-pitched tone. He held out his arms and asked, 'Can I hug you? Can I? Is that okay?'

I nodded. He wrapped his upper body around me as if he could go all the way around. Enveloped by his warm but damp skin, I closed my eyes and sighed. When he pulled away, I longed for it have lasted longer. He looked curiously at me, 'Hollie didn't say anything else about me, did she?'

'You can relax, Sandy. She didn't say anything. I even kind of liked her,' I lied. 'We're gonna hang out at school tomorrow.'

We walked inside and sat down. He ate corn chips. I bit my nails. He kept offering me some chips and I kept denying them.

It got dark. My dad still hadn't come to get me. Sandy slipped out of the room and I heard him on the phone. Concerned voice. Bewildered laughter ensued.

He came back into the room and said, 'He was at home. Ha. He forgot.'

My dad had actually forgotten about me. Forgotten. Me.

Sandy chugged the rest of his drink. 'I'll take you home.'

We rode along in darkness, our faces illuminated with the orange and green glow from the radio.

'Thanks for everything today, Sandy,' I said as I got out.

'No worries, mate. Any time. Want me to walk ya in?'

'I'm fine. I'll see you around.'

'That you will. All righty. See ya.'

'Bye.' I shut the door and waved as he drove off.

The porch light was on and Dad opened the door. I stood there for a while before he said, 'I am really sorry, Sprout.'

I limped past him and mumbled, 'I can't believe you forgot me.'

'How's ya knee, mate?'

I paused with my hand on my bedroom door then snarled, 'I'm not ya mate!' as I slammed the door.

In my bedroom, I paced, despite the tearing sensation in my knee. Fury kept the pain at bay. So mad I could pull on my hair and wrench it downwards with such force that I felt it ripping out of my scalp. I hated it here. What was the point of trying to get well? My mother dumped me. My father forgot me. I would never fit in. I would never have friends. Hollie was saying I was anno.

She's just jealous, said the voice in my head. *Jealous of your thinness. Every girl wants to be this skinny. They act like being anno is being bad but really, they're just jealous.*

I threw myself down onto my futon-bed and caressed my bones. I was better than her. She was just jealous.

In the morning, I decided to only walk one lap up to the highway and back, to give my knee a break. It had throbbed and ached all night but I was determined to exercise anyway. It was the only way I could face the day. Anorexia is an odd beast that lives inside your brain and works your body from the inside out, forcing you to do things that you don't actually want to. My knee was swollen and sore, but I continued to walk on it to make sure I was burning calories. Calories were something to be extinguished – or better yet, avoided altogether. Avoiding them gave me a high that made the world okay.

Upon arriving home after my lap of walking, I opened the door slowly, catching it from creaking and giving me away. I peered inside and gasped when I saw Dad's shadow moving around the kitchen. I could try to tip-toe down the hall to my bedroom and pretend like I'd been in bed this entire time, but I wanted to kick myself when I realised that I'd left my bedroom door wide open. Dad would have seen that I wasn't in bed. He would have realised I wasn't home. I sighed and decided to just confront the issue. Might as well. It was coming anyway.

'Morning,' I grumbled as I crept into the kitchen, favouring my knee.

'Morning!' He was too chipper. He was trying too hard. Bloody hell, this was going to be awkward.

'You're up early,' I said quietly.

'Wanted to catch you before you went.'

I slid down into the seat at the poxy kitchen table and mumbled, 'Okay.' What did he mean, before I went? Did he know about my leaving every morning anyway?

'Is this going to be a problem?'

'Is what going to be a problem?' I practically whispered.

'You. Running. Every morning.'

Oh, so he did know that I ran every morning. Sandy must have told him that he saw me.

I tried to be casual with a shrug. 'I like to exercise.'

'I know. Which is fair enough, but you hurt your knee yesterday.' He sipped at his coffee mug and leant against the bench, looking at me pointedly.

'That's why this morning I just went for a walk.'

'Or you could take a day off and just relax,' he suggested.

'I can walk,' I snapped.

He shook his head. 'It's one day. Don't let it be a problem, Daisy.'

I stared down at my running shoes. I mumbled but trailed off because I knew I couldn't even convince myself nor him, 'It won't be a...'

I heaved a sigh and took an apple from the bowl and began to peel the sticker off. I had to think of an exercise that could burn calories without hurting my knee, or look like I was trying to burn calories. Figure out a way I could be fit and maybe get muscles to look healthy. Hey, Sandy had muscles. I could ask him. He was pretty fit. Fit from surfing. That gave me an idea. An idea that could keep me fit, burn calories and possibly even get me in with the locals.

'Hey Dad?'

'What?' He sat down at the table across from me.

'Can I have a surfboard?'

We both looked at each other with wrinkled, concerned brows and then uniformly looked away. Dad rubbed at his stubble.

'Ha. Just joking.' I got up and got myself a glass of water.

'I'm working with Sandy today.'

I sculled the water to keep my face neutral, so I wouldn't give away that I knew he didn't really work with Sandy. It made me breathless.

'I'll ask him some questions about how we can get you started in surfing.'

I nodded. 'Okay.'

'I just have one favour.'

'What is it?' I asked.

'Eat more than that apple today.'

I walked into Ms. Gregg's class and handed her my weekly reading journal of *To Kill A Mockingbird*. She gleamed at me and thanked me. She said nothing about the beautifully measured, neat cursive and the colours I had written the title in. Nada. Feeling squelched, I made my way to a table by the window and stared glumly at Ms. Gregg, waiting for class to begin.

It took so much energy to just keep my head from falling to the tabletop and stop myself from falling asleep. I listened to what she told us all but did not really comprehend it. I meandered down the corridor to maths. Hollie was walking past and her shoulder bumped mine. I crashed into the locker and collapsed in a heap on the floor. Her mouth went wide open and she grabbed at me desperately.

'Oh my God. Sorry!' she cried as she helped me up.

'It's all right,' I muttered.

'I didn't mean to completely knock you down like that. It was just meant to be a friendly "hey girl" bump.' She laughed. 'Guess you're a lot lighter than a regular girl.'

She kept her hand on my shoulder and I began to believe her. I nodded. 'It's all right,' I repeated. I gave her a weak smile and limped away.

After maths, it was recess. *Eat more than that apple today*, echoed through my mind. Would it really be worth it? Surf and eat more? The whole point of surfing was to burn calories. Or was it? I looked over at the group of kids nearby; Hollie was laughing with all her friends. They all surfed. You had to surf to be in.

I sat alone and now my shoulder throbbed alongside my knee. To fit in, I had to surf, right? I wasn't completely averse to the idea of surfing. It looked fun. I'd never even thought about it before but the way Sandy was so addicted to it, made it appealing. Maybe it would help me to focus on something other than food for a change.

I pulled my usual recess apple out of my bag and rolled it in my hands as I contemplated eating it. Nobody was around. I could throw it away and just tell Dad I ate it. Two apples in a day, yeah. It seemed a bit too much to have eaten by 10:15am. The bell rang and I looked around in horror. I'd wrestled with eat it or chuck it for the entire recess break. I put it back into my bag and headed to my next class where Hollie hurriedly slid into the seat next to me.

'I saw you at recess.'

'Really?' I asked, wrinkling my face. 'So?'

'Look. You haven't made a single friend, right?'

I crossed my arms and refused to answer her.

'I figured you might be feeling a bit,' she shrugged, 'you know…lonely.'

We sat there, eyeing each other. Was it an olive branch? Was it a deception? After a moment, she cleared her throat and shrugged, turning her attention to getting out her stationery. Not willing to lose the opportunity, I piped up. 'What are you doing at lunch? Maybe I can hang with you?'

She brushed her hair behind her ear and nodded. 'That'd be cool.'

So, at lunch, I found myself loitering near the canteen with Hollie. She introduced me to her group of friends – all boys. They nodded and greeted me with monosyllabic greetings. Hollie bumped my shoulder as we sat chatting. 'Want something from the canteen? I can get you a chocolate milk or something.'

I shook my head. 'No, thank you, though. I've got lunch.' I pulled my sandwich out of my bag.

'All good then,' Hollie said and got up, bouncing into the canteen, leaving me with my sandwich and her friends Mitchell, Lockie, Blue, Ethan, Sam and Rusty. When Hollie came back with a cartoon of chocolate milk and some hot chips as well as a lollipop, I began to slowly eat. Nobody said anything. Nobody pointed at me and laughed. Nobody stared at me. It was like it was a normal thing to do.

After school, I began walking home but I was caught up to by Hollie. She came bolting up to me, school bag bouncing loudly on her back, hair wild and her shoelaces untied. She asked, 'Oi, will you be down the beach later?'

'No,' I replied, tightening the hold I had on my backpack straps as I walked neatly and quietly – unlike the shambles that was Hollie.

'Well…we'll be down there if you want to come hang, okay.' She squeezed me on the shoulder then galloped off. I pursed my lips and tried to walk as quickly as I could on my knee and in as straight a line as possible home.

When I got home, I collapsed onto the couch. I tried watching the television but there was nothing on. I had maths homework, but my brain was filled with a new voice screaming at me to *eat eat eat eat. You are so hungry. Eat eat.*

In a daze, I found myself in the kitchen, opening the pantry door and grabbing handfuls of chips, biscuits and crackers. I filled a cup with warm water and dunked the biscuits like a lady might dip a biscuit into her tea. I chewed and chewed. Swallowed. Mouth still full, I ate the cheese and onion chips. How many could I fit into my mouth at once? At the back of my mouth, the masticated, sloppy mess and at the front, the chips still crunchy. Swirling around in my mouth and squeezing down into my throat. Dunk. Chew. Dunk. Chew. Munch. Gnawing on crackers, biting rapidly like a rabbit. Still not enough!

I opened the fridge and saw leftover noodles. I avoided those. I'd learnt from a previous attempt. Inspired by my sandwich lunch, I hauled the bread out and slathered it with butter. Mushed it into a ball in my hands and stuffed it into my mouth. Next were pieces of chocolate. They didn't even get the chance to melt in my mouth before I swallowed them down. I didn't know how long I stood eating and dunking, refilling my cup and swallowing with force to get it all down. The moment of numb bliss and fullness suddenly gave way to an intense need to get it all out.

I whimpered as I ran to the bathroom, belly distended and painful. I hurriedly undressed and got into the shower and turned the water on. Mouth up, I swallowed lots of the water until I felt as though my stomach would burst. Head down, punching my belly, I expunged everything down the drain in a multi-coloured swirl of vomit. After I was sure it was all out, I sat down in the shower and rested my face on the cool tile, allowing the water to splash my face as it rained down. Completely shattered and exhausted, it took me a long time to get myself up and dressed again, my throat and nose burning, every limb trembling.

Later, Dad arrived home as I was trying to do my maths homework. He came home with some fresh vegetables and some sirloin steak. 'Daze! I'm cooking steak and veg tonight. Yummo!'

I wandered out from my bedroom and tried to look grateful. Dad took one look at my face and said, 'Jesus Christ. Who died?'

'Oh, nobody. I'm just tired,' I replied, my throat raw.

He studied me for a moment before walking into the kitchen. I wondered if Mum had thought to mention the signs that I had binged. Spotless kitchen that I'd scrubbed clean. Missing food. My malaise, bloodshot eyes, hoarse throat and puffy cheeks. If she had, Dad acted oblivious.

He cooked dinner and we ate (I forced mouthfuls) in silence. Because it seemed that he had no idea and I had gotten away with it, it became a regular thing. Every. Single. Damn. Day.

I wandered around school, bumping into things, completely buzzing around the edges as though I didn't exist. Not eating made me feel strong. Binging and purging made me feel weak and exhausted. I ate everything that Dad put in front of me. Eggs for breakfast. Apple for snack. Sandwich for lunch. Meat and vegetables, fish and chips, pizza, rice, tacos, barbequed sausages. I thought Dad was patting himself on the back a little.

46

One weekend, Mum called to check in and see how things were going. 'She's eating.' He beamed. He took the phone call out of the room. I pressed my ear against the door, so I could hear.

'Yeah, I don't know...I haven't noticed anything...Eggs, toast, whatever...She wants a surfboard, love...I think it's been a good motivator...She's eating...What do you mean? Some quack says so? The deal was I take her and she stops seeing those doctors. Fresh start. Maybe if you believed in her...Yeah, fine, fine, fine. Righto, righto. I'll take her. Bye.'

I leapt back onto the couch and pulled the throw blanket over me. Dad emerged and he said, 'Your mother wants me to take you to the doctor. Your doctors at home want an update.'

I looked down at my blue skeletal fingers and said quietly, 'But I'm fine, Dad...I'm eating.'

'I know, Sprout...I know,' he sighed.

I felt like a piece of crap for lying to him. I wouldn't ever get better until I was honest. Yet, I continued to lie. Wallowing in my lack of wellness.

At the doctor's office, the doctor ordered me to step on the scale. The doctor did not tell me my weight, but told me the BMI. Then breathed in a nasally voice as he said, 'Underweight.'

'Am I maintaining though?' I asked curiously.

'You've gained three kilograms from your last weight here in this file, so you are doing much better.'

It was like I'd been slapped in the face. I'd gained three kilos since being at Dad's. *I have to lose that right now*, my brain screamed. Outwardly, I nodded and smiled. 'So, I am doing well.'

'Yes, you are doing well.'

'That's great!' Dad exclaimed.

'Yes…' the doctor did not sound convinced. He felt around my thyroid glands and narrowed his eyes at me. 'Have you been vomiting?'

Dad crossed his arms and looked at me.

I looked away. Honesty, honesty, honesty. I mumbled, 'I'm trying not to.'

Dad's face burned red and I could see a vein pulsating in his forehead.

The doctor shook his head at me. 'That needs to stop, Daisy. You are never going to get well if you continue with these behaviours.'

I nodded. 'All right. I'll try harder.'

I knew he was right. I was trying. The urge to restrict what I ate after a binge was strong, and the feeling of being in control throughout the day was hard to resist. Whenever I got home and was left alone, the urge to binge took over. It was as if I wasn't in control of my own body anymore. Having the doctor tell me I would never recover, didn't really bother me and I pondered on why as we left the doctor's office.

As Dad started the car when we were leaving, he shook his head.

'I'm sorry,' I snapped. 'But I'm doing much better! You heard him. I've gained weight!'

'Yeah, well, if you don't gain three more by next month, I am not buying you a surfboard and you'll be banned from all exercise.'

Being banned from all exercise and not getting a surfboard made me shudder. I needed the surfboard. I needed something to be fit and burn calories without raising suspicions, but I also wanted to fit in with Hollie and her friends. It was okay to sit with them at school during lunchtimes, but every day after school, they would go off surfing at the beach, having the time of their lives, and I'd go home, alone, where I would succumb to the binge and purge as if it was a demon swallowing me whole. I couldn't keep doing this. I needed the surfboard.

I stared out the window on the way home, hoping Dad wouldn't notice the tears rolling silently down my cheeks.

Dad dropped me off at school and, instead of going straight to class, I went into the restroom and stared at myself in the mirror. I shrugged my shoulders up to expose my collarbones. I closed my thumb and forefinger together and looped it up my arm. I was thin, wasn't I? What difference would three more kilograms make? I turned left and right. I pulled up my shirt and studied my stomach. Did it really matter that I had hip bones sticking out? Which did I want more? My bones...or to fit in? I tugged on my hair as hard as I could as if ripping out my hair could give me the answer I so desperately could not find.

After school, instead of going home to greet the binge/purge monster, I walked down to the beach and sat on the picnic bench that provided the best view of the sea and the waves where Sandy and Hollie were below. The wind picked up around half past four and I watched the perfect turquoise walls become crumbly foam. The surfers, one by one, trekked up the stairs, muttering hi to me as they passed. The last ones to arise were Sandy and Hollie.

'Daisy,' Sandy said, sounding surprised. He had half of his wetsuit off and the arms dangled as though he was an octopus. Hollie shook her hair out of a braid, and I lusted for the luscious waves for a split second. 'What are you doing sitting here?'

'Just watching. Thinking.'

They both came over and sat on either side of me. I could feel the coolness of their wet bodies yet I felt warmed by their company.

'I didn't see you in maths this morning,' said Hollie. 'You doing okay?'

I nodded. 'Yeah, I just had a doctor's appointment. I was back for my other classes.'

Hollie smiled and said, 'That's good.'

49

We all looked at the water for a while before Sandy said, 'I've got some Milo back at my place. You girls coming?'

We both nodded, and we drifted up to Sandy's house and I decided to tell them both what I had to do. Maybe they could help me. Anorexia didn't mean I had to be alone all the time...did it?

I sat on the veranda while Sandy and Hollie were inside, changing their clothes. I rehearsed the conversation in my head. If it wasn't such a secret, maybe this eating thing would go away. It wouldn't be so addictive. I'd be able to let it go. For good. I'd look pretty and be fit, like Hollie. I'd have friends. I wouldn't randomly cough up bits of vomit at school and pretend like I had a bad cold when it was just my purged food blocking my septum.

Sandy and Hollie came out, laughing about their waves and excitedly sharing their rides. Hollie handed me a Milo and I lavished the warmth of the mug and the kindness they were showing me.

'I don't know how many times I've hit myself in the face with my board trying to do this god damn aerial, but oh my God, I really feel like I'm getting it,' Hollie said.

Sandy nodded. 'Just got to have a bit more of a gun up as you come out of your cutback at the bottom.'

Hollie nodded and glanced at me as though she had just remembered I was sitting there. 'You probably have no idea what we're talking about. Sorry, Daisy.'

'That's okay,' I said. 'I don't mind listening. I want to learn.'

'About surfing?' Sandy asked, with an eyebrow raised. 'Really.'

I nodded. 'Dad's going to buy me a surfboard.' I added with a sniffle, 'But only if I get better.'

Hollie cleared her throat. 'Well. Ain't that something.'

'That's great,' Sandy said. 'I guess I'll be teaching you then?'

I paused. He stared at me. Hollie stared at me. I'd honestly had no clue who would teach me. I thought I would just get in the water, follow them around and be included. I was such an idiot.

50

'I don't know,' I mumbled. I put the Milo down and stood up. 'I better be going. Thanks for the Milo.'

I scuttled out of there as fast as I could. *Stupid, stupid, stupid!*

Dad was home when I hurried in the door. 'Daze! Come in the kitchen.'

I rolled my eyes and expected to see him serving a banquet for dinner to get that weight on me and cure me. Stuff it. What was the point? No surfboard would get me friends. Bones were all that mattered to me anymore. But when I walked into the kitchen, I was stunned to see Dad standing above two brand-new surfboards. One was pale blue and humongous. The other, slightly smaller, was purple and white. Dad was attaching fins and leg ropes.

I laughed. 'Oh, my goodness. What happened to three kilos?'

He said, 'Call it my belief in you.' He grinned at me. 'Besides, I'm keen to try it with ya!'

The next morning was Saturday. As usual, I was awake before the sun came up and I lay in bed with my mind racing. What had I eaten yesterday? Had I ballooned up overnight? My body felt like lead but my brain sent electricity coursing through and I got out of bed and started doing crunches on the floor. 100 of them. Then 100 leg lifts. My hip flexors snatched painfully but I gritted my teeth and kept going anyway.

Dad made us both toast with peanut butter for breakfast. I promised him I'd eat it but only if he gave me one slice with a mere scrape of peanut butter. We compromised: *two* slices with a mere scrape of peanut butter.

We carried our surfboards to the car and I chewed my nails while watching Dad strap them down in the tray of his work ute. They were so long that they hung out the back.

'They're going to fall out, Dad,' I scoffed.

I imagined the chaos that would ensue. An angry driver punching my dad in the face because the surfboard smashed their windscreen. The boards broken into smithereens before either of us could even have a go. But we drove slowly the 750 metres down to Shelly Beach and my nerves began shifting from missing out on giving it a go because our boards were smashed, to being petrified of what could go wrong in the water.

'I asked Sandy which beach to go to. He said this one.' There were two beaches within a ten-minute walk of Dad's house – one was an open ocean beach and was where Hollie and Sandy mostly went, and one that was rockier but had less rips that could catch us out.

Dad and I carried the boards awkwardly to the soft part of the sand where the water fizzed in. We put our leg ropes on. Dad assured me that I had to put it on the leg that I wrote with. He'd read that on the Internet yesterday on How To Surf 101 on WikiHow. My hands shook as I picked up the board and walked it to the water beside Dad, the leg rope already shifting and spinning around my ankle no matter how tightly I wrapped it.

The water rushed up to greet us as though excited to see us. An icy jolt raced up my legs and I cried out. It stung and ached. Dad made a fuss about the water being *bloody* freezing but I felt a smile creep onto my face; it was a good cold. I was awake. I was alive.

Dad and I flailed around, mostly on our bellies in the whitewater. We spun around as fast as we could and waited for the waves to push us along then we fell off and shuffled our way back out. It was cold. It was exhausting. It was on the cusp of torture when you swallowed a whole bunch of burning salt water or miscalculated where the board needed to be in relation to the wave approaching and you went cartwheeling off the side. But it was the most fun I'd had in years.

After about an hour, Dad wrapped me in a big bear hug in the shallows. I could not stop smiling. We went home and collapsed on the couch, still in our bathing suits. My arms felt like wet noodles and I could see the salt crystallising on my eyelashes. Our boards lay abandoned on the front porch and neither of us cared that we had tracked sand through the house. We sighed with contentment and fell asleep on the couch together.

So, this is what living felt like, I thought as I closed my eyes in exhausted contentment. I could get used to living.

Chapter Four

On Monday morning, I got ready for school and listened to the surf report on the radio. It still made no sense, but I listened to the language and wondered if one day I'd be able to navigate the terms "bombs" and "big swells". I went to school and didn't even complain when Dad gave me two apples instead of one.

'What'd you get up to on the weekend?' Hollie asked at recess, peeling her orange.

I took her cue to eat and retrieved one of my apples out of my bag. 'Not much,' I said then added with a grin. 'My dad and I got surfboards and we went surfing.'

Hollie's eyes widened and she shrieked, 'Oh, that is great!'

'Really?'

'Yeah! Did you have a lesson or did you just go out playing?'

'Playing?' I said, feeling uncomfortable with the word. She did not take me seriously and it hurt my feelings.

'That is so good.' She nudged me with her shoulder and said, 'When you've learnt enough, you should totes come out with me.'

Acceptance. Invitation. I smiled and nodded, taking a careful bite of my apple.

I didn't understand where my issues came from exactly. A place deep in my chest, instead of my head like all the doctors surmised. I went to live with my dad to get well, determined to eat and that there was nothing wrong with me. The cliché of a "fresh start" made me almost roll my eyes, but the knot in my chest followed me. It manifested in the safety of exercise and apples. Loneliness. Having something to obsess over to keep me from noticing I was completely alone.

Being with Hollie at school made it less obvious I was alone. Going to school started to become routine, and so did eating. Each day I went to school on a full stomach from the breakfast Dad watched me eat. I obliged his demands out of a mixture of gratitude and embarrassment. Lumpy, cold porridge on Monday mornings. A slice of peanut butter toast on Tuesdays. Crunchy, stale muesli with a dollop of horribly tangy, though low-calorie and fat-free, Greek yoghurt on Wednesday mornings. Eggs on Thursdays. Fruit salads on Fridays. On Saturdays, we went surfing first thing and laughed at each other's failings and cheered for each other when we got it right.

Afterwards, we'd go to the little café across from the beach park and I'd pick at a healthy Bircher muesli served in a big mason jar, which made my eye twitch because I never had a say in whether I wanted it or not. So, I'd pick at it angrily, while Dad polished off a Big Breakfast.

Sunday mornings, however, Dad slept in. I went running. I left breadcrumbs on plates for him to find. Old habits died hard.

We'd go surfing again after my run and Dad had caught up on sleep, but my mind would be ruminating on the lunch we'd have.

Some days he'd merely raise an eyebrow if I ordered a salad. Some days he would order hot chips and a burger for me without asking what I wanted. Looking back, I think he was doing the best thing for me at the time. Allowing me the choice only sometimes so I could prove I was trying, but also keeping me alive.

School lunches were a different story. If I sat with Hollie and her group of friends, I'd find myself munching at my apple for snack and apple for lunch quite fine. If she had detention or was absent, I'd be too anxious to eat and both apples would find their way into a rubbish bin.

Lockie poked me one day when I sat there, arms crossed over my stomach. 'Gonna eat, Daisy? You look hungry as.'

I smiled, blushing. 'Nah, I'm okay.'

He offered me some of his food and asked me how I was going with surfing. He was really quite sweet. He had blonde hair that he often had to sweep back off his face, a relaxed laugh and a habit of picking up a book when the conversation turned to something that wasn't surfing.

After school, I'd pace around the house. If I ate alone, I would binge. If I binged, I would purge. If I hadn't eaten my apples that day, I'd be so hungry and the battle inside my head was vicious and unrelenting. If I had eaten my apples, I'd go into my room and work on perfecting my homework and school assignments.

If the surf conditions weren't great, Sandy would drop in to watch some surfing on TV, or eat some free food, and I'd go and hang out with him but I would not eat the food he ate – crumpets dripping with honey, potato chips, chocolate bars, protein bars, leftover Chinese. Whatever Dad had left in the fridge, Sandy would help himself to. I would wait to eat until dinner.

Monday dinners were spaghetti with a canned sauce. It was revolting so I scraped off as much sauce as possible or smeared it all over my lips to wipe off with my napkin. Tuesday dinners were Chinese or Thai that Dad brought home. Noodles with vegetables, occasionally sushi, I could handle. Wednesdays were fish and chips. I always ordered the same. A souvlaki with no meat, and no wrap. Often, I'd be too full to finish my dinners and half would be thrown out (the rest, masticated and spat out with it), but I was still trying to recover. I was eating.

Thursday nights, Dad attempted to cook. Woefully hopeless, we often had raw risotto, overcooked fish, burnt steaks and dried out roast potatoes. Mostly, we ended up with beans on toast. Friday nights, Dad finished work early and took me to the pub. Salad. A bowl of vegetables. Sometimes a parma, dissected and massacred into tiny pieces, of course. Sandy would pass us in the lobby of the pub with a smile, acting as though he didn't really know us that well. A polite 'how's it going' and a handshake. But my dad watched him at the bar, more than he watched what I was doing with the food. I'd leave the table early and go over to Sandy at the bar.

Saturday nights, I cooked. I made him things like chili, curries, lamb shanks, wraps. I would then pour myself a bowl of lettuce and douse it in salsa. Occasionally washed it down with a miso soup, dinner = 50 calories. Sunday nights, we had Mexican. I really loved Mexican, actually. I put a wall up in my brain and enjoyed a taco and ate too many frijoles so that my belly was swollen. My mouth would burn, and my eyes would water as I tried different spice levels. Maybe it was because I'd gotten away with no breakfast and had run sixteen kilometres earlier in the day, as well as gone surfing for an hour. Maybe that was why I loved Mexican so much. I could eat it without much fuss. Was Mexican the key to recovery? Wouldn't that make a funny story?

Whenever Dad tried to change what we'd eat once I was in my routine, I'd throw a tantrum. It wasn't what I'd counted on. I couldn't eat spaghetti on a Friday night. I couldn't have Mexican on a Tuesday. I could absolutely not have McDonald's or pizza instead of Chinese. I could not go to the pub on a Sunday night. That was Mexican night. During meltdowns, Dad stared at me with wide eyes and his mouth agape. I guess he was still new to the realm of anorexia nervosa, so I should not have called him a clueless idiot as much as I did.

But I was eating; I was eating; I was eating. Surely that meant I was recovering. What else mattered?

One Friday night, Dad and I went to the pub like we usually did and ate dinner together. Sandy was by the bar, as usual. I went up to him to say hello and he was already tipsy.

'Hey, Daze. How's it hanging?'

'Good.'

'Want a lemonade? My shout?'

'Can I get a soda water?'

'Sure!' He ordered it for me a little too loudly before he turned back to me and lowered his voice. 'Ask your dad if you can come to a party with me. I'm going in around five minutes.'

Me? A party? I froze. Sandy observed my expression and said, 'Only if you want to.'

'Is Hollie going to be there?'

He nodded. 'Whole bunch of that crew. Would be good for you to get out and about.'

The bar worker handed me the soda water and I nodded. 'I'll ask.'

I carried the glass of soda water back to the table where Dad was sitting, gazing around the room, casually stealing glances at Sandy by the bar with his surfer friends. He nodded at my drink. 'Did Sandy get ya that?'

I nodded.

'He's a top bloke, isn't he.'

I sipped at the soda water and revelled in the fizziness when it hit my tongue. It made my eyes water and it pained me to swallow but I loved every second of it. A sensory experience beyond bland water and stomach ache-inducing diet soft drinks. Calorie-free.

After I swallowed and sat back down opposite Dad, I brushed my hair off my face but found a few strands had come out and I stowed them in a ball in my fist. I asked, 'Why don't you two hang out in public?'

Dad frowned. Brow furrowed, he leant forwards and crossed his arms, resting his elbows on the table, looking down at the empty plate still in front of him. 'We run in different circles. There's an age-difference, and...' He sighed and his eyes flickered back and forth between Sandy and me. 'It's nice to have him to ourselves every now and then, isn't it?'

I nodded and smiled, taking another fizzy sip. I asked, 'Is it okay if I go to a party with him tonight?'

'Now?'

I shrugged.

Air escaped his lips and his upper body stiffened as he straightened up, stretching his arms out and folding them again as though he didn't know where to put them, eyes going back to Sandy with concern.

'I don't have to go,' I said in a quiet voice. 'It's just some kids from school who I know will be there, and I'm...' I stirred the soda water with the paper straw. 'I'm trying to fit in, you know.' I blinked my eyes slowly at him, hoping he would understand. 'If I fit in, I might get better.'

Dad swallowed and rubbed at his speckled stubble

'Please.'

He sighed and said, 'Okay.'

I jumped to my feet and bounced on my toes, hugging his shoulders, able to wrap my forearms all the way around him as my chest bones ached from bumping into the tip of his shoulder bone. 'Thanks, Dad. I'll get Sandy to bring me home.'

He nodded. 'I know. Have fun.'

I gave him a feeble wave over the shoulder as I trotted up to Sandy, who raised a hand politely at Dad as though they were nothing but polite acquaintances. I followed Sandy out to the dark, cold carpark and got into the passenger seat of his panelvan.

A man walking past raised an eyebrow and nudged a guy next to him. They watched us leave and I stared at them in the side mirror as we departed wondering what they were thinking and saying.

As I walked into the party, Lockie and Mitchell greeted me at the door and offered me drinks. Sandy put his hand out between us, and I watched him splay his fingers. He had such big hands.

'Nuh-uh. No booze. You two shouldn't even be drinking.'

Mitchell snorted and rolled his eyes. Lockie gave a sideways smile and said, 'Calm down, Sanderson. You're not her dad.'

I looked to Sandy. 'Sanderson?'

'It's his last name,' Mitchell said. 'His real name is Florian.'

Sandy's Adam's apple bobbed in his throat and I stepped backwards away from Lockie and Mitchell and asked, 'I'm fine for a drink, anyway, thanks though. Have you seen Hollie?'

Mitchell pointed through the hallway of the house. 'She's in there with her brother.'

I hadn't known Hollie had a brother. I walked through the hallway to a large entertainment area, where the walls were lined with surf posters and pictures of women with big breasts in bikinis. I looked up at one and glanced down at my own chest where my shirt went straight down. I pursed my lips and gazed around the room filled with people I barely knew or didn't know at all. My chest was pounding and I had to remember to breathe. I slipped between people towards the pool table where Hollie was holding a can of alcohol and laughing with her head tipped back, her braces glinting in the bright LED lights in the ceiling.

I grazed her arm and she looked down and smiled widely. 'Hi!' She mimicked giving me a hug – her left hand held the can still so her right hand went behind me but her fingers hovered above my back as though she was scared to touch me. 'I didn't know you were coming.'

I shrugged. 'Neither did I. Sandy brought me.'

Hollie's eyes found Sandy's across the room and she nodded a greeting at him, then she held my hand. 'Come on, let me introduce you to people – Wow, your fingers are freezing; you good?'

'Mm-hm,' I chirped and let her lead me around to people.

'This is Daisy; she's new.'

They would ask, 'Where are you from?'

'Victoria.'

'Ah, Vicco.' A knowing nod before they would inevitably ask, 'You surf?'

'I'm learning.'

'Neat.'

'Yeah.'

The conversation would end with an awkward smile and then Hollie would move me onto the next person. I couldn't remember anyone's names. I was weary by the third or fourth person. But I remembered her brother Chase. His eyes went up and down my body and he breathed, 'Jesus Fucking Christ, are you dying or something?'

Hollie shoved him. 'Be nice!'

He snapped, 'I am! Has she got cancer? Why is she so skinny?'

My fingers began circling my wrist, my forearm. My finger and thumb tapped each other comfortingly. I took a step back and swallowed the lump of shame in my throat.

Hollie rolled her eyes and said, 'Sorry, Daisy. He's thick as.'

'No worries,' I squeaked.

She led me outside to the deck where she introduced me to more people and before I knew it, Sandy was tapping me on the shoulder with a flinch. 'Time to go.'

'She hasn't even met everyone,' Hollie whined.

'There'll be plenty of time.'

'Why are we leaving so soon?' I asked.

Sandy said, 'I want to go.' He glanced at some guys – they were familiar; they were the guys that were in the car park when we had left. I watched them suspiciously and they kept glaring at Sandy. It was clear they had an issue with Sandy but he wasn't sharing, so I said bye to Hollie and followed him back out to his panelvan. He held the door open for me and as he closed it for me, those same guys came out to the front lawn of the house and watched him leave. He shook his head and rolled his eyes as he got in beside me.

'Who are those guys?' I asked.

'What? Who? What guys?'

'Those guys who followed us out and look annoyed.'

'I didn't see anyone.' He started the car and pulled out a bit jerkily, making my head slam back and forth on the headrest a few times.

He took me home and came inside, greeting Dad with a handshake. I didn't mention the men just in case it freaked Dad out. Maybe Sandy had gambling debts or something. I didn't want Dad to think Sandy was in trouble because he might not let me go to another party. The party hadn't been a complete waste of time, despite me only being there for around half an hour. I'd met people. Hollie had seemed really keen to integrate me with her group of friends. This could be my life if I recovered enough. Parties, surfing, friends…all I needed to do was eat. It sounded simple but it made me see a way out.

I retreated to my bedroom while Dad and Sandy sat on the couch together, watching a movie on the television, talking quietly every now and then. Instead of doing 100 crunches before climbing into bed, I did 50. I curled up under the blanket and rubbed my stomach, reassuring myself that I wasn't instantly fatter because I didn't do 100. I sighed and closed my eyes, willing myself to sleep.

The next morning, after our attempt at surfing, while eating in the café, Dad said, 'Spoke to Sandy last night. He can give us a lesson tomorrow.'

My stomach fluttered and my spine stiffened. I was too bad at surfing for anybody to see me do it, other than just people at the beach. I wanted to belong with that group. Not be the gawky beginner surfer, or "kook" they had to babysit. Besides, Sandy was an incredible surfer. What would be think of me and my hopeless dad?

I jiggled my leg and chewed my nails the whole way to the beach on Sunday morning before our lesson with Sandy.

'You right, Sprout?' my dad said as he parked the car. 'You look like you're crapping bricks.'

I nodded.

'He's not gonna think any less of us for being utter duffers, you know,' he smiled. I fought the urge to vomit and nodded again. 'Come on,' he said and we got out of the car and pulled on our wetsuits. We both gazed around, waiting for Sandy to arrive. He must have forgotten us, I thought, but then I thought of a worse possibility: he'd changed his mind. Despite being nervous for him to see me flailing around in the surf, I desperately wanted his help. My fears were allayed when Sandy's panelvan pulled into the carpark at high speed, his tyres screeching as they swung into the bay.

He leapt out and started pulling on the wetsuit he already had half on. 'Sorry, guys! Slept in.'

My dad cracked some jokes and I breathed out, relieved. Sandy and Dad walked side-by-side, matching footfalls down the path. I followed them silently down the thin sandy path to the waves.

The beach was stuffed with people despite it only being 7:00 am. The water was a brilliant blue, reflecting the sun as it shone rare winter warmth on it. The water was usually a cold desert this time of the morning but that morning it was as though it had decided to be an oasis or a mirage of summertime in July.

Dragging our large surfboards along the sand, Dad and I followed Sandy to the other end of the beach, which left us out of breath by the time we got to where Sandy said we'd surf.

'You want to surf down here because it's sand all through here; there are no rocks and you don't have a reef bringing big bombies down on top of you,' he explained. He pointed at where the reef was and the rocks.

'What are bombies?' Dad asked.

'Big waves from out there,' Sandy said, pointing out at the ocean. 'They break out there but they can still pack a punch when you're learning.'

Dad and I nodded, oh thank you, wise one. We'd taken some pretty big waves on our heads the previous week, which is probably what had prompted Dad to ask Sandy for lessons in the first place. I wondered if those were the bombies Sandy was referring to. Our lack of ocean understanding made it more and more obvious that even with practice, we were not ever going to improve without help.

'The waves at this beach are pretty friendly...but they can have a gnarly side to them too, if you're not careful,' Sandy explained.

'Kind of like a woman, eh,' my dad joked. Sandy chortled and rubbed his hands together, looking out at the water. I fixated on my feet. I guess I was pretty friendly and gnarly so could not be all that offended.

Sandy then told us to show him how we were getting up on our boards, lying on them and paddling. He touched my shoulder and said, 'Wow, not bad, Daisy; you're actually doing a pretty good job,' which made me blush like crazy. He had to tell Dad to keep his feet together and scoop instead of splash. I started to feel more confident. Maybe I wouldn't be a complete screw-up after all, but I was so nervous about nosediving in front of Sandy and looking silly.

After a few minutes, Sandy walked with us into the water, explaining how to get our boards over the top of the whitewater and to look at where the waves wall up so we would be in a good spot to catch the wave. As the whitewater surged towards me like fire up a hill, I clambered onto my board shakily and rushed it, which resulted in me wobbling and doing a belly-whacker straight off the board. I cringed with embarrassment and could have stayed under the water for the rest of the day, even happily drowned.

'Take your time, Daisy. You've got this.' Sandy had the patience of a saint, even if he did chuckle into his hand when he thought I couldn't see.

On the next wave, I took his advice and took my time. One step at a time, I was paddling, popping up, balancing and riding. I rode the wave until the surfboard bumped into the sand and I toppled off, smiling with victory. Dad also started to get some great moves. He had to work on not bending at the waist. His little belly pooched out and his middle-age butt sagged towards the board; It made me look down at my own butt and I wondered if I looked fat in my wetsuit. There was no time to really think about it very hard, though – which is what I liked I suppose. There was a relentless travelator of waves to get past. We were slugging it out to the very base of where they broke, to get on one wave and ride it, then start the process all over again. It was exhausting, but pure joy.

With Sandy's tips, I succeeded more times than I failed, and my knowledge of the waves increased.

After the lesson, Dad and I headed to the café; we were too tired to talk but saying everything with our smiles. We ate our breakfast and then headed home to nap on the couch.

I was awoken by a text notification.

Hey, got ur number off Sandy. Surf lesson went good? – Hollie x

I propped myself up on my elbow and read it about eight times before I computed that Hollie was really showing an interest in being friends and I wasn't imagining it.

Hey. Yeah it was awesome. Loved it, I replied.

Her reply came back: **That is so good. Glad you had a good time. Can't wait to surf with you,** and it was followed by a love heart emoji.

I laughed and ran my fingers through my dead, salty hair. Maybe everything was going to be okay after all.

Chapter Five

SEPTEMBER

'Daisy, get up! Hurry up, you're gonna be late!' Dad yelled.

I opened my eyes and yawned, rolling over to look at my phone to see the time. 7:00 am. I stretched and got out of bed. I'd been sleeping in a lot lately. I felt heavier, but it was okay. I was getting strong. I met Dad in the hallway to the bathroom to brush my teeth and do my makeup. Hollie had shown me how to do it and I had come to enjoy the routine of brushing and patting my face every morning before school.

'You want bacon and egg roll, or a toastie?' Dad called from the front door, heading out to the servo.

'Toastie,' I called back, pulling my hair into a high ponytail and swooping it into a bun. He'd go get the toastie for me while I got dressed and packed my school bag. Getting dressed took me a little time. I glanced at my reflection and noticed the outward curve of my thighs instead of the straight as a pin stick I used to have. My butt was rounded. Surfing multiple-times a week had given me a round little butt that I secretly adored and couldn't resist smiling when I saw it in reflections.

I sat on the couch with my phone, checking messages and the surf forecast. Dad came back with our breakfast and we ate together.

'Much on today, Sprout?' he asked between bites of his bacon and egg roll.

'Chemistry, English, drama, art, maths and literature,' I recited my timetable.

'You still like that literature teacher?' he asked.

I nodded and took little munches of the cheese and tomato toastie. I was doing great. I'd reached a healthy BMI of 20. Occasionally, the thought of my weight sent me into a frenzied attack of star-jumps but Dad would hold my arms, whispering how proud he was that I was finally living. I was no longer that crazy waif who had wafted into his life and lied to him. If Dad wasn't there to be my rock, Hollie was there with a hug and a pep talk. She had become my closest friend.

After breakfast, Dad would drop me off at Sandy's, then go on to work. Hollie and Sandy surfed together every morning, training for the competitions they would be doing soon. Hollie would be getting ready for school and Sandy would be getting ready for work, both still dripping wet but stoked out of their gills.

A week earlier, I'd gotten brave enough to paddle out in the rip to the spot where my whitewater rides formed. Sandy had talked me through how surfing the unbroken waves, or "green" waves was different. It was easier to pop up, but more challenging to be in position. Instead of travelling forward with the wave, I would now be dropping down it. He told me that as long as I avoided low-tide and huge swells, I would be fine. But it was proving more difficult than I had anticipated. Each time I felt the board drop beneath me, my heart went with it and I would freeze, going down in a gigantic splash of failure.

Hollie had promised she'd help me after school in the right conditions, but she'd been so busy all week focusing on the upcoming competition season to help.

This day she said to me as we walked to school: 'Today! I'll help you today.'

I nodded and smiled. Excited but suddenly terrified.

After school, we hoofed it to Sandy's, so she could pick up her stuff and hit the water at the ocean break.

The water was still. The mild spring day had no wind and the clouds cast a murky green overtone to the water. One hand at a time, I dug in and pushed my body along the surface of the water. It felt as though I was going nowhere but the rip picked me up along its way and sailed me out to sea where I needed to be to catch the waves where they formed. Hollie and I paddled across to the empty lineup and smiled up at the sky for giving us a beautiful afternoon, with the beach to ourselves.

'No matter how many times I come out here, I'm still blown away by how beautiful it is,' Hollie said.

'I know; it's absolutely incredible,' I agreed.

There was a lull in the waves that made me feel completely at peace. It was almost as though I had forgotten I even had issues when I moved here. The ocean was medication and nourishment, entwined with a pulse for life. I could not get enough of the sun on my face and the cool calm beneath my toes.

As a small wave walled up, Hollie said, 'Try this one.' She helped me spin my board around and gently pushed the tail of my board as I paddled. I got on the roll, felt the lift, and as my board dropped, I got to my feet and smoothly trailed along the face of the little slice of aqua heaven. I paddled back out to join Hollie, laughing and embracing her claps.

'Think you got it?' Hollie grinned.

'I think I got it,' I laughed.

'Want another one?'

'I want another one!'

We laughed and paddled further out so we could sit and wait for the water to rise and launch us both into space so we could fly. As we gazed at the smooth water out to sea, a fountain of water sprayed around two-hundred metres away on the horizon. Hollie reached her hand out to me and she clutched at mine.

'Ssh, ssh!'

Her eyes were wide and her mouth parted as she stared. Soon, a fluke of a whale rose above the water in slow-motion and we both screamed with joy. Hollie fell in the water as she bounced with excitement. Her mouth wide-open, her eyes glittering and laughter in her voice. She climbed back onto her board and put her arm around me so that I nearly fell, too. We wrapped our ankles around each other's and bobbed in the water, studying the sea and the whale out there that had come by to visit us as we played in its home.

Hollie's eyes glazed as she teared up. 'I love them, so much.'

I'd never really thought much about them but knowing that we shared the space with them gave me a tingle and a proud feeling. A fellow mammal at sea, living in the waves and riding the ocean currents. Endangered, but alive, just like me.

Over the next three weeks, Hollie and I went out every afternoon when it was mid- to high-tide, and not too big.

Almost every minute of my day was consumed with Hollie. She lived with her grandparents, but practically lived at my dad's house or Sandy's. Her older brother Chase would come knocking at dusk, telling her she had to come home. The one time I met her grandparents, her grandmother had shocked me with her abrasiveness, and her rank odour as though she had stopped showering six years ago.

Hollie and I were getting ready to go to a party, and we were getting ready at her grandparents' house because our only ride was her older brother Chase. Her grandmother had a habit of saying the c word when referring to her husband and her boobs seemed to hover down near her knees. She made me incredibly uncomfortable and I retreated into Hollie's bedroom where we brushed our wet, tangled hair together.

'Why do you live with your grandparents?' I asked.

Her face went stony and her lips narrowed. 'Because my parents suck. They chose drugs over me and Chase. We came to live here three years ago.'

'Where did you live before you lived here?' It shocked me that Hollie had once been an outsider, just like me. I wondered if she was teaching me how to fit in because she had once been in the same position.

'Adelaide,' she answered.

I raised my eyebrows. 'That's so far away!'

She shrugged.

'Is that when you started surfing?' I asked.

She picked at a spot on her lips and said without looking at me, 'Nah, my dad taught me.'

She must have missed her dad all the time when she surfed. He had obviously played some part in her life before he had got into drugs. The way the she clammed up told me to stop asking questions, but I wanted to know everything about her. She was my entire world, in the sea and on land. She was stunning. Perfect. Everything I wanted to be.

Her bedroom door opened suddenly and we both flinched and looked around. Chase stood in the doorway.

'You ready?' he asked. Hollie wiped a tear from her eye. I nodded.

'Well, hurry up, losers,' he said and left. We both followed him, mute.

We were heading out to a party of one of Hollie's friends. A guy from school. She had a lot of guy friends. I never paid much attention to the fact that I was her only close female friend. She had that outgoing personality that drew in guys.

I was finally normal. I had friends and was going to parties. Surfing was life. As long as I was surfing, I was choosing to live.

At the party, we stood together, nursing cans of soft drink, chatting about the day's surfing and about boys Hollie liked. She liked a lot of them. Lockie was her number one. He was "just too gorgeous to exist". I laughed when she asked which ones I liked. Sandy would walk by, with a few older mates, giving us a nod to check in – always making sure we were safe. I would watch him go by and want to follow him, but I forced myself to return to the conversation with Hollie.

The nights after these parties would always end the same. Walking home, bumping shoulders with Hollie, the night quiet, save the rustle of birds in their nests trying to sleep but our footsteps disturbing them. We'd go sit out on the ocean beach and peer into the murky grey that was the sea in the moonlight. Hollie rested her head on my shoulder and I ducked my head down to meet hers.

'I'm so glad you came to Short Point, Daisy,' she murmured. 'I was so lonely before I met you.'

'You? Lonely? You had heaps of friends.'

'Not really. They're just surf mates. We're a community. I didn't really have someone I could share stuff with.'

I thought about how she was so bubbly and extroverted around the kids at school, joking and mucking around compared with how serious and calm she was when she was with me. I guess the saying that gold only shines in the sunlight was true when it came to her. I cleared my throat and asked, 'What about Sandy?'

She shrugged, her hair tickling my ear. 'He's about the only one, but still, it's only about the surfing. I can talk to you about other stuff.'

71

'Like what?'

She was quiet for ages before she finally said, 'That I don't have a home...not really.'

I gazed at her and saw how alike we were. I had felt that way when I had moved to Short Point. My mother had kicked me out because of my mental illness – claiming it would help me but I didn't understand how at first. Now I knew I preferred living here. I loved the view over the river, loved the smell of the sea and getting to go to parties with Hollie and Sandy. Home wasn't where you lived all the time or where you grew up. It was difficult to leave what you knew. Leave the comfort of familiarity. Anorexia had been like that. It was daunting to recover because I knew the safety of control. Making friends with new people in a new town, new state, new sport. I missed Jessie terribly but everything here in Short Point was better. Better for me. It had to be better for Hollie, too. She didn't need to feel like she had nobody, nowhere. She had me, and I had her.

I sighed. 'I get what you mean.'

We lay spread-eagle out on the beach, shivering in the cool air and giggling.

'Life is shit, eh,' said Hollie with a grimace.

I wanted to tell her she should try a life with anorexia. You only felt good if you were slowly killing yourself, but then you didn't feel anything anyway. Except cold and alone, as though you were stranded in a desert of ice.

Instead, all I said was, 'Yes, it is.'

She rolled over to face me. 'But surfing is all right.'

I nodded. 'Yes, it is.'

'And you're all right.' She laughed.

I sniggered, 'So are you.'

The next morning, we went surfing at sunrise. Surfing at sunrise after a party was one of our favourite things to do. Hollie would duck dive under the waves and leave me for dead in the whitewash, but being in the icy water was all we needed.

The sun was a white orb, hazy morning fog reluctant to lift. The water vibrated under me and I stopped to gaze at Hollie in awe as she surfed. As if in slow motion, she would be in the perfect position, smoothly soar along the wave, face set in concentration. Her eyes met mine as she sailed past me and she smiled, her eyes glittering like the surface of the water in the yellow morning light. There was no sign of the self-doubt and depression that I knew was there, and there was no sign of that fake joviality she used as a mask. She was just Hollie. Hollie Matheson, teen surf legend and girl with a massive heart who didn't want me to feel alone the way she did.

Hollie was freedom and the reason for living. I'd thought surfing had helped get me mostly recovered, but it had been her all along.

When we were leaving that beach that day, I didn't utter a word. I dropped my board and I hugged her, our rib cages bashing together through our wetsuits.

Hollie laughed. 'You okay, Daisy?'

I nodded and wiped tears from my eyes. 'Yeah. I just…freaking love you.'

She hugged me back. 'I freaking love you, too.'

Surfing together every single day quickly became a thing, when it had only been a twice or three times a week fun activity. The more I went out with Hollie, the more I improved. I began going twice a day with Hollie when the conditions were good, and even when conditions were big or "woolly". Each time, I got braver and braver. I followed Hollie out the back to sit amongst the "real surfers" – the ones who cat-called us and tried to snake waves from us. Hollie and I would paddle off to the side, but a few men would follow us over and get in our way or wink at us, waggling their tongues occasionally through a V shape of two of their fingers, or occasionally grabbing at their crotches and saying dirty things, before asking, 'How ya going girls? Having a good time?'

Hollie would roll her eyes and call out, 'Yeah. You?'

We were constantly keeping the peace. If we reacted or pissed them off, they'd hound us all day.

One day, as we carried our boards back to my place, and three guys followed us. One crept up and pinched Hollie's behind, making her leap around and shove him.

'Fuck off!'

They followed us every time we encountered them, but only when Sandy wasn't around. If Sandy was around, they left us alone. They never touched me or even spoke to me, but they seemed obsessed with Hollie.

One day when Sandy wasn't around, we were not followed. They must have gone to a different surf spot for the day; it was blissful. Instead, we could concentrate on how our thighs chafed from the salt and the sand. It hurt a bit, and I wondered in awe why I wasn't bothered that my thighs touched when I walked.

At home, in the shower, I ran my hands down between my legs and smiled. Muscle. Rock hard. Sure, they touched, but I was proud of why: I was strong.

Later, Hollie and I sat out on the balcony, eating berries and pieces of mango for lunch. 'Why do those guys always follow you?' I asked.

She shrugged. 'I guess it's because I get the good waves.'

I sucked at the mango juice that dribbled down my arm. 'Does it bother you?'

Hollie chewed at her lip as she considered it. 'Yeah,' she admitted. Then nodded at me. 'Yeah, it really freaking does. They're pervs.'

We laughed. The days were getting longer as spring rolled in, and we spent longer at the beach now there was less wind.

Hollie started to feed herself while I fell asleep on the couch while she showered. She left me alone and would head home.

74

Dad woke me up one Saturday afternoon by placing his cool hand on my forehead. I jumped up, heart racing.

'Dad, what are you doing?'

He shrugged. 'You're sleeping a lot. Just checking if you have a fever.'

'I'm just tired. I've been surfing heaps, Dad. I'm getting pretty good.' He hadn't been out much since I'd started surfing with Hollie instead and I wished he could see how much I had improved.

He handed me a fun-sized chocolate bar with a raised eyebrow. Testing me. As if I was still the anorexic who would chuck a fit over chocolate. I lifted my chin at him, took it, unwrapped it and ate in one bite. *Take that. I'm fine.*

He said, 'Anyway, I'll make a doctor's appointment for you. Better to be safe than sorry.'

He made it for a week later. It filled me with dread. I was finally happy and doing well – going back to the doctor felt as though Dad didn't believe me and he had no faith in me. I was eating. I was surfing. I was finally happy. It niggled at me for days later. Soaring down faces of small waves and wobbling as my heart raced, it was as though I was leaving anorexia behind. Anorexia who? I wasn't Daisy the "anno" anymore. I was Daisy Cavill – Hollie Matheson's friend. Daisy, that girl who was trying to surf but wiped out all the time and star-fished under the swirling whitewash.

I surfaced, gasping and spluttering. All the surfers nearby chortled. 'Nice one, Daisy!' they teased. Later, if one of them wiped out, all the others would hoot and holler, 'Doing a Daisy!'

I didn't give up despite their teasing. I paddled harder and charged for those waves, even when Hollie tried calling me back, yelling it was too big for me. Determined to be like her, I'd ignore her and make the mistakes I was becoming famous for. Meanwhile, Hollie was getting famous for other things.

As we walked along the beach path, a guy ran up behind her and grabbed her by the hips to grind against her. She leapt forward, sending her board sliding forward onto the path. She fell onto her knees and her hands. I grabbed her and helped her stand. The guy laughed. 'Looking good, Hollie.' A wolf-whistle. A sneer. A cough disguising: slut.

Hollie picked up her board and tried to disguise tears in her eyes by sniffing and saying, 'Oof, I got so much salt in my eyes.'

I gaped at her and then glared at the guys who were walking away, laughing. I didn't know who they were. I hadn't seen them before. They were older, around twenty, and I didn't know whether to go after them and kick that guy in his balls or stay with Hollie. Fear and shock kept me rooted to the spot beside Hollie. I ran my hand down her arm and she dusted the pebbles from the path off her board, checking to see if it was scratched or damaged. Her hand trembled before she pushed her hair off her face and inhaled deeply with a shaky breath.

'Are you okay?' I asked.

Her lip trembled but she nodded and said, 'Let's wash off in the shower. I feel dirty.'

I nodded and followed her silently. Under the shower in the car park, she didn't pull off her wetsuit like she usually did, despite her face being red and her brow sweaty. Her eyes flicked constantly behind me as I stood next to her, washing the sand off my feet. I asked, 'Who are those guys?'

'Some of my brother's friends,' she muttered. 'Arseholes.'

'Why are they calling you a slut?'

She rolled her eyes. 'I gave head to a guy and now I'm the town slut, apparently.'

I laughed, assuming she was joking. 'When did you give a guy head?'

'Last week when I was up at Briars.'

Briars was a surf spot up the coast. She had gone with Chase. He went all the time with his friends. She must have ended up camping there that night because she did that sometimes when Chase wouldn't drive her back home. Chase was supposed to look after her, but he usually just got drunk or high with his friends instead.

'Who was it?' I gaped at her. I hoped she would say Lockie, because she had a crush on him. We had joked about what she had wanted to do with him before. She never held back on details. But she was being unusually cagey, so I had a daunting feeling that she hadn't enjoyed her time. She hadn't even told me she had done to surf at Briars, let alone camp there. She usually recounted every single second and then some.

Hollie sucked in water from the shower then spat it. 'Just one of them. I can't remember his name.'

My mouth dropped before I could stop it. 'Why?'

'Not like I had much of a choice.'

'What do you mean?' I shivered.

'It was a dare around the campfire. I had to suck him off or I had to strip nude and let all of them touch me.' She shook her head with a shudder, and started walking away. My entire body went cold. I jogged to keep up with her, reeling from these revelations and that she was only just telling me now. 'Just moron guys doing stupid shit,' she muttered, squinting back at the beach. 'Now they're teasing me about it, which is just…wonderful.'

I imagined her at a campfire, having to do that. Why hadn't her brother stepped in? A leaden-sensation filled my stomach and my head ached. I kept trying to think of something to say or do, but the nausea rose up in me and muted my voice. All I could think of to do was follow Hollie and be there for her.

That night at dinner, I waved away my food. 'I don't feel too good, Dad.'

'You've been quiet today,' he said, putting his fork down. 'I'm worried.'

'It's not the food…it's…something else.'

'What is this…something else?'

'Something that happened with Hollie.'

'You two have a fight?'

'No. But I don't want to talk about it.' I yearned to tell him. It seemed like something we should report. But I wasn't sure if Hollie wanted to do that or not. I didn't want to overstep our trust so I stayed quiet.

'Be sure to be ready by eight tomorrow. You've got the doctor's appointment, remember.'

I rolled my eyes and nodded. The leaden-sensation turned to dread.

On the scale in the sanitary doctor's office, I stood, gobsmacked. My weight had dropped significantly. I had stepped on with so much confidence. The last time I had been weighed, I had been a healthy BMI of 20. I was recovered!

My weight had dropped back to underweight. I didn't understand it.

Dad's shoulders slumped and his hand ran over his face as if he had been slapped. The doctor's mouth formed a thin, disapproving line as he tilted his head at me.

'Have you been restricting your food again, Daisy?'

'No.' But I had slept instead of eating lunch. I had eaten only fruit sometimes. I had surfed more and used more calories than I had eaten. But I hadn't restricted! On purpose.

'Have you been vomiting?'

'No.'

'Have you been skipping your meals?'

'No!'

'You didn't eat dinner last night,' Dad snapped.

'I didn't feel well,' I wailed. I sat back in the chair and threw my hands in the air. 'I don't understand it!'

'You have a deadly disease, Daisy.' The doctor breathed out through his nostrils and my face burned red. I wished I could hit him. I wasn't an idiot. I knew anorexia was deadly. I just hadn't cared when I had it. I didn't care if I lived or died. Back then. When I had anorexia.

'You need to eat more than the average person. You need to eat often. You need to regain your nutrition. If you don't follow the meal plan the dietitian set for you, you will not gain weight. You will be a very sick young lady, indeed. No more lying to your poor dad here.'

'I'm not lying!' I screamed.

'The results beg to differ. You have lost a significant amount of weight. You need to start taking this seriously, or you will die.'

Dad muttered with a deep breath, 'Jesus Christ.'

I knew the doctor was right. Despite me trying so hard, I had lost weight. I started to cry and all I could do was pledge innocence.

'What happens if we can't get her weight up, doctor?' Dad asked.

'If she doesn't get her weight back up to what it was, I'll have to admit her to out-patient, at least. Worst case scenario, she's admitted to a hospital and gets a feeding tube. She has to eat.'

Dad shifted his weight and his face lost colour. He turned to me and asked with tears in his eyes, 'Daisy, I thought we were going okay. Why aren't you eating?'

I cried and cried as we left the doctor's office and got into his car.

'Well, there's no use bloody crying about it, Daisy,' scoffed Dad as we drove home.

'I have tried so hard. I am doing everything right so don't yell at me!'

'I'm not bloody yelling at you,' he shrieked back at me, taking a corner too fast making the tyres squeal. 'I've been bloody working with you on this. I thought surfing was helping. You've been eating fine – unless you're puking it up again.'

'My potassium levels were better,' I muttered, scrubbing my eyes so hard blotches of black and purple swarmed my vision.

Dad pulled into a servo with a sigh. I waited for him to say he was giving up. I was too hard. Even when I was trying, I was losing weight. I was a fuck-up. A no-hoper. Bound to go back to Mum in Melbourne and be locked away in an eating disorder ward for the next six months.

My weight wasn't shockingly low. That was the kicker. Any normal person would just be called skinny, but no. I had history. When you have a history, doctors and your community all panic and think you're trying to starve yourself to death.

With anorexia, it was sometimes about starving. Sometimes it was about something else. Sometimes it was about control. Sometimes it was about just having something else to focus on when something completely unrelated was niggling away at you.

The way the disease takes hold so differently of different people makes it difficult to empathise with other victims. You might develop it because you have no self-confidence. He might develop it because somebody called him fat. She might develop it because she was lonely and wanted some attention. Not to mention, the scores of people that got it just because it was in their genetics.

All this time later, the doctors all agreed with each other that I developed mine because of something called adjustment disorder, combined with grief and the ongoing stress of school, not feeling nurtured, missing that father figure in my disordered, fractured family. They might all agree with what caused it but they sure as hell didn't understand it.

I really did not understand it either, sitting in my dad's car, bawling my eyes out because I had truly believed I was turning the corner…and so had he. I hated that I had disappointed him but I hated even more that he thought I was lying all that time when I hadn't been.

Dad got out of the car and went into the servo. He came back with a big bottle of chocolate milk. The disorder suddenly raged in my mind, awake now that it had been acknowledged and challenged at the same time.

He flung off the cap of the bottle and dug his left hand into my shoulder as I sank against the door, lowering in the seat as Dad leant over me and shoved the bottle lip at me. 'Drink it.'

'No.'

'Drink it.'

'No.'

'Drink it!' He shook the bottle and a bit slopped out, wetting the front of my shirt.

'Get it the hell away from me!' I shouted, spittle hitting him in the face. Dad seemed to snap. His hands shook and a vein bulged in his forehead as he tried forcing it into my mouth.

'No! No! No! No!' I screamed. I karate-chopped the bottle and it flung out of his hands; the contents sloshed all over the dashboard and windscreen, like watery mud. Dad and I locked widened, surprised eyes before I fumbled away and out of the car.

'Daisy, stop!' he called, but I bolted. I sprinted away from the car and down the edge of the road, heading towards Hollie's grandparents' house which was not too far. The wind whipped into my eyes and made them tear up more than they already were and I gasped for breath through my mouth, making the back of my throat sore and raw.

He could not fucking force me to drink fucking chocolate milk. This was my fucking body. He could not fucking force me to do fucking anything.

I ran all the way to Hollie's where I banged on her door and fell into her open arms as she opened it.

'What?' she cried. 'What is it? What's happened?'

She held me as I sobbed uncontrollably, unable to explain what was wrong. Was I upset about the chocolate milk? Was I upset about Dad refusing to believe me? Or was I upset about the fact my own brain lied to me? I was anorexic. I was not that healthy, well-adjusted girl learning to surf and fitting into a close-knit group of friends. I was a demon.

I fell asleep on Hollie's bed, curled up beside her. I opened my eyes as the sun was setting, casting an orange hue over the side of Hollie's face and made her hair look almost red as she stood at her window, chewing her nails, with her back to me.

'Hol,' I croaked.

She turned and smiled at me. 'You're finally awake.' She sat down and caressed my head and hair like a mother would. 'Can you tell me what happened?'

I shrugged weakly, feeling silly for having such a big reaction over a chocolate milk. I clenched and unclenched my fists, watching the tendons and pale veins jut from my wrists as I curled my hands around. I mumbled, 'I'm not doing as well as I thought.'

Hollie gazed at me with a quizzical expression, waiting for me to explain but I didn't elaborate. My fingers found a lifting spot of skin on my lips and began picking at it, instead.

A moment of silence passed before Hollie cleared her throat and said, 'Daze, my nan called Sandy. He's coming to get you.'

'I don't want to go home,' I said.

'I know…' she paused. 'But your dad is worried sick about you after you ran off like you did.'

I took a deep breath. So, she knew. Sandy knew. Hollie's grandmother knew. Defeat and shame washed over me, making me feel less than human.

Hollie took my hand away from my lips and held it, squeezing it. Her hands were balmy whereas mine were frigid. She said, 'We all care about you.'

'Why can't I just stay here?'

She sprawled out next to me and said with a sigh, 'Two screwed up kids is enough for my grandparents to take; they don't need three.'

'I have anorexia, Hollie,' I whispered.

The silence was heavy before she finally said, 'I know.'

'I don't know how to get over it.'

She rolled over and looked me in the eye with a nod. 'Drink the chocolate milk.'

'How?' I croaked.

She rested her hand on my chest. 'Nourish your heart. Be true to who is in *here*.' Her hand moved to my forehead, where she tapped softly. 'Not who's in *there*.'

Sandy pulled up in Hollie's driveway and beeped the horn. Hollie hugged me at the door, waved to Sandy and went back inside. I ambled to the car, burning red with embarrassment and shame. He drove me home and turned off the ignition. As I placed my hand on the door to open it, he said gently, 'Daze, wait.'

I looked to him, expecting a lecture about how I needed to respect my dad and start eating again. I didn't think I could handle Sandy being mad at me and my heart pounded as I waited for him to speak.

'I knew a girl that had this thing once. She was in school.'

'Yeah?'

'Yeah,' he sighed. 'She was anorexic. Not even as deep in as you.'

I wondered where he was going with this. I raised my eyebrows. 'O...kay?'

He swallowed. 'She had a heart attack in the middle of class one day. Never saw her again.'

I collapsed into myself. 'She...died?'

'Mm-hm.'

My mind raced with the thought of what it would be like to have a heart attack at school. I didn't care about death. I didn't care about life. That's what anorexia did to me. Heart attacks were a common risk as we starved our muscles. It was something I pictured happening to someone much sicker than I was, deeper in the darkness. I sat back against the seat and uttered, 'Whoa.'

'Yeah…' We sat in silence for a moment before he looked at me with wet eyes. 'Don't even think of leavin' us like that, Daisy. Hollie, your dad, me? We'd be lost without you. You have to get through this.'

My face burned but my heart gave a little flutter at the thought of people missing me. I was one of them. I belonged. So, why did I still feel like an outsider? I stretched out my legs and rested my head in his lap, hugging his waist. He gripped my shoulder and I closed my eyes, listening to the silence of the night around us and feeling his body with mine.

When we went inside the house, Dad was pacing the kitchen and Sandy put a hand up to keep him away while he guided me into my bedroom. I sat on the bed and he took my shoes off and squatted beside the bed. His eyes were so green they reminded me of the seaweed at the beach, and the way the water changes to green when the clouds reflect off the blue.

'Now…tomorrow: you're gonna eat. You're gonna try. You can't surf if you're too weak. You'll end up bloody drowning, won't ya.' We both smiled. He squeezed my shoulder and left.

I lay there for a while, listening to him speak with Dad. I had to know what they were saying so I tiptoed down the hall to listen.

'It was like she was somebody else,' Dad said. 'Don't know who but it was bloody something. Like a split personality or something.'

'Bit of a shock.'

'Her mother said it was full-on. I just didn't see it. Didn't think it was this bad. Just when I think *she'll be right*, something else happens. Thought she was getting better.'

'We all did, mate. Stop beating yourself up.'

The chairs squeaked across the floor as they pulled them out and sat at the table. There was a hiss of beer bottles opening. I peeked around the corner and saw Dad with his head in his hands, staring at the table. Sandy sitting opposite him, fiddling with his keys.

'She ain't gonna eat tomorrow. I know it. I got this feeling.'

'You're not alone in this.' Sandy reached out and placed his hand on top of my dad's. 'You have me, and I'll help look after her, make sure she's eating; Hol will keep an eye on her, too.'

Dad shook his head. 'It's not enough. I gotta make sure she eats.' He breathed out what my weight was as if he had to convince himself. 'I've gotta…' He got up and started pacing again. I didn't want to risk being caught listening so I went back to my room and gently shut the door, then slid down it. How the hell had I managed to screw this up so badly when I had been trying? I'd been eating so well. It was like I couldn't breathe. I choked back tears until I fell asleep on my bedroom floor.

I woke up at 4:00 am. Dad was asleep on the couch, surrounded by beer bottles. He and Sandy had obviously had a couple of them together while I had still been awake, but then Dad must have kept the party going into the early hours of the morning. I pulled on some clothes and slipped outside into the dark.

My breath was white in the night, puffing out in a rhythm as I ran. It would be highly unlikely Dad would ever know I was gone when he was probably hung-over. A dog barked as I ran past and made me flinch. I ran until my muscles wobbled and then I staggered home, puffing hard, two hours later, and then crawled back into bed, shivering from the cool clamminess that sweat had left on me.

I closed my eyes and pretended to sleep until Dad was due to come get me up. His alarm wailed through the house and he got up. He grunted and yawned as he came down the hall. He knocked and swung the door open, leaning inwards as though he needed it to hold him upright.

'Time to get up, Daisy.' He shuffled away, allowing me my usual routine of shower, makeup, getting dressed. I did each thing, stressing about what I would say to him at the breakfast table, where he was setting down beans on soggy, buttery toast. I sat down in my chair and picked up my knife and fork, gripping them so tightly that my fingers ached. Dad ate his, alternating between his food and his black coffee. I had a mouthful. The toast made me want to gag. The beans were going cold. My hands shook. Why was I suddenly so damn apprehensive about frigging beans on toast?

A thud made us both jump and swing in our seats to see what had happened. A lorikeet had flown into the sliding door. I jumped up, and said, 'Poor bird!' whilst scooping up handfuls of the beans and bread into my serviettes and clutching them in my fist. I sat down again while Dad got up and investigated whether the bird was okay. It didn't move. I shoved the serviettes of beans into my school jumper pockets, picked up my knife and fork again, and spread the mess about so it wasn't obviously missing two giant scoops. Dad returned to the table and shook his head. 'Poor bugger.' He glanced at my plate. 'Nearly done?'

I scooped up most of what was left and put it in my mouth, chewed, swallowed with a grimace, but smiled at Dad. 'Done.' If he was so sure I had relapsed, I'd make it come true.

Afterwards, he dropped me off at Sandy's and I walked to school with Hollie. I was exhausted by second period. I threw my apple in the bin at recess, despite Hollie raising her eyebrows at me. *Stuff it*, I thought. *If they think I'm still anorexic, I may as well play the part. What was the point of eating if I wasn't getting better anyway?*

However, I soon learnt that nobody was going to let me starve without a fight. Five minutes before the lunch bell went, there was an announcement on the public address system, summoning me to the office. I wandered up, curious why I needed to go to the office. I was greeted by the first aid nurse who was also an office lady, and my dad. He was standing beside her, holding a sandwich from the service station. *Oh shit.*

The nurse sent Dad away, reassuring him that they would make sure I ate. She sat me in the staff room, unwrapped and put the sandwich in front of me. She sat down across from me and stared at me with a blank expression, waiting for me to start eating.

I laughed. 'This is ridiculous. My dad is overreacting. You don't need to supervise me.'

'He feels otherwise.'

I pushed the plate across the table, grabbed my bag and stood up. 'I don't have to eat the sandwich if I don't want to. You can't make me.' I hauled my school bag onto my shoulder and marched out of the staff room, kicking the door as I did.

My head thumped and my face prickled with rage. Each step was heavy and my throat constricted as I suppressed a scream. It was as though everyone was out to get me. Everyone had something to say about what I ate. It was embarrassing and belittling. I didn't want to stay there at school where now even the adults knew I had issues with food and Dad was making them feed me. Running away seemed like the best option so I headed for the school gate.

Hollie came running after me as I strode across the school carpark, heading for the gate. 'Daisy! Don't go!'

'I'm not staying here! Everyone sucks!' I yelled.

She walked briskly beside me. 'Well, can you talk to me? I'll help you.'

'Not right now,' I gasped.

'But please, eat something. I saw you throw your food away. Daisy, please.' Hollie tried to keep up with me but a manic energy made me faster than her. 'Daisy! Stop!'

'I'm not eating! If they think I don't eat, I won't!'

She grabbed my shoulder. I swung around and slapped her.

She reeled backwards and shouted, 'What the hell, Daisy? I'm just trying to help you.'

'I am fine!' I screeched, feeling the tears come squirting out of my eyes as I said it. My chest ached so I dropped my bag and to my knees in the carpark, where kids and teachers were starting to gather to watch my tantrum.

Everything took over me. I wasn't going to eat. They thought I was a failure. Failures didn't deserve to eat. They wanted to make me eat. It made me want to starve. I cried as though my life was over, rocking back and forth and Hollie held me, wrapping her arms around me and pressing her cheek against mine.

'I can't eat the sandwich. I can't eat the sandwich. I can't eat the sandwich.'

'Ssssshhhh,' she comforted and hugged me tightly.

As my sobs lessened, I slumped against her warm, muscular body and sniffed, depleted of energy. She pushed hair off my face and wiped my tears with her sleeve. She whispered, 'You can. You absolutely can.'

She walked with me to first aid, so I could lie on the bed. Hollie sat on the edge of the bed beside me. I curled up and we listened to the nurse on the phone with my dad explaining that I had become rather volatile and if he could possibly be the one to supervise me tomorrow. Hollie and I exchanged awkward looks. When the nurse came in, she told Hollie that she could stay but only if I ate my lunch; that my dad was coming to pick me up and take me to the doctor.

Hollie glanced at me hopefully, thinking I might eat if she stayed. I loved her, but I wanted the comfort of an empty stomach more.

'Bye Hollie,' I said coldly. She stood up and left, with glances back over her shoulder at me.

The nurse crossed her arms over her chest and glared down at me. 'Now, Daisy, this is silly. You don't need to lose any weight. Why are you doing this?'

'You actually think this is about losing weight?' I spat. I shook my head at her and her face went red as she looked away, her hands smoothing out the lines of her midriff under her blouse.

Becoming the monster in my mind was surprisingly easy. The words flew out of my mouth, my hand swung out and hit, punched, slapped. My mouth only opened to bite the hands that fed me. Or tried to feed me. The way it morphed into my body from the invisible crevices of my brain startled others but it made me quiet inside with relief. *Take the reins for a while, anorexia. Absolve me of decisions and responsibility. I'm so tired of fighting.*

In the quiet of the first aid office, I closed my eyes and dozed until the bell went. I sat up, looking for my bag to go to class, which was with Ms. Gregg.

The nurse said, 'You're not going to class, Daisy.'

I asked feebly, 'So, do I just wait here for my dad?'

'No,' the nurse sniffed. She added under her breath, 'This room is for people that actually *want* to be helped.'

I scowled at her. 'Then where do I go?'

She had me wait in the school foyer, so the office staff could supervise me. I sat on the hard red chair in the office and that was where Ms. Gregg spotted me as she was passing by in the corridor, arms full of books and papers, on her way to go teach the class I would be missing. 'Daisy?' she said, doubling back. 'Are you all right?'

'Yeah,' I said, instantly embarrassed. I hoped the nurse hadn't told her that I was being a downright brat. Anorexia went quiet while I had to face the shame of my behaviour. *Thanks, anorexia, for letting me down* – it wasn't the first time and it wouldn't be the last.

'Are you going home?'

'Yeah,' I repeated, wishing I could be swallowed by the floor.

'That means you're missing our class.' She sounded so disappointed that my heart gave a little sad palpitation. It made me feel even worse. 'What about your reading of Sylvia Plath to the class and your analysis?'

I had actually been looking forward to that. I had enjoyed studying Sylvia Plath's writing. The rest of the class hadn't understood much of it, or thought she was just crazy, but my brain had lit up and I'd read her collections of poetry with ravishing melancholy. Ms. Gregg had given me a little nod and a smile when she'd seen me poring over her words on the page. I had the feeling she had assigned her just for me.

I said, 'I'm not feeling well, but I have my analysis here, if you want it?'

I reached for my school bag but she put her hand on mine and said with a smile, 'Just give it to me when you're feeling better. You need to go home and get some rest.'

She walked away and then my dad walked in and looked down at me with a measured exhale. 'Looks like we've got ourselves a bit of a problem, Sprout.'

I sighed. 'Yeah. Looks like.'

I followed Dad out of the school office and down the steps to where his ute was parked. I slid into his car, not bothering where I placed my school bag. It thumped awkwardly against my back and the back of the car seat and made me grimace as it smacked against my bones. As I adjusted it so I could sit comfortably, Dad shook his head. I turned my attention to him but he looked out his window so I couldn't read his facial expressions.

He said, 'If we don't get this right, you have to go back to your mother and she'll put you in the hospital.' He looked around at me. 'Do you think you need to be in the hospital?'

'Dad, no,' I whined. 'I was really trying. You know I was trying!'

He gestured at the stained dashboard. The remnants of chocolate milk remained in white patches. 'That didn't look like trying, Daisy.' He pointed at the school building. 'And what you did in there did not sound like trying.'

I began to hyperventilate. 'It freaked me out.'

'You have to try harder.'

I nodded and smeared my tears across my cheek as I tried brushing them away.

'You have to do everything the doctors tell you to do.'

I bit my lip.

'You have to get well. If you don't…Well, I don't want to even think about that. I don't want to lose you.'

'Okay, Dad, okay!' I whimpered. 'I'll do it. I'll get better.'

He drove me home in silence and I pressed my hands against my heart to feel it beating in its odd rhythm. Sometimes it lurched from my chest and sometimes it beat so faintly I worried it had stopped.

Chapter Six

We went to the dietitian and they gave me a meal plan that was stacked full of three meals and six snacks a day. Yes... *six snacks*. It seemed excessive but I didn't say boo.

It'll be okay, the voice in my head said. *Play the part and they'll leave you alone. They won't notice you purge or hide food if they think you're doing well. Your weight is not too low, baby. If anything, it's too high. You can lose a kilo or two. But that would put you at an even ten, and that zero looks too round, so maybe you can get back to the next odd number, or two, or three, ooh, maybe you can reach the next ten. Who knows? You just have to act like you're trying your best.*

I accepted all the advice and meal plan like a boss, with a serene smile on my face. But then they said I could not exercise until my weight was up again, my smile disappeared.

'Does that include surfing?' asked Dad.

'Absolutely. I suggest following the plan or she risks losing more weight.'

I nodded slowly; agree, agree, agree…

As we left, I stormed to my dad's car, doubling back to re-join him then powering ahead.

I slammed the door as I got into the car and I yelled through gritted teeth, 'I am going surfing and you can't stop me.'

Dad blinked at me and started the car with shaky hands.

I held up the meal plan. 'I will tear this in half. I will eat, but only if I can surf.'

Dad nodded, 'All right, all right, Daisy…just…calm down, will ya. I don't like it when you get like this.'

He started driving out of the carpark and onto the highway, and I tried not to notice the tear that rolled down his cheek. All I could think about was getting out and running to the beach with my surfboard and surfing for hours just to spite that dietitian. How dare they try to take away the one thing that made me want to live? I wanted to surf and never come back to shore, run away with the dolphins and the whales.

As soon as we got home, I grabbed my surfboard and ran to the beach, hitting the water with purposeful strokes. I got out in the empty lineup and stared at the flat horizon. There were no waves today to surf, so I sat on my board and just cried, instead.

I was shivering without my wetsuit and I didn't care. I just floated and cried. I don't know how long I was out there when Sandy and Hollie came paddling out and sat up on their boards on either side of me.

Hollie dropped into the water and rested on my board by my knees, looking up at me with her big round eyes. 'I've felt like this before,' she whispered.

I sniffed and shook my head. 'I have…'

'Swell coming,' said Sandy, paddling forward. It was the first wave all afternoon. He paddled away from us to get over it. Hollie glanced at it and we missed the impact zone by a metre; the water tipped us up and we fell off the back with a stomach-dropping momentum.

'Come on, Daze...this swell that's coming is too big for you. You need to go in. I'll come with you.'

I watched the next wave wall up and knew we were going to be smashed.

Hollie grabbed her board and pulled my leg rope. 'Let's go.'

'I'm going for it,' I shivered.

She let go and I angled my board to ride the wave. It was huge. Steep and huge. I was too cold and too hungry. The water sucked me straight back to the top of the wave without the paddle power I needed. I went over the falls and was driven hard into the sandy bottom. I surfaced with the feeling that I'd been dragged across sandpaper.

I resigned and tromped to the sand where I could sit and watch the masters at their game. To my surprise, I found my dad sitting there, waiting.

'How long have you been sitting there?' I asked.

I sat beside him and he wrapped me in a towel. He kept his arm around my shoulders and said, 'However long you've been out.'

'You were here the whole time?'

'I was worried,' he admitted.

'That I'd do something stupid?'

'Something like that.'

I wanted to sit there, lean into him, and bawl my eyes out. Why did this insidious demon always consume me and leave me so empty and dead? Instead, I swallowed the tears and pushed my shoulders back so Dad's hand slipped away. We watched Hollie and Sandy take off on the waves and come flying out of barrels of blue. They made it look so easy.

Without looking at him, I told Dad, 'I don't want to die. I do want to get better. I know I'm crazy when I yell at you. I'm sorry. I'm going to try...but you can't ask me to stop doing something

I enjoy. Without surfing…it's not worth me even bothering to get better. You can't make me stop.'

'I understand.'

'I'll eat…but only if I can still surf.'

'I know.'

Relapse for me should be called re-re-re-relapse. It was as though my body and mind had a stutter. Start again, fail, start again, fail and start again. I wondered if Dad had told Mum. My entire body tensed at the thought of her knowing that I was failing again. I got the feeling that Dad played it casual with her though. Their phone conversations were always short, and seemed on good terms. I listened in when I could, ears pricked for the mention of my name.

Recovery attempt 302. That's what it felt like. Only, in the back of my mind, this time I knew I definitely wasn't ready. I was "trying", yet I knew deep-down that I was only acting. But the anorexic voice in my head promised me that if I could pretend that I was doing what they wanted, I could get more freedom. And it worked. Everyone thought I was trying. Sandy, Hollie, Dad and even the school nurses. Dad came to school every day to help the nurse supervise me eat a stupid sandwich. I cringed with embarrassment on the days Dad couldn't get out of work so he sent Sandy instead. Seeing him walk into the staff room behind the school nurse made my shoulders droop and my cheeks burn. I wanted to make him proud of me. I was an inconvenience, needing baby-sitting just to eat lunch, and I was a disappointment.

It felt like all I did was eat and eat and eat.

My intake became as consistent to the hour as the behaviours I took to get rid of the energy they were putting into me. I'd wait for Dad to be asleep before I spent hours exercising on the patio outside my bedroom, before going in and taking too many laxatives and chugging a litre of Diet Coke. It would erupt out of me and I'd be in the toilet until 3:00 am before finally making it to bed, where I'd lie awake with a throbbing head and hoping to God that I wasn't gaining weight. I would get up in the morning and try not to crap my pants at school, and then do it all over again.

I was only allowed to surf on the weekends. That's the compromise Dad and I came to. Hollie and Sandy would take me out on the weekends and give me some "training".

Dad had stopped surfing and his surfboard gathered dust in the garage. It became my realm, instead of ours – something for him to be excluded from as he watched my friendship with Hollie deepen and my alliance with the group of surfers Hollie hung out with grow.

Saturday nights, I wouldn't go home. I'd go out to parties with Hollie and crash at Sandy's place. Dad knew Sandy would make sure I followed the meal plan, but Sandy just let Hollie look after me. Which she did, but not as eagle-eyed as a seventeen-year-old girl should ever have to. As far as everyone was concerned, I was following the meal plan anyway and doing such a great job. What an inspiration I was. Yeah right.

Hollie and I went to parties with or without Sandy. They were parties we probably should never have set foot into. Parties her brother went to were full of older guys, and Hollie would smoke and drink. I would take a few drags of a cigarette but I hated the taste that lingered on my tongue and the ashy sensation it gave my lips. I nursed one can of soft drink all night, too afraid of the calories to ever take a sip. At other parties, with our surf crew, I'd watch Hollie fall into the lap of one of the local surfer boys and watch the way his hands would find their way into her pants. She'd eventually disappear for a while and I'd have to pretend I was happy that she was off having sex with some guy in a garden shed, under a porch, in someone's little brother's bedroom. Sandy would also watch her go; his frown not hidden well enough from me.

I sat down with him on a couch on a porch at one particular party and said, 'I wonder what makes her act like this when she drinks.'

Sandy shook his head. 'We don't gossip, Daisy.'

'I didn't mean…' I stuttered.

He peered at my can of soft drink and said, 'That's still full. If you don't want to drink a soft drink, why don't you just get a water or something?'

'I want to fit in,' I muttered.

He stretched out on the couch and said, 'Man, I am so drunk.'

I laughed awkwardly and didn't know what to say. I wished I was like Hollie, so confident and able to act on my desires. I wished Sandy would kiss me. It made it obvious I was a failure at romance when Hollie went off with someone and left me by myself. Sandy was also by himself. I pictured him wrapping his arms around me and kissing me.

He said, 'You're looking good out in the water these days.'

'Thanks,' I blushed.

'You'll be hot stuff when you're all better.' He closed his eyes and licked his lips.

I leant forward and kissed him on the lips.

He shot up and pulled away as though I'd vomited on him. His hand flew to his lip as if it was burnt. 'Daisy, what the hell was that?'

'I like you, Sandy,' I whispered.

'Mate…I'm too old, for you. You're like a little sister.'

'But age doesn't matter to me. You're not that old.'

'Oh fuck.'

'Oh shit,' I whined and I got up but he grabbed my wrist and said, 'I'm sorry, kiddo. I'm not that guy for you.'

'Whatever,' I mumbled. 'It's okay. Don't worry about it.'

'I'm just too old. And your dad…'

'It's okay, Sandy,' I smiled, though I felt like crying. 'I understand.'

I played the conversation over and over in my head all week. The next weekend's party was at Sandy's place. I wasn't going to go, but Hollie begged me. We got ready at her house and she put makeup on me. 'Mitchell is into you,' she told me as she put highlighter on my bony cheeks.

'No...' I laughed. 'Really?' I played it off as something that entertained me, but the thought of a boy other than Sandy liking me or being interested in me was terrifying. It meant that I wasn't skinny enough. If I didn't repel boys, I was not skeletal. Boys didn't like skeletons. So, if a boy liked me, I was too much.

'Really.' Hollie applied my lipstick. 'He told Sandy he'd like to bend you over and Sandy decked him.'

I grabbed her hand and made her smear the lipstick. 'What?!'

She scowled as she fixed my lipstick. 'Last night! At the surf club. It was full-on.' Hollie put lipstick on herself, using the mirror.

'Hollie?'

'Mm?'

'Do you think I'd ever have a chance with him?'

'Of course,' she puckered her lips and kissed her reflection before turning back to me. 'He's into you.'

'Not Mitchell,' I said quietly. 'Sandy.'

She stopped and looked at me. 'No.'

I died a little inside. 'Oh.'

'Let me tell you something about Sandy.' She sat down beside me and said, 'He's not into girls.'

'He's gay?' I gasped.

Hollie nodded. 'You haven't realised it, eh.'

I pictured him talking to girls at the party, and how girls watched him as he surfed, the way he grinned sideways at them and it didn't make sense to me. I shook my head. 'No. He's so...' Hollie laughed and I laughed with her.

She said quietly, 'He doesn't like people to know. In fact, I think only I know...and, well, your dad.'

'They're pretty good mates,' I said, with a smile and put my heels on.

Hollie scratched the corner of her eye. 'Yeaahhhh. Mates.'

I glared at her. Was she telling me what I thought she was telling me? My heart began beating really fast and I stared at her, my face growing hot.

She stood up and said, 'All right. Let's go.'

We hung out at Sandy's for a low-key style party. At around eleven, a lot of people left to go to a raging party that would be at another guy's place a kilometre away. Soon it was just our regular gang of me, Hollie, Sandy, Lockie, Mitchell, Blue, Ethan, Sam and Rusty left.

Sandy made eye contact with Hollie and said, 'Ready?'

Hollie nodded. Sandy handed us all glowsticks.

'What are we doing?' I asked.

'We're going to do something that only the best people do,' Mitchell said. He snapped his glowstick and waved it around in circles above his head, making the light stay in the air and giving me a dizzy spell. My eyelids fluttered to regain my sense of balance and Hollie gripped my hand and squeezed it.

'It's awesome. You're going to love it.'

We walked down to the beach. I was lightheaded from all the exercising, vomiting and spending time in the toilet. Hollie was tipsy and held my hand as we navigated the rocky path in the dark.

'Where are we going?' I asked.

'To the caves.'

'What caves?'

Hollie spun me out like we were doing the tango. 'The greatest, most electrifying place on this earth. You'll love it!'

We continued walking along the beach for about half an hour and then we reached a crack in the cliff-face. It was so dark despite the full moon, and we only had the light from Mitchell's glowstick to guide us. Sandy and everyone else snapped their glowsticks so I snapped mine too. He led us into the cliff, the

99

ocean roaring and hissing as it slapped against the rocks below. I followed the group into the cave, bending down, feeling the top of the tight tunnel brush against my back. I wondered how the others were fitting. We edged along until the cave opened up. The walls reflected the green and yellow light from our glowsticks and our voices echoed, bouncing in the din and microphoning eerily.

'Oh my God,' I uttered. It was incredible. A cavernous hole in the rock like a cathedral.

Hollie pulled my hair playfully. 'This is nothing yet, Daze. Follow us!'

I followed them all further down a little track, stumbling on black rocks that were littered around the deep yellow sand. It was as though we had arrived on a different planet where the ground was the sky and the sky was all around us. Endless, deep and vividly black.

I followed everyone through a narrow uphill tunnel on our hands and knees and stood in a second cathedral, smaller than the last. Our voices echoed and gravity ceased to exist as my head spun in the darkness.

Ahead was a ledge. Sandy put a hand up to stop me and we peered down at the black water, recognisable as water only by the rushing and bubbling sounds it made.

'What is this place?' I asked.

'It's the blowhole,' explained Blue.

I could hear the water rushing in and bubbling out but I couldn't see it.

Sandy grinned back at everyone. 'Who wants to go first?'

Lockie and Mitchell leant over and said, 'Not it'.

Ethan shook his head. Rusty whistled as he looked down. 'It's shallower this time.'

'It's no different to last time,' Hollie scoffed. 'It was even further down the last time I jumped.'

'Wait...you're not actually going to jump in, are you?' I asked.

'Out of my way, pussies!' Hollie took off her clothes so she was just in her underwear and leapt off.

'Hollie, no!' I screamed. She hit the water with a splash. We all leant over, peering at the green of her glowstick as she surfaced.

'Whoo!' she screamed. 'It's AMAZING! The current's great. I'll see you guys out there.'

She started floating towards where the rocks caved in. Sam, Blue and Ethan followed her, and Rusty jumped in, laughing until he hit the water and surfaced with a gasp. 'It's cold!'

Mitchell leapt in, squealing like a girl the entire way down, making Sandy and Lockie chuckle.

'Why do you do this?' I asked.

Lockie shrugged. 'Any way to feel alive, right, Daisy?' He tore off his shirt and jumped off the ledge.

Sandy took off his shirt. I grabbed his arm. 'Sandy, no...I don't wanna do this.'

He looked at me with sympathy. 'You can go out the way we came in if you're too scared, Daisy.'

'This is so stupid, though! It is so dangerous.' My teeth started chattering.

'Do it with me.' He smiled at me and held my hand tightly. 'I'll never let you go.'

I hesitated. 'Promise you won't let me go?'

'I promise,' he grinned. 'Come on, Daisy. You're young and alive. Time to act like it.'

I nodded.

'Three, two...one!' We jumped together into the blowhole pool. I surged up to the surface and sucked in air. I'd half expected to hit a rock on the way down but the bottom had been sandy, rippled by the currents that marched and blew through there like an army offensive. Sandy tugged at me and we swam together to the narrow part of the pool. The water rose up and my head touched the top of the rocks.

'Sandy?' I gasped.

101

'It's all right. It shoots us out.'

'What if it doesn't? Will we drown?'

'I've got you, Daze! Just enjoy the ride.'

The water was violent in its way of sucking our bodies. I gasped for air as I was sucked towards the exit with a high surge of water that roared in my ears. The last thing I saw before it went dark was Sandy never taking his eyes off me. My body cartwheeled and tumbled so violently it felt as though I was being pulled apart. Sandy's hand slipped off mine in the churning water. I surfaced out in the sea, the choppy water overwhelming me. I started to panic, gulping and sucking in big mouthfuls of salt water until Sandy came up behind me. His strong arms held me up and he side-paddled me towards the rocks, which I hadn't even thought about paddling towards in my panic.

Mitchell, Blue and Lockie pulled me up onto the outcrop of rocks and Sandy eased me up from behind.

Hollie hugged me as I gasped for air. She squealed, 'How amazing was that?!'

'I'm young…and alive…' I wheezed, trying not to cough and splutter.

Sandy slapped me on the back and said, 'Well done, kiddo.'

Hollie squeezed her head close to mine so our noses were touching. Her hands held my cheeks before one moved down to my chest where my heart was racing.

'Do you feel this?' she asked.

I nodded.

'This,' she whispered, 'is what living is.'

Hollie and I slept on Sandy's porch couch together that night, under a shared blanket. We woke up to the garbling of magpies in the morning and I shivered in the morning air.

Dad walked up the porch steps and said, 'Morning, ladies.' We smiled at him and mumbled good morning. He went inside to speak to Sandy. I got up and poked my head up sneakily so I could watch them together. Hollie smirked at me. It was impossible to tell if they were together or not.

Sandy handed my dad a cuppa and they stood in his little kitchen, drinking tea and chatting. No hugs. No kisses. In fact, Sandy had touched me more than I ever saw him touching my dad. Had Hollie just been messing with me?

I shook my head at Hollie. 'I don't believe you that they're more than mates.'

She shrugged. 'You can always ask one of them.'

'Nah,' I said. I yawned and I shuffled into the kitchen to join them. Hollie sprawled back on the couch and closed her eyes.

I had a cup of tea with Dad and Sandy, listening to the way they spoke about work and the weather.

'What do you talk about together when I'm not here?' I asked curiously.

'Same old shit,' Dad said with a chuckle. Sandy drank the rest of his tea.

'Would you talk about girlfriends?'

Dad coughed.

Sandy rinsed out his mug and said, 'I don't have girlfriends, Daze.' He kissed me on the cheek and said, 'I'm going surfing. See ya.'

I smiled at Dad.

'What?' he asked.

I laughed. 'Nothing.'

'Nothing, my foot. What are you up to?'

'Nothing!' I exclaimed.

'Did you have a good night, Sprout?'

'Yeah, I did. Did you?'

'Ahh some beers and the footy made it all right. Was pretty lonely without ya but knew Sandyboy'd look after ya.'

Sandyboy. I'd never heard him call Sandy that. Maybe Hollie was right. Maybe Sandy and my dad were together. An item.

103

Maybe that had been why Dad had left me and Mum all those years ago.

'Come on, Sprout. Time for brekky. Let's get Hollie up and at em and go to the café together.'

I rolled my eyes. Why did I always have to eat?

Monday morning my adventure in the cave was big news among our year level, and even some of the year twelves came up and fist bumped me. I was inducted, it seemed. I had groups of people in awe of my efforts. Everyone knew that I'd done the cave dive, even the teachers. The woodwork teacher Mr. Ham came up to me at recess on his duty and struck up a conversation about how kids had been doing that since he had been sixteen. I shook my head in disbelief as he walked off in his fluoro yellow vest, though warned us not to tell anyone that he approved because it was so dangerous.

Hollie laughed, 'I would love to see a teacher do it.'

We carried on with our day, and I told myself I had made it. Finally, I belonged. In fact, some kids told me so. You're one of us now, Daisy Cavill. You're ours. However, the entire thing felt like a farce. I hadn't done it. Not really. Sandy had done it with me. If it hadn't been for him, I would have been crawling out the way I had gone in, or, even scarier to think about, drowned in the wild waters at the blowhole because I had panicked and Sandy had rescued me. It gave me an uneasy queasiness in my stomach that made eating my lunch really difficult. It was like chewing on wood. Neither Dad nor Sandy could come that day so the nurse was already alert, ready to jump on me at any hesitation.

She noticed my apprehension and said, 'Eat faster, Daisy. Your dad says you need to finish the sandwich within twenty minutes. It's been twenty-five.'

I put the sandwich down and rubbed my eyes with my knuckles before resting my head on the table. 'I'm done,' I muttered.

'You're not done.'

'I'm done,' I repeated, my words slurring as my mouth struggled to form words while resting on the table surface. 'You can't force-feed somebody this much food. It's inhumane.'

'If you refuse, I'll have to call your dad.'

'I wanna go home,' I mumbled and closed my eyes.

Sandy came and picked me up, because Dad was too busy, and I also suspected that he didn't want to deal with me because I was refusing to eat once again.

Hollie saw me leaving with Sandy and rushed over. 'Daisy, why are you going?'

I mumbled, 'I just can't do it today, Hol. I'm sorry.'

She gave me a hug and said, 'I'll see you later, then.'

I nodded and sat with Sandy in his car, neither of us speaking.

At home, I lay on the couch and was too tired to move.

'What's the matter?' Dad asked when he got home and found me lying morosely on the couch. I sat up and shrugged. I wanted to say I feel like a fake. I'm a failure. A wuss. If anybody knew the real me, I'd be banished or set alight for being a witch.

'I'm making a curry for dinner. You used to like me curry when you were a kid.' He went into the kitchen with a sigh and started chopping all the ingredients for his curry. I followed him in, compelled to make sure he didn't put any extra oil in or use ghee which is pure lard. Olive oil only. And not too much.

He rolled his eyes as I studied how much he used with narrowed eyes. He ignored me and smashed up some ginger. I leant against the bench and said, 'Dad?'

'Mmm.'

'Are you and Sandy together?'

He stopped and gaped at me, aghast.

'Boyfriends.' I looked down at my feet.

He scoffed. 'Love…I'm…Do you think I'm gay?'

105

'Is Sandy?'

'Why would you even think that?'

'Hollie said he was gay.'

Dad took a deep breath and muttered, 'I gotta sit down.' He pulled a chair out and collapsed down into it, staring catatonically at the table.

I sat up on the bench, hands under my butt and waited for him to think about what he was about to tell me. It was about five minutes before he finally spoke. 'We keep it quiet; it's just...' he cleared his throat, 'sometimes you just meet people... Sandy is...we're two people who...'

'Love each other?'

'Yes.'

'But you're not in a relationship?'

'Yes, but not officially...'

'But you feel the same way about each other?'

He nodded.

I swung my legs back and forth, back and forth, kicking the back of the bench with each swing. Thinking, accepting, denying, questionning, accepting, denying all over again. Sandy was so popular around the town, and it wasn't like if he was gay, he wouldn't be accepted. I didn't understand why it was so secretive.

I asked, 'Is that why you left Mum and me?'

Dad's hands shook as he ran them over his face. He croaked, 'I didn't know Sandy then.'

'But was it?' He didn't answer, so I pushed for more. 'Were you realising you weren't straight anymore?'

Dad nodded.

'Why is Sandy so afraid of people knowing he is gay?' I asked.

'Sandy has a background...and a status in this town,' my dad whispered. 'I don't want to ruin it for him.'

I shook my head. 'If he loves you, he wouldn't care what people think.'

My dad looked at me and rubbed his head. 'You've got a lot to learn about the world yet, Daze…there's a lot more between levels you've never had the chance to see.'

I hopped off the bench. 'Whatever. I'm going surfing.' I grabbed my board and my wetsuit despite not being allowed to surf during the week. I walked out, leaving my dad there at the table alone with his food. To my surprise, he didn't try to call me back. I was furious with him. And Sandy. Why couldn't they just tell the truth about who they were and who they loved? I had all my secrets exposed to their entire town in the straight line of my legs, my pointy elbows and sunken cheekbones. Why should they get to hide what they were ashamed of? It was hypocritical, and it made me seethe.

I paddled out with long, slow strokes, feeling the rip run me out to the back. Usually, I was nervous about paddling out into the lineup, let alone completely alone. I had spite and frustration forging me on and I didn't care if I ate shit.

My caution was eradicated. Dad and Sandy were liars. I was a screw-up. I guess there was a part of me that knew I could take Dad's guilt and run with it.

I let the first wave wall up and I bobbed off the back of it. Next one would be mine. It started to surge towards me. I kicked and kicked, swivelled and used all my strength to turn my board around. My fingers squeaked across the deck and I gripped the rail to steady myself. I should have put more wax on.

The wave picked me up. I went to pop up but I had nowhere to go but straight down. I was in the completely wrong spot to take off. I was going over the falls on the biggest wave I'd ever seen in my life.

I closed my eyes and waited for my stomach to catch up with me as I fell. The wave wasn't done with me once it smashed me into the water. Around and around, I went. I was cartwheeling and flipping. My right leg was yanked straight back to the surface by the leg rope. My left leg was somewhere doing somersaults behind me – or was that my arm? Pulled and sucked in every direction, I went limp, my lungs on fire, and the wave eventually passed.

I pushed up to the surface and gulped in oxygen and gulped in salt water as I saw the next set rolling towards me. Curtain of white over a pane of turquoise, spitting out rainbow spray. I sprawled myself onto my board and paddled as hard as I could, struggling to take in enough air in my panic.

BOOM! The whitewater seemed to make the wave implode on itself and I was caught in it. My board lifted up and shot off like we had been ejected from a canon. The whitewater surrounded me, picking me up and flinging me towards the beach, blinding me with white spray. I bumped my way along the whitewater and rode the wave, not lifting up from my belly, ducking my head as if it would close in on me and engulf me. Once I reached the shore, I rolled over onto my back in the fizzing shallows and stared at the sky. I'm alive, I thought.

But there was a little voice that niggled at me.

You could have made that if you were skinnier.

The waves grew bigger and bigger but I paddled back out with quivering limbs. Hollie and Sandy and a few of the boys eventually joined me.

'What are you doin' out here, Daze?' Sandy called. 'It's too big. You're gonna get smashed.'

'I can be out here if I want to,' I snapped. 'You don't own the lineup!'

I paddled away from him, slapping the water with each paddle instead of gliding my hand through. Hollie lingered between me and Sandy, in the middle of us like an umpire, bobbing on her board, only visible from the waist-up like a mermaid.

A wave walled up. I was in the perfect spot. I lunged for it.

'Daisy, don't!' Hollie called. 'It's too big for you!'

As I paddled for it, there was a hard tug on the back of my board. The wave fell like a waterfall in front of the nose of my board but I was tugged backwards off the edge. Sandy had swum over and grabbed my leg rope to keep me from getting onto the wave.

'What do you think you are doing?' I screamed. I splashed water into his face.

He ducked away from my rain of rage and said, 'I'm not letting you get hurt.'

'I hate you!'

'I'm not letting you get hurt,' he repeated.

'You're a dog.'

'I'm not letting you get hurt.' Again.

'You are such an arsehole,' I steamed and paddled away. He bobbed there in the water, his board abandoned. He spat seawater out and ran his hand through his hair, squinting against the salt and the tears. I shuddered and shivered. Hollie watched me with a solemn expression.

'Don't look at me like that, Hol,' I whined.

She shook her head.

'I don't want to be like this,' I wailed to her.

She nodded. 'I know.'

'I just want to surf...and forget.'

'I know. Me too.' She lay on her board and paddled slowly away from me and the rest of the lineup. Sandy got back onto his board and watched the horizon.

Abandoned. Crestfallen, I waited for the swell to drop before I managed to catch one in with Sandy and Hollie. They didn't speak to me. They didn't look at me. They just slowly followed me up the beach until I got to Sandy's deck and I threw my board down.

'Why are you so mad at Sandy?' Hollie ventured to ask. Her nose wrinkled as though she smelled something bad.

'Because of him being so ashamed of being with my dad. Why don't you just own it, Sandy? Own that you're gay. Nobody cares!'

His jaw clenched and he glanced at Hollie as she drew in a deep breath and blew it again, muttering, 'Oh, boy.'

I glared at Sandy and puffed out my chest as far as I could to make myself bigger somehow, me, the bag of bones and brittle little bird body. He leant in closer to me and replied through gritted teeth, 'You don't know what I've been through; where I've come from. My sexuality is none of your business.' He said louder, 'Nobody's sexuality is anybody's business!'

I hissed, 'My dad deserves so much better than you.'

'He deserves better than you too,' he replied quietly.

I slapped him. None of us saw it coming. It just happened too quickly to predict. My hand flew across his face like a windscreen wiper on speed. I looked down at my stinging hand, the skin wrinkled from being so long in the water. Sandy held his own hand to his cheek, looking at me as though he was aching deeper than the surface level of his skin.

'I'm sorry,' I gasped.

He paused. 'Me too.'

Hollie grabbed my arm and tugged me along. 'We're going, Daisy. Let's go!'

I followed her, still carrying my board and staring at my stinging hand, leaving Sandy standing there, with his hand to his face. The cold and the saltwater made my hand sting even more, so I imagined Sandy's face was hurting, too. The tingling lasted and went on in my hand, as though my hand was reacting to the violation of slapping someone who cared about me so much.

'What the heck was all that about?' Hollie asked as we walked.

I shrugged and finally looked away from my blotchy palm.

'Something has happened between you two.'

'Yeah,' I murmured.

'What?'

'Never mind.'

'Tell me.'

'Hollie, I'm sorry, but…it's none of your business. It's just something between me, my dad and Sandy.'

She blinked and I watched the exclusion work its way into her head. We had an inside secret. She used to be the one sharing Sandy's secrets and keeping me in the dark, and then suddenly she was out in the blackness and I was bathed in the yellow glow of his light. I had his favour. His favour meant everything. She had nothing left.

Her voice cracked as she said, 'So, we lie to each other now?'

'No.'

'I told you what happened that night at the campground.' Her eyes went dark and her mouth shrank. 'I thought we told each other everything.'

'We do.'

'Except this, huh.' She sniffed and looked away.

I didn't know what to say so I stayed quiet. Hollie had already known about it, so I didn't see it as keeping it a secret. I couldn't tell her I'd tried to kiss Sandy – she'd laugh at me! Especially since she knew he was gay and he was hanging around with my dad, pretending to be friends but being so much more. I didn't see it as something to be embarrassed about or ashamed of. You loved who you loved. I couldn't think of a way to tell Hollie I was more upset that people I loved had kept things from me, even though I kept things from them about my eating disorder all the time. I felt hypocritical and embarrassed.

When we got back to my place, Hollie and I half-heartedly chatted about school and the science project we had to do on the upcoming school holidays. I felt dejected and depressed by the time she said she was not staying over tonight. She waved goodbye and kept walking, adjusting her board as she walked into the twilight. I made a mental image of her walking away, thinking this might be the last time we surf together because she was mad at me. Once she disappeared behind the bend to the main road,

I went inside, shattered with exhaustion, and chucked my board against the wall.

Dad met me by the door. 'Sandy called.'

'Thought he would've.'

'You hit him?' he cried incredulously, propping a hip and leaning into me.

'He needed it; he was out of line.'

'Doesn't matter; he has his reasons for keeping our relationship quiet.'

'Why?'

'It's not my place to tell you.'

I growled with frustration. 'So that gives him the right to keep me from catching waves?'

'He just wanted to make sure you were safe!'

I'd had enough. Rage ripped from my gut and out my mouth with the spittle I had spat in his face as I roared, 'Why does everyone care so much if I'm safe or not? Just leave me alone! If people really gave a damn, I wouldn't be living here in this piece of shit shack of a house!'

Dad shook his head and shrugged. He stuttered, 'I don't know what to tell you, Daisy. Your mother was at her wits end. She's a person too.'

I rolled my eyes and went to my room. Dad called after me, 'Daisy, you have to come have dinner.'

Stuff dinner, I thought, but I turned around and followed him into the kitchen. Rice, beans and boiled Brussels sprouts. Mm. Delectable. Not! Two lamb chops sat blackened and inedible on the bench.

'You are a terrible cook,' I muttered.

To my surprise, he laughed and said, 'Yeah, I know.'

I laughed too and pretended to eat the rice and beans but it all went down my pants along with the scalding hot Brussels sprouts. I had a red burn mark on my upper thigh for days.

A month later, school ended for the term and my strict supervision ended with it. The days began to get warm. The water was less icy and more temperate cool. I spent every single day with Hollie and Sandy, surfing. They had both chosen to act like our fight had never happened, and I was grateful. Over the school holidays, we surfed for hours and they'd forget to eat lunch while I sang a celebration song in my head each time they forgot to go in and eat.

Sometimes, Sandy would whistle at me and beckon me in. I'd think *damn, he's remembered today* and we'd go in together and have some food. I just ate it without complaint. The less fuss I made, the quicker I could get back into the water.

If we weren't surfing, we were snorkelling and digging through the rock pools at low tide, looking at all the crabs, small fish and antagonising the blue-ringed octopi. Leaping from slimy rock to barnacled rock, I would often find my legs, limber and lean as they were, failing me. They would buckle, and I'd scrape my ankles and shins as I slid into the fragile rockpools, causing the clarity of the water to be overwhelmed by churned sand, turning it a murky grey. Hollie would laugh at my clumsiness and I'd pretend to laugh too, but was horrified by my weakness. The strength I had gained a couple of months ago was gone and I kept catching glances at Hollie's toned muscular legs. I cringed with jealousy. Why couldn't I look good and be strong like her?

We'd watch the sun set at the end of the day, our skin sunburnt and crispy with salt from the sea. Our mouths were dry with dehydration; we'd just sit in silence and bliss. Hunger pangs echoed a cacophony in my belly. We'd sit until it grew dark, increasingly later and later.

Surfer boys from out of town would offer us beer and joy rides. Some days we'd take them. Some days we'd laugh in their faces and frolic off. I was gloriously happy, happier than I'd ever been. I confided in Hollie about the weirdness that was anorexia. How I didn't even want to be skinny. It wasn't fuelled by losing weight, not really, even though sometimes it was. She got that. She told me how she felt useless and hopeless, unable to succeed in school, worried about dropping out like her brother, and worried she would be incapable of becoming a pro-surfer. She needed to be sexy, have an arse that was good enough for modelling but could still fit into the smallest size wetsuit. She needed to be a strong, fit athlete, with powerful shoulders for paddling, yet she had to stay streamline and feminine. Even strong girls were expected to be weak, and they felt the pinch of body image pressures and were made to feel shitty about themselves, getting lost in the wicked, ridiculous expectations they had on them.

As Hollie charged hard at the lineup, men and boys would sneer and swear at her for getting to waves faster than they could, riding them harder and she landed clean aerials while they snarled behind her, lurking in the sea like sharks. Their tongues were just as venomous in the shallows. Calling her a slut all because she surfed better than they did. Muttering under their breaths at her for being a cocky little shit. She had once been cocky. But her demeanour had changed since she had gone camping that night with her brother and his friends. What they had made her do, and how they had harassed her afterwards changed her. But she still surfed better than they did. And it killed them inside that they couldn't squash her spirit.

We found sanctuary at Sandy's after surfing all day. He gave us Milo but I hated the grittiness and, whenever he wasn't looking, I tipped it out in random places, like in his pot plants, under dirty dishes in the sink, out the window, down the toilet, and even in a pair of shoes on the deck. He never said anything about it. Was he that oblivious or did he choose to let it slide? Maybe he didn't know what to say. I guess I wouldn't know what to say either if a kid came into my house and tipped Milo into my shoes.

Hollie and I hung out at Sandy's even while he was at work all day. He'd come back to find the two of us had made a mess of his house or raided his photo albums of surf trips he'd taken when he was a little older than we were. But mostly, Hollie and I spent our days at the sea, following the waves up and down the beach, getting swept out in currents and watching the horizon for signs of more migrating whales. I thought the whales had their priorities wrong. Going south was an error. South was where my brain had imploded – the land of when everything had gone so wrong. Endless hospital visits, weigh-ins, obsessing over becoming nothing, no friends, cold oh so cold. Winter. Perpetually frozen, I would manically bolt around the streets at 2 am, wrapped in blankets, sculling as many dollar coffees from the servo that I could afford. Aged fourteen but still a baby; not that I was any more grown up at seventeen with the weight of a ten-year-old. Childlike in the body, but aged and blackened in the mind and soul.

I felt a lot better living further north. I had freedom, friends, this span of ocean. Mostly…I had Hollie.

We would eat strawberries by the punnet. The anxiety of eating and feeling full would simmer low enough until I would be trying to sleep later that night and I would not be able to turn off; I couldn't rest. I'd do calorie calculations in my mind. Six big strawberries. I would work it out. Round it up to 100 to be safe, decided it wasn't a very wide margin of error so I'd round it to the next hundred just in case. Far too many calories, then. I had to get rid of it. I'd get up and do star-jumps until I would collapse. 2,000 star-jumps. Might be enough. Better do 3,000. Just in case.

I'd wake up in the morning feeling absolutely shattered and believing I was only too weak to move because I was too heavy. I had to fix that. I had to get lighter. What is lightness, anyway? The lighter I became, the heavier I felt.

One Saturday evening at dusk, we were all sitting out the back of the lineup on our boards. Hollie was absolutely firing. She was getting on waves like a dolphin and always seemed to have priority. The guys were getting pretty dark on her, because she could snake the wave just by getting in position faster.

'That girl is gonna get the shit beat outta her if she keeps doing that, Sandy,' growled Robbo. I recognised Robbo as being one of the guys who had followed Sandy outside at the party a few months ago. He and his mate Dazza.

'So, what are ya tellin' me for, ya kook?' Sandy retorted.

'She's your little cock sucker, ain't she? She blows you in the back of your panelvan.' Dazza mimed oral sex with his fist and his tongue poking inside his cheek. My mouth fell open and I wanted to say something but I looked to Sandy first. He shook his head but didn't say anything. He just paddled away from him without looking at me.

Guys around us all turned their heads with stunned expressions on their faces and looked at me. One of them nodded at me, and said, 'Yeah, I've seen them.'

The lineup was packed that day and when Hollie paddled back out all the guys wouldn't look at her. She sidled up beside Sandy but he shrugged her off and paddled away, creating distance. She came over to me and sat up on her board, a little out of breath and her forehead wrinkled. 'What's his problem?' she asked.

I rubbed at a tight spot on my neck and swallowed, glancing behind me to make sure the incoming wave wasn't going to pitch us towards the beach.

Hollie sensed it. She glanced around at the guys, who mostly looked away but one spat in the water. She rolled her eyes. 'What did I do now?'

'They're saying you suck Sandy off,' I whispered.

'What?' She laughed. 'That's ridiculous.'

'One of them said they saw you.'

'But...I don't.'

I sighed. 'Let's go in.'

We both timed our paddle in and guys called out to us. 'Yeah, go, you little whores!'

I flinched. I'd never been called that before and it hurt more than I thought it would. We met Sandy at the beach.

'You all right?' he asked.

Hollie and I nodded. I said, 'Why do they think that, Sandy?'

'Because I'm a twenty-seven-year-old hanging out with jailbait,' he glowered.

'It's not true, is it?' I asked.

'No!' They both exclaimed with disgusted expressions. They both swore it was a rumour. I was too fixated on starving to notice anything going on between them before, but I believed it. The guys were adamant that Sandy was having sex with a minor, and it broke Hollie's heart. They had finally done it; they broke her spirit. She crouched in the carpark with her board over her knees and wept, with her head down. Sandy lingered, glancing around, too scared to put a hand on her shoulder, so I did. We stayed close in the carpark, surrounding Hollie on either side, as if protecting her from anyone who walked past.

Surfing was meant to be fun. This wasn't fun.

Hollie slept over at my house every night after the rumour started, because even her grandparents had heard it. They had tried to ground her for being sexually active, and ban her from seeing Sandy, and she'd do a runner and land on my dad's doorstep – reminiscent of the way I had turned up at her door. She couldn't go to Sandy's, it would have been like admitting that the rumour was true. Those guys were such crooks. We surfed at the other beach, away from the surf squad of the ocean beach. But other guys would catcall her as she carried her board down to the beach. Hollie's skin would be blotchy red all over from embarrassment but she never gave up going surfing every day.

She never even gave up surfing when we saw a shark. It was the first and only time I have ever peed in my wetsuit.

I was paddling across the lineup to get a better position when, to my right, a dark grey mound rolled upwards, knocking my board slightly, tilting to the side, slowly. I didn't compute what it was until a fin surfaced. My heart leapt into my throat as I screamed, 'Shark! Shark!'

I couldn't move fast enough. I was uncoordinated at the best of times, but trying to get my body to paddle when a shark was checking me out from less than two metres away was a hard task. My screams had alerted everyone and there was a rapid exodus – the biggest party wave of the century. I had never been so relieved to reach the beach!

Sandy stood beside me and squinted at the water. 'Shit. Hollie's still out there.' I followed his eyeline to where Hollie was taking off on a wave. She did a cutback up to the lip, and soared along the face.

'Hollie!' I yelled. We both cupped our hands and bellowed to her but she ignored us, and the shark. She had the waves to herself and she could breathe.

'She is nuts,' Sandy muttered, shaking his head and walking away. I think he had to. He had to get distance from Hollie amid everyone in the town believing that he was doing something illegal with her. It was a wise choice, especially because the local coppers decided they had nothing better to do than make sure Sandy wasn't diddling underage girls. They did drive-pasts, where they seemed to always be going somewhere that had them on a route going past Sandy's house, the beach, whichever jobsite he was working on at the time.

While we were surfing one Saturday morning, Sandy noticed my arms shaking. He made me go in with him while Hollie continued surfing. I was sitting in the back of his panelvan, relieved to be out of the sun because I was getting sunburnt. It was a hot day for October. 36 degrees.

I nibbled reluctantly at the sandwich Dad had packed for me. Sandy practically inhaled his sandwich then moved on to a chocolate bar and a coffee milk.

My ears started ringing and I saw bright stabs of light in my eyes. I grabbed Sandy's bicep, but it was too late. I was gone. Passed out with terrible timing. Sandy leaned over me in the back of his panelvan just as the police drove by.

The next thing I was aware of was Sandy shouting, 'No, no – she has anorexia; she's just passed out...' and he was being handcuffed by one police officer while the other officer roused me. He pulled my limp body into a sitting position. Dizziness overwhelmed me and I vomited all over the front of myself, sticky lumps of the sandwich sticking to my bare stomach and legs. I got out of the back of the panelvan, trying to make it out before I vomited in Sandy's car more.

The bitumen of the carpark was so hot it scalded the soles of my feet as I stood, vomit smeared on my chin and my heart pounding in my ears, my toes and my spine.

'Are you okay?' asked the police officer and all I could do was lean into his smelly, moist armpit and groan. 'Should we get an ambo, Dave?' asked officer smelly armpit.

Officer Dave glanced at me and realised what state I was in. 'Shit, yeah.'

My little picnic lunch with Sandy had turned into an excursion to the hospital for me, and a trip to the police station for him. Hollie remained in blissful ignorance and kept surfing.

The keen-eyed observer of this story would recognise that I was underweight at this stage. The doctors should have taken this into consideration, however, they put my fainting turn down to sun/heat stroke. They stabbed my hand with an IV and proceeded to fill me with hydration to solve the problem, because that was an easy fix. The real problem was too complex for them to fathom at that point so they shrugged it off and just blamed the unseasonably warm day. A nurse named Mandy was suspicious, though. The jelly she brought to me on the ward stayed untouched.

'Don't you like jelly?' she asked in a bubbly voice. 'I can get you some ice cream if you prefer. You should eat something, darl.'

'Oh, it's fine; I tasted a bit. It was lovely. I'm just not hungry.'

Dad arrived as she was carrying the jelly out. He exhaled, 'Hey Sprout.'

'Hey.'

'What happened?'

A voice I didn't recognise blurted from me, snapping, 'I got too hot – that's all. Get off my back! You're a jerk for taking so long to pick me up!'

Dad blinked at me, struggling to find a reply before he eventually found it, but he bit his tongue and saved it for when we walked into the cop shop later to pick up Sandy.

The police asked me, 'Did he touch you in any way? Did he do anything?'

'No! I just fainted.'

'She is a mentally unwell anorexic that did not eat enough and fainted. Sandy was just looking out for her.' *Ouch. A mentally unwell anorexic. Thanks, Dad.*

The police couldn't charge Sandy with anything so we took him home. I'd never witnessed any affection between him and my dad before, but the way they looked at each other when we got home made me feel so alone.

Eventually, the heat on Sandy faded. It made a lot of sense that he would be able to escape the scrutiny. He was the local surfing legend, right. However, Hollie's flaws were not so invisible; she remained the town slut. Girls made fun of her. Guys intimidated her. She held her head high and continued to paddle out, even more determined to snake the bastards' waves and I fist bumped her with each ride.

However, Dad began to only let me surf if he watched me eat a bacon and egg roll from the bakery before he went to work.

He'd kiss me on the cheek, prickling me with his stubble, then head off to work.

I carried my board across the street, across the grass verge, down the track to the beach where I would make myself vomit into the scrub. Hollie pleaded for me to stop. I ignored her pleas to keep the food in me because I needed it.

'I don't like that you do that, Daisy; please stop,' she'd whine. 'It makes me feel like I'm helping you die or something.'

'Just shut up,' I'd snap. 'It's either this or you can't stay at my house anymore.'

She needed me; she needed a place to stay when she couldn't bear being with her grandparents and creepy brother anymore. So, she shut up. After purging, I would be jittery for around half an hour and then I'd be completely sapped of energy. I'd just lie flat on my board and listen to the erratic thumping of my heart reverberate through the sea and I wondered if marine life could hear me and were trying to translate the thumping.

Hollie began withdrawing from me. She let me purge by just walking off on me while I expunged my breakfast into the bushes. She would paddle out and be in position for a wave before my toes even touched the sand. She ignored me when I was too exhausted to go for a wave, too exhausted even to paddle in, lying there on my board like a mollusk.

Sandy also kept his distance but he would give us a lift to surf spots with trepidation. Hollie kept my secrets, watching on helplessly. Until one night, she couldn't anymore. I'd lost more weight. I hadn't caught a single wave all day because I was too weak.

Dad cooked us all burgers and Sandy made a salad. He drank beer at the table in silence with Hollie and me while Dad cooked. Dad placed a hamburger on my plate and turned back to the stove to get everybody else their meal. I quickly scrunched the entire burger in my fist, the hot oil searing my skin, and crammed it in my pocket. Sandy had been sipping at a beer bottle but he froze mid-sip, staring at my plate. Hollie's eyes went wide and her cheeks flushed. Dad came over with napkins and read the disappointment and embarrassment on Hollie's face as she avoided his eye contact; Sandy stared at my plate, squirming with indecision of should he say something or shouldn't he.

He didn't have to. Dad followed his eye line to my plate and put the napkins down, placing both hands on the edge of the table, closing his eyes as if to calm himself down. He lowered his head as though he was praying.

'Daisy,' he murmured in exasperation. He looked up at me. 'Where's your burger?'

'I ate it.'

'Where. Is. Your. Burger?' he repeated through gritted teeth.

'Are you deaf?' I spat. 'I fucking ate it!'

'You didn't fucking eat it because you couldn't have fucking ate it that fast!' he screamed. He never swore like that so I jumped to my feet and started screaming back at him, curse words flying across the table with my spit.

Most of my conversations at that time were a blur. I felt like I was an insect, rubbing its legs together inside my brain, cleaning out any common-sense receptors.

Sandy stood up and shouted, 'Guys, guys, calm down! Stop yelling. Stop! Please.'

Hollie watched with wide eyes as Dad stood over me yelling, 'You're lying!'

'No I'm not! I ate it!'

'You're going to die – is that what you want?'

Sandy flinched.

'You're lying and you're dying!' Dad shouted, throwing the napkins in the air, making them rain down around us.

Hollie yanked at her hair and stood up. 'It's in her pocket!'

I screeched at her that she was a bitch and fell into a heap, bawling my eyes out as Dad searched my pockets, finding and pulling out the balled-up bun and squashed meat patty. What an odd sensation it was to be out of one's body. I was utterly numb yet behaving as though my emotions ran deep. Maybe they did.

The disconnect was just as unbearable as the starvation. As I wailed in nothing but anguish, Sandy took off home with trembling hands and tear-stained cheeks. Hollie sat on the porch and bawled her eyes out, just like me.

Dad squatted beside me in the kitchen, hands trembling with the food I had hidden. His breath came jagged and he choked before he covered his face and sobbed for a few minutes. I became silent at the sound of him crying. Lost. He had lost. And he knew it.

I choked out, 'I'm sorry.'

'I need you to eat, Sprout,' he begged in an exhausted, hoarse voice.

'I can't...and if you try making me eat, I promise I'll never eat again.'

I went to bed, utterly spent. Hollie climbed in with me and we spooned like lovers. We didn't have to speak. Her tears made the back of my shirt soggy. She lovingly stroked my hair and my arms.

'Daisy, you're my best friend.'

'You're mine, too.' I sniffed.

'I love you...but I hate your anorexia.'

I didn't know what to say so I grunted in response. My anorexia was me, but I knew what she meant, except I hated me but loved my anorexia, so what else could a kid be but confused?

It was as though I had surrendered completely to anorexia after that. I stopped surfing. I stopped pretending to be eating the food they gave me. I lived on the minimal, controlled amount I could manage. I went back to school when the term started, and Hollie moved back home. I guess being slut-shamed and scolded by her grandparents was preferable to being around me and my craziness; the detonation zone that was my home with Dad.

Chapter Seven

NOVEMBER

'Sprout.'

I opened my heavy eyes but did not give Dad my bleary gaze; instead, I stared catatonically at the grey, pock-marked wall.

'You've got school.' It was nearing the end of the school year anyway. I didn't see why I had to go. I was so tired.

I moulded myself to a sitting position and nursed the heart murmur before jutting my skeletal legs from the heaviness of the doona, and moved them to the floor where my feet ached upon the contact with the shaggy carpet rug. I went to stand but my legs collapsed as the room spun and the floor went flying towards my face.

Dad lunged for me and caught me by the arm. The grip of his fingers felt like steel binders clasping into my skin, so close to the bone.

My days always started like this: Dad coming in to get me up and catching me before I fell. I was okay once my equilibrium adjusted but I avoided Dad's eyes. My feet ached mercilessly in my shoes; the padding was gone from the soles of my feet. Dad or Sandy would drive me to the school gate and walk me by the elbow to my first class where the school nurse would meet me to sit me down in a chair that sent cold, sharp pains up my coccyx bone. She would make sure I was sitting safely so I wouldn't fall. My class mates avoided me, except Hollie. Two girls in the year level below us named Ella and Devlin sat with us once, between me and Hollie. Ella kept glancing at me as I tried to write and had to keep stopping, as though I was out of breath. I stooped over the desk, the limp hair on my head parting to reveal a bald patch.

Ella spoke up with a shaky voice, 'Daisy, I don't know if you know this…but you have a bald patch just there.' She pointed at the spot.

Devlin's eyes flew from her work to my head, which I covered instantly, tears springing to my eyes.

Ella reached into her bag. 'I have something you can use. If you want.' She pulled out a headband. I took it with a shaky hand and placed it on my head. 'Does it hide it?'

She nodded and smiled. Devlin asked, 'Why don't you just eat something?'

Hollie, who was the furthest from me, snapped, 'Shut up!'

The teacher called, 'Problem in the back, ladies?'

'No, we're fine,' Hollie replied. We got back to work but I gave Ella a smile and she smiled back.

Classes with Hollie were the best. We would chat – mostly she would speak and I would listen, trying to rev up the energy to comprehend and engage in conversation but it was horrendously one-sided as she regaled me of her morning surf with her hair still wet.

One morning, she didn't show up until second period.

'Are you okay?' I asked.

She nodded, her head down, her face cloaked behind the curtain of hair. I longed to have her hair. Mine continued to come out in clumps and dangled listlessly from my flaky scalp. The apple on my school desk remained uneaten. I would twirl it by its stem and rub my fingers on its sleek green skin. Shiny, oh so shiny apple. You're no longer even a symbol of temptation; you're a symbol of hunger and misery.

I'd be listless until I ate something at lunch. After having to eat lunch with the school nurse, my energy levels would be higher than ever. My heart went from a putter to a churn. Downing the few bites of the yoghurt and the glass of Ensure, a powdered supplement mixed into milk that was designed to put weight on or give extra nutrition. I agreed to drink it under supervision but it filled me with manic energy that burned from nowhere. Hollie walked beside me, slightly behind, struggling to keep pace with me. 'Slow down, Daisy,' she mumbled.

'I won't.' Gotta burn off the yoghurt. Gotta burn off the Ensure. Gotta burn off *myself*.

Every day was the same. Start the day in a sloth-like speed, until at lunchtimes, I had to sit in the staffroom and eat that fucking yoghurt and drink the fucking Ensure. My foot jiggled madly away, jiggle, jiggle, jiggle.

That day Hollie missed the first class, Ms. Gregg came in to make her usual Chai tea and noticed me making a bigger than usual milk moustache with the Ensure. She approached me with caution and pressed her cheek to mine in a light embrace and whispered, 'I believe in you. You're worthy of recovery, Daisy. We're all rooting for you to choose life.'

Boy, was she talking to the wrong girl.

She patted me on the shoulder with a shy smile and left. Anorexia hated her. That's when I knew she was right. Choose life. What even was life? How could I choose it? I was alive, wasn't I? *Wasn't I?*

Outside, I jogged on the spot, out of the sight range of the yard duty teachers' keen eyes. Each step was torture with how exhausted I was. Hollie lay in the sun with her top pulled up, exposing her midriff. I jogged circles around her. Anorexia or life. Anorexia or life; a mantra that repeated in my head like a metronome after what Ms. Gregg had said to me. Anorexia was stronger.

Hollie pulled herself up onto her elbows and squinted at me. 'You're exercising too much. It's getting worse.'

'No,' I retorted, and slowed to a walk.

'You are,' she snorted.

'Where were you this morning if you care so much?' I snapped.

'I am so tired of being there for your issues, Daisy! I have a life too! I've got my own issues to deal with – and where is *my* help? Where is my listening ear? Where is my friend? I have nobody but myself! Everything is not just about you and your *bloody anorexia*!' She leapt up and shouted in my face, 'I mean, *God*! I matter too! I matter too!' She was off then, sprinting away from me.

Whatever, I thought, and started jogging in place again.

I should have gone after her. If I had been a good friend, I would have, but I was consumed by that point. We had classes together in the afternoon, but she didn't speak to me for the rest of the day, even when Sandy picked us both up from school.

He had their boards in the back and my heart sank. The worst part about relapsing so hard was that I couldn't surf anymore, even though I wanted to. The exclusion hit me like a heart palpitation. 'I guess you guys are going surfing,' I muttered.

'You could go surfing too if you'd just eat something,' snapped Hollie, throwing her bag into the back with the boards. She climbed into the back with them. I got into the front seat beside Sandy and craned my neck to face her as she started waxing her board, rubbing so hard the wax was squashing under her hand and not really spreading onto the deck.

'I do eat!'

She threw the block of wax at me. I fought the urge to bawl my eyes out and focused instead on wrapping my fingers around my thigh.

Sandy dropped me off home and I got out of the car, each movement arduous. My breath shook and I held onto the car door, willing my body to work like it used to. Having Hollie mad at me sapped me of strength and made me feel like I was walking death. Sandy rushed out of the car and put his arm around my body, ginger with where he placed his hands.

'Do you need help getting inside?'

I hated admitting it but I gave a quick nod. He held the crook of my arm and helped me to the front door. 'We can stay with you,' he whispered. I shook my head. He added, 'You shouldn't be alone.'

'I'd rather be alone,' I mumbled.

My knees weakened and Sandy's face became a blur as I sank to the ground. I gasped and Sandy shouted, 'Daisy!' I couldn't keep my eyes open and Sandy screamed, 'Hollie, help!'

My legs jerked and my hands tightened on Sandy's wrist. My teeth clenched and my muscles went into what felt like a cramp, but was more of a spasm. I arched my back and rolled over onto all-fours, opening my eyes and fighting the urge to vomit. The patio was too hard on my knees and hands so I gave up and lay flat on my stomach, but groaned as it made my hips and ribs ache. Hollie came running up the steps and her hands went to her mouth.

Sandy took off his shirt and put it under my head, rolling me over onto my side. I stared at my forearms, sinewy with veins popping. 'Call an ambulance, Hollie.'

'No,' I muttered, feeling as though my tongue was going numb. 'I'm okay.' I forced myself to sit up. 'Just got dizzy.'

'Nah, mate, that was not just being dizzy. You had a seizure or something.'

I clutched at the doorframe and hauled myself into a standing position, waiting for the static in my sight to dissipate before I said again, 'I'm okay.'

Sandy sighed and gave Hollie a knowing look. 'We're not going surfing.'

She nodded with a tight neck, her muscles popping out as she clenched her teeth.

'Please don't call an ambulance, Sandy,' I whispered. 'I don't want to go to hospital. I'll eat. I promise.'

Hollie and Sandy helped me inside with a sigh. Sandy poured a glass of orange juice and Hollie passed me a muesli bar. With shaking hands, I plucked out some oats off the bar and placed them slowly into my mouth then put the bar down. 'I'm done,' I sighed.

Sandy handed me the glass and I sipped it, placing it down. 'I'm done.'

Hollie chewed the inside of her lip manically and looked to Sandy with wide eyes, who stood there with his hands on his hips, a false bravado of confidence and authority. Nothing they could do would fix me. No matter how hard they tried.

Anorexia was winning. Alone. Weak. Helpless. Lowest weight ever. Lonely. Lying on the couch, I ignored Dad when he arrived home early because Sandy and Hollie had called him in a panic, wondering what to do. Hollie said with a sniff, 'We should call an ambulance.'

The three of them stood in the kitchen later talking about what to do. Was I going to get better on my own or were they going to have to take me to the hospital? Their voices rose and fell just as my heart rate did.

'How hard can it possibly be to eat?' my dad mused, despair causing his lip to tremble.

'I won't eat,' I whispered to myself, closing my eyes, content with my prize in the sick game. Anorexia had won. I lost four more kilos.

Shit got really serious. I stopped getting up in the morning. I couldn't go to school anymore. Dad stopped going to work. Ms. Gregg came by the house to visit and dropped off novels for me to read while resting. I think she had come by thinking I'd be grateful and excited to take some rest and get better. She left in tears with the reality finally hitting her that I was trying to die, not get better.

Hollie came by every day after school, doing her homework instead of surfing. I was barely conscious, intent on dying. She sat at my desk, glancing at me every few minutes as I pretended to sleep which was easy to do. I had no energy to talk.

She stared at me with cold vacancy and I recognised the despondency that anorexia had given to me.

'This is the last time I'm coming to see you, Daisy.'

I heaved myself into a sitting position and blinked rapidly so I wouldn't faint when the room spun on me again. 'What are you talking about? You can't not visit me. You're my best friend.'

Hollie said, 'You'll always be my best friend.'

I started to cry and clawed at her to hold her close. I hiccupped into her collarbones, so much fleshier than mine and warmer. She pulled herself away softly and whispered, 'I can't watch you do this to yourself any longer...It's killing you.'

I nodded. 'I understand.'

'No...' she swallowed and blinked before pulling at a thread on her jeans. She shook her head and stared up at the ceiling. 'You don't get this, Daisy.' She looked back at me and shook her head again. 'This is not only your thing. It's not just something in your head. It is real. It is something I have to watch happen to you. I have to tell you the truth.' Her lip wobbled and she folded as if in surrender, with her face in her hands. She sobbed from the gut. From the ribs. From that deep pit inside I was purposely making void to avoid the feelings. No, I'd never get it. I'd never understand how anorexia affected more than just me.

Hollie left, sobbing, begging me to get help and her words stayed with me for the rest of the night until at around midnight, I made my decision. I couldn't lose my best friend.

I made my way to Dad's bedroom and leant against the doorframe. 'Dad,' I croaked.

He snorted awake and asked in a panic, 'Whozzamatta?'

I took a slow breath in and answered, 'I need to go to the hospital.'

Dad turned his bedside lamp on and peered at me with bleary-eyes – the skeleton in his doorway at midnight. 'What is it?' he asked.

'I'm not getting better,' I admitted.

'I'll call triple zero,' he added, reaching for his phone.

I let my body slide down the length of the doorframe until I was on the floor in the foetal position, too weak to resist being a heap on the floor.

I must have passed out or fallen into a deep sleep, because I didn't remember the paramedics coming to get me, stabbing me with needles and putting an oxygen mask on my face, however I did remember arriving at the hospital, lying on the gurney without any blankets, staring at my bare purple legs, the width only of bone. My knees knobbled out of my skin like boulders on a barren, cold landscape. The space between them was vast. Air. Was there supposed to be so much air that it was intoxicating and breathless? My heart pattered. My veins throbbed from my hand to my shoulder with whatever they were pumping into me. It hurt. A lot. I winced and flinched from my own arm. What was that? I learnt later that it was a potassium drip.

Slowly, I raised my skeletal arm and observed wires clinging to me like jungle tendrils. Confused, I uttered, 'Wha…?' I looked around the bustling ward, the din made my head ache.

'We need an NG tube in here ASAP,' a nurse demanded, marching by, around, about. A part of me questioned if they were moving at sonic speed merely for the reason that I was moving in slow-motion the way my heart was. Ka-thump…thump…pitter…patter…kathump.

I supposed I was lucky to have it beating at all.

I felt the sudden, extreme urge to vomit and it exploded from my mouth and nose before I even had the chance to roll over. Steaming bile splattered back upon my face. I tried to wipe it off but found myself almost tangled in the vines connecting me to blinking, beeping monitors. Nurse NG wiped me it away off my cheek, causing me to wince and gasp. She snapped her fingers at her busy colleagues. 'Now!'

'I don't want the tube,' I stated, what I thought was quite clear but my voice slurred like I was drunk, and I burned with mortification. It's a funny thing: dignity. You take it for granted until you're toes up on a bed being held down by the burliest of security guards while a nurse shoves a horrid tube up your nose so hard it feels as though your brain is being prodded by a sharp stick.

Swallow. Swallow. They tell you over and over to swallow until the sensation eventually stops and that it will be done and over with. Over with. You'll worry about the life-saving liquid nutrients they're pumping into you later. Right then, you just want the pain to stop. You will cry. Wracking sobs will hinder the tube so the nurse will merely push harder. You will writhe and squirm, agonised by the tube, the process, the implications and what it all means. You've lost. Anorexia has won.

When it's all done, the nurses will tape it to your nose and your hollow cheek and you'll wear it like a badge into the ICU ward where you may or may not meet other anorexics. They see you as a good anorexic because you've needed the tube. It's too late to promise that you'll eat, because you know that it would have been a lie. The doctors had to save your life.

I was down to the weight of a child. Where the heck did the rest of my body go?

They finally put me on a ward and let Dad visit me after a week of bedrest and 24-hour supervision. The tube remained in. They wouldn't let me eat for fear of any "behaviours" putting my life at risk.

'I don't have any behaviours. I eat,' I whined. 'I will eat. I'm here to get better, aren't I?'

The nurses all shook their heads and I was left stuck with a tube taped on my face. It was itchy and gave me a rash. I'd never been tubed before. I'd been in the hospital before, but I'd never had to be tubed. I'd never been unconscious when they had taken me into emergency before, though. I guess that was the one-way ticket to Tubeville.

On the ward, I had less supervision. If I had any energy to exert any behaviours, I'm sure I would've tried to rip out the tube but I sat on the bed and read books between naps. Getting visits from Dad made it much easier to cope. My throat was too sore to speak much, but he held my hand, said he'd called Mum and she was driving up from Melbourne as we spoke. Too hard. I didn't want Mum to see how hard I had failed and that she had been right all those times she told me to go back into the inpatient program near her house. I had thought I was all right. I'd tried, hadn't I? I'd even been a bit happy – happy enough to be considered a normal teenager. But after all, what was normal?

I wasn't the only one dreading Mum's visit. Dad paced the room and clapped his hands together, picking at the callouses on his fingers whenever he did sit down beside my bed.

'Dad, stop. Relax.'

'I need you to not say anything to your mum about me and Sandy, Sprout,' Dad begged.

I rolled my eyes. I wished they would just stop being so secretive about it. But then again, I'm sure I wouldn't have anorexia nervosa if I had just not been stupid about it, too. We

133

couldn't really control the way we felt or expressed our anxiety. There was nothing stupid about it at the end of the day.

While the tube was in, I didn't have to eat. It was an odd sensation to feel full yet never eat. All I had to really do was to sit there on the ward, propped up on my bed, and rest. *Rest*. After two days on the ward, I was of the belief that rest was a false concept. I was bored out of my brain. My potassium was still too low yet the machines pumped it up hour by hour, the way the doctors and nurses expected the tube to pump my weight up. I tried not to think about it, but after the two days, my butt was numb and the voice in my head said it was all the fat on my butt already, cushioning the sensation to the bones. My legs were cramping worse than ever before. I clutched at them, moaning and sobbing, earning disapproving looks from the other patients.

The nurse who had put the tube in (I called her Nurse NG) came by constantly and offered no bedside manner. I hated her. There I was, so depressed and negative but she was more pessimistic and negative than I was!

She had experience treating anorexic patients. She was eagle-eyed and no-nonsense. Other nurses could be manipulated. Anorexia remained strong when the shifts would change. Nurse NG did nothing but piss it off, and me by extension.

The day Mum was coming to visit, Dad was a nervous wreck. He sat by my bed, cracking his knuckles, and continuously looking up at the hallway as though waiting for the Grim Reaper.

'Why are you freaking out so much?'

'Never mind.' Crack, pop, crack, went his knuckles.

'You didn't let me get like this, Dad,' I whispered, after a pause.

He let out a scoff and looked away to stop me seeing his eyes puddle up but I did. I saw.

Mum arrived at two o'clock in the afternoon. She strode into the ward with her face made up, hair curled; her heels clacked, her blazer blazed and skirt was pencil thin. My throat lumped up as soon as she strutted in. The failure was mine; it was not Dad's.

Mum had some time with anorexia as it had developed and grown. Dad had it in its pure manifestation – he had not much of me but had the lying, manipulative cold devil. What chance did a simple man like him even have in the face of such a destructive demon?

Mum swallowed. Hard. Slowly, she removed her sunglasses, revealing her teal-coloured eyes that were like steel and brazen in how they caught my attention. 'Daisy,' she scolded. She crossed her legs as she sat down beside my bed, making sure to adjust the hem of her skirt as it rode up and she smoothed out her stockings. She tutted. 'I am absolutely fuming with you and your father. I mean, this has clearly been a worsening problem and your dad should have called me when he couldn't get you to eat.'

'I did eat,' I grumbled. I didn't know why I bothered. It was exhausting to continuously tell people that I ate, trying to debunk the misconception about anorexia and how I must not eat anything at all but the truth was, I did eat. Once you're at a certain point though, the weight plummets because your body is trying to stay alive. The morsels I was giving it weren't enough. Energy is an elusive enigma. It's not a tangible thing the way an organ is. You don't notice the shift in the race towards death until your time is up.

Truthfully, and I mean truthfully, not anorexia truthfully, the only time I actually completely stopped eating altogether was in the hospital with that tube pumping milky, chalky nutrition in my nose, down the back of my throat, into my stomach. Eating? I didn't need to eat anymore. It was proving to be a relief. I no longer ate. What a reversal of a biological logic; I would not eat until I gained enough weight. It sounds like a riddle that needs to be solved; one I'm sure only other anorexics would understand…but we wouldn't laugh about it.

After Mum's visit, I couldn't lie still. The cramps in my legs had me kicking and the vines attached to me burned and made me itchy. Nurse NG warned me to lie still. I started crying and I couldn't stop.

'Do you want your mother to come back?' she asked. 'Visiting hours are over. You'll see her tomorrow.'

I didn't know how to tell her that I had just realised I hated my mother. I absolutely despised her. Blame goes in different directions when you're mentally unwell, I guess. I wanted Dad, just Dad.

Later, the psychologists would tell me that the only reason I wanted Dad instead was because it was easier to be anorexic when he was around – that he was the reason I had got so ill when I lived with him. I didn't care. Dad made anorexia easier but he also made my life easier.

Nurse NG gave me a muscle relaxant. I went to sleep and had fitful, alarming dreams of gargantuan waves rushing up the beach. I was running from them and screaming at Hollie to run, to get away. I was clutching at the sand dunes, my skin ripping open as the grass turned to razors, the noise in my ears the roar of an approaching tsunami. I woke up crying when I realised that I couldn't see Hollie, but I fell asleep again, running through the streets, freezing cold wearing a fur coat, sucking on a disposable cup of black coffee. Sandy offered me cake. I pushed him and he fell in the gutter of a street that was filling with my tears. As I tried to pull him up out of my tears, with my weak arms, my eye caught a whale, beached upon the pavement on the other side of the street. I screamed and woke up to a crowd of nurses around me and a shrieking heart rate monitor alarm.

'Wake up, wake up, wake up, that's a girl, that's a girl. Stay with us.'

My heartrate had dropped so low that they'd almost had to resuscitate me. I wondered why it didn't terrify me like it should have.

Once I became stable enough over the next couple of days, I was chauffeured in a wheelchair to the eating disorder ward where I had to attend group therapy sessions with the other patients. On the second day, I refused to sit in that chair and kicked it across the room, sending it sailing into the hallway and nearly taking out a few visitors and nurses.

For the thousandth time in my life, I sat in a plastic, ripped vinyl chair in group therapy, listening to older women so eloquently describe their anorexia. I half-heartedly hoped I'd be dead instead of still struggling at age 48. No offence, Karen. How accurately they could define what happened to them and explore the dark reasons for the development of their demon. They were raped. Molested. Never good enough. Had a death of a loved one. Just wanted to lose weight but got carried away. Had a fear of choking. One lady, about thirty, was sick all because her cat couldn't eat in its final days before it died, so she didn't deserve to eat either because she couldn't save the cat. Complex reasons, but reasons they could all express and process.

My cause was foggy. I was from a broken home, sure. Did I actually care about it? No. It wasn't that major to me. I'd never been that attached to my parents, even as a little kid. I was running off in shopping centres and walking past my mother in the street after school and on the weekends. So it wasn't that at its core. Sure, Dad leaving was traumatic enough but life had really just…gone on, so I didn't attribute it to that.

I'd always had tantrums about food, being a fussy kid, so maybe I always had a taste for not eating. My mother was a stubborn woman and I'd fallen asleep at the dining room table, refusing to eat the roast meat, the pumpkin, the fish, the Brussel sprouts, the broccoli, the bits of onion – whatever I had decided was inedible that day. But I'd eat tonnes of cookies and lollies, so it wasn't likely.

For a while, I thought it may have been because I knew a kid in grade one who was gravely ill and had died. She had been so thin – like a walking matchstick. I couldn't stop staring at her; I

137

saw how she wrote then had to lay her head on the table, to have the teacher come by and rub her back, uttering encouragement and praising how hard she was trying. My writing was messy. I didn't do my finger spaces correctly. I misspelled my own name as Daze. D. A. Z. E. I had been a phonetic speller.

I was never a good student. I got the giggles when I had to read aloud to the class, a book about a cat named Mopsy and I found the name too hilarious to cope with. Mopsy! I had cackled and was sternly told to go sit down at the back of the classroom and think about my actions…so of course I had mulled over what a doofus I was and how I couldn't do anything right. The sick girl, Skyla, was allowed to read alone. Her hair was always neatly braided. Mine was always in a scraggly pony tail with flyaway hairs because Mum didn't have much time in the mornings before work and I didn't like her touching me anyway.

Skyla was dying. I didn't understand that at the time. I was six. How could I?

At recess time, all of us would gallop outside like horses or pretend to be ninjas. I remember one playtime very clearly. I paused at the drink taps outside the classroom to get a drink from the fountain, the sound of the water rushing through the old pipes. I noticed Skyla lying at the classroom door, too weak to play. I went over to her and studied her thin legs in her bright blue woollen tights. She looked over her shoulder at me with her grey eyes, embedded in bruised, sunken eyelids.

'Why aren't you playing?' I had asked curiously.

I can't remember her answering. The next memory I had of her was her not being at school anymore, and my teacher sobbing, being led away by two other teachers when she received the news. Skyla had died. I was lost for an idol.

After school, I was in the Nippers for a bit but lost interest. Mum put me in piano but I had fat fingers. Then I wanted to do ballet so I could wear a tutu. Could the unethical expectations on ballerinas' bodies have been my trigger? No. I backed out of ballet after two months because I didn't practise outside of my weekly class because I just didn't care enough. I always felt like I had been floating, slightly engaged at times, but mostly detached from everyone else. Had that been my trigger?

But it always came back to Corey. When I first stopped eating. Two years ago, almost three. It was just me and Corey, hanging out at the beach, being typical bay brats, showing off and jumping off the edge of the pier. Gallivanting and sprucing our youth and young love. Corey jumped in. Wrong timing. Wrong place. He slammed his head into a submerged shopping trolley from the local supermarket. Vegetable. Instantly.

When school had started after the summer holidays, I had changed. Corey never came back to school. His best friend Luke focused on school. Went to church. Played footy for the local team. Checked on Corey every day, with either phone calls to his parents or by dropping in to say hi – even though he knew that Corey had no idea what was going on. Luke ate lunch with me every day while I chewed gum and jiggled my leg…

It had been my fault he'd jumped in because I called him a chicken and triple dog dared him. I never told Luke that. I never even apologised to Corey, or went to see him. Too scared. Maybe one day I would.

When it was my turn to speak up in group therapy about what I thought triggered my eating disorder, I wrapped my cardigan around myself with a shiver and shrugged, plucking imaginary pieces of dirt off my legs. I stayed quiet. The only person I could tell about things like that was Hollie, and I wasn't even sure I'd tell her.

The following morning, I was hit with an update from the doctors.

'Relocation forms?' I sputtered. The doctors all nodded. 'But why? I think I'm doing well here.'

'Your mother has got you a place in a very good inpatient program in Melbourne.'

'I don't want to go,' I said with a shrug.

139

'She's got a court order, Daisy,' replied one doctor with a very calm breath.

'That bitch!'

I paced my room all afternoon. Dad had to guide me to the bed to physically push me to sit down.

'I don't want to go with her!' I wailed. 'I am doing better here.'

He nodded. 'I know, I know.'

I grabbed his sleeves and begged him. 'Please, Dad, please. Let me stay here. Make her let me stay here. I'll be good. I'll eat.'

He pulled his arms away from me and rubbed his head as he admitted, 'I'd like to believe you, Sprout, but I just don't.' He shrugged. 'You've gotten sicker here.'

'But I feel better!'

'But you're not better.' He frowned and looked at me with a crinkled brow. He kissed my forehead and rubbed his hands together. 'So...let's pack your stuff up and I'll help you to the car.'

So, there I was. My last day. Sandy and Hollie were outside with my mum at her car. Hollie and I hugged, clutching each other and crying.

Sandy pulled her gently away to go as she shouted, 'Please get better! I need you.'

We waved goodbye. And that was it. That was the last time I saw my best friend.

Mum drove me all the way to Melbourne, torturing me with '80s pop music. We stopped at Cann River for a toilet break and so she could get some food. I sulked. I didn't want to get out of the car and have people stare at the NG tube, not to mention the fat that jiggled whenever we hit a bump in the road, but she made me sit down in the quaint little café where people did indeed stare.

'Come on, Daisy. You need to eat.'

I gestured at the tube. 'I don't have to, remember,' I snapped.

'You can still eat with that thing in,' she retorted. 'They'll only take it out once you start eating, you know.'

'Guess I'll be wearing it a while, won't I.'

'What is wrong with you?' she groaned with exasperation.

'You!' I cried. With all the nutrients I needed going straight to my organs, my brain was more aware of my heartache and despair, and I cried at the slightest upset. I sat there in the quaint country café, sobbing with a tube up my nose, with my mother sitting opposite me, pushing her own food away, too awkward and unnerved by the raw emotion I was displaying.

When we arrived at the clinic eight hours later, my bag was searched. My hairbrush was taken off me...my freaking hairbrush.

The nurses told me I had to pee into a tray because they wanted to measure the output of millilitres and they told me to tell them how much water I had drank that day already. I shrugged. Mum, obviously feeling very prepared, held up the water bottle she'd given me on the beginning of our trip. 'Approximately 200 millilitres in around nine hours.'

I felt fat just for having someone point out that I'd ingested so much.

'Eaten?'

'Nothing,' said my mother. That gave me a bit of pride and I smiled serenely, until they poured a big glass of Ensure.

'Drink this,' they said.

'But I have a tube!' I exclaimed.

'Yes, we'll be taking that out tomorrow morning. Here, we focus more on remembering how to eat instead of just being tubed. We think you'll be much better that way.'

The room closed in around me with its yellow walls and white tiles that went halfway up the wall like a bathroom. The fluorescent light above us glimmered and buzzed, giving me a headache. Amongst the buzz of the light, I heard Hollie's voice. *Please get better. I need you.* The only way I was going to get to go home and be with her, and surf again, was to get better. I heaved a sigh as I took the glass with trembling hands. *Don't do it*, my mind screamed, but I took a little sip for Hollie, then started to cry all over again.

Chapter Eight

The nurses placed a heart rate monitor on me, which stuck to me like a root system and I was taken to my room in a wheelchair – they couldn't risk me losing more weight by allowing me the simple freedom that was walking. I shared a room with a girl called Avery. She was tall and much skinnier than I was. She had wild, red hair down to her waist. She was quiet, and I understood. Speaking took too much energy. She lived on a farm with her older sister, her parents and a collection of animals. She liked horses – their photos were adhered to the wall above her bed.

I asked, 'How long have you been here?'

A tear ran down her cheek. 'Six months,' she whispered, wiping her eye with the back of her hand, a slight tinge of blue.

My mind calculated how much she must have weighed when she'd arrived and I shuddered. I wondered how close to death she had been. One moment I pitied her, then a moment later I was jealous of her for being better at anorexia than I was.

I went with Avery in my wheelchair to dinner only about an hour after unpacking my clothes. She inched me along the hallway to the dinner room, pausing for short gasps of breath. I twiddled my thumbs and wondered why I had to sit in the wheelchair when I could walk. There was Avery, a twig of a thing, heaving me through the reflective corridor to dinner when she was clearly struggling.

'Should you be pushing me?' I asked.

She nodded. 'I'm fine. You need to rest.'

Dinner was served in a small room and we were all perched on a bench-style seat. Our hip bones knocked each other's and I was welcomed warmly, albeit with competitive, jealous stares. I stared at the plate of potato, peas, corn, beans, macaroni, cheese, and roasted chicken. I had already had an Ensure, plus the tube. There was no way I could eat all that as well. I'd explode.

The girls around me started eating. Around the table, trembling hands moved to mouths – some slowly, some hastily.

'Daisy, you have to eat,' Avery whispered as she spooned her peas and corn into a corral under her chicken.

'Daisy!' screeched a nurse.

We all looked up and froze.

'You need to start eating because if that plate isn't cleared in half an hour, you will have a glass of Ensure.'

'I've already *had* an Ensure,' I moaned. 'Plus, I have this tube. You can't expect me to eat all this on top of everything else? I'll be sick!'

'If you are sick, you will be put on 24-hour supervision. Is that what you want?'

'No,' I huffed. The nurses always loved to threaten 24-hour supervision or the tube. When they couldn't use the tube threat, they used the supervision. Privacy is a luxury at hospitals anyway

– having it taken away by a nurse watching you around the clock was just as terrifying to me as the tube.

Avery tucked a piece of chicken behind her ear, into her frizzy hair. I glanced at her and she smiled. 'You can do it. Be strong.'

I stared incredulously at her and wondered if I should tell someone that she was hiding food. She was the first friend I'd made in here, so I didn't want to upset her. Besides, upsetting her would make it harder for her to recover. I would keep the peace. I looked up at the nurses and then looked around at the other girls, all pretending to eat but watching to see what I'd do in inconspicuous glances. I felt like crying all over again, but I picked up my fork and ate the chicken as fast as I could. Next the potato. Then the corn.

'Daisy!' screeched the nurse again.

I jumped with my mouth full of mashed corn. 'What?'

'Mix your vegetables together. Don't separate them. That's a behaviour.'

I blended it all together and shovelled it into my mouth, swallowed with great effort and got a start on the beans, which were cold and rubbery. My stomach gave a sharp stab. I stopped. I took deep breaths and began rubbing my stomach gently. Avery "finished" her plate and showed it victoriously to the nurse who nodded and let her leave the table with a swish of her orange hair.

The nurse turned her attention back to me. 'Keep eating, Daisy.'

I took another bite. I couldn't swallow it. It was coming up…all of it. I lunged for the nearby sink but I projectile vomited all over the kitchen floor, my tube snatching in my throat and burning.

I sank down to the floor and gasped for fresh air. The tube dwarfed my airways. It was all too difficult. I wanted to go home. The nurses wiped me up like a baby, gently wiping the vomit off my hands and face. The girls all stood, staring at me, some sad, some disgusted and dry-reaching themselves.

145

Just as the nurse had threatened me that if I threw up, I spent my first night in the observation ward for 24-hour observation.

I curled up in the bed and stared at the wall, shivering under the thin blanket. I rolled over again – where my bones dug into the springs. I tossed over again and sighed. Closed my eyes but light from the window shone in. I rolled over again, to face the nurse and they glared at me and told me to lie still.

I rolled my eyes and pulled the blanket higher up to my chin. Getting to sleep seemed to take hours. When I did eventually fall asleep, my heart rate dropped below forty, so they woke me up and forced me to drink electrolytes and then I couldn't get back to sleep. Even though only one night had passed, it felt as though I'd been there for months – and all I wanted to do was go home and see Dad, Sandy and most of all, Hollie.

Every morning at 6am, we were weighed. We were collected by orderlies carrying clipboards with a running list of names. I was wheeled out in my wheelchair and I had to sit there and wait with the other girls who looked me up and down like I wasn't skinny enough to be in a wheelchair and tubed. Girls skinnier than I was.

When it was time for my weigh-in, I had to sit on a chair, facing away from the digital read-out. There were disapproving murmurs that I had lost 0.2 kilograms. By 7:00 am, the doctors had made the decision not to take the tube out since I had lost weight. They would be leaving the tube in, just in case they needed to unexpectedly boost my calories. *Unexpectedly*. I didn't like the sound of that.

At 8:00 am, I had to eat breakfast with a nurse named Louise. She explained that I'd join a different group for meals than I had been in last night once they were sure that I would eat by myself and not vomit it back up. In the meantime, I needed to be monitored one-on-one. They timed me eating with an actual timer instead of a verbal time limit. They gave me a bowl of cereal and set the timer for half an hour to clear the bowl. If I couldn't do it, I'd have an Ensure. Motivated to clear the bowl, I set to work, even though my jaw was tired after the big effort of dinner the night before; my stomach was queasy. I broke a sweat. The milk on the cereal coated my tongue like oil. I hyperventilated when I saw my half hour was nearly up and I'd be given another Ensure.

I begged for mercy as Louise poured the Ensure, turning off the alarm with a wince.

Later, in the day room, I tried to jiggle my foot and move my arms so the nurse in charge of my 24-hour supervision wouldn't see. Avery watched me.

Lunchtime was at 12:40 and I had to eat a bowl of pasta and sauce. I actually loved pasta. I managed to eat the lot. Louise cheered for me and gave me a high five. I was wheeled back into the day room, beaming, as everyone else was returning from their lunches.

'Did you get pasta?' A girl called Bronte exclaimed. 'How disgusting is it?'

'So gross! I want to purge so badly.' Melinda acted out sticking her fingers down the back of her throat.

'It's disgusting,' Evie wailed.

'They're really trying to just give us such unhealthy foods!' Emily shook her head.

My pride of eating the full meal without feeling ill evaporated with their disgust. Pasta. Ew. I felt dirty for eating the entire bowl.

Snack was a plate of crackers with cheese and some avocado. I pushed it away. Dinner was a big cashew stir-fry with noodles, dripping in oil. I pushed it away. Dessert was cream pie. I pushed it away. I got the lecture and they fed me through the tube. So that was what they meant by "unexpectedly". It meant when they couldn't control me. Lesson learnt.

After my 24-hour supervision ended, I got to spend my first night with Avery. I complained that they had fed me through the tube even though they didn't believe in the tube. What hypocrites. Controlling hypocrites. I paced the room.

She watched me from her bed. 'You should try to get better.'

'I am,' I replied, stopping my pacing. 'I'm trying. They're just annoying me!' They weren't the only ones. Who did she think she was to tell me that? She was the one hiding food. But I shrugged it off. It wasn't my problem; it wasn't my business. So, I got on with it. I got into the routine. I liked routine.

Eventually, I was going well with the meals. The food sometimes got jammed in my throat and I vomited again once and was given a warning. I couldn't help it. I was just too full.

Mum visited every night. She brought me books and tried giving me a surfing magazine but the Gestapo confiscated it because it had images of skinny girls in bikinis. Mum campaigned against it, furiously trying to wave her feminism in their faces. 'Strong, healthy girls! How is that triggering?'

But it was a no. She wondered aloud how would I learn to adjust to the world outside if I couldn't even be permitted to see healthy girls in case I might be triggered. I agreed with her. The tired old "it was the super model's fault". How dare there be skinny people in the world? They must cause anorexia.

I missed Hollie so much. I dreamt of starving again. I missed the emptiness as much as I missed my friend. Dad and Sandy popped into my mind every now and again, mostly when I noticed the dads and brothers and uncles visiting the ward. Everybody felt so far away and my only purpose seemed to be to clean my bowl at each meal time. Sometimes it felt like I wasn't even there.

Avery's sister visited every day, bringing homework from her university course and silently studying while Avery watched. They chatted easily together, as if Avery didn't have a severe mental problem and they weren't in a hospital being studied by every other anorexic. Truth be told, Avery was easily the skinniest there, therefore we all idolised her, which gave her both power and a target on her back. But if she noticed, she never let on. She went on chatting with her sister. It hurt to see them together as I sat alone with a book or a colouring book, wishing I could see Hollie. *Please get better. I need you.*

It took two weeks just to put on a half a kilo. My NG tube was finally taken out. I started finishing meals in time and started to eat in the main dining room, but that had its own challenges, of course. Remember how I said we all idolised Avery? How she had a target on her back? Well, I couldn't help shouting one Tuesday lunchtime, 'Her serving size is smaller than mine!'

That outburst got me an Ensure.

I tried squashing my potato under the table. That got me an Ensure and no visiting hours for two days. I spat my peas into my napkin, so they confiscated my books. I cried and cried. I complained in therapy that it was unfair because Avery got away with everything and she was skinnier than me. I was told I had to focus on my own recovery.

I did leg lifts at 5:00 am while everyone was sleeping. I couldn't help it. I had to destroy myself and it didn't seem to matter if I was trying to get better or not.

It took another two weeks to get phone privileges.

The phone booth was a little office with a yellow phone with the spiral cord. Awfully vintage. The line crackled and hissed but our parents and friends could call us after dinner. I'd been desperate to get a phone call from someone – and as soon as Dad knew I had finally got my phone privileges, he must have told Hollie because she was the first person to call me.

'Phone call for Daisy!'

I sprinted to the phone room and took the phone from the nurse so fast I couldn't even remember saying hello to find out who it was. I was so eager to hear from anyone that wasn't my mother or a nurse.

'Daisy!' Hollie's voice echoed down the line.

Tears sprung to my eyes at the sound of her voice.

'I miss you!' I exclaimed.

She sighed. 'You have no idea how much I miss you.' She sounded different. Older. Removed.

'Are you catching loads of waves?' I asked.

She avoided the question. 'Are you getting better? Will you be home soon?'

'Yeah, totally. I've gained frigging two kilos, Hol!' I laughed.

'What do you need to weigh before they let you come home?'

'They'll let me go to a day program if I gain four more kilos…after that, they'll let me home at two more than that, I think. It's a lot…but I can do it.'

Hollie was quiet. I strained my ears to hear if she was still there, but the phone pressing so hard against the top of my ear hurt.

'Hollie?'

'Yeah,' came her voice as though she was far away.

'You there?'

'Yeah, I…' With a sigh she said, 'I just miss you. It's hard being here without you. Things are…well, they're how they are. It is what it is.'

'I'll be home soon.'

'I can't wait.'

'Yeah, me neither.' I grinned.

She said, 'I'll, um…I've – I've got to go, Daze. I love you.'

'Love you, too. Bye.' I skipped back to my room, more positive than I had been in weeks just hearing her voice. I could get over this. No amount of weight gain was going to stop me.

On Christmas Day I was allowed to go home for the day – home as in my mother's home, not my home-home. Mum picked me up for 8:00 am and was given a long debriefing on what to feed me and how much. I sat in my wheelchair, rolling my eyes.

150

The wheelchair had been non-negotiable. I was not allowed out of it in fear of the kilograms that I had put on might melt away. I felt okay at the weight I was at that point. The goal weight they had set for me was an even number, and I knew I'd have to be either a kilo under or a kilo over because I didn't like being an even number. I had to be an odd number. I was determined to gain just enough weight to get out, and stay at that weight for the rest of my life, no matter what those yuppies were saying about my goal weight. I just needed to be functional enough to go home and surf. That was it.

Mum drove me back to my old home, following the highway along the bay. Mobs of cyclists dominated the road. 'Don't they have families to be with?' she muttered.

I shrugged, trying to engage but not really knowing what I could say. My family was in New South Wales and I wasn't with them.

Jessie met me at the front door with a high-pitched whine and yelp frenzy. Gold fur flew as she danced with joy, her tail wagging so hard it wound round and round. I went to get out of the chair to play with her, tears in my eyes – I hadn't realised I missed her so much – but Mum gently pushed me back into the chair. The anorexia raged. I remained seated, caging the beast – heal – get better – she needs you.

It surprised me how easy it was to shut that part of my brain off. I thought I'd be straight back to starving in my old environment but I sat on the couch and allowed my mother to wait hand and foot on me as I cuddled with Jessie, whose tail thumped lazily at the leather. I got out of the chair and slid onto the floor in order to get closer cuddles with my dog.

I thought of Hollie and wondered what she was doing for Christmas. I wished I could be with her and share gifts instead of here with my mother with the greasy scent of a roast chicken permeating the house. This sucked.

151

I kissed the top of Jessie's head and she reached up to lick my cheek and I giggled. I hugged her closer. 'Jessie, can I tell you a secret?'

She rolled onto her back, crushing me with her portly Golden Retriever weight. She pawed at the air, waiting for me to waggle them, which I obliged. She had always enjoyed me peddling her paws like she was riding a bike.

'I don't ever want to come back to live here.' A tear plopped out onto her snout and she sneezed. I hugged her again. 'I wish you could come with me, though. I love you.'

Mum came back into the living room and tutted at me on the floor with Jessie. She helped me get into the wheelchair and wheeled me to the kitchen table for a very lonely lunch with just the two of us. We pulled a bonbon. I was too weak to pull it but Mum let me win anyway. She put the paper crown on my head and I forced a laugh, vowing to never come back to that house.

I ate everything she fed me and she beamed. I simmered as she gloated that she shouldn't have sent me to Short Point. She'd been so silly to leave me in Dad's care. He didn't know what he was doing and had allowed me to get so sick. She was so glad I was home for the day. I sighed and swallowed my last bite of potato salad. I couldn't wait to go home. My real home in Short Point.

Christmas and New Years set off a frenzy in the ward. It was a skipping record of girls wailing *I want to go home; I'm fat; that's too much food; no!* I stopped singing on the record in chorus, and I started listening, instead.

Avery went home after her seven-month stint on the ward, still sickly thin and barely strong enough to walk. Her sister wheeled her out in a wheelchair but Avery smiled and said, 'I won't be back. I'm better.'

The glint in her eye told a different story. I stood at the door with my arms folded, and stayed until she disappeared. It would be good to see her again. I knew if I didn't – she'd be dead.

That afternoon, I got a new roommate. Her name was Steph. Steph was a bulimic. I flinched as she bounced off the walls, laughing from the back of her throat like a braying donkey.

She unpacked all her clothes and took over our closet.

'How are you allowed to bring that many clothes?' I muttered.

'What'd you say?' she snapped.

'Nothing.'

Steph wrestled with the carpet until it came up with a sound like a zipper. I peered in around her shoulder.

'What are you doing?'

Her hands dove down the front of her pants and she dug around in her underwear, making me cast my eyes aside to save her dignity. She retrieved a baggie of pills.

'Lax. If they make me eat too much, I'll take these.' She winked. 'Our secret, roomie.'

Steph tucked the laxatives under the carpet and smoothed it out.

'Why don't you just try to get better?' I asked. 'It's what you're here to do.'

She snorted. 'What – then everything will be hunky dory once we get to go home?' She clapped a hand on my shoulder and my clavicle trembled – if she'd done it any harder, it would have snapped, I was sure.

'Flower, you've got a lot to learn about having an eating disorder.'

My face burnt and my teeth clacked. 'My name is Daisy, not Flower.'

'Whatever. Point is…' Steph shook her head. 'You'll never get better. It's with us for life.'

A bead of sweat rolled from her forehead to her temple and I studied it as it fell. As it hit the floor, an overwhelming wave of sadness hit me. Was she right? Would I be like this forever?

153

I sat in the day room that afternoon, gnawing at my fingernails and jiggling my leg. I couldn't be like this forever. I couldn't keep it up. I wanted to be like how I was when I'd been surfing all the time with Sandy and Hollie. I had been strong. Happy. My eyes went to a nurse as he approached and I paused my leg jiggles so it wouldn't look as though I was burning calories.

He came over to me and said, 'Great news, Daisy. You've just been cleared for a weekend privilege next week.'

'What does that mean?' I asked.

He clapped his hands together. 'You get to go out for the weekend.'

'As in more than just a day?'

'As in the whole weekend.'

Air filled me. Light shone. I could have sung.

I called Dad that night. He hollered and yipped and I laughed myself giddy.

'I know, I know. I'm so excited.'

'We'll come down. Make a proper weekend of it.'

'What will Mum say?' I asked.

'Mum Schmum,' he laughed. 'She's got to see you every day. I reckon I can have ya for at least a day.'

I beamed. 'I can't wait.'

Going to bed that night, I told Steph my exciting news. Avery and I had shared something good about the day before we had said good night. I would regret trying to keep up that tradition with Steph.

She scoffed. 'You know it's a test.'

'What do you mean?'

'It's a test to see if you can still gain weight when you're out of here for the weekend. You'll have to eat twice as much to make sure you don't lose weight. Otherwise, they'll keep you in here longer.'

I stared at her from across the room in the dark. How dare she? She always brought me down and made me upset.

She grinned. 'Good night.'

I lay in bed and scowled at the ceiling. I couldn't sleep. I started doing leg lifts once Steph began to snore.

Every night that week, I compulsively exercised in the room, freezing each time I heard Steph stir in the stiff hospital bed. On Thursday morning during the weigh-in, the nurses tutted.

'Daisy, have you been hiding food?'

'What? No. Of course not. You see me – I eat everything you give me.'

'Have you been vomiting?'

'No!'

'Have you been exercising?'

I blinked. My throat closed a bit as I said, 'No.'

She sighed. 'You've lost weight.'

I stepped off the scale and despite losing weight, felt heavier on my feet. I pushed my hair off my face so the nurse could see my eyes. 'So, what happens now?'

She scribbled her notes and took my blood pressure. Scribbled more notes and shook her head. 'I don't know what to tell you, Daisy. You're going to die if you don't start giving this a good go.'

'But I am,' I whispered. I wanted to tell her how I really felt. I was trying, but Steph was awful to stay with. She was negative, destructive and she seemed to really hate the hospital and she made me exercise out of anxiety. I thought of the laxatives under the carpet. I could get rid of her and get my own recovery back on track. But I stayed quiet.

The nurse said, 'You were meant to have a weekend privilege this weekend, weren't you?'

I nodded.

She clucked her tongue. 'Well, I'm afraid you can't have those privileges until your weight comes back up.'

There was a roaring in my ears and black specks appeared in my sight. People surrounded me, calling my name and telling me to breathe. My chest ached and my hip stung. I looked up at the door and saw the concerned faces of girls waiting in line to be

155

weighed. I cleared my throat and tried to stand but three nurses held me back down. Where had those three nurses come from?

'What happened?' I croaked.

'You fainted,' replied a nurse. A senior nurse with thick thighs and a jingling key chain on her belt marched into the room with a plastic cup of orange juice. I drank it down with a thick throat.

Afterwards, lying on my bed in the middle of the day, reading, Steph bounced into the room, always trying to burn calories.

'You are a total dork,' she teased. 'Passing out at weigh-in. So many of us nearly wet ourselves having to hold on that long.' She laughed her donkey laugh.

I glared at her. 'You shouldn't be water loading. It's cheating.'

Steph held out her arms as though crucified. 'Gotta do what we gotta do to get out, Flower.'

'Stop calling me that,' I snapped. I was in no mood to put up with her always triggering me. I'd lost weight, lost consciousness, lost my weekend trip and now I'd lost my patience.

'What do you want me to call you then?' Her eyes glittered. '*Weed?*'

I slammed my book closed and threw it at her with a wail. It was only a paperback so it clumped into her chest pathetically before falling to the floor. She shrugged at me.

'I really don't like you,' I admitted. 'If you don't leave me alone, I'm going to tell them what you've been doing.'

Her throat moved as she swallowed and she looked me up and down as though trying to work out if I would. I didn't blink. She nodded and walked away. Finally – I had some peace from her. I got up to retrieve the book and whimpered as I realised that I'd lost which page I was up to, as well.

That night, I called Dad crying that I'd lost weight, so I'd lost my upcoming weekend privilege. He, Sandy and Hollie had been planning on coming to Melbourne. They were going to take me for a day trip to Bells Beach. The trip would have to be cancelled. I was embarrassed and ashamed. Devastated.

Dad was an angel on the other end of the phone line. 'Sprout, don't worry about it. We'll still come visit you.'

'I don't want you to just visit – I want to go to Bells Beach with you!' I sobbed.

Hollie took the phone from my dad and she shouted into the phone, 'Daisy, I'll come visit.'

'No, no, no,' I whined. 'I don't want you to see me in this place.' My voice came out as though it was filled with helium. Even strangled. Protecting my dignity was getting harder and harder.

Her voice cracked as she said, 'Then I'll go camping with Chase, instead.'

'Do you want to?'

Tears laced her voice like a thick poison as she whined, 'It doesn't matter what I want to do, Daisy. What I want is you to just come home and be better.'

The tears in Hollie's voice had prickled at my skin and my conscience. Now that I was getting better, my brain was getting clearer. Guilt about my behaviour made my insides quake and shudder. Having anorexia was like having my body and mind split into separate entities. I was not my body and it was something that could be punished, denied or flagellated. The mind was me, most of the time, but succumbing to the illogical thoughts and actions of a mental illness nobody really understood yet claimed they did. While the body had been punished for so long, the mind had switched off and didn't feel so bad. The hurt and abandonment in Hollie's voice prickled the body and the mind together. Re-joining them. Painfully. I went to bed thinking it was the worst day of my life to turn her down and disappoint her so much. Boy, was I wrong.

Chapter Nine

Something was wrong. Hollie didn't call to tell me about what she did on the camping trip. Monday morning weigh-in was delayed. I stood outside the door of the weight room with the other patients and we yawned and shifted our weight from one foot to the other. Staff was having a meeting.

'Someone's died,' Steph said.

'Who?' Melanie cried.

'Everyone is here,' Evie said with an eyeroll. She had just as much patience with Steph's crap as I did.

'Maybe it's someone that already left,' Steph said.

My mind went to Avery. She was still ill when she'd been discharged. The time allowed by health insurance companies to recover was no match for eating disorders. Health insurance lasted weeks, or months if the patient was wealthy. Anorexia had a stamina that lasted years. It stole years. It stole lives.

My hand went to my mouth, having convinced myself Avery was now dead. Oh God.

Staff came out of the office and with their heads down, then commenced the weigh-ins with closed lips. Nobody was brave enough to ask what had happened even though we all wanted to ask: Why were they having an emergency meeting? Who had died?

In the hallway while I was still lining up, Nurse Louise put her hand on my upper arm and I flinched. 'Daisy, could we have a private word with you, please?' Her voice was so quiet I needed to tilt my head towards her mouth to hear her properly. My heart lurched. Oh no. It must have been Avery!

I nodded and followed Louise into the office where I was met by the chief doctor that I rarely met, my therapist, and to my surprise, my mum. My pulse hammered in my throat and my toes crunched inside my slippers.

'Mum, what are you doing here?'

She avoided looking at me, confirming that something was wrong.

'Daisy, we have some concerning news that you may not want to hear,' the doctor said.

'Is it Avery? Is she okay?'

Louise pulled out a chair for me. 'You should really sit down, Daisy.' I obeyed and waited for them to tell me the news that my ex-roommate had died. She was too sick when she had left. I was ready to be angry that they had let her go in that condition. It was on them! This was all their fault.

'We are concerned this will impact your recovery, and we want you to know that we are here to support you in any way you need,' the doctor said in a slow, soothing voice.

'What is it?'

159

'Your dad called last night,' Mum said. 'Honey...your friend Hollie is missing.'

'Wait – what?' It was as though I'd been splashed in the face with boiling water because it burned. I thought that Avery passing away would have been bad, but now they were saying Hollie's name, and that was worse.

'This isn't about Avery?' I croaked.

'No, this is about Hollie.'

'Hollie?'

'Hollie,' my mum repeated.

'Hollie is...' It made no sense. I couldn't comprehend what she was telling me.

'Missing,' she finished.

The material on my cardigan had a loose thread. I pinched and plucked at it, my mind working through what *missing* meant. How could someone be missing? You were in the world, or you weren't. Missing only meant people didn't know where she was. That didn't mean she ceased being. *I bet I could find her*, I thought. I knew all the places where Hollie could be. I knew her the best.

My mum handed me her phone to read the news report.

Teenage Girl Missing from New South Wales South Coast

Seventeen-year-old Hollie Matheson disappeared Friday night and was last seen leaving Whitehill Park campground. Police continue to search the area and local bushland after her brother returned home on 9:18 am on Saturday morning and discovered she had not returned home.

'Hollie said she was going home just after we had dinner, around nine. She didn't want to stay. She said she was going back to the road and a friend was picking her up. That was the last I saw her,' claims her older brother.

Family and police are concerned about Matheson due to her age and the rugged and isolated area. None of her friends admitted to picking her up.

She is described as Caucasian appearance, about 170 centimetres tall, *with an athletic build and wavy brown hair. Hollie was last seen wearing* *black leggings, pink sneakers, and was carrying a light blue backpack.*

Police believe Hollie might still be in the area, or may have gone north *towards Byron Bay.*

Anyone with information of her whereabouts is urged to contact Crime *Stoppers.*

She had been on a camping trip. Numb all over, I knew what that meant. There was no friend picking her up. She wouldn't have left unless her brother's friends were there, the ones who had harassed her. She wouldn't have left the campground if she had felt safe.

I ran a shaky hand over my eyes a few times and I gripped the arms of the chair. I coughed as I tried to breathe. 'I think I need to speak to the police.'

'What do you mean?' the doctor asked.

'I want to know more.'

He looked to my therapist and she shook her head. 'I don't think that's a good idea, Daisy. You need to focus on getting well. We'll give you updates as we get them. We assure you.'

'No, I need to go home.'

'You can't come home with me,' Mum said. 'You're not ready.'

'That's not home!' I snapped.

Mum crossed her arms, tucking her phone to her chest. I ran my tongue over my teeth to stop myself from screaming at her and the doctors. I had to do something. I knew Hollie would never just leave that campground; I knew it and nobody was listening.

My recovery meant nothing to me in that moment. I was recovered enough! I couldn't bear staying and sitting on my hands, doing nothing but gaining weight while my best friend was out there somewhere in the world, last seen in the forest, needing to be found and taken home.

I crossed my arms and pouted. 'I am not going to eat another morsel unless you let me out of here and let me go look for her.' I narrowed my eyes as if daring them to doubt me. 'I bet I can find her.'

The powers that be collectively groaned and rolled their eyes. I knew they were thinking: This was typical Daisy Cavill. Giving an ultimatum to try to keep control of the situation. Another excuse to not eat. What they were worried about.

'That's not going to happen, Daisy,' the doctor said, folding his arms across his chest and leaning back in the lush office chair to mirror my own position. 'Your health is paramount. Leave finding your friend to the police. It's what they're trained to do, after all.'

'Oh yeah?' I snapped. 'Well, your job is to make me better and I'm telling you – you're doing a shit job if you don't let me go.'

They still didn't let me leave. Mum left, well, tried to. I gripped her by the wrists and she continued walking to the exit, dragging me along the linoleum floors with me begging. 'Mum! Please! You have to let me out so I can find her! I'm the only one who can! She wouldn't have left. She didn't leave. She's still out there. Her brother knows more than he's letting on, Mum, please!'

Mum shook me off at the door with the help of the nurses and doctors. 'Daisy, come on, now! Get well and they'll find her. Hollie will be fine.' She walked out, her heels clacking on the concrete steps outside the glass door, then out of sight.

As the nurses and doctors held me from behind, I balled my fists and clamped my legs together. Everything inside me burbled up like a volcano and I screamed with my teeth clenched, eyes fixed on the exit that I should have been going through. Once I strained free of the nurses, I spun on my heel and shoved them away, hoping that the pain in my throat would go away, too. I sucked in air and screamed until my throat bled.

I was allowed to skip weigh-in that morning. I was not, however, allowed to skip breakfast. The girls all stared at my tears and got into a state when I refused to eat. Staff had to remove me into the smaller kitchen to give me an Ensure, but I was too stressed to drink it.

'Daisy,' said Louise. 'You really need this.'

I gulped down tears and replied, 'No, what I need is to leave here and find my friend. She needs me.'

She lowered her head so I wouldn't see the tears springing into her brown eyes but I saw them pooling in her eyelids.

That night, instead of sleeping, I smothered my face with my pillow and wrote a mental letter to Hollie.

We were meant to be going on a trip to Bells Beach, and I stuffed up. You were still going to come down for the weekend, but I said no. You went camping with Chase again, and disappeared. It's all my fault. If I hadn't have stuffed up and if I hadn't have turned you away, you would not have been in the bush with your brother and his psycho mates.

I dropped the pillow and gasped for air, staring up the ceiling. Chase had been on that camping trip, but he never camped with just Hollie. Why would he say that he was the only one there with her? He knew more. He was not alone. Something had happened to make Hollie want to leave. If she even did. Maybe she went and hid from them and got lost. I curled into the foetal position despite my hip bones aching from being on the mattress springs. I closed my eyes and sniffed, trying to stop crying but it was difficult.

Steph uttered into the oppressive darkness of the room, 'Hey, Daisy?'

'What?' I snapped.

She flicked her lamp on and perched herself up on her side, her hand supported her ear and one rested on the curve of her hip. She was so pale that she seemed to glow beside her lamp light.

'You know what you have to do.'

163

'What?'

She widened her eyes at me. 'You have to get better. At least…enough to get out of here. And quick.'

My acid reflux sat in my chest, burning and ever-present from having to eat so much. She was right. It would hurt, but I had to get better to get out. Quicker than what would actually heal me. Play by their rules. Even break them to make it look like I was gaining faster. I had to get out of there.

I nodded at her and she gave me an awkward smile before settling back down and switching off her lamp, plunging me into the dark again. My heart broke as I thought about Hollie being alone in the bush, lost. She needed me and I was stuck in this stupid hospital. Her voice filled my head. *Please get better. I need you.* I opened my eyes to her voice – it was like she was in the room with me. Morning light squeezed in under the blind. I had fallen asleep. I sat up, glancing around at Steph, still asleep and snoring. I yearned to have Hollie in the room instead of Steph, but Steph had a point, after all. I had to get better. I had to.

Chapter Ten

I hogged the phone all day, every day, waiting for updates on Hollie. The girls clucked and tutted at me each time it rang and I shoved them aside to answer it. *Please be my dad calling to say they'd found Hollie. Please.* But it never was. It was always someone's parent or friend and I'd have to give them the phone, anxious that Dad would call while it was engaged and I'd miss it.

My weight over the next few days steadily dropped and I agreed to get the tube re-inserted. I'd started eating again but the nervous energy was combusting all the calories. It stagnated for three days while I dived to the phone, desperate to hear something. Mum visited at night and let me read the news reports on her phone.

Police Still Searching for Lost Teen. Biological Parents Investigated for Missing Daughter. Matheson, 17, Still Missing. Where is Hollie Matheson?

I gained 0.2 of a kilogram. It gave me the heebie jeebies for a second, but then I reminded myself that I was meant to celebrate weight gain. I wanted weight gain. I was on the right track if I gained more weight because then I could go look for Hollie.

It went up steadily then. 0.2 a day. It was finally working.

I made progress and they released me. I went back to Mum's, still underweight. I promised to attend a day program, but as soon as I was left alone in the house, I kissed Jessie goodbye, grabbed my bag, got on a bus to the train station, and went home. It took twelve hours. I didn't eat or drink anything.

I arrived in the town at 6:00 am, lugging my suitcase. Its wheels rattling and scraping on the bitumen on the road through the reserve to the ocean beach. I stood over it and observed its emptiness. Fog hung in the air and I rubbed my bare arms, too stubborn to wear a jacket because it was too complicated to rifle through my luggage to get it out.

The sky was like a watercolour painting; orange, pink and loaded grey, blended at the horizon with the aqua of the water and disappearing into the distance just like Hollie had. *Right, Hollie...where are you?*

An icy breeze cut along the entire coastline; Summer, and all of its brightness and fearlessness, was over. Too much time had passed. I'd missed it.

I wandered to the shoreline and let the water rush to my feet, saturating my socks and leaving me soggy and cold. Part of me grieved for the time wasted. Part of me grieved Hollie. I stopped myself – I couldn't grieve for her. She wasn't dead. I would find her. I refused to think the worst.

I wrapped my noodle-thin arms around myself, caging my heart and walked along, my luggage abandoned and being sucked

166

into the sea by the incoming tide. I let it go. The ocean took my belongings and I barely glanced back.

When I made it to Dad's, finally back home, he was getting ready to go to work, packing his lunch in a paper-bag. I let myself in and leant against the doorway frame of the kitchen. Startled, he stared at me, his shoulders visibly dropping before he came to me, and hugged me so tightly I thought I'd never breathe again. My heartbeat pulsed in my eardrums.

He let me go and cupped my cheek with his palm. 'Welcome home, Sprout.'

'Thanks.' My voice was tight.

The sun shone through the window and caught me in the eye so brightly I had to squint. I sighed, weary from the trip.

'Your mum called me last night. Said you ran off. She was going to call the police. I called the bus and train services. They spotted you at Bairnsdale and I knew you were coming home.' His eyes ran over my face as if looking for an apology or a sign that I was not recovered. He added with a smile, 'Been waiting for you to walk in that door, actually.'

'Thanks for not calling the police,' I murmured.

'I can call the guys at work and let them know I'm not coming in,' he offered. 'We can catch up.'

I shook my head and told him I was going to be fine – I just needed to go to sleep so he may as well go. We could catch up after I slept. He watched me for a moment and I could guess he was struggling with should he go or should he stay. Should he feed me or should he trust me?

'I'll be fine,' I promised. He tapped his pockets and kissed me goodbye, carrying his lunch with him.

The sounds of the morning surrounded me. The sound of Short Point. Home. Birds, the breeze rustling the gum and fruit trees, Dad's car choking to life and driving away, his car motor blending with the rumble of a boat motor on the river. The neighbour's dog barking and a cockatoo shrieking in response.

167

I stripped off all my clothes and stood in the bathroom, scrutinizing my new body in the mirror. *Hello? Are you there? Anorexia?* She was there. Sleeping.

I showered quickly to avoid waking her up and pulled my soggy clothes back on and then curled up on Dad's couch and immediately fell into a deep sleep.

Dad woke me up when he got home in the early afternoon. He placed a flat hand on the middle of my back. I opened my eyes. My neck had stiffened and it made me nauseous.

'Daisy,' he whispered. 'I need you to eat something.'

The metallic queasiness hit my throat. It was now or never wasn't it. Eat something and get better for good, or starve and stay this way. Eat something and be able to go find Hollie.

I nodded. He helped me up and I followed him to the kitchen. He handed me a banana and I choked it down, swallowing as quickly as I could.

Get out, get out, get out – I wasn't sure if I was thinking to anorexia or to the banana. Everything blurred except my desire to find Hollie. Dad smiled at me and squeezed my shoulder once I was finished with the banana. I finished chewing and stood up, running my hands down my arms, linking fingers, an old habit.

I asked, 'Is it okay if I go see Sandy tomorrow?'

Dad studied my face, as I studied his in return. There was tightness in his jaw and a sadness in his eyes. Something was different but I couldn't put my finger on it. Dad nodded and squeaked, 'Sure.' I wondered what had changed, but I needed to focus on finding Hollie first. Sandy was the only person I could talk to who I knew wanted to find Hollie as much as I did.

The next morning at sunrise, I laced up my sneakers, still damp from yesterday, and walked to the beach. A fog hung in the air, and trees loomed like skeletons in the darkness until the orange sunlight illuminated their green or red leaves. At the beach, I blew out a misty breath. It was cold but I was bundled up in multiple layers that felt tight against my skin. Vestiges of the night clung to the horizon in a velvet curtain. Stars lingered. Dots of black drifted behind the waves. Surfers. My people.

I combed through the car park until I found Sandy's panelvan. It faced the waves, like a beacon over the beach. I sat on the bonnet and watched Sandy out in the surf, feeling the loneliness smother me on the overlook.

When he finally came in, jogging up the steps carrying his board, blonde hair plastered to his forehead, fingers blue from the water, I called out for him. 'Sandy!'

He glanced up then his eyes widened as though startled. His face softened and he beamed at me. 'Daze!' He climbed up the scrub, throwing his board into the bushes and gave me a tight hug as I jumped off his car. He blinked at me. 'You look amazing.' A.K.A fat.

I wrung my hands and tried to smile.

'The swell is picking up,' he said with a seaman's blow. 'Have to get you back out there.'

'Yeah,' I agreed. 'It'll be good.'

'Yeah.'

'Yeah.'

We lingered. Awkward in the cacophony of each other's shyness and unease with the unspoken name.

'Um, I've been...' I said but Sandy spoke at the same time, 'Has your dad...Oh, sorry.' He blushed. 'Go on.'

'I've come to look for Hollie.'

His voice cracked and his eyes went back to the sea, as though he wished he could get back out there. 'We've looked everywhere, Daisy.'

'But there's something I know.'

His eyes narrowed and he leant in closer. 'What?'

I glanced at some other surfers making their way up the track. I would have to make it quick, and quiet, because it was approaching high tide, and they were retreating out from the fat, weak waves in droves. I took a deep breath but the air escaped me and I ended up more breathless than before. I tried again. 'I know Chase and Hollie weren't alone out there.'

Sandy took a step back, putting distance between us. His shoulders squared and a nerve ticked in his temple as he chewed his inner lip. He glanced at the guys walking by and his mouth wrinkled. 'Are you telling me that her brother has been lying to the police, and to me, for the last two months?'

I nodded, not blinking, too scared to miss any reaction. I could be wrong. Maybe it had just been Chase, but I knew, I *knew*, there was no way she would have left and gone off with a "friend" who none of us knew.

Sandy sucked in a gasp of air and blew it out through his nostrils, making it whistle. 'You didn't tell the police?'

I shook my head.

He couldn't hide tears from me. 'I don't...I can't talk about this...right now, Daze.' His voice shuddered and he stared out at the ocean. 'I just...' He turned back to me. 'We could have found her by now! I mean...Damn! Jesus Christ, Daisy! You should have told me or your dad, at least!'

My lip trembled and I stepped back from him, surprised at his anger. 'I tried,' I whispered. 'Nobody listened.'

He pointed to his chest. 'You should have told me! *Me*! I would have listened!'

'You never called!' I shouted.

'I can't talk to you. I can't. Okay.' He grabbed his board from the bushes and chucked it into the car, wiped his face with a towel and drove away still wearing his wetsuit. A spinning sensation overwhelmed me and I realised I had stopped breathing. I squatted down with a gasp and was overcome with wracking sobs that I'd held in for too long.

I dawdled home in a daze. I sat on the steps and succumbed to the throbbing headache that you get from crying too hard – the kind that make you want to puke and think you've fractured your skull or have a tumour growing inside your brain and you're about to die of an aneurysm.

Part of me wished I could die on the steps because I deserved it. Sandy was right. I should have told him. I should have told Dad. What had I been thinking? We could have found her by now. Had Sandy really looked everywhere for Hollie? Why hadn't she come back by now to let us all know she was okay? A heavy and dark feeling of dread nagged at me.

Dad opened the front door. 'Where have you been?'

'The beach,' I murmured, not looking up from where I had my head in my hands.

'Not bloody exercising, I hope,' he grumbled.

'No, I went to see Sandy,' I sniffled.

'Oh.' He was quiet for a while before he asked, 'So I take it he is still struggling with Hollie going missing, too.'

I answered by vomiting in the softly packed black dirt. 'Dad,' I groaned.

He sat with me.

'Why did she have to go missing?' I wailed. The tears came again. Thick and blindingly hot. I sobbed and Dad pulled me into a hug, even though I got spew on him. He pulled me up and took me to my bedroom. I laid down and he pulled off my shoes and pants. I was emotionally done. Cooked. I could barely blink. Dad covered me with the blanket and stroked my head which brought back memories of him doing that to me when I was a little kid, just before he left us and moved up here. My breath rattled as I took in air with the memory, surprised by how much comfort and hurt it brought me at the same time.

'Maybe stay away from Sandy and the beach for a while, Daze. It might remind you too much of Hollie…more than you can cope with at the moment, anyway.'

I swallowed hard. 'Dad...I know her brother is lying about what happened the night she disappeared.'

'Oh?'

'Dad...' I winced with the effort of sitting up. He had to know. I had to tell him. 'Dad, her brother has some really bad friends. She told me once that they forced her to give them oral sex.' His eyes widened and hand went to his mouth momentarily before he regained his composure in order to stay calm for me. I went on with a hurried whisper, 'I think something bad happened to her and her brother is covering up for his friends.'

I lost control of my breathing and my eyes rolled uncomfortably in the panic. I knew it. I knew something had happened to her. Admitting it made my heart beat too fast. Dad squeezed my shoulder and helped me breathe properly again when I wanted to scream. I shouldn't have gone into the hospital. I should have stayed. She had needed me. I couldn't let Dad know how I felt, despite the thoughts circling around my head endlessly like a gnat or mosquito.

Dad nodded.

'I had to tell someone. What do we do now?'

'I think we should go speak to her grandparents first,' he replied. 'I think they ought to know if her brother is lying or not. He might be telling the truth.'

He couldn't do that. Chase would find out I was suspicious and he would dig in even deeper. I shook my head and said, 'No, Dad. We can't. We should go to the police!'

'But you don't know he's covering something up. Not for sure.'

'I know Hollie.' My jaw ached from clenching my teeth so hard. 'I know she wouldn't have tried to leave unless something really bad happened to her, and even then, she wouldn't have got into a stranger's car.'

'Things like this never stay a secret forever, Daisy. Especially in such a small town like Short Point. Someone will come forward.'

'Not if Chase is covering for them!' My knees wobbled as I stood up but I was determined to go to the police, no matter what Dad said. I started walking down the steps towards the street. It would be a long walk, but I used to run that far and back multiple times. I could do it on my own.

'Daisy, stop,' Dad called. 'You should be resting.'

'I spent months resting!' I roared, spittle flying in white globs through the air. Nobody seemed to care where Hollie was. They had got bored. Lost hope. Lost cause. I refused to let her be lost any longer.

I shook my head at Dad and said, 'I'm going to find her if it kills me. You can help me or not. Either way, I'm going.'

Sandy had been right. I should have told the police months ago. My mind hadn't been working the best, or even at all. Everything had always been about me. Now it was time for everything to be about Hollie.

Dad and I walked into the police station at Short Point, the overhead fans circling despite the cool autumn weather. The lime green walls made noise to my eyes and I had to look at the dark grey linoleum to settle my headache. There were three other people waiting around with furtive glances and crossed arms, shifting from toe to heel. They clutched at paperwork, purses and key collections that rivalled jailors. I kept my body close to Dad's, my hip bones bumping into the side of his leg as we waited for the window to be answered after Dad pushed the metallic plate of buttons screwed to the wall.

The police officer, a man with clipped white hair and a stern eyebrow, sighed as though we were interrupting his dinner. 'What can I do for you, folks?'

'My daughter has information to offer regarding Hollie Matheson.'

The police man's grey eyes turned to me and widened but his face remained unimpressed. 'Oh? Does she now.'

Eyes around me looked up. Hollie's name was famous these days. Everyone wondered where the wayward teen had gone. Where she had run off to after the town ran her out.

I nodded, my voice freezing under the glare of the police man's eyes. Maybe I was wrong. What if I gave them the wrong information? No. I had to do something. Hollie needed me.

'Do you know where she is?'

The eyes of everyone else were on me then. Not a single person in the room looked anywhere else. Dad put his arm around my shoulder, sensing the attention, too. I swallowed and shook my head.

'What do you have to say, then?'

I pulled back but Dad supported me by placing his palm in the middle of my spine. 'She was my daughter's best friend. You might like to hear what she has to say.'

The police man's eyes softened and gestured us towards the side door. He opened it and closed it behind us as we stepped in. He smiled. Tough exterior gone. 'Sorry about the guardedness. You'd be surprised how many looky-loos we've had coming in to claim they know something.' He smiled at me. 'Come with me.'

Dad and I followed him to a room where he gave us cups of water and sat down beside a younger police officer, with wavy black hair and bulging biceps. Liquid-like dark eyes and a smooth complexion that made me falter in my breath. He nodded at me. 'How ya garn.'

Dad wasted no time. 'My daughter Daisy was in hospital at the time Hollie went missing.' The police officers didn't look up as they wrote down everything Dad said. 'She was recently discharged and she's come straight home and told me that Hollie's older brother and his friends forced Hollie to do something quite vulgar on a previous camping trip.'

'What was it?' The younger police officer looked up at me. 'Could you tell us?'

174

I balked under his gaze. I looked to Dad. He nudged me.

I cleared my throat and whispered, 'She said her brother's friends forced her to give them oral sex.' My cheeks burned red. It was so private and I squirmed having to divulge what happened to Hollie without her permission. The boys hadn't kept it a secret, and had given Hollie an awful reputation, yet nobody seemed to be mentioning it. I wondered if any of those guys had told the police what they thought of Hollie, and if me telling the police this information would help get her back home or not.

The police officers cleared their throats.

'When did this happen, Daisy?'

I told them. I added, 'There were rumours about her after that. They all said she wanted to do it. They lied.'

The police officers exchanged a glance. Perhaps they had heard the rumours and just like most of the other males in the community, they believed it. Maybe they had given up looking for her thinking she had got what she wanted. I couldn't let Hollie be remembered in that way – a false way. The more I thought about it, Chase and his cronies needed to be punished anyway, even if they weren't bald-face lying about what happened the night Hollie disappeared.

I sat at the table, clutching the Styrofoam cup of water, jiggling my leg, resolved to find her. She was out there somewhere. Somebody knew something. At least I was somebody and I was sharing something. Anything could help. I would be damn sure those rumours were not how Hollie was remembered by this town.

'Thank you for letting us know.'

'Is that it?' Dad asked with uncertainty.

'That's it.'

That's it? That was it!

Dad shook the hands with the police officers and got to his feet, but I shook my head and uttered, 'No,' over and over until they all gazed down at me as if I had lost my marbles.

I planted my index finger firmly on the tabletop. 'I am not leaving here until I know that you're going to investigate Hollie's brother and his friends.'

'Sprout, we can't —'

'I am not moving!' I hissed. 'He was the last person to see her. He knows more than he says he does.'

The police officers assured me they would go and re-check with Chase that he had really been alone that night. Dad had to practically drag me from the police station. I was hoping that speaking to the police would get things rolling. I had expected them to be as convinced as I was that those boys were lying flat-out. Chase had not been out there alone. I knew it.

In the car on the drive home, Dad asked, 'Did that help?'

My skin stretched all over, my thighs tremored, my throat ached, my eyes burned and my ears rang. No. It did not help. I cringed at the thought of the boys surrounding Hollie and then lying about what they had done to her, whatever it had been. My head throbbed and I squeezed the bridge of my nose to try to relieve the tension.

'Dad,' I muttered. 'Nobody ever listens to me. They're lying! I know they are. Nobody is even doing anything.'

Dad pulled the car over and sighed, not looking at me. 'Daisy...'

I waited. His mouth kept pulling downwards as though he was about to cry before he finally said, 'The entire town looked for her. You keep thinking nobody cared or nobody did anything.' He took off his cap, ran a hand over his scalp then re-positioned the cap. 'Sandy and I looked for weeks. He was, and still is, destroying himself about it. Like I'm worried you will.'

I sat back in the seat and placed my hands over the lap section of my seatbelt. Holding on. Listening. Absorbing.

'People looked. People searched. Helicopters. Horses. Dogs. People from as far as Sydney.' He shook his head. 'Nobody found anything. It was as if she had never even been out there.'

My eye twitched.

'She left that campground because she was sure as hell not there anymore.' He gripped the steering wheel but didn't look at me as he added, 'I know you want closure – we all do – but I'm worried that if we do find her, and she's…'

He looked at me, aghast.

'Dead,' I whispered for him.

He nodded. 'I love Hollie, but I don't want this to destroy you.'

A sensation of being removed from my body took over me. It was as though I was watching from outside the car. Maybe it was anorexia looking on, waiting for a new way in. Split from myself, I heard myself say, 'I don't care if it destroys me – I have to find her. She needs me. Take me to where she disappeared and I'll see if she was there or not.'

Dad took a deep, rattling breath in and said, 'Righto. I'll take you first thing in the morning, Sprout.'

We drove up through the winding roads to where the campground was nestled in amongst the blue gum trees. Strings of bark wept from the branches and the wind disturbed the leaves in a hushing sound that made it sound as though an audience awaited. It was at the foot of a mountain. I looked up and was met with the green foliage and the overpowering scent of earth and eucalyptus. Bell birds whipped out their distinctive calls. The distant sound of a laughing kookaburra faded as Dad and I ambled around the campground. I stood and shuffled in a circle, looking up, around and down. Dad scuffed his Blundstones on the gravel. I stepped off the gravel into the grass and tripped over a tree root. Dad caught my arm but my knee grazed the grass. The place all looked so normal. A space where good times were meant to be had. But it was isolated. Empty. Wild. But normal.

As we walked back to the car, a wind picked up and I stopped, gazing back at the trees – surprisingly still. Chills ran up the back of my neck and down my arms. I closed my eyes. It was as though the wind was calling me back.

'No, I'm not leaving. I'll stay,' I whispered.

Then the wind stopped. Dad studied the trees and frowned. 'That was weird.'

Even this campground knew I had to get the answers. I turned to Dad. 'I want to know exactly what Chase said. Do you think the police will let me read his statement?'

Dad shrugged. 'He was on the news – so I reckon it would be the same thing. I'll find the videos.'

I clapped my fist into my hand and nodded, peering around at the trees again as if to reassure them. Reassure Hollie. 'Excellent. I'm going to figure this out. Don't worry, Hollie. I'm going to find you, even if it kills me.'

Chapter Eleven

Chase's eyes flicked to the right of the camera before he spoke. His voice was rushed. 'She walked down that path,' he pointed and the camera panned to where Dad and I had driven in. The camera returned to Chase's face as he said, 'She got into a white car. Told me she was going with a friend, and yeah, that's it…that's the last I saw her.'

I paused the video and scrubbed it back on the phone screen, peering intently at his mouth as he mimed "a white car…told me she was going with a friend". Where had Chase been standing when she had told him she was going with a friend? A friend of Hollie's? No, we had ruled that out. It had to be a friend of Chase's. A white car. Did any of his friends drive a white car?

Had Hollie even told him she was going or was that just him trying to cover something up?

I asked Dad these questions over and over with an eating utensil raised at my lips before putting it down again. Dad waited expectantly with a raised eyebrow until I caught his expression.

'Oh.' I placed the food in my mouth, chewed and swallowed, before I asked the questions all over again.

As he and I did the dishes side-by-side in the cramped kitchen in the low-orange glow of the fluorescent light, Dad said, 'I think you should still go see Hollie's grandparents.'

I placed a dry plate in the cupboard and eyed him. 'Why?'

He shrugged, rinsing the sink. 'It might be helpful for you to talk over these things with them.'

'Yeah, but what if I see Chase?'

He took the tea-towel off me and dried his hands. 'What if?'

Dad got a beer out of the fridge and retreated to the couch but I remained by the cupboard, scratching my head. I ran through scenarios in my mind. If I saw him, I could ask him those questions myself. Get answers. But I'd need to act as though I didn't blame him for her disappearance. My stomach and chest tightened with the thought of it, but I swallowed the tenseness and started a plan.

I zipped my phone into my coat pocket and rode my bike over to Hollie's grandparents' house the next day, hands trembling with my plan. If I saw Chase, I would ask him the questions, like a concerned friend – which I was, but I would pretend to believe every word he said, even if it made me sick. If I didn't see Chase, I would see if Hollie's grandparents had any ideas, or see if they were suspicious, all while acting as though I was a friend to them. I cringed. I hated going to their house.

I stopped on the footpath outside and peered up at the house. A fibro house on the main road, upon a hill. Gnomes in the yard, littered as though they'd been caught coming to life and been frozen; some had chipped heads and missing limbs. I straddled my bike and sighed. If I went up there, I'd have to act better than I'd even acted while battling anorexia.

I lay my bike in the driveway and walked up to the front mesh screen door and knocked, dreading the answer. They weren't bad people. They just made me uncomfortable. Hollie's grandparents were enigmas. Her grandmother was friendly enough, but rough around the edges. Her boobs sagged down to her belt, and her brown hair was dull, frizzy and laced with white hairs. Not enough for someone her age. She called everyone love, or darl but called them the c-word in the same breath. Hollie's grandfather was white-haired, fit, wore gumboots over his jeans and had a tattoo of a snake running down the side of his neck. He pretended to be hard of hearing, saying 'eh?' after anything that was said, but he always had the slight smile as though he knew exactly what you had been talking about.

Hollie's grandma answered the door. 'Daisy Cavill – what are you doin' here darl; ya back from the nuthouse, are ya?'

I cringed and wanted to turn around and run but I stayed for Hollie. Taking a deep breath in, I replied, 'Sure am. I'm here just to see how you're going.'

She invited me in and I loitered in the cramped foyer of the house. 'Bernie,' said Hollie's grandma, and Hollie's grandfather looked up from his armchair. 'Eh?'

'Bernie, Daisy is here for a visit.'

'Have they found Hollie?' He half-got up from his chair.

'Sit down you deaf old bastard. No! DAISY...IS...HERE.'

'Who the bloody hell is Daisy?'

Hollie's grandmother rolled her eyes and snickered and I joined in, unsure if I was meant to or not then returned to only taking shallow breaths through my mouth to avoid the bad smell of the house. The stench of mold and mildew perforated my sinuses and made me want to vomit. The scent of old was difficult to describe. Musty and damp as the rotting, faded wooden wall panelling. There was pilling on Hollie's grandma's cardigan and I was tempted to pluck it off and smooth it, but she probably would have slapped me into the wall.

'Daisy, cuppa tea, love?'

'No, thank you.'

'So about time yer out of the nut house. I couldn't believe yer was gone when Hollie went missing. Prolly a good thing fer yer mind, I guess. The stress has been bloody…' She sighed as she searched her mind for the word to use. I understood. There was not a lot of words that could be used to describe how it felt. How we felt. Missing Hollie. It was as though life had stopped even though it went on around us.

I gingerly placed a hand on hers and nodded with a grim expression, trying to show support and that I cared. Tears glazed her eyes and she pulled away from me with a sniffle, looking away, seeing through me.

I cleared my throat and thought carefully through my words. 'I want to help find Hollie very much since I didn't get to join in on the big, initial search.'

Her grandma shrugged. 'What can ya do?' She sighed. 'She's out there somewhere. We just can't find her.'

I nodded slowly. 'Mm-hm, mm-hm. The police said that, too. But I want to help.'

Hollie's grandma and I stared at each other for what felt like hours. Finally, she said with pursed lips, 'You think we don't care and we've given up.'

'No!' I yelped. 'I just think…fresh eyes, and all that.'

She narrowed her eyes at me. 'Mm.'

Plan B. 'I want to talk to Chase. Hear it from him about what happened.'

'He told the police everything he knows.'

I shrugged. 'I don't know. I just…I've got to do something, you know.'

Her face tensed as though I was physically twisting her arm and making her beg for mercy. She gazed around the small house and at the school photos of Hollie littered here to there. Toothless ones from primary school and sullen ones from high school. I longed to see her smile again. All I had was the memory of her mouth erupting and revealing her braces as she laughed, guffawing while slapping her knee. When I relapsed, that smile had disappeared. It had been too long since I had seen it. I was determined to see it again.

'Daisy?' Hollie's grandma's voice echoed.

'Huh?' I tore my eyes from the photo of Hollie and looked back to Hollie's grandma.

'I said, he doesn't like to talk about it.'

No, I bet he doesn't. I swallowed and nodded.

She added with a flippant wave of her hand, 'Besides, he's busy at work.'

I had begun walking to the door, but stopped. Turned. 'Where does he work?'

Dad absolutely refused to drive me to Chase's work. He worked at a panel beating shop in a town an hour away. There was no way I could walk or ride my bike that far, and I didn't want to go on my own in case Chase thought it was weird that I was asking questions about Hollie and what he remembered.

My only other option was Sandy, but he wasn't talking to me.

I decided to leave a note on his door while he was out surfing. He would come home in a good mood and read it.

I dug around Dad's closet for a notebook and pen so I could write my note. I came across a brown leather journal and opened it up. *Daisy eating* was written on the first page. I turned the page and saw that it was dated the day I had moved in with Dad. I flipped through. It was like a novel of all his concerns.

I'm making sure she's eating but she lost more weight. Don't know what I'm doing wrong! Sandy sandwich. Likes rice — make sure to buy more so she eats. No longer eating rice. Caught her hiding food – Hollie told on her. Scared she's going to die.

The newer entries looked like less food but I knew it was simply for the fact I wasn't hiding it. I was actually eating it. The latest note was dated for the day before.

I can't protect her if Hollie is dead. I don't know what to do.

I shivered in the cool air; it was like a poisonous gas, affecting me with gloom and lethargy. My chest ached as I read Dad's entry. No, he couldn't protect me. I would have to protect myself. If Hollie was dead, I'd relapse. If I relapsed again, I would probably die.

I wiped a tear away and ripped out a sheet of paper so I could write my note to Sandy.

Dear Sandy,
Hollie is our friend. I miss her so much. Please don't stop reading this letter. I need your help to find her. I am living with the guilt of not telling the police and don't know what I can say or do to make that better. But I have an idea on how to find her. Please speak to me. I will come to your house at 8 o'clock tonight. Please be home, and talk to me.
    Love,
    Daisy.

With a hammering heart, I went to Sandy's front door at eight. He opened it before I had a chance to knock. His feet never planted as he shifted them. 'Come in,' he said, avoiding my eyes.

I went to his kitchen – following the script of times before when he'd make me Milo and we'd stare out at the ocean, but this time was different. Stiff. Detached. It was as though mental illness in its corporeal form lingered in the room, hovering between us.

'Thank you,' I said as he handed me a cup of Milo. He held his coffee mug and leant against his fridge, away from me. I got straight to the point.

'Hollie told me something one day about what happened to her once when she went camping with her brother.' I swallowed some Milo and sat at the bar on a rickety stool.

Sandy didn't say anything so I continued. 'Chase's friends forced her to give them oral sex.'

Sandy's face went pale and his eyes moved up to stare at the ceiling. His chest heaved deeper and deeper with each breath, as a vein protruded from his temple. His fists bunched and his neck tensed. Then he snapped. He bellowed a swear word and stormed into the hallway. I stood up and followed, metres behind him, my heart rate rising and making me tremble. I watched Sandy roar and double over, before he reared back and railed his fist into the wall. I screamed and covered my mouth to mute the sound, cringing. He panted, with his eyes frozen in place to the wall. I knew how he felt. I understood what it was like to be out of control like that. Was it rage or sadness that made us implode, ricocheting ourselves so much that even our physical space and surroundings began to suffer? I could have asked if he was okay, but I knew the answer. No. He was not okay.

He turned, removing his fist, blood dripping from his knuckles. He narrowed his fierce eyes at me before they softened again and filled with tears. 'I'm sorry you had to see me like this.' His voice trembled. 'Are you okay?'

I stepped forward and hugged him.

Chapter Twelve

We left the hole in Sandy's wall and went for a walk to the beach. A belief in my mind that Chase knew more, was slowly developing in Sandy's, too. We sat on the first step leading to the bushy track, the cold seeping through our backsides, and we spoke about Hollie. Sandy blamed himself for not going with her on the camping trips, her last one but also that one where she had been violated. I reminded him that we had never been invited along. I brought up the rumours that circulated the town before I got sick again. Sandy was a pedo because he was hanging around with that slut. I pointed out that the rumours would have been even worse if he had gone along with her to the camping trips. Who knows what people would have thought?

Sandy admitted that my dad had even stressed to him that he needed to stay away from Hollie. People were talking and it wasn't nice things they were saying. For a long while, the entire town thought he had done something, and my heart faltered.

'The cops even reckoned I did something to her. They interviewed me and everything. Kept going on and on about the last time I saw her.' He shook his head and clucked his tongue, having to look out over the black water to calm himself down again. His grazed hand trembled in his lap. The bandage he'd wrapped around it was already loose and dangling at the end. Sandy was so tense in the upper body that I began to wonder. What had happened the last time he saw Hollie? I needed the entire picture. Every second, every minute of every hour so I could figure out what happened.

'When did you see her last?'

He glared at me, his cheeks going red. 'Just in case you decide Chase and his friends are actually telling the truth? You have someone else to blame?'

'I never said that,' I sputtered. 'I just want to know!'

'It was at your dad's place, all right. Your dad was stressed out about you, and we had to cancel the trip to Bells Beach. We all had a big fight about it in the kitchen. Hollie screamed at me for being a jerk because we could still go and surprise you but your dad put a stop to it and said if we stopped or affected your recovery, he wouldn't be able to forgive us. I said that was a bit extreme – a visit would do you good. We fought about it for hours. Hollie called us both cowards and walked out. I said she was right. She went camping the following night.'

I could understand how awful it would have felt to have their last interaction being a fight.

Sandy tutted to himself. 'I should have gone after her and taken her to see you anyway. It was all she wanted. To see you.'

My stomach fluttered and my heart broke with guilt. I asked, 'Would you go back?'

'What do you mean?' he murmured, filtering flecks of sand through the gaps in his fingers on his uninjured hand.

'To that day.'

He squinted at the water and took a long while to answer. 'I'd go back a lot further than that. When she first moved here to live with her grandparents, I would have adopted her and kept her away from her brother. Kept her away from what was going on in this town. How everyone falls the way they do.'

My nose prickled, unsure if he meant the way they had ganged up on her or the way my own mental illness had disrupted everything.

Sandy did not elaborate or pause for me to ask. He said, 'She was already a goner the second she moved here.'

I agreed with him, thinking of the humming sensation I had each time Chase opened his mouth to speak on all the videos on the news. Freeze-frame after freeze-frame, each night before I went to bed, I'd stare at him, searching for the truth.

That night after watching Chase on my mobile phone over and over, I fell asleep with pure exhaustion and dreamt that I was standing in the clearing of the campground and gazing at the picnic bench with the triangle roof. I picked at its green paint and it peeled off as though it were made of loose threads. A wind howled but my hair didn't budge. There was a scratching sound behind me in the trees, and I yelped and spun to see a goanna climbing the trunk of the closest gum tree. Our eyes locked and we stared at each other until its tongue poked out at me, and one of its cumbersome legs reached up and its black talons gripped the bark of the tree, tearing it away. It fell but was caught by the wind. Bark flew up into my face and I jolted awake, panicked and gasping in my dark bedroom, thinking for a moment that I was back in the hospital. I was home. But it didn't feel like it anymore. Not without Hollie.

The next day, Sandy drove me to Chase's work. He was adamant that I wasn't to accuse him of lying, not to accuse him of having friends there and to definitely not, absolutely not, mention that I knew about the time he let his friends use his little sister.

As we pulled in at the kerb, Sandy and I peered around the carpark for a white car. Surely the cops had determined it hadn't belonged to Chase, but I was convinced it may have been a friend of his who had picked her up. But who? There was no white car in the workshop carpark.

Sandy said, 'Be careful.'

I swallowed hard, pressed record on my phone, slipped it into my pocket and made my way into the reception. A bell tinkled above my head and a woman in her 40s looked up at me with a warm smile.

'G'day, love. How can I help you?'

'I'm here to see Chase. His grandma told me he works here.'

'I'll yell out to him.' She got down off her chair, and waddled with a limp. One of her legs didn't bend properly. She walked all the way to the back of the room and opened the door to the workshop. I felt bad that I'd made her get up off her seat.

I peered outside at Sandy sitting in his panelvan. His long blonde hair curled out under his beanie, and his sunglasses sat atop the bridge of his nose. He clutched the back of the passenger seat as if holding on for life and stared in my direction. I gave him a subtle flat hand signal to say *chill* and he sat back and glanced at his phone.

Chase shuffled into the office, followed by the waddling receptionist. His eyes narrowed when he saw me. 'Daisy? What are you doing here?'

'Chase,' I gushed, stepping towards him, trying to make sure he and the receptionist couldn't see my hands trembling. 'I've been away. I'm so sorry about Hollie.'

He swallowed and threw a cautionary glance at the receptionist. She tucked her head and looked as though she was trying to disappear behind the computer monitors, but still listen to every word.

Chase wiped his hands over the front of his coveralls and nodded. 'Yeah, been a bit rough. Sorry to you, too. She was your...' He cleared his throat and scratched his chin. 'She's your friend.'

'I need to know what happened.' I didn't blink. I hoped the phone was still recording and had caught his words.

Chase took a deep breath. 'I told the police everything. Maybe ask them.'

'I did. But I want you to tell me. Please.' I battered my eyelashes. I probably looked ridiculous to the receptionist. This skinny girl in baggy capri pants, oversized hoodie and beanie, wearing thongs, coming in and alternating between not blinking and over-blinking. A strange, quirky girl begging for answers from an apprentice panel beater about the day his sister went missing. Sure, that happened every day – not.

Chase whispered, 'I don't want to talk about it here.'

'Where then?'

'I'll meet you at the pub for dinner tonight at seven.' He widened his eyes as though daring me. 'Kay?'

'Okay.'

'It's a date.'

I nodded and hurried out of there, my skin crawling at the thought of it being a date, but eager to tell Sandy that he was coming with me to the pub tonight whether he wanted to or not.

We argued about it on the drive back to town.

'You shouldn't be going on a date with someone anyway when you're still recovering – least of all with him.'

I rolled my eyes. 'It's not a real date. I'm only pretending to get him to open up and talk to me about Hollie.'

Sandy shook his head. 'You're taking too much of a risk here. What if he tries something with you?'

'You'll be there.'

His Adam's apple bobbed and his forehead crinkled. His knuckles were purple on the steering wheel. I was giving him too much responsibility. I knew it. It had started as a conversation to merely drive me to see Chase at his work, and now I was lumping him with the responsibility of looking after me in the company of someone we suspected covering up the disappearance of his sister.

'Maybe I should ask your dad…'

'No! You can't tell him what we're doing. All he cares about is my recovery. He's so worried that this entire thing is going to set me back into anorexia and I'll die.'

Sandy raised an eyebrow but didn't look at me as he asked, 'Well, aren't you worried it will?'

I groaned. 'I'm so sick of everyone treating me like glass. It's like I'm never going to live it down. I will never recover while you guys don't let me.'

Sandy was quiet, and I wondered if it was because he couldn't think of a decent comeback to that. Or if he agreed with my dad and didn't want me to know it. I was so sick of it always being about me. It had always been about me and I resented it. Hollie never got any attention, even when she was practically raped on a camping trip by older guys that were meant to be looking after her. The only attention she ever got was the nasty rumour around town that she would sleep with anyone and everyone, and that she was being screwed by a pedo. Even then, all the attention was still on me as I tried killing myself in slow-motion, one meal at a time. I wasn't going to let anorexia take attention off her, ever again.

Sandy pulled up at my house to drop me off. 'Don't dress too nicely. Don't give him any reason to think he can have you.'

A shiver ran from my hip to my ears as I imagined being with him. His freckles loomed in my mind, not evenly scattered over his nose the way Hollie's were, but dense over his face, receding into his spiked brown hair. I imagined Chase trying to hit on me. The outward curve of his cheek and his flat nose, his calloused, meaty hands; I almost gagged. Sandy was right. I wanted answers badly, and I was determined to get them, but Chase would be determined to get something else and I would have to be careful. I nodded at Sandy and waved goodbye. 'See you at seven.'

Dad was peeling potatoes at the kitchen sink when I walked in.

'I'm home,' I uttered.

He beamed and said, stating the obvious, 'I'm making spuds for dinner.'

'Actually,' I said with a grimace, knowing he wouldn't believe me but I continued, 'I'm going to hang out with friends from school.'

Dad stared at me but didn't stop peeling the potatoes. His face was fixed on me, looking for the lie. I added, 'I haven't seen them since I got sick.'

'What are their names?'

I rattled off the names of the only two other girls I spoke to at school. 'Ella and Devlin.'

Ella and Devlin weren't exactly friends, but I knew who they were and they knew who I was. I hadn't returned to school yet, but Dad had already told me I'd be starting the following week. They were the two girls I hoped to gravitate towards. If they would have me. I was not all that keen to hang out with the boys again without Hollie to buffer me from their bold jokes and loud laughter.

'Where are you going?' Dad asked.

'Just having dinner at the pub and then maybe we'll go for a walk around town or to the skate park, or something.'

'Want me to drive you? I could come with you.' He wanted to keep me safe, and made sure I ate at the pub.

'No, it's okay. Sandy's taking me.'

Dad's face softened. Sandy would look after me. I hoped.

I swallowed hard as I left the house into the darkness, going downstairs to meet Sandy in the driveway. He never came inside the house anymore. I wondered if he and Dad had broken up. I wanted to ask, but didn't want to upset either of them. I would wait until they told me what had gone on between them. Maybe it was nothing. Dad had said Sandy had changed when Hollie had gone missing, and it made her disappearance all the more noticeable. Everything had changed in Short Point.

On the way to the pub, Sandy prepped me by telling me what to do in certain situations then quizzed me once he parked in the dark carpark. I squinted out of the window but only saw my pale face looming back at me.

'Daisy, concentrate.'

'Sorry.' I clasped my hands together in my lap and returned my gaze to Sandy. His eyebrows were pinched together and his lip wobbled slightly.

'What do you do if he touches your hand?'

'Smile, but drop something so he has to let go.'

'What if he tries kissing you?'

'Tell him it's too soon.'

'What if he gets mad or you get worried?'

'I tell him I'm going to the ladies' room but come straight to you,' I replied with a nod. I was ready. In theory. But it didn't stop my hands trembling in my lap.

'Where will I be?'

'At the bar.'

Sandy nodded. 'Okay.' He put his hand on my shoulder and said, 'Godspeed.'

My stomach churned as though I'd sucked down multiple laxatives as I walked into the pub and met Chase in the foyer. The cologne he wore made me sweat, even though it was a blustery, cool night, the clouds massing above threatened rain. My teeth chattered as Chase greeted me with a light hug. He had put effort in to look good, and it made me feel a twinge of guilt that I was leading him on. He was clean-shaven, his hair was gelled up and his fingernails were spotless and well-trimmed. His eyes were shiny and warm as he smiled, and I doubted for a second that he had been lying.

'It's so good to see you, Daisy. I hope I didn't make you feel unwelcome earlier today – just being at work, you know. Got to focus.'

I shrugged. 'That's okay. You must be a hard worker.'

He beamed. 'I am…I really am.' He gestured over his shoulder, 'Shall we?'

I nodded and followed him through to the bistro section of the pub. The televisions in every corner of the room broadcasted rugby or keno. I stared at them, transfixed, despite not being interested in either. Chase picked up the menu so I followed his cue and cast my eyes over it, too.

'I'm getting the steak,' he said.

'I'll get the risotto,' I added.

He blinked at me. 'You're eating?'

I flushed. 'Yeah?'

He shrugged. 'Thought this would be a cheap date.' He laughed.

I could have collapsed inwards into the universe. I folded my hands in my lap and hunched over my ribcage, waiting for him to realise it was not funny. Any comment on what I ate was dangerous. I was determined to be recovered for Hollie, but things like that sure made it difficult. Of course, I was going to eat. Did he really expect me just sit there and watch him eat?

Chase caught the look on my face and stopped laughing and cleared his throat. 'I was joking.'

I breathed a laugh through my nostrils, unimpressed.

He adjusted his jacket and said, 'I'll go up and order for us. You stay here.'

While he went up and ordered, I peered around for Sandy. He was there. Wearing a baseball cap and a leather jacket, with aviator sunglasses on. I suppressed a giggle. He looked utterly ridiculous – nothing like his usual bohemian self.

As Chase and I waited for food, he chatted and devoured three bread rolls. 'I never expected you'd go out with me. I had my eye on ya for a while.'

'Really.'

'Yeah. Always wanted to invite you to come camping with us but didn't know how to do it without revealing that I liked ya.' He chewed loudly and smacked his lips. 'Hollie would've died if she knew.'

I winced but Chase didn't notice – he was too busy looking for another packet of butter to spread on his bread. 'She would've made sure I didn't go out with ya.' He chortled. 'Look at us now. She'd be rolling,' he choked on a bit of bread but cleared his throat to add, 'laughing her head off.'

I rolled my shoulders back and my shoulders made crunching noises that reverberated up my neck and into my head. My hands stayed in my lap, not touching the bread roll in front of me. It made me nauseous to think Chase found it amusing that Hollie didn't approve of us dating. I didn't approve of us dating either. Nobody did, but him. I knew he hoped I wouldn't notice that the choke was fake. He almost said rolling in her grave, I was sure of it. He knew more. He absolutely knew more. A headache drilled into my eye as I glared at him from across the table, trying to relax my face into looking passive.

Our food arrived and we ate in silence. I hated every bite because it sucked – it just sucked – that my first date was with him. I hated him. Thinking about how he knew more than he let on and he cut into his steak and took bite after bite. After he had finished and I'd made it through half of my risotto, he sat back and sighed. 'That was good.'

'Yeah, mine is good too,' I lied.

'So! You wanted me to tell you about when she left the campground, huh.' His eyes bored into mine, again as though daring me to say yes.

I nodded, my throat too thick to speak.

195

He shrugged. 'She walked down a path. She got into a white car. Told me she was going with a friend, and yeah, that's it…that's the last I saw her.'

The number of times I'd watched him tell the news crew that exact same thing rang in my ears. It was word-for-word. I couldn't help a twitch in my eye. *Liar. You're a liar. You're lying.* I sucked on my tongue for a moment to stop myself shouting those words in his face, then asked, 'Why did she leave?'

He shrugged. 'She just wanted to.'

'Where do you think she went? Where do you think she is?'

Chase scanned the room. 'I don't know where she is.' He looked back at me. 'Where do you think she is?'

I pulled my ponytail around and twisted it around my finger, thinking, before I held it against my lips. I wanted to tell him what I really thought but I couldn't. I dropped my hair and leant forward, pushing my bowl of risotto aside. 'I don't know.'

A glass smashed behind him, making us both jump. I looked up as Chase spun to see what had happened. Sandy had dropped his glass on the counter. Chase scoffed. 'What an idiot.' He squinted as he realised it was Sandy.

I said quickly, 'Do you know whose car it was she got into?'

Chase looked back at me but gestured his thumb back over in Sandy's direction. 'That guy used to hang around her. Sandy.'

I nodded. 'I know.'

'He's a pedo. I trust him as far as I can throw him.'

'Do you think he had something to do with it?' I whispered.

Chase's eyes met mine and I was put-off by their emptiness. It was like staring into a desert. Nothing was there. He asked, 'Does your old man know you hang out with that bloke?'

I gritted my teeth so hard it made me flinch. Had he made Sandy and me out? My mind galloped through scenarios. A bead of sweat dripped down my back and made me squirm in my seat. Chase continued, 'If you're hanging out with him, you ought to know a few things.'

Curiosity piqued, I couldn't resist asking, 'Like what?'

Chase crossed his arms and chewed his lip as he surveyed my face. 'Depends. Are you hanging out with him or not?'

'Of course not. I just know him from surfing with Hollie,' I breathed.

He reached forward and latched onto my hand. Oh no. He was already breaking one of Sandy's rules. I scanned the table for something to drop but the waiter had already taken everything away, and I couldn't reach the glass of water. I shook my head, staying silent. I told myself to calm down, act cool. *Act like you don't mind the feel of his hand on yours, even though it feels scratchy and as though it's turning my hand to rust with how sweaty it is.*

'He's not someone a girl like you should be hanging around.'

'Why?' I squeaked. I cleared my throat so I could repeat myself, stronger, firmer – more confident.

Chase leant forward, which encouraged me to lean forward to hear him. Everything inside me screamed not to but I relented. He whispered, 'He takes advantage of girls like you. He groped my sister.'

I pulled my hand away, out of his grasp, with a curl of the lip, unable to handle his sweaty grip anymore. He was lying. There was no way. How bold he must have been to lie to my face. He grinned. 'Didn't Hollie tell you that?'

I shook my head. 'No.'

He sucked air in through his teeth with a triumphant tilt of the head as he sat back. 'Guess Hollie didn't tell you much after all.'

We looked at each other for a long moment. Was this a challenge? I wondered if he was trying to make me doubt myself because he knew I knew more than he let on, or he was trying to make sure Hollie was discredited with everything she told me. Or might have told me. He wouldn't have known that I knew about that camping trip. He would have assumed she'd stayed quiet, too embarrassed. He was that brazen.

He said, 'So, I'd stay away from that Sandy bloke if I were you. Or you'll end up like my sister.'

197

I couldn't take him anymore. I pushed back my chair and said, 'I can make my own decisions, Chase.'

I began walking away but he retorted, 'You starved yourself almost to death. I reckon that's a clear sign you can't.'

I stopped and snarled at him, 'I bet you loved knowing she was helpless out there with you and all your friends, huh.'

Fellow diners paused their dull chatter and gazed over in my direction. Chase studied them with the sides of his eyes but kept his face and chest directed at me. He replied, 'Sit down before you embarrass yourself. You don't know everything, Daisy. You could be in danger.'

I glanced over at Sandy. He stood up and had a pinched expression. I shook my head and sat back down. I needed to know more. Chase leant forward again but I purposely scooted my chair back a few inches so I was out of his reach.

He whispered, 'There are some real pieces of shit around.'

'Yeah, and I reckon you might be one of them,' I muttered.

He slammed his palm down on the table. 'Daisy, listen to me.' His lip trembled. 'My sister is missing! Don't hang out with pervs like him. I don't know why you're acting this way.'

I shook my head and gobbed – words gone before they came to my mind.

'She got into a white car.' He pointed to Sandy and hissed, 'That guy drives a white car.'

I remained quiet, my shoulders slumping. He had a point. Sandy's car was indeed white. But I knew Sandy. He loved Hollie. He would do anything for her. I said softly, 'The police already looked into him. He's not the one who took her.'

Chase pointed to his chest with a vein popping from his temple. 'And you think they didn't look into me? Don't be stupid, Daisy. As if I would touch my own sister.'

'I'm not saying you did.' *Your friends did*, I wanted to add but my voice faded into the din of the dining room bistro. Now that we were quietly having a discussion together again, the crowd had forgotten about us and got back to chatting.

Chase shook his head and rested an elbow upon the tabletop and rested his cheek in his palm. 'It feels like you think I know something.'

'Well, what did you mean that I don't know everything?'

'I meant about the world. About this town. You've been in your own head since I've known you.' His voice cracked and he looked away to re-compose himself. He said with a sigh. 'I've told you all I can.'

My nose ran and my eyes prickled. *Oh no. Don't cry. Don't you dare cry.* I stared down at my lap and pursed my lips.

'I promise…Look at me,' he said, and I did. 'I promise with all my heart. Hollie said she wanted to go home. She called a friend. I watched her walk down that path and get into a white car. She waved goodbye and she was gone. I haven't seen her since.'

A tear leaked out and I desperately swiped at my cheek to smear it away. Chase didn't bother to wipe away a tear of his own. He said, 'I have to believe she's out there, still. She's alive. She's even okay.'

I shuddered as I took a deep breath, willing my tears to stop. Chase sniffed. 'Okay?'

I nodded and said, 'Okay.'

'We can believe that together.'

'I have to find her, Chase. I have to.'

He stood up and approached me. I stayed seated. He rested his head in my lap like a little boy, and sobbed. I raised my hands up to not touch him. I cringed, feeling his tears soaking my legs. Real tears. Not faked. My mind raced with thoughts.

When he stood up, he blew his nose into a napkin. I didn't speak until we said our goodbyes and swore to meet up again so we could talk about Hollie and get through this "together". I met Sandy outside.

'He definitely knows something,' I said. Sandy handed me the rest of his hot chips that he'd ordered at the bar. He watched my ritual of separating them by consistency. I continued, 'He was awfully concerned about me being with you and he told me there are a lot of pieces of shit around.'

'Pieces of shit being me?'

I thumped my fist on the hood of Sandy's car. 'Damn it, why are all these chips so crispy? I can only eat the soggy ones!'

'Daisy!' Sandy snapped. 'Just eat them and tell me what you want to do.'

'I want you to go make friends with him,' I said.

'He hates me.'

'Well, I'll make friends with him, then.'

'No, you will not!' Sandy puffed out his chest. 'I'm responsible if something happens to you.'

I paused mid-chew of a chip and raised an eyebrow at him. 'Nothing will happen to me. I'm impervious. If I can survive anorexia, I can survive Chase Matheson.'

We paused. The words seemed to hang in the air in front of our faces. Was it possible that Hollie survived? I smoothed out my hand along Sandy's car where I'd thumped it. Chase had been right. It was white. I shuddered and shook my head. Nope. Not even going to go there. It was definitely not Sandy. It couldn't have been. I knew in my heart that Sandy would rather die than hurt Hollie.

Chapter Thirteen

I went back to school two days later. Nerves chattered my teeth and made eating my toast that morning difficult but I managed two slices with butter and vegemite. Dad patted me on the back and drove me to the school gate.

'Want me to walk you inside?'

I shook my head and said with a shaky voice, 'Dad, no offence, but that'll make it more obvious that I missed a whole bunch of school. I don't want people to think I'm weak anymore. I'm not frail.'

'No, you're not.' A smile crept onto his face.

'I'll come get you at the end of the day.' He went to shift the car into drive, but I held steady to the open door and didn't move until he looked back at me with a questionning expression.

'Sandy is going to pick me up. Don't be mad.'

He scoffed. 'Why would I be mad?'

I tightened my chapped lips together and nibbled at a peeling bit.

He asked 'When did you two organise that?'

I replied with a smirk, 'It's a secret.'

'Righto,' said Dad. I waved goodbye and closed the door, watching his ute amble down the road, black smoke puttering out of the exhaust pipe and the gears moaning as he changed them.

Walking back into the school made me numb. I concentrated on placing one leg at a time in front of the other, eyes on the timetable in my fingers. First up was maths. Remedial. Great. The principal had assured me and my dad last week that my classes could change depending how I coped with the course load. I had always been good at maths – counting calories could be thanked for that, at least. There was the chance they could switch me out and put me into the mainstream maths class at least.

Walking into the classroom that morning, I was met with silence. Heads went down after they saw me. The teacher fixed any extended glances with a stern bark of their name. I realised they had been warned to not stare at me and make me uncomfortable. Mission not accomplished.

I trembled as I sat at a table between a boy I didn't know and Blue, whom I had sat with at lunchtimes the year before. He nodded at me and said quietly, 'Good to see you, Daisy.'

'Thanks. You too. Good to see you. Too.' I cringed. 'Sorry.'

He gave me a sideways grin that made my legs warm and my cheeks flush. I started to think maybe being in this remedial maths class wouldn't be so bad after all.

'I'm glad you're here.'

I giggled and said, 'So am I.'

I squeezed my legs together and tried to take up the least amount of space before I caught myself. I was not too big. I deserved to take up space just like other people did. I sighed and studied the way Blue's curly blonde hair fell over his face as he took notes from the board. He licked his thumb and turned to the page in the text book we needed to work from. He slid it across the table.

'Here – you can share my book.'

I smiled and thanked him. He jiggled his leg and licked his lips as he studied me back. An unusual feeling came over me. Admiration. Pride. I felt special for a reason that didn't involve me killing myself in slow motion. I smiled so hard that my cheeks hurt.

After maths ended, Blue met my eyes – and I saw how he got his nickname. His eyes were like the ocean on a sunny day. When they landed on mine, I felt like a star.

'What's your next class?'

'Drama.' I frowned. 'Yuck.'

Blue chuckled, adjusting his school bag on his shoulder. My eyes fell on the way his shirt moved on his tight chest muscles. He said, 'Don't envy you. None of our group took that elective. Might see ya at recess? Wanna hang out?'

I nodded. 'Yeah, yeah, of course.'

'Same place, same time. See ya.' He winked and walked away. I found the performance room where drama was held, and was put off by the darkness. The teacher was an eclectic, overweight man in his forties.

'Welcome back to school, Daisy Cavill. I've heard about your back story. I'll go out of my way to make sure you adjust quickly to our program. We're ten weeks out from putting on the biggest production our school has ever done. Now, there's no role for you.' He paused for dramatic effect. 'So sorry if you wanted one…there's none.'

I shook my head and laughed. 'That's fine. I'm happy to be backstage.' If he only knew how happy he had made me.

'Excellent. Here's the script. Highlight the stage directions.' He handed me a wad of papers coming loose from the binding and I almost dropped six pages. I glanced over at the group of students standing together. Devlin spotted me and waved. I waved back. I sat in the corner with the script and started reading, highlighter in my hand. I glanced up every now and then to watch the group of students rehearsing. Devlin delivered her lines in a monotone expression and drove the teacher nuts because he got redder and redder in the face each time that he had to correct her.

'More emotion, Devlin!'

'MORE emotion, Devlin!'

'Emotion, Devlin! More of it!'

'DEVLIN FOR GOODNESS SAKES, PUT SOME OOMPH INTO IT!'

Devlin rolled her eyes and I chuckled.

At recess, I met Blue with Ethan and Sam and Rusty. They all greeted me, awkwardly avoiding mentioning Hollie, but the quietness was evident without Hollie's endless chatter and how loudly she would laugh with them. I hesitated to eat my sandwich.

Blue nudged me. 'Come on, Daze. Eat.'

I pulled the slices of bread apart, pulled the tomato off and nibbled at it. It was all too easy to relapse. Sitting with boys and eating in front of them made me nervous. Blue leant in closer to me and whispered, 'Want to go sit somewhere else? With me?'

I nodded.

We stood up and left, leaving Ethan to wolf-whistle and it made me blush while Blue snapped, 'Shut up. Stop.'

We sat together on the edge of a school garden tree that was growing lemon and orange trees. The scent of the leaves was bitter.

'How are you?' he asked.

'I'm okay.'

'Can I ask you something about Hollie or will it upset you?'

I shrugged. 'Depends what you're asking, I guess.'

'Have you spoken to Sandy about it?'

'Why?'

Blue lowered his voice. 'With all the rumours going around about him, and he has a white car. Her brother said she went off in a white car.'

'Sandy had nothing to do with it,' I said with a swallow.

He raised an eyebrow. 'How can you be so sure?'

'How can you not be?' I snapped. 'You're meant to be his friend. You just bought into all those rumours?'

Blue leant back and raised his hands in submission. 'Hey, I'm sorry. It's just been crazy here. Hard not to get caught up in all the rumours.'

My voice shook as I asked, 'Did you believe everything they said about Hollie, too?'

His face slackened. His lips closed tightly and his denim eyes went down, hidden behind his almost-white eyelashes. He rubbed at the dirt in the garden behind us. I waited for him to answer. It was as though he didn't want to because he knew that Hollie being slut-shamed was a sore spot for me that would make me hate him. All the good, nice feelings I'd had for him earlier in the morning were evaporating, disappearing into the air like a mist in the sunshine.

Blue finally answered, 'No, I didn't.'

'Why did you take so long to say that? Are you lying?'

He shook his head and looked up at me. 'I didn't believe any of the rumours. I just didn't think about it like that. Like the rumours being the same.'

I crossed my arms over my stomach. 'Yeah, well, it's interesting because the rumours were started by the same group of guys.'

'Who?'

'Chase's friends.'

Blue's eyebrows pinched together as he thought through what I had told him.

I muttered, 'It's like they're out to get him or something.'

Blue nodded. 'You could see if they are.'

'What do you mean?'

205

Blue's grin had returned. 'Get them to think Sandy is doing something to you. See what they do.'

'Sandy would never do anything to me,' I scoffed, uncomfortably reminded of the disgust on his face when I had tried to kiss him.

'They don't know that,' Blue said.

I chewed on my lip. 'No, you're right.'

'Get him to hit on you or pretend to try to…' he laughed and rubbed at the back of his neck, a blush going from his neck to his cheeks, 'try to have sex with you.'

'In front of them?'

'Yeah, but,' he placed his hand on my thigh, 'don't. Obviously.'

I looked down at his hand and he removed it. 'Sorry.'

'Why not?'

He laughed again. 'Sorry, it's not up to me. You can…you know…with whoever you want. I have no say in it. Not like I want to.'

'Want to what?'

'Huh?' His eyes widened at me and the warmness returned.

'Want to have a say or want to have sex with me?'

He scoffed and put a strand of hair back over his ear before he shrugged and said with a goofy smile, 'I'm just saying…maybe it's a bit of both.'

I almost fainted. The colour must have drained from my face because Blue instantly asked, 'Are you okay, Daisy?'

I nodded and smiled, trying to hide it but unable to.

'Do you want to…go around with me?' he asked.

I took a deep breath and hesitated. Corey flashed in front of my eyes. All the pain that came from that. Then Hollie. Her obsession with Lockie. Neither of us had ever paid Blue any mind. But he was gorgeous. I imagined having a date with Blue and found myself wondering what it would be like. What it would be like to be with a boy. But all my thoughts returned to Hollie. All I could think about was finding her.

206

'Can I...' I paused. 'Can I get back to you on that?'

He nodded, shoulders deflating.

I explained, 'I just really want to find Hollie.'

'I get it. Yeah nah. I do. It's okay.'

I asked, 'Want to help?'

'Sure.'

After school, Blue walked me out to Sandy's car in the car park. He shook hands with Sandy. 'How you been?'

'You all right, mate?'

'Yeah.' Blue nodded at me. 'Daisy and I had an idea on how to see what those bloody idiots would do if you did something to her. Whether they believe their lies about you.'

'Lies you believed, you mean,' Sandy muttered.

Blue's jaw tightened. Instead of saying sorry, he said, 'She'll fill you in, eh. Catch ya.'

'Yeah, see ya,' Sandy said. I got into the car and filled him in. He asked, 'Where can we do this that they'll see us?'

'Blue said that the surf lifesaving club is showing the rugby State of Origin and having a big party. He said all the guys are going.'

'Yeah,' Sandy shrugged, 'so am I. So what?'

'Then, I'm going, too.'

Sandy ran his hand through his hair and whistled. 'This might be tough, Daisy. It's a big deal. Can you do it?'

'Can *you*?' I turned it back on him. All I had to do was be the victim. I'd felt like one my entire life.

'We'd have to make sure it's only them that see it,' Sandy pointed his finger on the dashboard of his car as he spoke, 'otherwise people are really going to believe I'm a perv pedo, sick jerk.'

I nodded. 'We only do it if we're alone with them. Deal.'

Sandy and I concocted the plan over the following week while sitting in his car when he came to pick me up from school each day.

Finally, on the following Wednesday night, Short Point Surf Lifesaving Club held a big party to host the pay-tv viewing of a State of Origin. The State of Origin was the rugby game played between the states of Queensland and New South Wales. It was held every year and fans were either diehard Maroons (Queenslanders) or Blues (New South Welshmen). Short Point was a dedicated Blues fan.

Every person I knew from town was at the surf lifesaving club, in a sea of blue jerseys. Sandy and I walked in, hand-in-hand, almost like couples. He was only making sure I got to the bar without being lost in the blue sea, but eyes still went to us. Drinks went to lips. Murmurs reverberated around the room. It felt like holding hands with an older brother.

It was a temperate winter night and the flow of alcohol was keeping drinkers unseasonably warm. The ocean outside rolled out in a low-tide, black and vast on the edge of the horizon, at the end of the world. Music was playing but the game was louder. Groups of guys swore with raised schooners and pots, burly and blunt. WAGs (Wives and Girlfriends) lingered together by the floor-to-ceiling windows, champers and cocktail dresses giving them faux class and demure. The scent of their coconut spray tans and floral perfumes, laced with vanilla, wafted towards me, making me dizzy with hunger.

Girls from school, older sisters and city girls greeted me. 'Daisy, wow, you're looking so amazing.' 'You look so healthy now.' 'I love your dress.' 'Wish I was skinny enough to wear that.' Impish laughter and awkward glances combined with envy followed me through the room.

A woman in her early 20s named Chloe stopped me by the ladies' room and asked in a rushed, hushed voice, 'Are you and Sandy together now?'

I shot her a piercing glare. 'I'm not with anyone.' If I was going to be with anyone, it would be Blue, I wanted to add.

'You walked in with him,' she whispered. 'Don't you know that he was with your friend Hollie when she went missing?'

I looked her up and down. 'How would you know?'

She scoffed. 'Daisy...I'm not stupid. Who do you think was out there camping with her? He was!'

I walked into the ladies' room, pulling her with me. I glanced around at the closed toilet doors and whispered, 'What are you talking about? Sandy wasn't out there. Chase was.'

Chloe shook her head with wide eyes. 'You have no idea, do you.'

'No idea about what?' I snapped. My feet were already aching in my platform wedges and the sleeve of the black dress I was wearing kept digging into my armpit.

'That campground. Whitehill Park. What guys like Sandy do out there to girls.'

She waited for me to get it, but I didn't. Yes, that was the campground Hollie had disappeared from and where Dad had taken me to look around. It was where she had walked down the path and got into that white car. Whitehill Park was a forest reserve and was famous for the gumtrees, wildlife and great camping. It was isolated and quiet, protected from the heat and its creeks and streams ran for kilometres.

Chloe said, 'That's where Sandy took me.'

I studied her face. She did not blink. She merely waited for me to catch up.

'Took you?'

'Didn't you know?'

'What?'

The conversation was making my forehead ache. *Spit it out*, I wanted to say. What was I supposed to have been missing?

Her face darkened. 'Sandy took me there three years ago. Drugged me. I woke up in the clearing – my pants were down and I had jizz all over my hair.'

This was news to me. Chloe had never been part of our friendship group. She'd never hung around with Sandy. She was never part of the cool gang. She surfed, sure, but she stayed on the outer banks and never came to our parties. She was pretty much a loner. The jealousy she had was so strong, and now she was clutching at the false belief that Sandy was guilty.

'You're lying.'

Her lip trembled and she snapped, 'I'm not telling you this just to bloody bullshit you. I went out there with Sandy and his mate. Next thing I knew, I was by myself. You're telling me I would lie about something like that?' Her face screwed up as she pointed to her chest. 'I know exactly what must have happened to Hollie out there. It's not a coincidence that that happened to me at that campground after hanging out with Sandy, and she was hanging around with him. He must have drugged her, done something to her. I don't know for sure but I know you can't trust him!'

I took a step back away from her but bumped into the hair dryer and jumped as it blared. A toilet flushed and a woman came out and washed her hands, avoiding eye contact with us. We watched her leave.

Chloe's eyes roved over my body and I hunched my shoulders. 'After Hollie and everything? You hanging out with Sandy? Not cool, Daisy. Not cool.'

'It's none of your business,' I croaked.

Chloe shook her head and left me leaning against the wall, trembling. Was she right? There was so much being said against Sandy. Did I really know him? Hollie had got into a white car, and he had taken Chloe out there to…to do what? It made no sense. Sandy was gay. There was no way he would have assaulted Chloe. I shivered as I began to think I was making excuses.

I wanted to find Hollie. I couldn't allow myself to be steered in the wrong direction. I walked out of the bathroom and found Sandy in the crowd. He was high-fiving and fist-bumping guys. Male eyes took in my body and I pulled the hem of my dress down, suddenly worried it was too short. Chase was right. There were pieces of shit everywhere. If that had happened to Chloe…

210

I was in a wolf den. I reminded myself why I was persisting in staying here at the party. Hollie. Chase. I needed to test Chase and his mates. But I had goosebumps all over my body, dreading that I was walking into a trap and maybe Sandy would take it too far.

But I had to do this. I had to know. I scanned the room. Where was Chase? And his group of block-headed heathen friends. I stopped a guy walking past. 'Hey, have you seen Chase?'

'Yeah, he's out at the boat shed.'

'The boat shed?' I asked, puzzled. Why was he out there? There was no lighting and it was right at the water level. I thanked the guy and made my way over to Sandy. He put his arm around me when I got to him.

'He's out in the boat shed,' I said in his ear.

He nodded. 'All right. This is it. Are you ready? Are you sure you want to do this?'

'Yeah,' I lied, my body vibrating with anxiety. I would never really be ready for what we were about to do. Sandy was going to pretend to assault me to try to either get Chase to defend me and get me on his side, or for Chase's true colours to come out and he'd ally himself with a fellow predator. Hearing what Chloe had just told me about Sandy and that night at the campground made me want to bolt out of there at the speed of light.

I set my jaw as Sandy guided me outside, his hand placed firmly on my back. I wondered if I faltered and backed out, if that hand would fall away or if it would push me out to the boat shed to meet my fate. I guessed I was about to find out.

We walked until we were in plain sight of the group of guys in the boat shed, all circled around a cooktop and some bottles. Sandy pulled me around – I almost lost my balance. He was so much stronger than I was. His lips mashed to mine and he stuck his tongue down my throat. Kissing your dad's former lover was probably equivalent to kissing your cousin. I was easily repulsed into the role I had to play.

Sandy grabbed my butt and breathed heavily into my neck. I squirmed away and fell dramatically to the sand. Sandy straddled me and began hiking up my dress, trying not to tremble. Those trembling hands reassured me and broke me from my paralysed fear.

'No, Sandy!' I yelled. 'I'm not ready!'

He played along and argued. 'Well, when?'

'I don't know!'

'A man has needs,' he shouted, glancing at the growing captivation of our audience, their faces still shrouded in shadow, but their figures large, standing up and shaking bottles of something.

I squeaked, 'I just don't want to.'

'Then we're done here. You're dumped.' He got off me and frog-marched away through the sand. He was a terrible actor – it made me feel better about Chloe's accusations. I shook my head and clambered to my feet. Chase rushed over and helped me up.

'I fucking told you to not to trust him,' he whispered, 'but get out of here. Now. Right now.'

I wasn't expecting that response. 'Huh?'

'Get out of here,' he said urgently.

'Oi! Chase, bring her over!' yelled one of Chase's friends. The voice was empty and made me cold.

'Run,' Chase yowled like a cat.

The blood rushed to my face at the terror in his voice. I did as he said. My legs wobbled, but I bolted, breathing hard and glancing back behind me at the silhouettes of Chase and his friends, now standing on the beach watching my departure.

I dove down a sandy track and tripped over Sandy, who was crouching on the track. He held me in a tight hug. 'I'm so sorry. Are you okay? I hated that. I'm sorry.'

'I'm fine…It…' I struggled to catch my breath. I shuddered. 'What is it?'

'I just had a bad feeling. It was…something about that voice.'

'What voice?'

'The voice that called out to Chase.' I shivered and Sandy rushed to take off his jacket to give to me. 'Chase…told me to run.' I swallowed, tasting the bile fear in my mouth as I reached my conclusion. I was chasing the wrong cat up the wrong tree. I said, 'Chase didn't do it. But he definitely knows something.'

Sandy peered out at the group with trepidation before looking down at me as I snuggled into his chest, sinking into the warmth and safety. How could I have ever doubted Sandy? Sandy was golden. He would never hurt a fly.

'Who were they?' he asked.

'I don't think I know them but I couldn't see them. Do you know them? I've seen them around, I mean…but I don't know them. Only Chase.' I gagged. I could feel my last meal sloshing in my gut, churned with the cold sensation that walloped me like a baseball bat. Hollie was missing, and there were real pieces of shit out there. A big group of guys – one of them a creep. One of them a liar. Or all of them? My teeth chattered and Sandy helped me stand.

'Come on. I'm taking you home.'

The drive home was quiet in the dark as we passed the paddocks and fields, swollen and gasping for air under the overflow of the river. I considered asking Sandy about what Chloe had said but my throat closed up. I wondered what would have happened if Chase had brought me over there to his mates. Were they the ones who forced Hollie into giving them oral sex?

When Sandy and I pulled up outside my dad's house, the yellow paint looked white in the street light, Sandy asked, 'Do you think we should keep looking into this, Daisy?'

I could feel my entire body drooping and I imagined I resembled a Basset Hound or a melting ice cream in his passenger seat. 'I can't give up on her Sandy. She never gave up on me.'

He forced a smile and said, 'Me neither. Come on; I'll walk you up.'

Sandy followed me up the stairs and inside, to where Dad was asleep on the couch by the coonarra. The post-game talk was on the television but the sound was muted. Sandy looked down at my father with a longing, sad expression. He leant down and kissed him on the forehead but Dad didn't stir. Sandy placed a hand on my shoulder and whispered, 'You're my family. I hate not being here with youse.'

'You could come back,' I whispered.

He shook his head. 'Nah. I burnt all the bridges. Not sure if I could handle building another one.'

Sandy left me standing there over Dad as I fought the urge to shake him awake and scream at him to make up with Sandy because at least if we were a family again, no matter how irregular, we could be okay. I needed a family again.

The next morning, I woke up to the sound of a lawnmower. I peered out the window at the white light of the winter sunshine and my forehead throbbed. The late night lingered over me like a lace veil. I scratched at my scalp, finding comfort in the way my fingernails raked over my sensitive skin. My toes twitched. It was a still morning, good for surfing if there was any swell. I got dressed and carried my board down to the beach.

As I predicted, the water was clean and offshore. The whitewash rushed at me with a bubbling flow. I carried my board in and gasped at the icy water. I paddled out into the lineup, where only a few older men on long boards sat like buoys.

'G'day, love,' some of them called.

'Good morning,' I called in return. You had to respect the old men in Short Point. If you didn't, they'd go from pale white to bright red and give you a stern talking to in the language of board riding – they cut you off on every wave. I'd seen these old guys out plenty of times. They were all right. They were only threatening if you pissed them off.

I let them all take waves before I went for one, and they called me on and whooped and hollered for me as I fumbled and wobbled down the face and along the wave. Freedom once felt like surfing – it was synonymous with being alive and choosing life over anorexia. Finishing the wave and slapping my belly back down on the board to paddle out the back for a second wave, to a lineup filled with old men and no Hollie, it hit me with a shuddering slap. This could be my life now. Without Hollie. Life went on, wherever she was, whether alive or dead.

I straddled my board and let the old men have all the waves. They glanced at me quizzically as I allowed them in front of me for waves when it should have been my turn. I waved them on. I needed to sit with the sea for a while and watch the horizon as I bobbed and swayed with a shiver from the cold. Wondering if I'd ever feel joy again.

Chapter Fourteen

The school cracked down on me after I stopped eating again. One of the teachers noticed I wasn't eating lunch. The principal, assistant principal, business manager and head of year eleven called me into the office for a meeting with Dad. They said I could only keep coming to school on the condition I go to an outpatient program once a week for six weeks to ensure I was staying on track with my recovery. They passed a pamphlet across the desk towards Dad, whose hands shook as he opened it.

He read it briefly before he asked, 'So if I don't sign Daisy up for this – you won't let her come to school?'

'It's a health risk, Mr. Cavill,' sneered the head of year eleven. 'Exams are coming up. We want to ensure Daisy all the success – she can only do this if she is healthy.'

'But can't she just eat lunch in the staff room again? That worked well last year.'

'No, Mr. Cavill,' the principal said, looking at me. 'It did not.'

Dad sighed and they had him sign the agreement before they passed it to me. Resigned, I signed it. Whatever it took. I had to do this. I had become a health hazard and an insurance risk to the school. They could swear all they liked that it was for my own good, but I knew better. They didn't want a student wasting away on their campus and then having a court case from my dad claiming that the stress of their exams made me relapse. Whatever. I got it. It was one day a week. I could do that.

However, the outpatient turned out to be in Batemans Bay, which was quite far north from Short Point. Dad had to rent a holiday house and we stayed there for two nights a week. We would head up there straight after school on a Tuesday night, stay the night; I'd attend the day program on Wednesday, and then we'd stay another night. We got up at four in the morning on Thursday and Dad would drive me to school and go to work. Dad was eager to make it work but I saw it wearing thin after we did it for two weeks.

'Dad, why don't you stay here and ask Sandy to take me or pick me up?' Something – anything – to get them speaking to each other again.

'Sandy is always welcome but it's not going to be how it used to be, Sprout.'

'Why?' I whined.

'He changed when Hollie went missing.'

I had to agree with him on that. Sandy *had* changed. He was pretty reclusive except for going surfing, and even that he didn't do much of anymore. Since we'd faked having a moment on the beach to entice Chase, we hadn't even spoken. I'd gone out surfing, hoping to see him, but he was rarely there, or when he was, and I managed to catch him, he was just leaving.

As much as I wanted things to go back to how they were, it would never be the case. Hollie had gone and things could never be the same. Sandy had changed. School was different. Surfing wasn't the same, and I was like a new person. A person that was no longer the anorexic friend of Hollie Matheson. Now I was the friend left-behind, the girl who wanted to find her best friend. Finding her was my goal. As Dad and I made tracks up and down the highway to Batemans Bay and back, I found myself staring into the trees and out to sea, up the hills and down into the creeks, wondering if I may just spot her hitchhiking or bushwalking.

When the six-week outpatient program was complete, my weight was the same. They weren't keen on letting me go. I was furious. I had been compliant. My weight hadn't dropped, yet they seemed more concerned than the hospital had been. They expressed concerns that I was not dealing with my issues, merely accepting that I had to eat. I had to attend therapy. I didn't really want to get better. I just had to.

'Well, duh! No anorexic actually wants to get better, but we know we have to,' I said with an eyeroll. 'How else do we actually get better?' I had them stumped with that point. They couldn't offer me an answer but they said they wanted me to do another six weeks.

'My dad needs to go back to working full-time. We can't afford to keep renting here and making trips up and down the coast. That's ridiculous.'

They compromised. I had to continue for another three weeks.

'Is it actually helping you, Daisy?' asked Dad as he dropped me off in the morning. I still felt exactly the same when it came to food, but at least I was healthier. I was enjoying being back at school four days a week, even though it was lonely without Hollie. Hanging out with Blue often heated up on Tuesdays and

218

being gone on the Wednesday made it slow down again. Having a boyfriend was the last thing I needed, but the way his hand brushed my hair off my face or the way he leant in close to whisper an inside joke had my defences lowering and my hope rising.

I nodded. 'Yeah, Dad…I think it is helping.'

Dad worked on the weekends to make up for the Wednesdays off. Ms. Gregg embarrassed me every time she saw me sitting in class on Friday morning for her literature class. The first time I had walked into the classroom, she had cried; she had wiped her eyes and boys had called her a sooky old woman, but affectionately so. Everyone loved her.

'Hi,' I had mumbled, smiling, looking down.

She had touched a hand to her heart and said through streaming tears, 'Daisy, you have no idea how much it warms my heart to see you after everything you've been through.'

We read Shakespeare and I gnawed on my apple in class. Nobody complained about the crunching because they all knew I was on a special diet. Lockie sat next to me, giving me painful reminders of how much Hollie had liked him.

He was surprisingly smart. Brighter than I had ever thought. Most of the guys in our friendship group were contemplating dropping out, or were doing trade classes so they could get apprenticeships straight out of school. Nobody was thinking about university or further education in the academic fields. Except Lockie, as it turned out.

He was quiet and stoic in class, always the last one to make a comment but blowing us away with an analysis that stunned even Ms. Gregg. It would have been my favourite class if Blue was in there, too.

He'd meet me after the class, fist bump Lockie then put his arm around me and I felt like I was the safest girl in the entire school between those two surf bums. I only wished Hollie could have felt that safe.

That night, I woke up halfway through a nightmare. My tongue was sticking to the roof of my mouth and it took a while to place myself in my bedroom. I wasn't in the hospital, and it wasn't the campground that I had been dreaming about. In my dream, I'd woken up without my clothes and had to run through the eucalyptus trees with bare feet, sounds of boys running after me like wild dogs.

I'd tripped as I heard the voice from the beach, 'Oi Chase; bring her over here then,' and woken myself up, the safety I had felt with Lockie and Blue earlier that day had evaporated in the dark, post-dream disorientation.

I mopped sweat from my forehead with the back of my palm and got out of bed, the floorboards were so cold that they sent shockwaves up my ankles. I meandered, drunk with fatigue, to the kitchen to pour myself a glass of water to quench my dry mouth. I shut the fridge and gulped my water down, but a light from outside caught my eye. I moved to the window and peeked out through the horizontal blinds, trying to see what it was. It looked like light from a mobile phone screen. There was someone standing outside the door. Their silhouette hunched over their phone screen. They turned to look around at me and I gasped and shrank back from the window.

I had still been half-asleep but now I was wide awake. I counted to three and went to look again, trying to figure out who it was. There was a soft knock at the door. I ducked down, my knees crunching as I crouched too quickly.

'Daisy, it's me,' came a hushed voice from the outside. 'Chase.'

I trembled and shivered.

'I just want to talk to you.'

I considered going to wake up Dad. If Chase was waiting outside my house, there was something wrong. I was worried he'd found out that Sandy and I had faked our little event on the beach, but more afraid of the fact that he knew that I knew more than he was letting on and needed to make sure I didn't learn any more.

'I really want to talk to you.' His voice through the door was calm and sad. 'Please?'

I didn't answer.

'Is that even you? I waited until a light came on. I think it was you I saw through the window.'

Resigned to the fact he knew I was there, I cracked open the door. 'What do you want?'

'Are you alone?'

A shiver ran through my body. 'Why?'

'I want to talk to you.'

'Why do you care if I'm alone or not?'

He sighed and leant against the side of the door. 'I'm in big trouble. I don't know where else I can turn.'

'I'll get my dad.' I turned to leave but he shoved his hand through the tiny gap and latched onto the bottom of my pyjama top.

I yelped.

He tugged. 'Daisy, no, no, no. Please don't. Just talk to me. Come out.'

'No frigging way,' I hissed. I tried peeling his fingers off from my top. I took a deep breath and threw a cautious glance down the hall to Dad's bedroom. I opened the door more to ease myself from the gap. Chase grunted with the effort then latched onto my arm.

I screamed. 'DAAAAAAAAAAAAAAAAAD!'

Dad came out of his room like an elephant, crashing through the door. 'What? What is it? What's wrong?' His eyes widened at the sight of me tugging my arm away from Chase. I slammed the door on Chase's hand and heard him run off.

'Hey!' Dad barked and bolted for the door and leapt outside in just his boxer shorts and his night shirt. His old man chicken legs and knobble knees looked ridiculous as he rushed out the door after Chase, swearing and shouting. Chase disappeared into the shrubs opposite our house, and into the swampy banks of the river. Dad came back inside.

'Who was that?' he shouted. 'Out of the way – lock the door – I'm calling the cops!'

The police came quicker than I thought they would. I was still pacing the balcony in my pyjamas, trying to glimpse any movement in the scrub that would tell me where Chase was. The police car pulled up without their lights going and I bolted inside to get dressed. Dad met them and pointed at the scrub and the police officers spoke into their radios.

By the time I went downstairs to speak to them, they were already knee-deep in the overgrown grass, shining torches and a second vehicle pulled up – an unmarked Amarok with a barking Belgian Malinois in the back. My impression of the police in Short Point was that they had been slow, hopeless, judgemental and not helpful at all, but they had arrived so quickly and prepared that I began to realise that I had been wrong. Maybe they had searched hard for Hollie after all.

One police officer yelled to us, over the noise of an approaching helicopter, to go back inside and lock the doors. Dad bundled me inside and locked the door and we listened together to the search going on around the house and in the river. I wondered if it had been like this when Hollie had been reported missing.

Dad looked at me in the darkness. 'They'll find him.'

'They didn't find Hollie,' I mumbled.

Dad swallowed. It sounded like a war out there. A search light shone through the blinds and illuminated our faces, making us flinch. The dog was barking and there was a buzzing and crackling hive of radio chatter. Before long, the dog's barks became constant, high-pitched and interrupted by snarls and growls. Police officers yelled and the helicopter hummed as it hovered.

'Sounds like they got him,' Dad said, peering out the window. I joined him there. We watched as two police officers wrestled

Chase into a waiting patrol car. Handcuffed and his pants sliding down to his thighs. His arm bled from where the dog had bitten him.

Dad squinted. 'That's Hollie's brother, isn't it.'

I nodded.

'Did you know it was him?'

I nodded again.

He ran a hand over his face and muttered, 'Jesus.'

After the police officers had Chase in the back of the car, and the dog had jumped back into the Amarok, the two original police officers came up to the house and Dad opened the door to invite them inside. Now in the light from the porch, I could see the sweat running down the side of Dad's neck.

'We've got him. Was there definitely only one person?' The police officer got right to business.

Dad looked to me and I nodded, though I couldn't be sure. I had only seen Chase, but I did wonder if the owner of that voice "bring her over here then" had been lingering in the shadows out of sight. A gut feeling told me he was, but at least with the police coming, he would have left. I hoped.

'An officer will come by later on in the morning to take your statement about what happened, and we'll get the detectives to come and take fingerprints and photos, just to clarify that it was definitely only this one perpetrator. In the meantime, go eat some breakfast, make some coffee. But stay inside your house.'

Dad and I nodded, both stunned. After the police officers left with Chase in the back, Dad rounded on me. 'You hesitated.'

'What do you mean?'

'When they asked if there was definitely only one. You hesitated.'

I shrugged. 'I don't know for sure.'

'So, you only saw Hollie's brother.'

I nodded.

'But why would you hesitate? There's another person you're worried about, isn't there?'

I took a deep breath. 'I can't be sure.'

'Did he say anything to you?'

The police asked me the exact same question later in the morning. I brushed the crumbs from breakfast off our kitchen table where we were seated.

'He said he wanted to talk to me.'

'What did he want to talk to you about?' the officer asked.

I had to think back to the hours when Chase had been at the door. What had he said? I'd been so nervous that it had gone a bit blurry in my memory. I shrugged. 'I don't remember. I just remember that he said he wanted to talk to me.'

'He didn't try to enter the house?'

'No, but he…' I acted out what Chase had done, '…grabbed my shirt, and my arm, and pulled a bit. I got scared and screamed.'

'You know him, don't you?'

Dad and I nodded.

'He's my best friend's brother.'

Dad added, 'We used to know him kind of well.'

The police officers both looked at each other and shifted their weights in the small kitchen chairs. Their holsters and vests made them cumbersome and stiff; it was almost as if they didn't fit inside the kitchen.

'You know this guy "kind of well", but still got scared?' He whistled. 'Must be a good reason for that.'

My ramrod back softened like a noodle and I sat back. I sighed. 'Are you actually going to listen to me about him now?'

They were different officers to the ones I had spoken with at the station, but I still wanted to scream.

'What do you mean?'

Dad put a hand on my forearm and explained, 'Something happened to Daisy's best friend and she's concerned that her brother isn't being very truthful about it. We came down to the station to give you that information, and uh…not much was done with it.'

'Hollie Matheson,' breathed one of the officers. 'Yes. We're aware.'

'Do you think it's at all possible he was more involved than he said he was?' Dad asked. 'I mean…it's a bit weird, don't you think? Weird that he'd show up here in the middle of the night looking for my daughter and wanting to talk to her.'

'It is a bit strange,' the other officer admitted, taking notes in the notepad.

I sat up straight again with the memory of what Chase had said. 'He kept asking if I was alone.'

Dad turned his entire torso to face me. I stared straight ahead at the police officers. They blinked back at me, unable to contain their concerned expressions. I shrugged. 'Why would he have done that?'

One of the police officers stood up and stretched, looking behind him to see the progress of the detectives as they fingerprinted the door jamb.

I folded my arms and sighed. 'This is all just…weird.'

The police officer agreed and approached the detective team. He whispered, but I could still hear him. 'There might have been more than one person here. Go wider.'

Dad put his arm around me and hugged me, and I found myself wishing he had been there to protect Hollie because there was something so secure and safe in the weight of his arms.

Chapter Fifteen

Brother of Missing Girl Slapped with AVO

Chase Matheson, 22, was given an Apprehended Violence Order this week after a disturbing incident in which he waited outside of a 17-year-old girl's home in the middle of the night. The girl is said to be a close friend of his sister, and was unnerved by the 22-year-old's actions and alerted her father, who called the police. The dog squad was called to retrieve Matheson who was hiding nearby the Short Point home. Matheson offered no comment.

"Unnerved" was an interesting way to describe it. Thanks, News Media. Sandy knocked on the door the following morning. Dad let him in, and they stood awkwardly for a moment before shaking hands.

'I read about what happened in the paper. This is...this is...'

Dad nodded. 'It is.'

Sandy looked like he was gasping for air. A fish on land. It wasn't the first time I'd got that impression of him. He soon turned to me and asked if I was all right. I nodded.

It had scared me having Chase arrive at the house that way, and it was alarming to think that he might not have been alone, but it made me even more determined to figure out what was going on.

'He said he wanted to talk to her,' Dad said. Sandy raised an eyebrow. 'I know. It's just weird.'

Sandy rubbed at the back of his neck and I knew he was troubled by our secret. *Don't tell him, Sandy. Don't.*

'We've got to come clean about something, mate.'

Damn it.

I crossed my arms and scowled as Sandy gestured for my dad to sit down.

'Daisy and I...we think...Chase is involved in Hollie's disappearance. Or he at least knows more than he's letting on.'

'I'm aware Daisy feels that way. We even went to the police. We've reported this.'

'Yeah, uh...' Sandy scrubbed at his neck harder. 'I've been helping Daisy get closer to Chase so we can get more information out of him.' He flinched as my dad levelled a glare at him.

'You've been what?' He turned to look in my direction and my arms collapsed from their folded position and I held up my hands in resignation.

'How could you both be that stupid?'

Being stupid had nothing to do with it. Life was void of warmth not knowing where Hollie was or what had happened to her. There was a coldness in me that lingered, no matter how many layers I surrounded myself with. When I was starving, it had been the same. I could never get warm. Since Hollie had gone missing, I was cold all the time in the same way. Nothing could warm me. It was indescribable. Dad wouldn't understand it.

Maybe he thought he could, but he would never really comprehend how it was for me and Sandy. We were empty without her. To me, it wouldn't be stupid to try anything to get answers. We had to know. We needed to.

Sandy and I sighed, as though we were thinking the same thing. There was nothing in our futures except finding her. Bringing her home. Being with her again.

Sandy was solemn. 'We have to find her, mate.'

'Sandy, we've been over this.' Dad stood and gesticulated. 'Let the police find her! Let them do their jobs. Why do you both need to put yourselves in danger to find answers to things that the police will find?' He began pacing the room. 'I mean – what happens if you're right? What if her brother really did do something or know something and you've tipped him off? Now he's going to dig in and nobody will find anything at all.'

Sandy and I both tucked our heads down. He was right. But it was a risk we were willing to take. Finding Hollie was the most important thing. We couldn't go on living without her. We couldn't breathe without knowing where she was and what had happened.

Dad sighed. 'How are we supposed to move on from this?'

Sandy shrugged. 'I can't, mate...not until I know what happened to her.'

'Or where she is,' I added.

Sandy reached a hand out to Dad, but he turned away and muttered, 'You put my daughter in danger, Sandy.'

Sandy cleared his throat and stood. 'I guess...I'll go, then.'

I followed Sandy to the door because Dad didn't. He hugged me extra tight and left. Dad continued to pace.

'Dad –' I said but he held up a hand to stop me.

'I don't want to hear it, Daisy. I'm tempted to go to the police and tell them to call off that AVO since you wanted to talk to Chase Matheson that badly in the first place.'

I gaped at him. If he did that, Chase could come talk to me, and possibly drag me out the door like I had the feeling he had been trying to. 'You can't be serious.'

Dad held his palms face up and said, 'Well, if you wanted to get close enough to him to get answers about what happened to Hollie, it sounds to me like you wanted him to take you the same way he took Hollie and then you'd really know wouldn't you? If he did to you what he did to Hollie, you'd finally understand. I can't believe Sandy *helped* you do that. This is just…ridiculous. I can't believe you'd both do this!'

I swallowed a sob and asked, 'Does this mean you agree with us? You think Chase knows something?'

Dad grabbed both my hands and pulled me into his chest and hugged me. His chest was heaving and his heart racing. He patted my hair like I was a cat. 'I never doubted you.' He took a deep breath and his chest moved my entire body. 'I'm just so worried that you could disappear like she did. I don't ever want to lose you again.'

I didn't want to admit he was right to be worried. I had the same fear. He was right that I was so curious to see what would happen if I let Chase play out what he wanted. It was terrifying to think that I would never be seen again. Now I guessed I would have to do that without Chase. Or Sandy. I would have to rely on Dad to take me back to the campground and let me look around. I was sure that I would see something, or feel something, the police and search teams would have missed. I knew Hollie better than anyone, except maybe Sandy. I couldn't believe there was no trace.

'Let me go back out there again, Dad,' I murmured. 'I have to see if I can find something. Anything.'

'No,' he said with a gulp. 'I think you should just focus on school and getting better.'

The midyear exams were coming up. Everyone expected me to be able to focus on school work but they didn't get it. I was missing a massive part of myself. I would be reading a book and at each full stop, I would stop and think of Hollie, as though she was in that little dot on the page. Nothing started again. It was the end. Having to force myself to read on, I lost what the prior sentence said or meant. Reading homework took ten times more effort than it should have. I was flailing, and my recovery started to take a hit alongside my desperate grabs to "get it".

Dad asked if I wanted a tutor. I said I didn't. He was too short on savings to be able to afford one anyway.

Stress got to me. I didn't even notice that I was squirrelling toast in my gums until I noticed it swirling down the sink hole when I brushed my teeth. It was a little slip at first. Not a big deal. It was okay. I'd have to forgive myself. I was going through a lot. I was trying to recover from anorexia, missing my friend and trying to study for exams. At recess on the same day, I got caught up reading, stopping, reading, stopping, re-reading and forgot to eat my rice crackers with avocado slices.

The bell went and I gasped at my food in shock.

'You okay?' Blue asked, standing and putting his school bag over his shoulder, holding a hand out to help me up. We both stared at the food I had forgotten to eat. I considered shoving one into my mouth but the avocado was beginning to oxidise and I couldn't bear the thought of eating rotten food, so the crackers and the avocado went into the bin. At lunch, Blue had detention. To avoid slipping even further into my bad habit, I made my way to the staff room where they let me eat if I wasn't doing too well. All the teachers knew who I was and what I was doing in there and it made me burn with embarrassment. Silly Daisy Cavill. Has had every opportunity to flourish but still can't eat her frigging lunch.

I lingered awkwardly amongst the teachers but was determined to not give up. I ate my muesli bar and told myself I was being good because I was eating to make up for the snack I'd missed.

After I ate the muesli bar, I glanced at my sandwich. I was too full. My hands shook as I put it in the bin. I wouldn't be able to eat it, and I couldn't let Dad see I'd missed food. I buried it under the rest of the rubbish and looked around furtively. The staff had become complacent. I wondered if anorexia knew this and had been merely biding its time.

In the common room, I found Ella and Devlin, who were sitting with Rusty and Ethan, as well as a few guys from the year below me. Their names were Oliver, Lennox and Fraser. I stood behind them as they lounged on the couch, tracing fingers along inner thighs and lips.

'Camping this weekend is going to be amazing,' Ella sighed.

'Yeah, it'll be good as,' chuckled Rusty.

Hearing the word camping made my skin crawl.

'Camping?'

They all looked up at me, stunned. The entire common room went silent. The boys all looked up at me and their faces went a greyish tinge.

'Where are you going camping?' I asked, trying to sound bright.

Rusty brushed something off his hand and he and the girls sat up, twisting their bodies to face me. Fraser shrugged. Oliver looked down at his shoes.

Lennox zipped up his grey hoodie, glared at me and asked, 'Why do you want to know?'

Fraser nudged him and whispered, 'Her friend went missing. Dude. Shut up.'

Ella took a deep breath and said, 'We're going camping with a few friends at Whitehill Park.'

'Oh?' The blood disappeared from my face. The room swam and swirled around me like a breaking wave.

'You should come with us.'

Rusty shook his head. 'She doesn't have to come.' He looked up at me and touched my hand. 'Daisy, you don't have to come.'

Ella's eyebrows raised noticing the way I was slowly drawing deep breaths without answering, and her eyes noticed my fingers clutching the back of the couch.

She said, 'It'll be more fun if you come, Daisy.'

Devlin added slowly, 'Yeah. The more the merrier.' She cleared her throat. 'If you want to.'

I grimaced. Dad would never let me go alone, and he wouldn't camp with me. But it was my only shot at getting out there and having another look around, especially at night, and I could keep Ella and Devlin safe just in case.

I nodded. 'Sounds fun.'

'Good. Then you're coming.' Ella smiled.

Blue came in, as the bell went, dismissed from his detention. He took in the sight of all of us with tense shoulders and grey faces. Ella looked at me as I chewed the inside of my cheek. She said, 'Sorry. You did want to come, right?'

'Come where?' Blue asked.

'Camping,' Ethan said as he stood up. He raised an eyebrow at Blue pointedly. 'Daisy's coming camping.'

Blue scoffed. 'No, she's not.'

I said, 'Yes, I am.'

Blue scoffed again. 'Daisy, no.' He paused when he noticed I was being serious. 'You can't go camping.'

'You can't tell me what I can't do,' I snapped.

'No, but I'm telling you not to go,' he hissed.

I shook my head at him and turned away.

'Daisy,' he cried, lunging for my hand but I snatched it away from him and glared at him.

'Leave me alone.'

I walked to where the school bus was waiting for our outdoor ed kayaking excursion. Blue didn't try to speak to me again until we arrived at the river.

We loaded ourselves into the kayaks with bulky life-vests. My vest bounced up and down with each stroke with the oar and made my teeth bang into each other as it clunked up into my chin. Bone on bone and I grew bitter.

'What's up with you today?' Blue asked.

'You have no say in what I do, Blue. Even if we were dating.' My teeth chattered.

'You're right, I'm sorry.' He sidled his kayak beside mine. 'But I do know you don't want to go camping there with them.'

'Why not?'

He sighed. 'I can't say anything. But…those guys…'

'Our friends,' I corrected.

His face was solemn. 'They're not our friends anymore. Not since Hollie.'

I adjusted my vest and gave him a quizzical look. We sat with them at school. They surfed with us sometimes. I had no inclination why Blue thought they weren't our friends.

'Just please don't go. Please.'

I rolled my eyes. 'Either give me a good reason or leave me alone, Blue.'

'I love you.'

I tutted and paddled away. He wouldn't distract me. He couldn't control me. I paddled and paddled until he was too far away to hear.

My stomach growled as I paddled and my arms quivered, and I was furious with myself, just as much as I was with him. How dare I let anorexia in again?

I stroked harder and harder, and the outdoor ed teachers had to call me back because I'd gone too far. I stopped paddling, out of breath and looked back at them. They were the size of little beetles in the distance. The water was shaded where I was, murky and the bank lined with tree roots. Looking up, I could see the riverside houses. I was almost to Dad's house near its mouth to the sea.

The river ran between the sea and the mountains where Hollie had gone missing. I had been paddling closer to the sea when I was supposed to be paddling in circles. A speck that was a teacher in an ugly vibrant green rash vest was paddling towards me, probably thinking I had got myself caught in a current.

I sighed and my lungs burned as I allowed the kayak to drift to the middle of the river. I'd let myself take a rest and then I'd start paddling back to where I was supposed to be, but I didn't really want to return. I didn't want to have to deal with Blue telling me what I couldn't do and trying to trick me by saying he loved me.

Being alone on the river was preferred, peaceful. The sun peering through the clouds warmed my face, but all I could think about was Hollie. I was floating in the middle of the river and heading to sea, when I knew she was further inland. She had to be. She was somewhere in those mountains. My heart rate doubled and I couldn't breathe. I started to gasp for air. I didn't notice that the water had become slick.

I gripped the edge of my kayak as water slapped at the sides and rocked me gently side-to-side. I gazed at the rippled water then noticed a smooth section, as if part of the water had been ironed out. Wondering why that section of water was different, I reached down with my hand but drew it back in terror. A black shape emerged from below. It moved slowly, encumbered with barnacles and seaweed.

I froze and inhaled air with a cough. Tears came to my eyes. A stream of rainbow water expelled upwards like a fountain and I laughed. A cow-like eye rolled upwards. The eye was black, with a blue circle in the middle that shimmered like an air bubble. I peered into the eye, thinking it to be a hallucination, but it blinked; its owner was staring back at me.

I pinched myself. This could not be happening.

The behemoth beside me huffed and breathed, making the water surge around me. The eye disappeared under the water, and its long body arched above the water as it submerged itself under the water again.

A southern right whale.

I sat there, stunned, hardly daring to believe my luck. This whale had come to visit me in the mouth of the river when I had been close to falling apart.

A cool breeze whipped up and made me shiver, even in my wetsuit. I picked up the paddle and I paddled back to my school group, debating whether I would share what I had seen. I wasn't sure if it had actually been there or not. Something in its eye told me to keep going. *Keep fighting. Get better. She needs you.*

Chapter Sixteen

Dad was furious when I told him I was going camping. No place other than the exact same place Hollie went missing from.

As I packed my overnight bag, he shouted, 'Don't think I'll drop you off.'

'It's all good,' I said, trying to act nonchalant. 'They know an older guy. He can drive me.'

'Who?'

Who, exactly. When Ella and Devlin had told me where to meet them so the guys' older friend could pick them up, my heart rate had doubled. I said, 'Don't tell them who I am. I don't want to talk about what happened to Hollie. I just want to have a good time.'

They'd winked and nodded. Now I was having to tell Dad that I was going into the bush to camp with an unknown older guy and somehow still get out the door and go. I sighed. I couldn't do it to him. I couldn't disappear.

I said, 'I've messaged Sandy. He's going to meet me there, but they don't know. He's going to camp a bit further down and keep an eye on us.'

'I should come by and check on you, too.'

I nodded. 'I'll text you every hour. If I stop texting you…come get us.'

Later, I stood on the street corner near the highway with Ella and Devlin. Ella really liked rabbits and wore a sweater with a Kawaii bunny on it. Devlin wore large pink-framed glasses and socks over her pink leggings, her curly brown hair in a messy bun atop her head.

She adjusted her glasses while we waited. 'I can't believe you're coming. This is the last thing I thought you'd want to do considering what happened to your friend. I wasn't expecting you to actually come.'

I shifted my weight and sighed. 'Yeah, well…It's the only way I can figure out what happened to her.'

Both girls stared at me.

Ella said, 'Wait – you think these guys had something to do with Hollie Matheson disappearing?'

I nodded. 'I want to know who this older guy is, as well as the others.'

Ella and Devlin exchanged glances before Devlin asked, 'Should we actually be going?'

Ella added, 'If you think that, Daisy, why are you coming? I mean,' she looked to Devlin, 'we're going because we like those guys and they said they'll give us booze.' She giggled. 'You don't really think they had anything to do with Hollie, do you?'

I shrugged.

'Those guys from school had nothing to do with it,' Devlin decided. Behind her glasses, she looked down.

'You don't sound very convinced,' I observed.

She shrugged. 'I just don't think they did.'

My phone buzzed and I glanced at it. It was a picture message from Sandy, showing me exactly where he had set up camp. He was deep into the forest, but close to the creek that ran off the river. I pinched the screen and zoomed into the shape of the trees. The two trees near his car were close together and the branches made a Y shape, while the one closest to the creek was bent, falling down. If I ran into the forest and needed him, I knew to look for the Y and the bent over tree by the creek.

A text message followed soon after, **down from main track; right of the fork.**

I sent a thumbs up emoji.

'Is that your boyfriend?' Ella asked, peeling open a lollipop and sticking it into her mouth with a clack against her teeth that made me flinch.

I shook my head. 'No. He's just a friend. He's camping too.'

'With us?'

I nodded but put my finger to the lips. 'But don't tell the other guys. He's out there just in case.'

'Just in case what?' Devlin squeaked.

We all looked up as a car drove down the road with a rattling exhaust. It was banged up and rusted. The car stopped and an older guy wound down his window.

Ella peered in at him. 'Are you Oliver's friend?'

He nodded and gestured for us to get in. I'd never seen him before. I gulped and the three of us climbed into the backseat and I couldn't stop my hands from shaking as I put my seatbelt on.

I asked, 'What's your name?' But he didn't speak. Ella and Devlin looked to me with concerned faces but I couldn't reassure them. I had no idea who this man was. He was around thirty. Tanned, short hair, narrow face and had buck-teeth. His cheeks were littered with acne scars and he bobbed his head to the electronica music as he drove. My throat was sealing up and I had to keep opening my mouth for more air. What if he never even took us to the campground? I suddenly felt very stupid for following through on this plan. Trying to squash the panic rising in my chest, I studied the road ahead, peering around out of all the windows to look for landmarks. Everything looked right. We were heading into the hills to where the campground was, where Sandy awaited in the deeper section off a fire trail, hidden by the gumtrees and on guard with the goannas from my dreams.

We arrived at the campground and Ella went to open the door, but it was locked. She yanked at the handle. The guy grinned but didn't say anything, as though we were idiots for not realising that he had child-locks on his car. We breathed a sigh of relief as he opened the door from the outside and we stepped out into the fresh air.

The guys greeted us. Looking around the campground, I saw two other guys – Lockie and Mitchell. With relief, I rushed over and hugged them and their eyes lit up. 'Good to see ya.'

'Yeah, you too.'

Nobody mentioned Hollie.

'Who is that guy?' I asked.

'His name's Cain. He's going to go buy us some more beer. He'll be back later,' explained Lockie.

We watched Cain as he drove off, and the girls and I began to relax. Maybe this would be fine. I texted Dad to let him know we'd arrived. I gave him the names of all the guys and told him I felt safe because Lockie and Mitchell were there. I texted Sandy the same.

Weird that Lockie and Mitchell are there? Came Sandy's response.

Why?

They stopped hanging out with Rusty and Ethan ages ago. Said they all had a big fight about something. Never found out what.

I'll ask? I suggested.

No, DON'T.

I studied Rusty and Ethan in the corner of my eye. Then turned my attention back at my phone when it buzzed again from Sandy.

Is Chase there?

No, I sent back.

Lennox glanced at my phone as he walked past. 'Who are you texting?'

'My dad,' I said. 'He's a bit overprotective.'

'Is that because your friend ran away from here?'

I raised my eyebrows. 'She didn't run away.'

'Oh…my bad.' He frowned. 'I thought she ran away.'

'No, she went missing,' I said slowly. 'She didn't leave of her own choice.'

'Her brother said she did.'

I took a deep breath, trying to stay calm. 'Do you speak to her brother much?'

'All the time,' he said with a smile. 'He's coming by later. That's when it gets fun. When Chase gets here, the party will really begin.'

My feet rooted to the ground and I swayed for a moment before I texted Sandy. **Chase coming later. What do I do?**

Lennox playfully grabbed at my phone and I un-rooted myself and dodged him with a quizzical expression. 'Why are you trying to touch my phone?'

Devlin looked over from her camp chair by the firepit and stood up. Ella glanced at her from beside her and then followed her gaze to me. I shook my head at them. They sat back down. We were okay. I would make sure we were okay.

'Who do you keep texting? You should be present in the moment,' Lennox replied. He grinned and his eyes glittered. 'That's what camping is about.'

My phone buzzed. **Call me one ring when he arrives.**

I tucked my phone into my underwear and tilted my chin up at Lennox. He nodded. 'Good. Now come on. Enjoy yourself.' He grinned. 'You're so tense.'

240

I went and stood by the fire pit. It had no fire yet but Oliver and Fraser were collecting kindling on the outskirts of the site. Lockie and Mitchell were setting up tents for everyone. Rusty and Ethan sat talking with Ella and Devlin.

Ella called to the boys, 'What do you want us to do?'

'Sit still and look pretty,' Lennox said with a big smile. 'Don't stress girls. We've got it sorted.' He turned his back and unzipped his jeans and a trickling sound met our ears.

Devlin tugged on my sleeve and whispered, 'I don't think I want to stay. I've got a bad feeling about this.'

Ella shook her head. Her eyes were wide. 'Me neither. This isn't for me.'

A bird call made them both jump. The boys all looked up and rolled their eyes at each other. Lennox, Rusty and Ethan went off and helped Lockie and Mitchell set up the tents. The girls and I loitered, unsure what to do. The boys mostly ignored us, and I wasn't sure if that was a good thing or whether it was a ploy to lull us into a false sense of security. I wanted to look around the nearby area, look for clues and hints that might tell me where Hollie had gone, but I also didn't want to leave the girls alone with the boys. I shook out my hands and decided that I would make them come with me.

'Guys,' I said loudly. They looked up. 'The girls and I are just going to take a bit of a walk.'

'No, no, no. Stay,' Lockie whined. He rushed over and held my hands. 'Daisy, stay.'

'We're not leaving,' I said, narrowing my eyes at him and pulling away. Ella and Devlin stood up again. 'We're just going to go for a walk.'

Fraser threw down a heavy branch into the firepit and smaller twigs crunched under its weight. Ella and Devlin leapt backwards. He shouted across the campground, 'Go then.'

Ella and Devlin grabbed my hands and we walked. I stared at Fraser as we walked off down the closest walking trail until we disappeared from his eyeline in the cathedral of eucalyptus trees.

This was the path to the creek. I knew it from walking it so often looking for Hollie before. I'd never seen anything along this trail but hadn't gone deeper than a thirty-minute walk.

Ella said in a hushed voice, 'Why am I freaking out so much?' Devlin gave a nervous laugh. Ella added, 'No, I'm serious. This should be fun but it feels really weird.'

'Because Daisy freaked us out,' Devlin muttered.

I stopped. They stopped too and gazed blankly at me. It made my stomach tighten to hear how negatively they saw me, but she was right. I couldn't feel bad about it, though. We would be okay. I'd taken precautions. We weren't alone; we had Sandy waiting nearby, and my dad was waiting for those hourly text messages. Ella and Devlin's parents knew where we were. We had six people aware of our exact locations. We weren't going in innocently or naively. We were prepared. But I couldn't reassure them. They were sitting like little ducks while I hoped to get proof the boys were up to no good. Technically, the only nefarious person was me. The boys might have been legitimately wanting to take us camping. There was nothing wrong with that. But Blue's insistence that I don't go camping with them, saying they weren't friends anymore, and learning that Lockie and Mitchell had also removed themselves from Rusty and Ethan all hung over my mind. But here were Lockie and Mitchell. Camping with Rusty and Ethan. They looked like they had buried whatever hatchet they had and were mates again. I wondered what it was they had fought about.

A twig snapped nearby. We all jumped and clutched at each other's wrists, eyes trained on the never-ending mess of twigs and green. Nobody appeared and we heard nothing else except the wind in the trees.

I sighed. 'It must have been an animal or something. Maybe a goanna.'

We continued walking. Ella and Devlin started chatting about people they knew and videos they saw on their social medias, laughing. I followed behind slowly, eyeing the trees. I didn't

242

expect to see anything but looked for a trace of Hollie anyway. A necklace, a bracelet, a shoe, a jacket – anything.

Devlin and Ella got so far ahead that I lost them. I started to walk quicker to catch up but stepped on the edge of a rabbit hole. My ankle cracked and I fell to my knees. I gasped as I hit the ground, grazing my palms on the dirt track.

Swearing to myself, I sat up and nursed my ankle. It ached, but wasn't broken. I jiggled it side-to-side with my hand and it made grinding sounds and hurt, but nothing super bad.

To help myself stand up, I grabbed onto the trunk of the closest tree, clawing at it with my nails. I snapped my hands back when I spotted scratch marks in the tree that matched mine. Spreading my fingers wide, I placed my hand upon it, matching my fingers with the finger marks. Someone had clutched at this tree as if hugging it. I looked from the left to the right, then noticed a black shoe up above. Someone had not only clung to this tree, but climbed it. I stepped back from the tree and gazed up at the rubber thong. It was wedged between two branches that came together like a fulcrum.

It looked a lot like a thong I swear I'd seen Hollie wear before.

Footsteps approaching from ahead snapped me out of my staring daze. Ella and Devlin had realised I was no longer with them and had run back to make sure I was okay. They bent over with relief when they saw me. 'Oh, thank God.'

Devlin said, 'Are you okay?'

I nodded and pointed, wordless, at the shoe in the tree.

Devlin and Ella looked up and screwed their noses up.

'Why is there a thong up in that tree?' Devlin wondered aloud.

'Someone climbed the tree,' I whispered. I matched my nails again to the scratches in the tree. The goanna in my dream climbing the tree came to me and I murmured, 'Like a goanna.'

A bird nearby whistled and chirped like a siren and the girls and I stood transfixed, staring at the shoe before we started walking slowly back to the campsite.

As I limped along, I sent Sandy the GPS location of where the thong was wedged up in the tree. He was going to go look and see if it was worth calling the police about. It could have possibly been thrown up there; we didn't know for sure. I kept thinking about the dream I had of the goanna and felt as though it meant something. Had Hollie climbed the tree and lost her shoe? But then I began wondering why she would have climbed a tree. There were no serious predators out there in the forest, except for maybe a wild pig here or there – or a person.

'How was your walk, girls?'

I stopped when I noticed Chase was sitting on the bonnet of a Landcruiser. He was wearing an Akubra hat and had his elbows resting upon his knees.

'It was good,' Ella and Devlin muttered. 'Yeah, it was good.'

'Find anything, Daisy?' Chase challenged.

I shook my head. Ella and Devlin cleared their throats and we gazed around at our camp set-up. It was late afternoon and the fog was beginning to roll in. Sandy wouldn't be able to find the shoe if it got too dense. I imagined him fumbling around in the dark looking for a black thong up in a tree and was disheartened. If he didn't find it and make the call as soon as possible, I didn't think I could hold back my own suspicions.

'Aren't you gonna say anything about me being here?' Chase asked loudly with narrowed eyes. 'Tattle on me to the police for breaching the AVO?'

I took a deep breath to make myself seem calmer than I felt. 'No, Chase. It's fine.'

He jumped down off the Landcruiser, his boots sliding in the gravel a little and he almost fell. I crossed my arms, then decided that probably looked too defensive so I uncrossed them again and crossed my throbbing ankle over my good one. *Be calm.* I thought of the whale that had visited me in the river while kayaking. It was probably looking for a safe place to rest, away from the great whites and orcas that hunted along our ocean shores. I couldn't be weak like potential prey.

Lennox laughed. 'Mate, she asked about ya when she got here. Reckon she wants a piece.' He sniggered and all the guys laughed too. Ella and Devlin's faces fell. I wanted to say "don't worry" but being only three girls, surrounded by eight guys took away my confidence.

I concentrated on the bird calls. Whipbirds and rosellas, encircled by the constant nattering of the white-throated tree creeper with cockatoos in the distance. I never noticed how noisy the bush was until I focused purely on the sounds of the birds. It was like Bourke Street, Kings Cross, or Times Square, out there amongst the trees. Whistling, whipping, whirring, rattling and cooing. It gave me comfort to know that Hollie had at least heard such a beautiful chorus the last time she was here. If she ever really did leave.

Chase snarled, 'As long as I don't have to leave because of your stupid AVO.' He stalked past me and lit the fire.

The guys all stood around it later, pelvises jutted forward with their wide-stances, arms crossed over their chests. Ella, Devlin and my pelvises tucked inwards, collapsing into ourselves, making ourselves smaller as we sat by the fire and applied insect repellent to our clothes. Chase handed out cans of beer. Ella and Devlin took one each and sipped at the cans politely.

Chase waved the can in front of my face and I said, 'No, thank you.'

He shoved it into my lap. 'I said no, Chase,' I snapped.

'You've got it in case you change your mind.' He slurped from his own can and moved away, barely lifting his feet from the ground as he shuffled around. Oliver started a conversation about something that got Ella and Devlin talking with animation. I couldn't listen. I ended up opening the beer can and sloshing it into my mouth. I realised I had forgotten to give Sandy the one ring, so pulled out my phone again.

Lennox groaned loudly. 'This one and her bloody phone.'

'Take it off her,' Fraser muttered.

245

Lennox made a grab for it but I raised my arm out of his reach. He wasn't as tall as I was so he missed. The tips of his ears flushed red and his upper lip lowered so that it smoothed over his teeth. 'Give it here, you moll.'

'No!'

He jumped to reach it, but I spun away, unable to believe that he was actually trying to take my phone off me. That phone was our lifeline – there was no way I was going to give it to him. I pulled up my call screen and tapped Sandy's name to call. One ring, and then I was face down in the dust, gasping for air but coughing as I inhaled dirt.

Lennox straddled my back and his knees dug into the sides of my ribs which made me squeal. He'd bumped into me so hard that we had both fallen. He held me down and I squirmed from under him. He rolled onto my hands, crushing them and making me wince, so I couldn't grab my phone. Fraser darted over and grabbed the phone from the ground. Ella pulled at Lennox's shirt.

Devlin lunged for my phone but Fraser held it up out of her reach, laughed and scrolled through my phone. 'Ahhh who are we texting? Who's your boyfriend?' He grinned at me. 'Sandy.'

Lockie said too loudly, 'Nah. Sandy's gay.'

Chase's head tilted. I wet my lips and realised little pebbles were stuck to the side of my mouth so I spat them out discreetly. The realisation was on Chase's face. He knew Sandy and I had faked it that night. He walked over and shoved Lennox off me. 'Leave her alone.'

'Just mucking around.'

Chase held his hand out to Fraser who frowned as he handed Chase my phone. I pleaded silently for him not to scroll through and see my suspicious messages with Sandy and that he wouldn't see the message about the thongs in the tree. *Please, don't look at my phone, Chase.*

He didn't. He handed it to me.

I swallowed hard and mumbled, 'Thanks.'

Ella and Devlin helped me stand up. My ankle hurt even more now.

Chase nodded at my ankle and asked, 'Need ice for that?'

I shook my head, but Chase was already busying himself in the tray of the Landcruiser ute, shoving ice from the esky into a plastic bag. He guided me to the camp chair and dragged another chair over for me to prop my ankle on and slapped the make-do icepack onto my ankle, which was starting to swell.

Chase shoved Lennox roughly so he had to catch himself from falling. 'The hell are you doing, Lenny? Ya hurt her ankle.'

Ella snapped, 'I want to go home. You guys are too rough.'

Devlin piped up. 'Yeah, this is really crap.'

'Will you relax?' Lennox shouted. 'You're all fine. Why are you acting like we're going to do something to you?'

Chase was in the middle of rubbing his eyebrow but stopped when Lennox said that, and his mouth formed a thin line and his eyes narrowed. Lennox glanced at him and his eyes fell to the ground and he walked away.

Chase inhaled deeply to relax his face, then squatted beside me. 'Are you okay?'

I nodded. 'I'm fine.' I rallied the girls with a few shrugs and nods. 'It'll be okay. We're fine. We're going to camp and we're going to have a good time.'

Lockie held up his beer and said, 'Here, here. Cheers.'

My ankle ached, throbbed and swelled but sitting down for a while made it feel a bit better.

The beers the boys gave me washed away the pain, but the swelling in my stomach made me stiff and uncomfortable. Anorexia never would let me be free. We were technically breaking the law by drinking under-age, but that made it exciting.

Oliver doted on Ella and by the time it was completely dark, she was sitting on his lap and they were kissing in the firelight. All fears she held were long abandoned under his tender touch and soft smiles. Devlin's reserves remained, judging by the side-eyes she made at me as I, like Ella, relaxed into the evening and chatted with the boys.

I checked my phone and messaged Dad every hour as per his request. Sandy texted that he had found the shoe in the fog but couldn't get it down. He would mention it to the police. He said to text him if I needed him.

I texted back **actually having a bit of fun**. And I was. Rusty made us all laugh with stories and jokes. Fraser ripped open a bag of marshmallows and gave everyone a stick. I turned them down so he shrugged and said, 'More for us, then.'

Chase kept glancing at me. I tried to avoid him but he came over and sat beside me.

'I wanted to apologise,' he said over the hooting laughter of the other guys.

'For?'

'Scaring the shit out of you that night.'

I shrugged even though the memory of him grabbing me through the door made me shiver.

'I got myself into a bit of trouble,' he said quietly and I had to lean closer to hear him. He gestured at the other guys. 'All of us did. We got in too deep.'

'What do you mean?'

He hesitated, then shrugged, shaking his head. 'Doesn't matter now. I'm just...' he swallowed hard, looking off into the distance, 'I'm sorry for everything.'

My phone buzzed. I glanced down and saw a kiss emoji from Sandy, replying to my last text about having fun. I smiled, remembering the awkwardness of the night I had tried kissing him, but the warmth faded as I recalled Hollie having to tell me he was gay. Hollie knew everything about everyone. She wouldn't have come back out here if she had been worried about the guys Chase hung out with. It was sobering to think of Hollie out here again and I was furious with myself for having forgotten why I was even there. But here was Chase, apologising. Maybe I had been wrong about him the entire time. But I needed to focus.

I poured out the last of my beer and Lennox's eyes went to me as soon as I did. He shook his head at me and stalked off into the dark fog beyond the campsite, at the opposite end.

When he returned, there was the sound of a car engine and crunching gravel. We shielded our eyes as headlights pored through the fog and shut off. The car door squeaked as it was opened then slammed.

'Who's that?' Devlin murmured beside me.

Two figures walked through the fog and I noticed they were smoking crack pipes before I saw their faces. One was Lennox. The other was Cain – the guy who had driven us. He still didn't say a word, just greeted the guys with a handshake.

Chase deflated beside me. 'I didn't know he was coming.'

Cain's eyes lasered onto me and Devlin as he drew in the smoke from his crack pipe. Chase sniffed and Cain passed his crack pipe around. The only guy didn't take a hit of it was Oliver, because he was still kissing Ella. It got to Chase and he hesitated before muttering, 'What the hell,' and sucking on the pipe.

I stared at all of them, gobsmacked. Drugs. Chase did drugs. Lockie did drugs. Mitchell did drugs. I wanted to take that crack pipe off them and smash it.

Cain tried again to give the pipe to Oliver, but he waved it away, placing his hand instead on Ella's breast, making her giggle.

'You two should go in the tent,' Lennox teased. 'Looks like she's pretty keen.' He caressed the side of Ella's leg and she pulled away. 'At least leave some of her lips for us.' He cackled with laughter.

Ella got off Oliver's lap and wiped her mouth as if only just realising what she had been doing. Her cheeks blushed and she looked down, avoiding eye contact with everyone. Oliver went to pull her back in but she squirmed away and said, 'No.'

He said, 'Later then.'

She stepped back with a shy nod and came to sit between me and Devlin, looking up at Cain with wide eyes. The happy atmosphere had disappeared.

Fraser nodded towards the car and asked, 'Different car to before?'

Cain took another hit of meth and laughed, high-pitched and squirrelly. 'Yeah – stole it.'

His voice made me gasp. That was the man that I had heard on the beach. My stomach churned and I almost threw up. Devlin touched the top of my right hand and I noticed I had curled it into a tight fist.

Her eyes went wide when she realised that I wasn't breathing normally. I was panting. I didn't even have a logical reason to panic. I had no evidence that Cain was not good news, but I knew he wasn't going to be a friendly person.

The three of us girls stayed silent for the rest of the night while the guys got high and their behaviour became erratic. Chase retreated to his car and fell asleep in the backseat. Everyone else slumped in their camp chairs, as the fire died off into a flicker. Devlin, Ella and I stood up and walked to our respective tents.

'What a night,' Ella sighed.

Devlin grunted. I stayed silent. I only wanted morning to come.

I got changed and got into my sleeping bag, zipping it up tightly to my chin, teeth chattering and feeling as though I had uncovered a dirty, dark secret and I knew Blue had been right to try to stop me coming. Drugs. It had all been because of drugs. I thought of Hollie and realised she had known all along, too. Maybe she had been involved? I hoped she hadn't. I longed to ask her. Where was she?

I wiped away a tear and sniffed. She was out there somewhere. She had to be.

Devlin came into my tent soon after we had all gone to bed. She had changed into her long-johns and wore a pink over-sized hoodie. She shivered in the torch light and whispered, 'Daisy, are you awake?'

I rolled over in my sleeping bag and she climbed down to all-fours to lie beside me. 'Where's Ella?' I asked.

'She went into Oliver's tent,' she whispered back. 'I told her not to; she's drunk; she'll regret it, but she didn't care.'

I thought of the way Oliver had his arm around Ella all night and how she swayed in the darkness, drunk. I should've stopped her drinking so much. I was such an idiot! What had I been thinking?

I counted to ten to work up the nerve before sitting up and pulling on my puffer jacket. 'Come on. Let's get her out of there.'

We strode across the campsite to Oliver's tent. Devlin and I both stopped when we noticed the zipper and door of the tent was open.

Oliver was standing inside the tent, watching over Ella, his hand on his groin. We stepped up beside him. Someone else was in the tent with her. My brain didn't quite understand what was going on before me.

Devlin muttered, 'Oh God.'

Cain was standing, his head cricked to the side to stop hitting the ceiling of the tent. Devlin and I froze. Cain had his face close to Ella's cheek, one hand around her neck and one hand on her hip. He breathed in deeply before blowing out the methamphetamine smoke into her face, making her grunt and revolt.

'Let her go,' Devlin demanded.

'Nah,' Cain said with a grin. One weedy arm swooped down as he hand burrowed into Ella's pants, making her squirm and weep. I couldn't move. Devlin didn't move either so I think she was as terrified as I was.

Devlin grabbed Ella's arm and yanked her towards us. I flew at Cain. I knew it. I knew it. I knew it. He was the one. He had done something to Hollie.

I punched his chest, and it echoed back in my own. I couldn't move fast enough. I was so angry that I couldn't get my arms to swing hard enough and it came out in my teeth instead. He pushed me out of the tent and I somehow managed to stay upright despite him trying to push me down. I may have nibbled at food, but I gnawed and gnashed at Cain so hard that he bled. He didn't even seem to react. He just laughed and threw his crack pipe onto the ground where it smashed.

While I pounded at his scrawny chest, Ella and Devlin ran out into the darkness, down the furthest track. Cain grabbed my arm and twisted it behind me and it crunched and wrenched out of position.

Pain lit me on fire. I cried out at the burning surge through my neck and arm. It hurt so much that vomit lurched up and I spat orange globs of chewed up carrot and bread onto the ground. I staggered away, clutching at my shoulder, heaving for air. I gazed around at the campground and wondered how all the boys could be so casual and not do anything. They had all come out of their tents and stood watching with perplexed expressions.

Cain shoved Chase, Lennox and Fraser. 'Go after the two that ran off, you idiots.'

He squatted to pick up the crack pipe pieces, and I bolted for Sandy down the narrow track where I had found the shoe. Each footfall made a searing bolt of pain radiate through my neck and arm. I clutched at my useless hand and it was so cold. I had a terrifying moment where I thought I'd have to get it amputated. But I had to get to Sandy. I didn't think of Ella and Devlin. I only thought of Sandy. If I got to him, I'd be safe.

There was pressure in my chest that felt like an elephant as I gasped for air and my ankle wobbled under me, threatening to send me down to the dirt again. I passed the tree and was blinded by my tears. Had Hollie run this way too?

I arrived at the creek clearing, which led to the fire trail where Sandy had parked. *Look for the trees. Look for the trees*, I told myself as I gasped for air. Sandy had to be out here somewhere, camping in his panelvan. He'd promised.

I found the trees and circled the area, but it was empty. I cried out and wailed at the fog that surrounded me. I couldn't see past the trees. I couldn't even hear the creek but there was the Y. There it was, but no sign of Sandy.

I fell to my knees in the clearing and wailed. Alone. I was drowning in the forest, in the fog. I didn't care if Cain heard me and found me. Killed me. Anything to end this pain. Anything to end being alone.

There were hands on me suddenly and I lashed out, roaring and squealing, hitting with my uninjured arm. There were arms around me. A familiar face blurred in front of me as though he was at the surface of the water as I was drowning. Sandy.

I couldn't speak without sobbing. I got into his panelvan and he drove through the white fog down the fire track, dodging and swerving around logs and potholes to make the trip easier for me. I could only think of the pain in my shoulder. My arm must have been dislocated or broken. Either way, it was agony.

'Wait here.' Sandy parked the panelvan and the windscreen wipers screeched and grinded across the windscreen. I squinted and saw we were back at the campground. *No...No, no, no.*

I got out and stumbled after Sandy, following the sound of his voice as he bellowed, 'What the hell are you guys doing?'

'What are you doing here – lurking in the woods like the fucking pedo you are?' Cain cackled.

'Tell me what happened.'

'Nothin' happened. Dunno what ya on about. Get outta here.'

Sandy kicked him in the knee and pinned him to the ground. Cain was too stoned to react now and relented without a struggle.

'What did you do to her?' Sandy cried.

'Who?'

'The girls!'

'The girl? Oh, she ran off.'

'What did you do?' Sandy growled, twisting Cain's arm the way he had done to me.

'Sandy, stop!' Lockie called from the firepit.

Sandy asked, 'Where are the other girls?'

'What other girls?' Cain asked.

'Don't bull shit me!' Sandy's voice went up several octaves and spittle flung from his mouth.

'Sandy, mate,' Cain droned. 'We're just mates having a good time out here.'

'Stop lying. Tell me what you did to Daisy. Tell me why the girls ran. Tell me what you mother-fucking did to Hollie!' He burst into tears and lost his grip on Cain, who pulled away but made no attempts to retaliate.

'I don't know what you're on about.'

Sandy spat at him and marched back to the panelvan, placing both hands on my back to propel me forward.

He sniffled as he drove us out of there. Three kilometres down the winding road, he slowed. Ella and Devlin were walking on the narrow edge of the road and looked at us with wide eyes. When they saw me in the car, they hurriedly grabbed at the panelvan door as Sandy stopped. They climbed in and hugged each other and sobbed.

The lights at the hospital were too bright. I shielded my eyes when I came to from the sedation. My arm was in a sling and Sandy, Ella and Devlin were around me.

'I've been eating,' I whined before my brain could register that I was in hospital for my arm, not my anorexia. As the minutes went by, the memory of what had happened at the campground came back to me, and I chewed with an open mouth as though it was a rotten taste that I could get rid of with a breath mint.

I sighed loudly and Ella said suddenly, 'I feel sick.'

She grabbed for the sick bag that it was in my lap and doubled over, puking all the beer out. She had almost drunk an entire six-pack.

A nurse attended to Ella, taking her out of the bay ward I was in.

Devlin wiped her nose on a tissue with shaking hands. She shook her head down at me and said, 'I hope you got what you needed.'

I recalled the shoe in the tree. I tugged at Sandy's arm and whispered, 'You have to go get the shoe before they find it.'

He retracted himself from my grip. 'I'm going to the police as soon as I know you and the girls are okay.'

'You're going to the police?' Devlin cried. 'I'm coming with you. I want to report that sicko for what he did to Ella!' She pointed to where Ella sat in a chair and spoke with the nurse. She had a blood pressure cuff wrapped around her arm like a python and she continued to spit into my sick bag.

My stomach started to churn as the sedation they had given me to set my shoulder back into place gave its after-glow. I put my hand to my mouth and tapped at my tingling lips. Everything was numb. I closed my eyes and focused on my breathing, which was starting to increase. I was going to vomit. Again. For the second time in the night.

'Sick bag?' Sandy asked.

I nodded frantically and he bolted to the nurse station. Devlin lingered between me and Ella, before she eventually went to stay with Ella.

Alone again. I couldn't blame her. I would have chosen Hollie if she had been there. But the thought made me want to cry all over again. I knew she wasn't missing, anymore. Before, I'd thought maybe she was alive somewhere, but now I knew. Hollie was gone. She was not alive. Hollie was dead. Now it was just going to be about finding her body and making sure the police knew what happened to her...and it wasn't something good.

Chapter Seventeen

I met Sandy down at the beach the next day at sunset. Dad fell asleep in front of the television and I snuck out. He'd grounded me for my own sakes. My shoulder felt surprisingly good. A few pain killers in me and a sling, and it almost felt good as new. Used. Bargain bin. But at least I wasn't in pain.

Sandy emerged from the surf and wrenched his torso out of his wetsuit and seemed out of breath. I waved with my good hand and he padded through the damp sand towards me.

'How are you feeling?' he asked, snorting some snot out of one nostril, then the other.

'Fine. How did you go at the police station?'

'They took Ella and Devlin's statements. They're looking into it.'

He gritted his teeth together and avoided looking at me as he said, 'Ella's denying it happened the way you and Devlin said though. Think the cretin may have got to her.'

My teeth ground together as I remembered what Cain had done to Ella. I had been in so much pain that I hadn't really processed it until the early hours of the morning, lying awake in bed, staring at the ceiling, replaying the scene in my mind. I couldn't imagine being in her position. It was bad enough to be physically hurt, but to feel that encroached upon...it made me shiver. Unbearable.

'I told them about the shoe in the tree,' he added and I ceased breathing while I waited for him to tell me what they would do.

He shrugged. 'They said they'd look into it but they're not convinced it would be evidence.'

I rolled my eyes. 'I will go out there again and get it myself.'

'How?' His eyes glittered, teasing. 'You've got one arm.'

'I'll be fine.'

He tousled my hair and said, 'Yeah, I know you will be, Daze.'

We began walking up to the carpark but when Sandy stopped, I looked up at him, confused. I'd been so busy watching my feet as we walked through the sand that I hadn't seen who was in front of us on the track.

'You've got nerve being here,' Sandy hollered.

I locked eyes with Chase who was standing in the middle of the track. His mouth was ajar. I sidled up to Sandy, bumping my arm into his hip but I didn't care if it hurt. I was never getting close to any of those guys ever again.

'I wanted to come say sorry,' Chase called, tilting his head as if his voice needed to bend around Sandy for me to hear it as I cowered behind him.

'To apologise about Cain's behaviour last night.'

Sandy strode forwards and I followed, scuttling to the other side of him to put Sandy between me and Chase. He stepped towards me and Sandy nudged him with his surfboard, making him step back.

'We've got nothing to hear from you,' Sandy hissed as we walked away.

I refused to look back at him but I could feel his eyes on my back like an arrow on a target.

The next day, Sandy went and got the shoe. He walked into the police station with it and slapped it down on the service desk like a trophy he had won. 'Investigate it!' He told me about it afterwards. I hugged him and thanked him.

A month later, there were whispers around town that there had been an anonymous tip from Gould, a town to the south of Short Point. People had been talking about a body discovered in a creek. A body of a girl.

I waited. And I waited. I waited for the answer to come to me that I knew to be the truth. That body was Hollie's.

When that phone call came in from the police officers to let Dad know, he withheld a gasp and a sob as his eyes went to me. Wrinkling at the edges, never losing their blue light, yet filling with water that would never fall. I had expected it. I knew it, but it didn't stop it hitting me like a wrecking ball.

Before he could tell me, I was gone. I was running out of the house and straight to the beach. I stripped off my jeans and shirt. I sprinted into the water and freestyled – meeting the incoming waves on the head and being pushed back to shore.

A rogue big set came through and I couldn't get past it. I swam and it pushed me back with such violence that I cartwheeled underneath the shallow water, skidded along the sandy bottom and sat up in the overflow, dumped upon by the reformed shore break.

Salty water lined my face, combining with my tears. I sat in the puddle of saltwater and its liquification under me and I willed it to suck me down, too. *Please. Soften like quicksand and gloop me under the world so I don't have to comprehend that my best friend is dead.*

Dead.

Gone forever.

Dad ran down the beach to me. Limping in his old man way. He pulled me to my feet but I collapsed to my knees and fell into his thighs as I gasped for air. Dad hunched over me, his nails digging into the soft part of the flesh on my back that was new to me. I cried harder than I ever thought I could. I would never get over this. Never.

The days passed and I shivered under the blankets, refusing to eat more than an apple a day. Dad was right. This was going to destroy me, but it would have destroyed me anyway whether I had recovered or not. Dad brought me sandwiches, hot chocolates, Milo, sticky cinnamon buns, bananas – anything he thought would entice me to eat on top of my apple a day. I wouldn't. At first.

Hollie's funeral was a fortnight after we had got the news that it was her body in that creek. I crawled out of bed that morning and across the floor to my wardrobe. I was determined to go. I wrapped a robe around my shivering body, and forced myself to shower, confined with the intrusive thoughts of anorexia screaming at me again. If I couldn't have Hollie, at least I had my anorexia, right?

The thought sickened me. No. I needed to survive. Hollie needed me to survive.

Dad looked up from his toast at the table as I stumbled into the room, making a chair slide across the hardwood floor. 'Wow,' he said, pausing as he chewed the toast in a circular motion. 'Sprout, you're up.'

I nodded and grasped at the refrigerator and heaved it open. Eyed off the orange juice in the door. Liquid calories. *No,* anorexia warned in a low voice but I grabbed and gulped a few mouthfuls from the bottle as the voice raged in my head.

Dad hurriedly chopped me up an apple, and watched as I choked it down. I asked, 'Can I have some toast, too?'

He nodded and made it. Dry. He knew not to test me when I was making the choice to eat more. I wouldn't let myself be destroyed after all. I could make sure I didn't succumb to a fate that would have me in the ground alongside Hollie.

Dad held my elbow as we made our way down to his ute to go to the funeral. I was positive he was petrified that I would faint at any second and hit my head on the steps, but I was going to that funeral. Nobody, especially not anorexia, was going to stop me from saying goodbye to Hollie.

The funeral was held inside an Anglican church. Hollie was not Anglican. But the local government had pitched in with other local donations to ensure Hollie had a proper memorial service. Her grandparents were wretchedly poor, and there was no way her estranged parents would pay. I gazed around the crowd, scanning the faces, wondering if her parents were even there. If they even knew.

Whispers followed me. 'She's skinny again.' 'Looks like death.' 'Poor girl.' 'I wish she'd just eat something.' 'Better hope she doesn't die, too.'

Everything had a slight haze around it, like the aura of an ocular migraine. My vision wavered sometimes like I was under water, or like everything was a mirage in a desert as I shivered from the cold. Dad wrapped a blanket around my shoulders and I normally would have died of embarrassment, but I was so weak that I didn't care – I laid my head down on his lap as soon as we were seated.

Anorexia infantilised me. It didn't matter that I was a seventeen-year-old girl. I was stunted. *Protect me from life*, I wanted to whisper to Dad. *Protect me from all this*. I closed my eyes, which were so heavy, and I remembered that he was trying to protect me, all this time, but I hadn't let him.

I opened my eyes as Sandy sat beside me. I reached out a hand for him to hold and he did; he squeezed it with a teary smile.

There was an electronic hum as the projector switched on. Photos of Hollie displayed on the projector with a flicker and our attentions all turned to the grainy images of her smile. Girls from our year level at school sobbed. I sat up and looked around to see if Ella or Devlin had come, but couldn't find them in the sea of grey faces. Sandy put his arm around me and his hand landed upon Dad's shoulder. Dad's body stiffened next to me then eventually relaxed with a sigh.

As the priest rambled on, I continued to look around to see the people who had turned out to pay their respects. I had a checklist in my mind that I needed to tick off. People who cared. People I could trust. There were more people than the church had space for. There was a line, four-deep, at the back of the church, and straining eyes and ears from the foyer. My head swam and I caught the edge of the pew to steady myself. I was so grateful for a seat. Further along the pew, Hollie's grandparents sat. Quiet. Drawn. Looking much the way I did – like they were somewhere else but grasping to reality, fighting to stay, just to say goodbye.

Lockie and Mitchell caught my eye then looked away. Our encounter at the camping trip still fresh in our minds. They looked bigger, more grown up, than they had before. Suits did that, I supposed.

Further back in the pews, Blue sat with his mum. His face blotchy and his leg bouncing like he couldn't wait to leave. I tried to catch his eye but he only had eyes for Hollie on the projector. I hated myself for feeling disappointed that we couldn't talk to each other. Rusty and Ethan were nowhere to be seen. Teachers from school stood at the back of the church, trying to keep their composure but I saw the tears glistening in the sunlight even from a distance.

I turned my attention back to the priest and tried to focus on what he was saying, but my cheeks were sagging away from my eyes as I tried to stay awake. It wasn't anything like Hollie would have wanted. Finally, the priest stepped down to allow the mayor

261

to speak. A white rose pinned to his lapel. He didn't know Hollie, yet he was up there telling us all what an incredibly bright and "sparky" young woman our town had just lost. It wasn't our town that lost her, last I checked. It was her family. It was me. Dad. Sandy. Looking around at the attendees again, I saw strangers. Looky-loos. Come to say goodbye to the poor murdered girl. Cynicism wrapped around me like the blanket on my shoulders.

I stopped breathing when I noticed it for the first time. The coffin. God, it was huge. It loomed towards me and my breath was gone. It was drenched with flowers, under the projector, so I hadn't noticed it with my blurred vision. I edged closer to Dad and he knew. He knew I had only just noticed it. On the projector screen, Hollie's school photo came up and her name was in cursive writing, too extravagant for the bogan she prided herself on being. Numbers below for her birthday and the date she was found. She'd died long before that. It was wrong. The police had said she had died in that creek. Drowned. A surfer like her didn't just drown in a little creek. I shook my head to myself, knowing I couldn't think about that right now – this was time to think about Hollie and only Hollie.

Her picture at the front of the room showed her thick, wavy brown hair and the glint of her braces. The grin was bold and cheesy, but I liked the way it made her eyes glow. She'd stay the same for the rest of my life while I would change. She'd be seventeen forever.

Once the politician stepped down from the podium, Hollie's grandma got up. I wasn't sure if I could handle the pain so I stared at the crisscrossed beams of the church. The timber was thick and I marvelled how it almost looked medieval.

I swallowed hard to quell my tears as music began playing; it was sweet upbeat music with a ukulele. The photos on the projector went around in a carousel. Hollie as a kid, a baby, surfing. People cried, yet I stared at the photos, wishing I had had her in my life longer. It was a blip of time, though we'd been so close; as if I'd known her forever. I rested my head on Dad's shoulder and he dabbed away his tears. A photo of Hollie standing in front of her grandparents' house came onto the screen. With Chase. He stood beside her, hands behind his back and his mouth in an odd shape as if he'd been saying something. Hollie ignoring him, blissfully free in spirit and life.

A louder sob than the others in the church rang out. Chase. His voice was breaking as he wailed like a toddler to his grandparents. 'I've got to leave. Let me leave.'

He stood up and shoved his way through the crush of crowd. 'Leave me alone!' he shrieked. People stood and watched him go, Sandy, Dad and I included. Chase disappeared into the grey daylight and we all looked back at the projector to see a video of Hollie, Sandy and me sitting on the beach together, waxing our boards and laughing about something. My heart collapsed inwards and I fell into Sandy and Dad, and my eyes glazed over with tears. Then it was my turn to break down, diving for the exit, after Chase. Sandy following behind to make sure I was okay. People cleared the way for me like the parting of the Red Sea and I fell on all fours on the lawn of the church, pitching downhill. I threw up the food and orange juice. My mouth and nose on fire from the citrus.

I grabbed at my stomach as it cramped in revolt against the grief. Sandy squatted beside me and rubbed my back.

We didn't speak. Blue came over but Sandy kept him away from me with a silent palm up. Once I stopped vomiting, I looked up. Blue stood back with a greenish tinge to his tanned face, but my eyes went to where Chase was sitting on the fence of the church, staring at me, wiping away tears. Sandy noticed him and his entire body tensed. He jerked up like a spring. 'Let's go back inside,' he murmured.

I nodded and I allowed him and Blue to help me up and lead me back inside, leaving Chase alone with his guilt.

The funeral ended and people either dispersed into groups or left. I expected to speak to Lockie and Mitchell, but they walked out of the church yard with only a glance at Chase as they passed him where he was still perched on the fence. His head remained down, even when his grandma went over to talk to him. She dismissed him with a wave of the hand and went back to her husband and spoke with other attendees.

I was glad he was feeling guilty. He knew Cain was responsible this entire time but he remained silent, protecting his mate – all for drugs. I wanted him to feel as guilty as he could. Sandy brought me a cup of water and a banana. I pushed them away but he didn't relent. 'You need this.'

I sipped at the water and bit the banana. With my mouth full, I snapped, 'Happy?'

'You know I'm not.'

I chewed and swallowed, hating myself for being such a bitch. I couldn't keep blaming anorexia for my outbursts of savagery. Hollie had put up with it and I hated myself for it. It had to stop. I took another bite of the banana and chewed slowly. I would make it better with Sandy. I would make myself better.

Sandy said, 'There's a vigil at the beach tonight for Hol. I'm gonna go.'

'I want to go, too.'

Sandy pointed at the banana. 'You have to eat that whole banana first or your dad and I aren't gonna let ya go anywhere except for the hospital, kid.'

I ate the whole banana and sighed. 'I'm never going to hospital for anorexia again. I'm going to survive.'

The vigil was held an hour before sunset. Dad had organised it. He was one of the hosts. He drove me down to the top of the beach and parked the car. Sandy found us and we walked solemnly down to the beach, where the president of the surf lifesaving club was handing out tealight candles. Blue, Mitchell and Lockie stood either side of the president and nodded at everyone, mumbling their thanks for coming.

We took the candles and they nodded at us. Sandy and Dad led me to a smooth part of sand to sit with our candles. A guy I'd never seen before traipsed down the beach with a guitar, and a girl followed with a wireless microphone. Everything was so organised. I recognised people from school, teachers and students alike. Surfers in our little community, the old guys I'd found myself out with that day. Everyone looked so different in the setting sun. An amber glow across their faces as if they were turning to rust in the salty air. Media crews jogged down the path and wasted no time sticking their microphones under the mouths of people.

'It's tragic; it's so sad; This was her favourite beach so we've all come here because she's probably still here in spirit, you know.'

Then the kicker line from the reporter: 'In this devastated beach community, there is an air of unease. Among their closeknit community, there is a killer...who still remains to be caught.'

I rolled my eyes and stomped off. They didn't care about Hollie. They only cared about the murder. I pushed past people making their way down to the beach, surprising even myself how strong I was when I felt so weak. I bumped into one woman and flowers and a teddy bear went flying. I apologised under my breath but kept walking.

'Daisy! Daisy!' Sandy was trying to call me back. I didn't so much as glance back at him. I would go pay respects to Hollie the way she would want me to. Without fakers that hadn't sniggered behind her back calling her a wharf rat and a slut. As I walked through the narrow street, I began to be aware that someone was behind me. I slowed my frantic steps and tuned into my hearing. Yes, there were footsteps behind me, crunching on the gravel road. I peeked over my shoulder and began jogging when I realised it was Chase.

'Daisy, stop!'

I broke into a sprint, my breath ragged and my chest tight. My legs went into spasm and I fought back a frightened wail as I forced them to keep going. Keep moving. Get home. Get away from Chase.

As he caught up with me, I heard someone else's footsteps. My heart pounded and my head spun from the exertion. Why was it so hard to breathe? There was a scuffle and grunts behind me so I stopped and turned.

It was Sandy. He had caught up with Chase and grabbed him by the neck.

'What are you thinking?' he hissed in Chase's face.

'Nothing. Just wanted to talk to Daisy.'

'Bull shit!' Sandy hissed. 'Stop lying. Did you do it?'

'No!'

'You're lying!'

'I didn't do it!'

'Just bloody come clean, Chase. You know something!' Sandy roared.

Chase sobbed. Sandy let him go. I stepped closer and noticed the snot and tears smothering his face. 'I didn't know that they would do it.'

'Who?'

'My mates!'

'Your mates that forced Hollie to suck them off that time?' I spoke up.

His eyes met mine and widened.

I nodded. 'Yeah, she told me about that.'

Chase said shakily, 'I told her to leave because I didn't think she was safe. They said they'd do something to her if I didn't pay, and I hadn't paid.'

'What is "something"?' Sandy asked.

'Rape her.' He sighed. 'Ah, I'm sorry.' Chase swallowed and said, 'I tried to explain to you, Daisy, that night at your house. I was the one that made her leave the campground. I wasn't lying about her leaving in a white car.'

'Who was it? Cain?' Sandy pushed.

Chase sniffed, looked up at Sandy and replied, 'I can't say. He'd kill me.'

'Did he…rape Hollie?' I asked, my legs wouldn't stop shaking. Chase's skin glistened in the street light, soaking his shirt in his armpits. His eyes darted from me to Sandy. He took a deep breath and admitted, 'I took her out there hoping she could work off my debt, but the longer we were there, the weirder they got…I just…told her to leave. I chickened out. I thought I saved her by getting her out of there. I thought I saved her!'

Chase gagged and put his head between his knees. My shaking legs suddenly buckled and Sandy had to catch me and lower me onto my hands and knees beside Chase. I grabbed Chase's jacket collar and shook him feebly. 'Did they rape her?'

'I don't know. I wasn't there.' He began to sob. 'I have a problem. I was using too much meth. So were all of us.'

I glared at him as tears rolled down his cheeks. 'I told her to leave. I called Lockie and Mitchell to come get her. She got into the white car. I went to bed. I thought she was safe.'

'You've got to be joking,' Sandy mumbled.

'They're rough guys, Sandy – I couldn't have done anything.'

'You could have HELPED her! Got her out yourself!'

'I'm sorry,' he sobbed. 'Like I said, I'd had too much. I couldn't drive. I'm sorry!'

'She's dead and you're sorry? Jesus Christ!' Sandy spun away and paced. I succumbed to my tears and curled my back up, straightening through my arms. It was becoming a lot clearer and I couldn't bear the images that were running through my mind. When I hadn't known, I thought it would be better to know. But hearing Chase explain the event more clearly, I wished I hadn't known at all. My tears fell upon my hands, hot on my cold skin.

267

Sandy rounded on him again. 'You're going to the police. Right now. You're going to tell them what you did.'

'Okay.'

He started off to get his car and he doubled back, swearing to himself. 'I can't leave you with him, Daisy. Both of you, get up. Come with me.'

While Chase gave his statement, Sandy and I waited outside the police station in his panelvan. I thought of Hollie being surrounded by Cain, Lennox, Fraser and Oliver out there in the trees. Whether they had raped her not, the terror she must have felt made me rock side to side in my seat subconsciously. There were so many predators that took advantage of girls. It made me think of the accusations Chloe had levelled to me about Sandy. I glanced at him, his elbow resting on his steering wheel and fingers massaging his temple.

'Sandy?' I whispered.

'Hm.'

'Did you ever take a girl named Chloe camping?'

His hand fell away from his face as he turned his eyes to me. 'Why?'

'She told me she went camping with you and she woke up, in a…vulnerable position.'

He sighed and rubbed his neck. 'I did…but…it happened differently for me than that."

'How do you mean?' I asked in a high voice, goosebumps popping up all over my skin.

'I took her camping, back when I was trying to convince myself I wasn't gay. It was years ago.' He swallowed hard. 'I went with Cain and his girlfriend.'

'Who was his girlfriend?'

'I don't know…some girl from Queensland who was down for a holiday. It was a summer fling I guess.'

'Oh.' He didn't explain any more so I probed. 'What happened?'

He shrugged. 'Nothing happened. We drank. We went to bed. Chloe and I tried...' He glanced at me and cleared his throat, turning red. 'It didn't happen. I had to kind of come out to myself, then.'

I studied his furrowed brow and the yellow light that made him look so much older, as though he was my dad's age. Emboldened, I asked, 'Why are you so afraid of people knowing you're gay, Sandy?'

He blew out of his mouth so that a strand of blonde hair bounced away from his narrowed eyes. He placed a hand to his chest. 'My parents were very religious. *Very* traditional Catholic. I wasn't even allowed to sit next to a girl at school, and all our women teachers and girls had to wear dresses and veils. We said prayers every hour...Being gay was not accepted at all. The values were just...ingrained in me. Parents disowned me when I told them.'

I widened my eyes and said, 'No offence, Sandy, but that doesn't sound Catholic. That sounds like a cult.'

He snickered. 'I know,' then he sighed, 'just some things stay with you, Daisy, and it makes it pretty hard to be kind to yourself for being the way you are.'

'I know what that's like,' I murmured with a swallow. 'So, what happened after you...you know?'

'So, we went to sleep. I woke up in the morning and she had left. Gone home. I figured it was because...Well...you know.'

'She said she had...stuff...in her hair.' My tongue had turned into lead. It was so awkward talking about that stuff with Sandy. I coughed. 'Jizz?' I immediately wished I could take it back. I squirmed in my seat and looked away.

Sandy was silent for a long time. 'Ha.'

'Why do you say HA?' I asked.

'Bit odd, is all. I couldn't even get a hard-on for her, so how was I supposed to have been the one that cum on her hair?' He noticed the embarrassed expression on my face and said, 'Sorry, I shouldn't be talking about this stuff with you.'

'It's okay,' I said with a smile. 'It's as weird for me as it is for you.'

We were quiet for a moment before Sandy uttered, 'Cain.'

'What?'

'It must have been Cain.'

'Do you think he's the one that killed Hollie?' I asked in a small voice.

Sandy nodded. 'Yeah. I hope the police do, too.'

'But Chase said Lockie and Mitchell were the ones to pick Hollie up.'

'In whose car, though, Daze?' He squinted at me. 'Something stinks.'

A police officer emerged from the police station. It was the young guy whom I met when I reported that Chase knew more than he let on. Sandy wound down his window, making loud squeaking sounds and the officer stood outside awkwardly. Nobody had wind-down windows anymore. Sandy was a special kind of guy with his ancient panelvan.

Once the window was open, the police officer leant on the window frame and said, 'He's made a statement. We've got some names. Did you guys want to come in now or come back tomorrow? It's getting late.'

'Did Cain do it?' My voice was louder than it had been in weeks.

He gazed across to me and blinked slowly. He would have told me if he could. His face was soft and his eyes empathetic. He looked back to Sandy, who replied that we could make our statements now. See if it all corroborated. The officer smiled. 'Good man.'

We got out and Sandy locked the panelvan's doors, put an arm around me and we ventured inside the police station behind the officer, who locked the door behind us. It wasn't a 24/7 cop shop like the one in the main town.

'Daisy, could you tell us everything Hollie told you about the night she was sexually assaulted?'

The other police officer, a woman this time, got right to business and I nodded and spoke as clearly as I could.

'She told me she went up to a surfing spot, then went camping with Chase and his friends. There was a dare. It was either suck one of the guys off...'

It was as though I was back with Hollie standing at the beach shower, washing her mouth out as she told me what had happened. I panicked a little, remembering everything we said or did that day on the beach. 'Uh...sorry, I...' I covered my face and made myself breathe.

'It's all right. Take your time.'

After a few deep breaths, I looked up and said, 'The dare was to suck this one guy off or strip nude.' It had never occurred to me she'd chosen what I thought of now as the most uncomfortable and degrading option. After being at the campsite with those eyes on me and the way I had felt like game prey, I understood. She'd known all along. If she'd chosen the other option, they all would have pounced on her. Vulnerable. Skin. Human. I began to cry and apologised to the police officer, who did not react, save for reaching for the box of tissues to hand to me.

'I'm sorry, it's just...I'm figuring out some things...I...didn't understand before.'

She smiled gently. 'I understand. Did Hollie tell you who had dared her?'

I shook my head. 'Just one of Chase's friends.'

'And who are Chase's friends – that you can list?'

I counted them on my fingers. Their faces swarming at me at the campsite. Thumb, Cain. Index finger, Lennox. Middle finger, Oliver. Ring finger, Fraser. I got to my pinkie and paused. Two others. Two others that I always seemed to overlook. Quiet ones. Ones who disappeared into the background. Ones who appeared harmless but had been close to Hollie the entire time. Ones who

271

had picked her up in a white car and nobody had seen her alive again.

I added in a confused tone, 'Lockie and Mitchell – but…they were her friends, too…that's why she…' I took in a sharp breath that made me wince. 'That's why she would have gone with them. She felt safe with them.'

'So, you're thinking these two boys were there when she went missing? Lockie and Mitchell.'

'I don't know,' I murmured, gazing down at my shoes. I added with a whisper, 'They were there when I went out there…so maybe. With Rusty and Ethan, too.' I didn't understand why it had never occurred to me before. Why I had even trusted them? But I knew why. Because Hollie had.

The police officer nodded. 'Thank you, Daisy. You've filled in a couple of gaps. Your story matches with Chase's. We'll be in contact. You may be called into court to testify. Is that something you're comfortable with?'

I nodded. 'I want whoever killed Hollie to be caught and punished.' I had a salty, almost pickle-like, taste in my mouth at the thought of it not being Cain. It must have been Cain. It surely couldn't have been friends of Hollie. Confusion set in, disbelief. There were hurts needing repairs as it was but throwing in the loss of more friends. I was tired of always being damaged. Broken friendships and broken trust. Had I really been blind enough to not notice it was Lockie and Mitchell all that time?

Meeting Sandy again out in the foyer, I hugged him tightly. I was a weak person, but I never gave up. Pain never stayed with me long enough because I starved myself to get rid of it. I was beginning to realise I would never be all right. I would always live in this undignified state of helplessness. If I could just let go of everything, I might be happy one day. But for now, everything stayed with me and it made living so…damn…hard.

Chapter Eighteen

'She was happy to surf. Happy to stay out and surf into the sunset like some wild and reckless nomad. No bed for the night but the sand under her feet. She didn't want to come back to the campsite with us. We were smoking too much meth. We shouldn't have. But we did. Hollie hated that we were using.'

I was in the courtroom, listening to Lockie make his argument, statement, testament – whatever they were called. He was telling his side of the story. Everyone in the courtroom was silent, listening intently, to the firsthand account of one of the boys up on a murder charge. Was he guilty or innocent? His blonde, long hair and icy eyes set within the tanned face suggested he spent more time in the sun than killing girls in the forest. Time would tell.

'She was happy to stay with Mitchell and me, surfing late. The moon was already up and the sun was going down, flattening like it does. Its last rays spewing in rows across the golden banks of the sea. But her brother made her get into his car. I smoked more meth. She was trying to be happy and make jokes, but the whites of her eyes were a bit too big, you know. I knew she was scared. She was worried about going back to the campsite with all of them.'

'Who are all of them?' asked the lawyer.

'Her brother. Chase.' His eyes went upwards as though trying to remember who was there. 'There were some other guys there. Chase's friends.'

'You were called to pick Miss Matheson up, weren't you?' The lawyer wore a grim expression. 'Who called you, and why did she need to be picked up?'

Lockie nodded. 'Chase called. He said he was falling asleep and he wanted Hollie to get out of there, because, uh...' His head went down. 'He was worried he couldn't keep her safe if he was too out of it.'

'When you got there, was Miss Matheson in good spirits?'

Lockie nodded.

'For the record, please.'

'Yes, she was okay. Bit nervy. But fine.'

'Where did her brother go?'

'He went to bed, in his tent, I mean. I'd had a bit too much to smoke, too. Everything got blurry after that. What else do you want me to say?'

His lawyers whispered to him what he needed to explain.

'After I picked her up? She was...ha...funny. Was it rape? No. Absolutely not. We never had sex with her. Never. Just fun. How did her shoe get up a tree? I have no idea. Last I saw her, she was down on the ground. Missing shoe? Nah, she wasn't missing a shoe.'

The lawyer asked, 'How did you pick her up? Records show you don't own a vehicle, Lockie.'

He sniffed.

'No, it wasn't my car.'

The judge asked who owned the car.

'Whose car? I don't know. It was stolen.'

'You stole a car?' The judge raised his eyebrow.

A whistle ran through his teeth and his hands ran through his floppy, long hair. Lockie shrugged and looked down. I sucked in a deep breath of air. It was unbelievable. Lockie, the kid who excelled in school, spoke like a poet. It was shocking enough to hear that he was a drug user, but the fact he was out stealing cars was too much for me to hear in one sitting. Sandy reached over and squeezed my icy hand.

'No further questions, Your Honour,' the lawyer murmured. Mitchell was called up to answer the same questions. While Lockie had given long, well-thought answers right up until he had picked Hollie up, Mitchell was matter-of-fact with his answers and didn't avoid anyone's eyes, especially mine.

'What happened after you picked up Miss Matheson? Because you did not drive her home, did you?'

Mitchell shook his head and said, 'We stopped at a spot in the road that a little track went down to the creek. She and Lockie got a bit heavy on, if you know what I mean.' The lawyer looked at him blankly, prompting him to roll his eyes and say, 'Sex. They had sex in the backseat. I just had a smoke.'

'Then what happened?'

'Then Cain showed up. Said he wanted to scare her because her brother owed him money. He made her walk down to a creek with a knife to her neck, her arm twisted behind her back. Cain asked if we wanted to – and I quote "fuck her". We both said no and went back to the car. We waited in the car for them to be done.' He shrugged. 'We thought she was good for it given her reputation.'

Lockie choked. My breathing became raspy. Sandy's hand shook upon mine. I wanted to leap to him and claw his eyes out.

How dare he bring her reputation into this? How dare he try to explain away what he let happen to her?

'You left…a vulnerable teenage girl, alone with an older man who had intentions of having sex with her, by force, with a weapon in his hand?'

Mitchell swallowed. 'I'm not proud of myself. Cain came back and told us she ran away.'

'Why didn't you tell police that this Cain person was the last person to see Miss Matheson alive?'

Mitchell shrugged, chewing the insides of his cheek in a way that made his face ghastly and ghoulish. I knew why. He was frightened of Cain. He supplied the drugs to them. He was shutting down any suspicions of him, but at least he had told the court that it was Cain who was last with Hollie.

The lawyer asked, 'What did you do when Cain returned to the car?'

'We went home.' He exhaled deeply. 'I had no reason not to believe him that Hollie had run off.'

Lockie looked up at him with a confused expression. The lawyer didn't miss this. 'You don't agree, Lockie?'

Lockie shrugged and crossed his arms. 'Who am I to say how Mitchell feels? He's not me.'

'Did you have reason not to believe Cain?'

Lockie scoffed. 'He said he'd raped a girl before. You'd have to ask him though.' It made me shiver uncontrollably to hear him say that he'd raped some girl before. I knew this was when they'd bring Chloe into it. Chloe who would blame Sandy.

Sandy whispered, 'Want to leave?' I shook my head.

Chloe took the stand. 'About three years ago, I went camping with Cain and his girlfriend.'

'Not his wife?'

'No.'

'Noted, please continue.'

'And Sandy. Um, sorry. He goes by that name.' She took a deep breath. 'Florian Sanderson.'

Sandy shuddered next to me and I placed my cold hand over his and wrapped my fingers around each of his.

'Could you tell us what happened?'

'We had a good time, and then we went to our respective tents to…you know.' Chloe blushed and looked down.

'Were you?'

'Was I what?'

'Were you intimate with Florian Sanderson?'

'No. He must have been too drunk or something because he couldn't…perform.'

There was a wave of whispering in the court room. The judge glared at everyone and they snapped back into silence, reprimanded by her stern, brown eyes. Sandy's cheeks went bright red next to me.

Chloe continued, 'I woke up in the middle of the campground, with…ejaculated matter…all over me. In my hair! And my pants were down at my knees.'

I rolled my eyes. There was no way they could pin that on Sandy, and I was relieved when the lawyer proclaimed, 'Let the court be aware that Florian Sanderson has later come out as homosexual.' He turned back to Chloe and asked in a firm voice, 'You don't actually know who it was that assaulted you that way, do you?'

Chloe opened her mouth to reply but reconsidered whatever she was about to argue. She thought for a moment before answering, 'No, but I've thought it was him who did it all these years, so I'm not convinced it wasn't.'

I held Sandy's hand and smiled weakly at him. It was just stupid of Chloe. There were two guys at that campsite. One was now being investigated for murder and she was still not convinced. I couldn't bear her ignorance.

'Thank you, Chloe. You can sit down.'

Cain was called next to the stand. Everyone stared, watching his every move as he sat down, folded a hanky in his lap and crossed his legs, almost looking feminine or elderly. Dainty, even.

He sniffed and hardened his stare at the courtroom crowd, even narrowing his eyes at me which made me tremble and sink down low in my seat. I dreaded to hear the lies he would spin to the courtroom to convince everyone he had nothing to do with Hollie going missing, and nothing to do with the murder. My shoulder aching was evidence enough of him being a sociopath. I wouldn't let him get away free. I glanced at Sandy's expression – his jaw muscle was clenched and his eye twitched.

We knew. We *just knew*. Why couldn't they find him guilty based on our judgment?

'Really makes me upset. I've been blamed unfairly for all this. Mitchell and Lockie wanted to have sex with the girl. They told me themselves ages before all this happened. I've camped with them in the past. Camped with the girl's brother. A bit. Yeah. But I wasn't there that night. I was with me missus and me kids. Just ask them. I have an alibi.

I saw Lockie and Mitchell the next day and they said they'd camped out with her and then her friend Sandy had picked her up. Saw Chase on the news the next night. Assumed the coppers would find her. I didn't have a single thing to do with it except knowing the guys.' He shook his head with its razored surface and sniffed. 'I was as shocked as anyone else was.'

'Do you think Lockie or Mitchell would have harmed her?'

Cain stared across the courtroom at Lockie, who looked down at the floor and Mitchell, who stared back at him. 'They're good boys.' He shrugged. 'But then again…you don't really know, do ya. I was stunned to hear Mitchell's story. I wasn't even there. He seemed to know a lot about how it all happened.'

I looked at Mitchell, whose face had gone red and his teeth had clenched. Cain was allowed to sit back on the bench, far apart from Lockie and Mitchell.

'Besides, it wasn't *my* seminal DNA they found, was it?' he added with a smirk.

Sandy whispered, 'He's lying through his teeth. He was there. He did it.'

We were hushed and we sat in silence as judges and lawyers whispered together. It was finally time to see evidence. The Detective Inspector took the stand and talked us through all the small hints that it had been more than one person involved.

'The victim's brother stated he got his sister to leave. These men were high on ice, and were not in the best states of minds to make good decisions. They might have been carried away, but the fact of the matter is the victim's brother became afraid, indicating he did not feel that she was safe in the presence of those men, long before she got into the car and was driven to the area where her body was found. The victim was taken away from the campsite where her brother was. She was meant to be taken home. Instead, she was taken to an isolated space, where she was threatened with a knife – it remains unknown whom held the knife but DNA suggests that both Mitchell and Lockie did hold the knife at some point – she engaged in sexual activity, likely forced, with Lockie, because only his DNA was found, and her head had traumatic injury as though she had been kicked or hit in the head, and she drowned after falling unconscious into the creek. There was no DNA of Mr. Cain Brewer found at the scene.'

Lockie glared at Mitchell, whose head hung low. Sandy's hand squeezed mine so hard that my knuckles cracked. A hiccough escaped my lips as I tried to suppress a gasp. I hadn't known all the details. Dad had warned against me coming for this reason. I would hear everything that had happened to Hollie, and I probably would regret hearing every detail, but an urge forced me to go, in the same way it must have forced Sandy. We needed to know, as much as it hurt.

The Detective Inspector's chest crushed inwards as he gave his account of the day he walked down to that creek and saw Hollie's body there in the shallow water, based on the tip he had received.

His voice shook. 'I have daughters. When I saw Hollie Matheson's body, I was devastated. This was not an accidental drowning. This was a violent crime and a murder which should never have happened. It was opportunistic, and fuelled by drugs. There was no way in which the victim could have escaped. This girl was surrounded by wolves. Worse. Monsters. Words cannot describe the pain I feel for that young girl. Her life hadn't even begun. The best years of her life were ahead of her.'

He paused, overcome by tears. We all waited in silence as he apologised and dabbed at his eyes with a wad of tissues. Breathing stopped being automatic. I had to remind myself to inhale and exhale. *Keep breathing. Be alive. Stay here. Be here. She needs you.*

The Detective Inspector composed himself and cleared his throat. He continued to show evidence. Photos of a firepit in Mitchell's backyard. Hollie's clothes. He had burned them. My head swam and I went woozy. I leant into Sandy's forearm and he put his arm around me as if he could protect me from what we were hearing.

The Detective Inspector held up a knife. Divers had recovered it from the river. He showed photos of the finger prints. Despite the fact that he had broken down minutes ago, he was now level-headed and calm as he pointed out the minor marks on the handle. It was lucky whoever disposed of the knife had thrown it in the river where the water was shallow with the tides and it had submerged itself in a pocket of sand. It was unknown if the knife had been thrown into the river from up in the hills near where Hollie had been killed, and it had come downstream, or if it was thrown in from the bank. A satellite image displayed on the screen next, with a path leading to the river, directly from Lockie's house, right on the river bank. I flinched when I realised where the knife was discovered was where I had been kayaking and encountered the whale. A dull thump in my chest reminded me again I was alive, so I kept breathing. I was choosing life by breathing. No matter what, I would hear what happened to Hollie, and I would make sure I knew the entire story.

Lockie and Mitchell squirmed in their seats, handcuffed, and were gazing up at the Detective Inspector with resignation.

'The finger prints matched Mitchell's and Lockie's. The knife was discarded right by Lockie's house. That's why it's compelling evidence to say that it was Lockie and Mitchell.'

But not Chase. And not Cain.

Lockie and Mitchell were led away and the jury left the courtroom to decide. Cain stood and walked out, wiping a hand over his head as if in relief. Sandy and I watched him leave and shook our heads in disgust.

'Do you think it was Lockie and Mitchell?' Dad asked when Sandy and I got back home. I sank into the couch, too weak to keep my eyes open. Dad handed me a cup of Ensure and I begrudgingly sat back up to down it. Upping my calories each day seemed to be relentless. Recovery even in times of my best friend's murder trial – I couldn't escape it. In a way, it made things consistent. It gave me a routine of familiarity the way starving and running used to.

Dad hadn't wanted to go to the trial. He didn't want to hear what had happened to Hollie. She was like a second daughter.

'It looks like it was,' replied Sandy. He sighed and sat on the couch beside me. 'It just feels off. I know Cain had something to do with it. Guy's a predator. Through and through.'

'You even stopped hanging out with him as a mate,' I observed, wiping the milk-moustache off with my sleeve and handing the empty cup back to Dad.

Dad gave Sandy a quizzical look. 'You hung out with Cain?'

'Years ago,' Sandy said. He cleared his throat. 'Not something I broadcast, Daze. Thanks.'

Dad put the dishes down on the coffee table and crossed his arms. 'You mean you kept it a secret.'

Sandy shrugged.

'Well, why?' Dad asked.

'Because he got into the drug scene.' Sandy shuddered. 'Went through all that in my teens – kids droppin' like flies from heroin. Nah, mate. Not it. Didn't wanna be associated with that stuff, and people who get into it. I just wanna surf.'

'That's all Hollie wanted to do, too,' I murmured. Sandy and Dad looked to me and stopped talking. 'They even said it. Lockie said it. "She was happy to surf. Happy to stay out and surf into the sunset like some wild and reckless nomad." I sighed. 'He said it so poetically…I still can't believe he could do that to her.'

Sandy sucked on his teeth for a moment before he shook his head. 'I don't think he did. I think he and Mitchell are Cain's scapegoats. Hopefully the jury sees that, too.'

The jury, however, did not see that. They came back the next day and said Lockie was guilty and Mitchell was guilty. Cain had an alibi and hadn't left DNA, so it must not have been him.

Upon hearing his guilty charge, Lockie burst into tears and cried, 'No, but I didn't! I went back to the car! We only had sex!'

Mitchell stood stoically and allowed himself to be led away to be put into jail while Lockie had a conniption. He flung himself on the floor and screamed, sobbing he would never hurt Hollie. He loved her. He was innocent. It was not him. He was out of it on drugs. He didn't know what was going on. He loved her. He didn't do it.

The security guards wrestled him up and dragged him out, his shoes kicking and scraping on the tile floor. The jury made anxious chatter and Lockie's mum sobbed and called after Lockie that she loved him and to be a good boy. She caught my eye and looked away instantly, perhaps unable to bear the judgement on my face, but if she had taken long enough to really look at me, she may have recognised pity. I didn't think Lockie had done it, either.

Sandy stood with his mouth in a thin line and said, 'Come on.'

I followed him out and we went home, trying to feel like justice had been served but it really hadn't.

Chapter Nineteen

Lockie and Mitchell went to prison for murder. I didn't go to their sentencing trials, but I heard about it on the news. I went back to school and concentrated on my studies and getting well. The school was an emptier place, feeling hollow. Fellow students had lost some shine, knowing that two killers had walked those same halls and courtyards. Blue and I nodded politely at each other, but the connection we'd had was gone.

After final exams, Ms. Gregg pulled me aside to ask how I was going. I nodded, awkward with the topic of discussion: me. I should have been used to people always asking me how I was, given all my time struggling with the most fatal mental illness, but it had been different since Hollie had died. People weren't asking how I was going and expecting me to merely nod and say, 'Yeah,

I'm going well; I'm eating and being healthy. I'm going to really kick this illness's butt. I've got this. I can do this. I'm a survivor.' Instead, they were asking how I was with being alone, lost in the void that was losing your best friend. Losing your trust in people you knew as friends.

Joy disappeared from my life and everything seemed grey and dull around the edges. Anorexia had numbed me, but grief blinded me. There was no burning motive to stay alive anymore. No sleuthing to be done. No answers to be had. It was over. Now, I just had to live. As simple as that. It was a simple thing but it made the back of my throat feel full and ache.

Ms. Gregg frowned and waited for me to speak. It was difficult to get my voice past that lump in my throat but I answered, 'I'm...alive.'

Her face moved in a way that told me her teacher-empathy was in red alert, and I recalled the way she had left my house after visiting me at my lowest weight. Crying. This teacher was worth her weight in gold and I couldn't bear to see her cry again.

I added, 'I'm sorry.'

Ms. Gregg touched my arm gently and smiled through watering eyes. 'Don't ever say you're sorry, Daisy. I'm incredibly proud of you.'

I tucked a strand of hair back behind my ear to distract myself from her warmth. I couldn't allow myself to feel it when Hollie was gone. I deserved to be in the cold all my life. I wanted to reassure Ms. Gregg that I was going to be okay, but I couldn't say another word.

She said, 'I hope you're still doing the things you enjoyed doing with Hollie. She would have really wanted that for you.'

Hollie had wanted me to get better. I gazed into Ms. Gregg's eyes and replied, 'Yeah, you're right. And I am...I am.' I will.

After school, I carried my surfboard down the beach and paddled out past the golden boulders that freckled the shoreline. My hands cupped the water and I pushed the water behind me, hearing it rush behind, under, toward and through me. Life blood.

The sun was low on the horizon. It would set soon. The waves were quiet. I caught the first one that stood up behind me and I rode it while squatting low on my board, pushing my weight into my front foot to gather speed, but it was a slow wave, powerless. It only gave me a short ride and I paddled for the next. It was also too small.

My shoulders ached as I put all my strength into paddling, digging and shovelling but power eluded me. The wave fell under me and skittered to shore. I spun my board around and waited. I let waves go until the sky went pink and my lips were shuddering. Caught the last one that came up. Rode it to shore. Almost feeling my heart heal.

As I carried my board home, I paused outside Sandy's place. I watched for the lights to come on, but they didn't. He'd withdrawn from Dad and me again. His white fibro house glowed in the dark but no lights came on.

I'd leave him alone. My ears ached as I walked home, my fingers and toes burning as though I was getting frostbite. I couldn't wait to get home and eat the soup Dad was making. My mouth watered as I made my way home.

The water became Hollie, and she became water. Her ashes were dropped out at our favourite part of the beach. A paddle-out. I was given the honour of being the one to tip the urn. The surf lifesaving club members and I paddled out slowly one calm Saturday morning. Hollie's grandparents and Chase stood on the beach to watch.

'You orright, love?' one of the old guys said.

I nodded as I straddled my board, keeping Hollie's urn securely upon the deck of my board. I unscrewed it as the others around me tossed flowers into the middle. Sandy paddled in behind us. I smiled at him, relieved he had come. He didn't smile back but he nodded.

I took a deep breath and gazed down at the urn, and the grey ashes inside. Tears sprang to my eyes and I considered hugging the urn to my chest one last time. One last hug, but I remembered she was only ashes. It made me shiver. I sniffled. Everyone in the ring of boards called out encouragement. I counted to three and flung the urn upwards so Hollie's ashes surged through the air towards the centre of our surfboard ring. They seemed to hover for a moment before falling to the sea, where she needed to be.

Be with the whales, my best friend. Be with the whales.

Chapter Twenty

Sandy met me at the track to the beach one morning, jogging to catch up to me. 'Hey.'

'Hi,' I said, stopping.

I waited for him to apologise for shutting me and Dad out, but instead he said, 'I think we can still prove Cain had something to do with it.'

I squinted at him in the early morning sunshine and asked, 'Oh yeah?'

'They never brought up your shoulder in court.'

I replied, 'No, the lawyers said it was inadmissible because it wasn't along the same lines of what happened to Hollie.'

Sandy ran his hand through his hair and said, 'Well, what about what he did to Ella?'

'She is still claiming it never happened.'

He chewed on the inside of his cheek and swore to himself.

I shifted my board under my opposite arm to ease the bruising sensation of it banging my armpit. 'I don't think we can prove Cain was involved, Sandy.'

He shook his head. 'I don't...I *can't* accept that.'

It physically hurt to reply, 'Well, we need to, and we need to move on.'

His eyes narrowed and his jaw clenched. 'How on earth can we move on, Daisy?' He gestured around us. 'I mean, this place isn't the same without Hollie. You can't deny that. Don't you want to get justice?'

'Of course,' I whined. 'But we need to move on.'

'But...' He looked away as his voice cracked. 'How?'

'We do what Hollie would have wanted us to do. We surf.'

And we did. We went out together and caught wave after wave. Sandy began to light up again. His jaw bone usually pulsed with tension, but it finally slackened and opened into a grin as we caught clean green waves and he could charge up and down a face and do aerials, with the booming of the waves breaking becoming his applause.

We surfed for three hours. With jelly arms and a light heart, we made our way back up the track to the carpark. It was beginning to feel as though we could move on, riding waves into the new parts of our lives, but instead, life stopped as we came face to face with Cain, standing with a man I didn't know.

Sandy's grin disappeared. I was icy all over.

'Heard you got a problem with me.' Cain glared at Sandy.

Sandy muttered, 'Yeah, I do.'

'You think I killed her,' Cain sneered.

'Somethin' like that.'

Cain spread his arms like an angel, inviting Sandy to punch him in his chest. 'Well, let's sort it like men.'

Sandy shook his head. 'I'm not hitting you, Cain.'

Cain's mate lunged towards me and grabbed me, yanking me towards him.

I dropped my surfboard and I was too shocked to scream. I squirmed hopelessly like a goldfish.

Sandy dropped his board too and reared back, punching Cain so hard in the face he spun around and hit the asphalt, completely out cold. The back of his head made a crunching sound on the ground.

Cain's mate shook me until I fell beside Cain, grazing my knees and hands, but I didn't feel anything. All I could do was stare at Sandy's shadow on the ground as it loomed towards us.

No, don't do it, I thought.

You're about to make the biggest mistake of your life.

Don't do it.

I winced as Sandy lifted his surfboard and brought it crashing down into Cain's head.

Shouting and screaming filled my ears as well as ringing. My screams. I couldn't stop them erupting from my chest.

Sandy pulled me up and we stared at Cain. At the pooling blood from his ears.

Cain's mate sprinted away.

I gazed down at Cain. He wasn't moving.

I murmured, 'I think you fractured his skull.'

I couldn't read my surroundings at first. I staggered away, wiping the blood from my hands. I glanced at Sandy and noticed his nose was bleeding. Cain must have hit him too but I hadn't seen it.

I looked back down at Cain and kicked at his thigh, half-hoping he would move and half-hoping he wouldn't. He didn't. He didn't even blink.

I got down on all-fours, choking back tears. I held my breath to listen for a breath, like I had learnt from first aid classes at school. No sounds came out except my own heartbeat.

He was nothing. No more.

'Sandy,' I groaned, 'I think he's dead!'

In response, Sandy gave a shudder and gagged.

He lunged for Cain and rolled him into a recovery position, muttering, 'Shit, shit, shit,' over and over.

Bystanders began to surround us.

Sandy glanced up with glassy eyes. 'Somebody, please! Call an ambulance!'

He crouched beside that piece of shit Cain, trying to recover him. I trembled as laid a hand on the chest of the devil and didn't hope to feel a heartbeat.

'Oh, fuuuuck,' Sandy sobbed. He shook his head. 'I shouldn't have hit him.' We locked eyes over Cain's body. 'I've killed him.'

I slowly crossed my hands over his heart, ready to do chest compressions but hesitated. *Do I do this? Should I do this? This man killed my best friend. He might have gotten away with it, but I know he did it.*

I began chest compressions. I was not a murderer.

You piece of shit, I thought. *You better live. Don't you dare take someone else I love. Don't you make Sandy go to prison when it should have been you. Don't...you...dare.*

I continued chest compressions even when the ambulance arrived. Sandy walked in circles around me, holding his hands to his head, ripping out his hair and periodically breaking down. I didn't stop until the police arrived and took Sandy away in handcuffs.

The fight was fought. It was over. Cain had lost his life, tearing out the heart of a good man's heart along the way. There was nothing in the way on his trip to Hell, now.

'You son of a bitch,' I muttered, staring down at his gaping mouth and the blood around his head. 'I hate you.'

I watched the paramedics black sack him. They touched my elbow tenderly as I crossed my arms.

'Well done for trying, lass,' they told me.

I wrinkled my nose and shook my head. 'Don't you feel bad for him. I don't. He deserved it.'

Once they left with him in the ambulance and the police took Sandy away, I ran home. I left our surfboards in the carpark and bolted home to Dad as fast as I could. Each breath in felt like it was slashing my lungs to shreds, and each step pounded my chest. Cain deserved it. He deserved it. He deserved it. So why was my blood bubbling up at me?

I erupted into the house, screaming, 'DAAAAAAAAAAD!'

He looked up from his phone in a panic. 'What? What? God, what's happened?' He stood and his eyes went up and down me. I had bare feet, and was still in my wetsuit that dripped on the wooden floors. My hands were stained red.

'Sandy's been arrested!'

'What? Why?'

Gasping, overheating, I peeled off my wetsuit. The blood bubbling hadn't stopped. 'I can't breathe,' I cried as I yanked at my sleeves.

Dad helped me peel out of the wetsuit that was like a sticky glove. He forced me to sit on the floor.

I blubbered, 'We have to get Sandy out of jail.'

'Daisy,' Dad said in a firm voice that made me look him in the eyes. 'What…happened?'

I averted my eyes from his to the window, grasping at a way I could tell Dad without breaking him. I sobbed, regretting everything I had told Sandy about Chase. I should have stayed quiet. No good had come from it. The wrong guy went to prison – Lockie – I wasn't sure about Mitchell, and a guy I was pretty sure did it got away with it. I ruined everything. It was all my fault. If I hadn't been sick in the first place, Hollie would have been safe because I would have been with her. Now I was going to lose someone else very close to me because he'd been so upset.

A ball caught in my throat as I explained, 'He killed him, Dad…' I looked back into his alarmed face and noticed how much he had aged since I had come to live with him. He was too young to look that old – as old as I felt.

I sighed and repeated myself, 'He killed him.' I put my face in my hands as I cried, 'Holy crap, Sandy killed him.'

Dad fell backwards on the floor and gaped at me, wordless. We sat in silence except for the sounds of our sobbing.

Chapter Twenty-One

AUGUST

On our last day together, Sandy and I walked down the beach carrying our surfboards and wearing our wetsuits. It was late, almost five, and the sun was sinking. We wouldn't be out very long. We didn't have time. One wave, Sandy had told me. Catch one wave together and we would be all right.

I had a strange heart rate. Excited, nervous. Or was I about to have a heart attack because of refeeding syndrome? I'd avoided heart issues all through my eating disorder – maybe my luck was about to run out.

I thought of Hollie and where Sandy was headed and corrected myself: no, my luck ran out a long time ago.

My toes hit the liquification and I lit up like a disco ball. Joy. This is what it was. My toes and fingers froze and my teeth chattered, but I smiled as I paddled out behind Sandy on the emerald ripples. A stripe gleamed on the surface, reflecting the narrow, setting sun. Soon all the sea would be navy, then black. We didn't have much time.

We caught our one wave. One wave, and it was over. An end of an era. An end of time.

The sun set so quickly and I was out of breath before the water even met me at the shore. One wave. All we could have together was that one wave.

Tomorrow he would start his sentence in prison for manslaughter. I wished that one wave could have lasted forever.

Afterwards, we walked through the shallows, up to the beach in silence, stepping gingerly on the frigid sand, both of us as changed as the other. Was it melancholy I was feeling or dread? I couldn't even tell; all I knew was that I was on an unfamiliar edge. My feelings were thrown out by the eating disorder but the leftover vestiges of anorexia dangled, a highway to oblivion but I didn't get on it. I wasn't going left anymore. I was going right, just for a change. Right.

What even was right? It was considering Sandy more in that moment than how I felt. Was it really my fault? I thought it was. Sandy said it absolutely wasn't.

'Do as I tell you, Daisy…' he said, stopping at the water line, looking nervously around.

'What?'

'I'll be who I am. You need to be who you are. Hollie was always herself. I think we need to be more like her.'

'But…I don't understand.'

He pulled me close and my bones banged against his muscles. I whispered, 'Please…stay.'

He let out a wracking sob that shook my entire body. 'I can't.'

'You're my hero, Sandy,' I whispered. I couldn't bear our imminent parting.

He sniffled and laughed through his sadness. 'A hero, eh?'

I gripped him tighter. 'Yep.'

The wind picked up and blew into us but couldn't tear us apart. We shivered by the sea and stayed together despite the growing desert between us.

The remaining weeks of winter were hard on me. By September, I learned that Unanderra Jail had visiting days and I pondered how to ask Dad to take me. *Please take me. Dad, take me. Sandy – wouldn't it be nice to go see him? Could you drive me? Please, pretty please. I promise I'll eat if you take me. If you don't take me, I'll stop eating. Please, pretty please. Take me to visit Sandy.*

The truth was, I couldn't use manipulation anymore. I would eat whether Dad took me or not. It was just the two of us now. Sitting across from each other in the muted, flickering light of the television, my dinner balanced precariously on my lap. I stared, unblinking at my father. He ate methodically. Carrots. Peas. Potato. Lamb chop. He sawed at the lamb chop and watched the television screen, chewing rapidly like a goat, swallowing between forkfuls. It was almost meditative to watch him eat without thinking about each bite. He finished before I'd eaten three mouthfuls.

He stood, stretching, arching his back and I observed the dirty pants getting baggier. He'd lost weight since Sandy got sent to jail. I had hoped he would get out of it because he'd been trying to defend me, and the victim was a piece of shit murderer anyway. But he had been charged with excessive self-defence, and was imprisoned on a manslaughter charge and had to serve eight years. Dad, Sandy and I had broken down in the courtroom and cried so hard we were all sick. But Sandy had accepted it – he had made a stupid choice.

KING HIT the local papers had squawked. *Poor* Cain was killed by a local surf hoodlum. Statements claimed it was a severe case of localism – testosterone-fuelled crazy idiots fighting over a surf spot. There was no mention of the fact Cain came looking for trouble, and no mention of the fact his friend had grabbed me.

I really wanted to visit Sandy to make sure he was going okay. I had to make sure Dad could take me though.

Dad glanced down and noticed I hadn't finished.

'You all right, Sprout?' he asked quietly.

Anorexia wanted me to throw my plate against the wall and demand I get my way. But I was not ever listening to that bitch again. It may have given me control over my emotions and even other people, but it had been a strangulation. Logic was returning to me.

A tear trickled my cheek and I hurriedly wiped it away. I whispered, 'I just miss Sandy.'

Dad hugged me. 'We can go see him if you want to?'

I nodded. 'I'd like that.'

Chapter Twenty-Two

A YEAR LATER

The rush and boom of the waves on the coastline woke me up at night. Any minute now the house would be flooded and I'd be lost, trapped yet unwilling to fight the tide.

I tiptoed across the house, the floorboards achingly cold on my feet. I hugged my slight frame, so much larger and softer than it had been the last time the whales came to Short Point, and I peeked out of the kitchen window. It took a while for my eyes to adjust to the dark but I soon made out the king tide. It swept up high on the beach and lapped at the cobbled, planked, jutted earth.

I spied the path that led to the dilapidated staircase, tracked religiously by the local surfers. The lowest steps would be out to sea by morning.

The window began to fog up from my breath – a reminder I was still alive. What a time and place to be alive, after all. I wiped the window clear again with my sleeve. I'd been staying at Sandy's a few nights a week to get it ready with Dad to be sold.

The cold went to my bones but I stayed put at the window, before I forced my legs into sweat pants and jogged to the point. Some habits never ceased.

It was the storm of the century, and they warned of a king tide, caused by a storm cell coming up from down south. It had been a year since Hollie had disappeared, and almost a year since Sandy was sentenced. One down, seven to go. I almost cried thinking I would be in my mid-twenties before I could surf with Sandy again. It made me run harder into the wind.

I arrived at the point above the blowhole, completely breathless and winded, clutching my pitter-pattering heart. The sun would be back soon. And when it came back, I'd be waiting.

I huddled and crouched, shivering, waiting. The sun would come up and I would be there to see it. I would welcome a change and roll with this rotation of time. I had graduated high school without Hollie. I'd eventually got around to kissing Blue and saying yes to a date with him. I refused to be stuck the way I'd been the last few years. I was breaking out, crawling and lumbering, of the shattering exterior.

Sunrise was still hours away, and I wanted to stay and wait. If I could weather this storm, I could weather life. It took hours of shivering in agony and sobbing at my own stupidity. What was I doing? Trying to die out there on the point, freeze to death with the winter wind of the Pacific Ocean, strangling and constricting my lungs and chest?

But then it appeared. A mirage at first, peeping between the smothering grey clouds that resembled vast, lumpy cushions of meringue, stained with dust and depression. It wouldn't be too late. It would never be too late as long as I could make the choice myself. Here was me, accepting recovery. Truly wanting it – willing to shiver my arse off for it. I was ready to live.

I rubbed my bluer-than-the-sky hands together to summon some warmth. The sun gleamed in pockets of orange light with purple and red hues upon me.

I closed my eyes and whispered, 'I'm alive. I'm alive.' I opened my eyes again slowly and was rewarded with a cold desert of water before me, the horizon finally clear. The wind had gone, and left behind a perfect rolling wave.

I imagined Hollie and Sandy riding the wave, one going left and one going right. What a spectacular sight. I smiled at the thought and was about to turn when I caught a glimpse of a spout of water. Whales.

The pod came through slowly at first, but they increased with energy and athleticism as they crossed the head, leaping from their cold playground with simple bliss and joy. I gazed at them, awe-struck, until they passed from my sight.

Then, as simply as we live and die, I went home...and got something to eat.

ACKNOWLEDGMENTS

I'm indebted to my fiancé, Rick, who has not only seen me through writing three novels and supporting me by bringing me coffees and reminding me that I can, indeed, do this writing gig, but has also seen me through the many years I've been plagued by eating disorders and disordered eating. I may never have been as sick as Daisy Cavill, but our mindsets were intertwined for many years. A part of me wanted to write this just to get my mindset down on paper, so others may understand what it is like to suffer with an eating disorder.

I am incredibly grateful to my sensitivity reader Kristina for reading this novel in its early days and making sure I wasn't being too triggering with Daisy's mindset and her extreme behaviours. It was extremely important to me that I delivered a book that could educate others on the illness and bring understanding to an incredibly misunderstood disease.

Thank you to Lel for your incredible insights as a reader and pointing out things that were clear in my head and might not have been very clear to a reader. Thank you to Nathalie for being a great supporter and critic – I knew when I first met you teaching you to how to ride horses that you were an incredible woman and we'd be friends. Thank you also to Nicole, Vanda and Sam.

Thank you to Jodi Gibson for all your encouragement and for creating our little Write Squad. I wrote this book daily, but meeting every Thursday morning on your Instagram lives was a great motivator to keep going.

Last but not least, thank you to the reader. Your support is the world to me!

ABOUT THE AUTHOR

Ava Dunn is an Australian author of books that explore surviving adversity and coming of age. She is a passionate advocate for raising awareness for eating disorders and the lack of criminal justice for victims.

Her second novel, *Salt*, was short-listed for the Faber Academy Scholarship and explores issues of overcoming the trauma of sexual assault and having to fight for custody with a sexual predator.

Ava Dunn is a teacher and currently resides in Victoria, Australia with her fiancé, cats and horses.

You can follow Ava Dunn on Instagram to stay updated on her upcoming novels @ava.dunn.author.

Available to buy now
SALT

"Touching and tragic"
"Heartwarming"

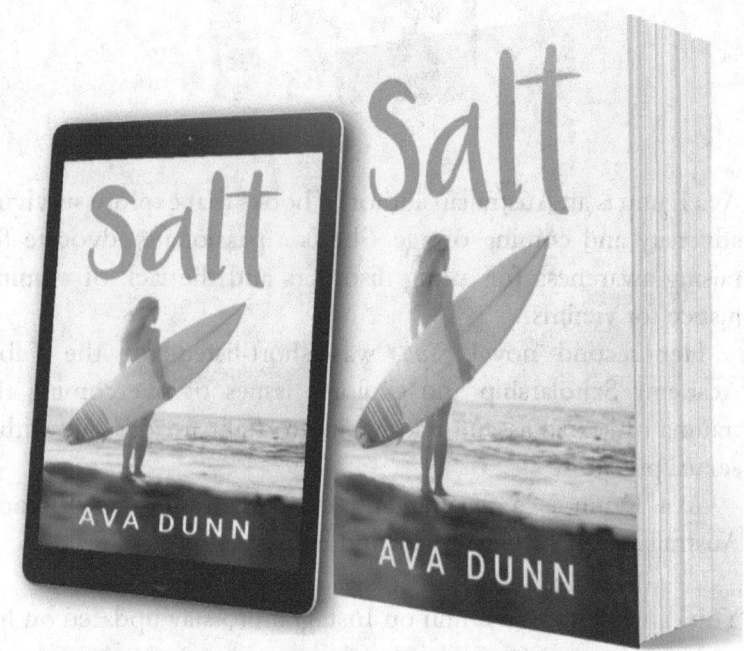

AVAILABLE NOW